e toi   W. Perry

'A satisfyingly convoluted plot.' *Sunday Times*

'No-one is better than S. W. Perry at leading us through the squalid streets of London in the sixteenth century.'

Andrew Swanston

'The writing is of such a quality, the characters so engaging and the setting so persuasive that, only two books in, S. W. Perry's ingeniously plotted novels have become my favourite historical crime series.' S G MacLean

'*The Serpent's Mark* is an excellent evocation of Elizabethan England, with espionage, intricate conspiracies, strange medical practises and a gripping story. A rattling good read.' William Ryan

'The second in [Perry's] series about the Elizabethan doctor-cum-sleuth Nicholas Shelby... is as elegantly written as the first.'

The Times

'A gorgeous book – rich, intelligent and dark in equal measure. It immerses you in the late 16th century and leaves you wrung out with terror. This is historical fiction at its most sumptuous.'

Rory Clements

'Wonderful! Beautiful writing, and Perry's Elizabethan London is so skilfully evoked, so real that one can almost smell it.'

Giles Kristian

'A strong and convincing debut.' Antonia Senior, *The Times*

'I knew before I got to the bottom of the first page that *The Angel's Mark* was th... ...is one is going to

The Serpent's Mark

S. W. PERRY

CORVUS

First published in hardback Great Britain in 2019 by Corvus,
an imprint of Atlantic Books Ltd.

This paperback edition published in 2019

10 9 8 7 6 5 4 3 2 1

A CIP catalogue record for this book is available from the British Library.

Paperback ISBN: 978 1 78649 498 6
E-book ISBN: 978 1 78649 499 3

Corvus
An imprint of Atlantic Books Ltd
Ormond House
26–27 Boswell Street
London
WC1N 3JZ

www.corvus-books.co.uk

Printed and bound by CPI Group (UK) Ltd, Croydon CR0 4YY

For Lilian and Vera Jones

Hic locus est ubi mors gaudet succurrere vitae.
(This is a place where the dead are pleased to help the living.)

INSCRIPTION IN THE ORIGINAL THEATRE OF
ANATOMY AT THE UNIVERSITY OF PADUA
1594

Physicians are like kings – they brook no contradiction.

JOHN WEBSTER
The Duchess of Malfi
1614

Tilbury, England. Winter 1591

In the dusk of a desolate November evening an urchin in a mud-stained and threadbare jerkin, long-since stolen from its rightful owner, hurries along the Thames foreshore beneath the grim ramparts of Tilbury Fort. The chill east wind claws at his puckered pale flesh. The hunger that has driven him down to the narrowing band of shingle gnaws within him, as if it would tear itself out of his belly and go crawling off by itself in search of sustenance elsewhere. He is risking the tide because he knows a place where the oysters are plump and good. On balance, the strand is a safer route than striking inland in the gathering darkness.

His destination is a small channel that runs deep into the Essex shore, a wilderness of marsh and reed, of dead-end tracks that lead to creeks where you can drown in stinking mud before you can get to the *Amen* at the end of the Lord's Prayer. He knows this because the wasteland is where he lives, on its southern fringe, in a ramshackle camp of vagabonds and peddlers, swelled by the destitute and the maimed from the wars in Holland and by discharged sailors from the queen's fleet.

The river is the colour of the lead coffin he once saw when he broke into a private chapel to get out of a storm. It is studded with ships: hoys and flyboats from Antwerp and Flushing, barques from the Hansa ports of Lübeck and Hamburg, fur traders from the white wastes of Muscovy. As night approaches, they are begin-ning to dissolve before his eyes, like old coins tossed into oil of vitriol. All they leave behind is the tarry smell of caulked timber and the tormenting scent of food cooking on galley hearths.

Before the boy can reach the channel he must first climb over the great iron chain that runs out into the water, the boom that blocks the river lest the Spanish come again, as they did in '88.

He is unwilling to jump the chain because the hunger has given him cramps in the stomach. He'd crawl under it, but that would mean slithering through pools of rank green slime. So instead he puts one tattered boot into a slippery iron link and starts to ease himself over.

And as he does so, something amongst the rotting kelp that clings to the chain detaches itself and drops to the pebbles.

A crab! A dead crab.

Dare he eat it? He's ravenous enough. But how long has it been there, trapped amongst the weeds and the barnacles? The urchin knows you can die from eating bad food. It makes you double up like a sprat being fried in a pan. It makes you scream. He's seen it happen.

But famine has made him canny. He knows exactly what to do. He'll wash the crab clean of mud in the nearest pool, take a long sniff beneath the carapace and judge then if it's worth breaking open.

It is only when he lifts the crab from the pebbles that the boy realizes it is not a crab at all.

It is a human hand.

PART 1

The Physician from Basle

1

Nine months earlier. 23rd February 1591

It is a day made for second chances, a day ripe for confession, for penitence, for admitting your sins and seizing that unexpected God-given chance to start afresh. A dying storm has left thin wracks of ripped black cloud hanging in the saturated air, above a pale empty world awaiting the first brushstroke. It is simply a matter of applying the paint to the canvas. Let today slip by unused, and Nicholas Shelby – lapsed physician and reluctant sometime spy – knows he must return to London, no nearer to accepting the new life he's been so cruelly dealt than when he left.

His father has sensed it, too.

'Your Eleanor died in August last,' Yeoman Shelby observes with devastating calmness, as the two men shelter from the last of the downpour in the farm's apple press. 'It's now almost March. *Seven* months. Where were you, boy? Where did you go?'

How much of an answer does a father need? Nicholas wonders, close to shivering inside his white canvas doublet. Would it help to know that for a while I was busy drinking myself stupid in any tavern I could find that hadn't already banned me? Or that I was losing every patient I had, because word had soon spread that Dr Shelby was raging in his grief like a deranged shabberoon? Or that I was busy rejecting everything I learned at Cambridge – attended at a cost you could scarcely bear – because when the time came and Eleanor and the child she was carrying had need of it, my medical knowledge turned out to be little more than superstition? Or that, on top of everything else, there had been a murderer I had to stop from killing again?

There are some questions, Nicholas thinks, that should remain for ever unanswered, if only for the sake of those who ask them.

'How could you do that to us, boy – vanishing off the face of God's good earth like that?' his father is saying, his words delivered to the dying rain's slow drumbeat. 'Your brother wore himself thin, searching that godless place called London for a sign of you. Your mother wept like we'd never heard her weep before. Do you not know *we* loved Eleanor, too?'

Nicholas has been dreading this moment ever since he returned to Suffolk and the Shelby farm. Now he sits on the cold stone rim of the press, straight-backed, head up, a damp curl of wiry black hair slick against his brow, unable to give in to the desire to slump, because a Suffolk yeoman's son is not grown to wilt, even if the weight of all that's happened since Lammas Day last is almost too much for his broad countryman's shoulders to bear. Sickened by the excuses he hasn't even tried to make yet, at first all he can bring himself to say is 'I know. I'm sorry.'

Yeoman Shelby has rarely struck either of his sons, and not at all since they've grown to manhood. But as he comes closer, Nicholas wonders if he's about to land a blow in payment for the extra pain his youngest has caused the family by his vanishing. He catches the heavy, musty smell of his father's woollen coat, the one he's worn in winter for as long as Nicholas can remember. Dyed a now-faded grey, it smells as though it's been buried in a seed basket for all of Nicholas's twenty-nine years. But the scent is oddly comforting. Nicholas has the overwhelming urge to reach out and cling to the hem, as if he were an infant again.

'The only way I can explain it is this,' he says, staring at his hands and thinking how his fingers, nicked and coarsened by boyhood summers helping with the harvest, seem so unsuited to healing work. 'Imagine if you woke up one morning and discovered that all the wisdom accumulated over fifteen hundred years of husbanding the land didn't work any longer – that you couldn't grow anything any more; that you couldn't feed your family.'

'It's called an evil harvest, boy. It's happened before.'

'Exactly! And there was absolutely nothing you could do about it, was there?'

Nicholas looks up at his father with moistening eyes. He snorts back the tears, frightened that he's about to weep in the presence of a man who has always seemed immune to sentiment. 'That's how it was when I tried to save Eleanor and our child,' he says thinly.

His father lays a hand on his son's shoulder. 'I know you well enough, Nick. You would have moved heaven and earth, if you but could. But sometimes, boy, it's just the way God wants things to happen.'

Nicholas gives a cruel laugh. 'Oh, I've heard *that* said before. Did you know the great Martin Luther – fount of this new religion we're all supposed to embrace so unquestioningly – tells me in his writings that God *designed* women to die in childbirth! He says it's what they're for! Well, for the record, I'll have none of such *knowledge*.'

'Parson Olicott would say that what you learned at Cambridge is God's wisdom revealed through man,' his father replies, caution in his runnelled face. 'He'd say our Lord would offer us no false remedies. He'd call you a blasphemer for suggesting otherwise.'

'The remedies Parson Olicott gets called upon to administer, Father,' says Nicholas, running his fingers through a tangle of hair that the rain has flattened to his scalp like black ribbons discarded in a ditch, 'are for ills of the soul, not the body.'

'But if the soul is in good health, does not the body follow?'

Though a humble farmer, a man who only learned to write when he was forty, his father has just summed up the current thinking of the College of Physicians in a nutshell.

'That's what we've thought for centuries,' Nicholas says. 'That's what the books tell us: bring the body into a balance pleasing to God. They instruct us to bleed the patient from a particular part of his body if the sanguine and choleric humours are out of kilter; purge him if the melancholic humour suppresses the phlegmatic; read the colour of his water – and always make sure the stars and the planets are in favourable alignment, before you do any of it. Then present the bill. And if it all goes wrong, say it was God's will – or the stars were inauspicious.'

His father kneels and stares into his son's eyes with the stoic acceptance of the cycle of life and death, of hope and disappointment, that a man who relies on the fickleness of the earth for his survival must learn. His face looks carved out of holm oak. You're barely fifty, thinks Nicholas, yet you look like an old man. Is it the toil? Or have my own actions aged you? He settles for what his mother and his sister-in-law, Faith, have always claimed: grubbing away at the earth makes Shelby men look older than their years.

'Listen to me, boy,' his father says with a surprisingly gentle smile that looks out of place on such a hard-used face. 'Thrice in my lifetime I've heard Parson Olicott tell me I'm to forget my religion and believe in a different one. Every Sunday – until I was about fourteen – he'd tell me the Pope was a fine Christian man, an' that for my spiritual education I was to study the pictures of the saints in St Mary's...'

Nicholas wonders what that weathered stone Saxon barnacle, where the Shelby family now have their own pew almost within touching distance of the altar, has to do with his present agony; but he's learned long ago that when his father embarks on one of his homilies it's best not to interrupt.

8

His father continues. 'Then one Sunday shortly after King Henry died, I hear Parson Olicott announce, "King Edward says the Pope is the Antichrist!" Well, you could have knocked me down with a feather. After the sermon, Parson Olicott hands us lads a bucket of whitewash.' He makes a painting gesture with one hand, the fist clenched. '"Cover up those paintings of the saints," orders old Olicott, "'cause now they be heretical!"'

Nicholas has stared at the plain walls of St Mary's every Sunday for as long as he can recall, usually with intense boredom. It has never occurred to him that his father was one of those who'd done the whitewashing.

'Took us lads ages, I can tell you,' Yeoman Shelby says. 'But the next thing I know – around the time I was paying court to your mother – there's Parson Olicott proclaiming that Edward is dead, Mary is queen, and the Pope is once more our father in Christ. Imagine it!'

Nicholas indulges his father and imagines.

'"Change the prayer book!" says Olicott. "Bring out the choir screens again" – we'd hidden them in Jed Arrowsmith's barn. "Scrub off the whitewash! The bishops what made us paint over those saints are all now heretics and must burn for it!"' Yeoman Shelby sighs, as though all this variable theology is beyond the understanding of a simple man. 'To tell the truth, Nick, when we got the whitewash off, I was surprised those paintings had survived. But survive they had. Stubborn buggers, those Catholic saints. Didn't last, of course. Barely five years on, Bloody Mary is dead, we're all singing hosannas for Queen Elizabeth, and the Pope is the Devil's arse-licker again. And what's old Olicott preaching?'

'Fetch the whitewash?'

His father nods. 'Exactly. What I'm saying to you is this: there ain't ever such a thing as *certainty*, boy. Maybe in the next world, but not in this. So don't you worry your young head about whether or not your old father can handle it when his clever physician son has a crisis of belief. Because what really grieves us, Nick – what *really* makes us weep – is that when *your* world was turned on its head, when you had need of us most, you didn't come home.'

For a moment there is only the slow dripping of water on the pressing stone. Then Nicholas is in his father's arms, his chest heaving like a man drowning, sobbing with a child's bewilderment at unjustified injury.

Outside, the rain is starting to ease. The old thatched houses of Barnthorpe are beginning to take on their newborn, sharper forms. When the two men walk back to the Shelby farmhouse, Nicholas feels somehow lighter. Certainly more resolute. Confession has done him good – even if it's only a partial confession.

Because there's something else Nicholas hasn't admitted to his father. He hasn't told Yeoman Shelby that a part of his son – a small part to be sure, but even the smallest canker can still presage a greater infection – now belongs to one Robert Cecil.

✠

'Careful now, Ned. Master Nicholas is not here to set your bones if you fall!'

Bianca Merton grasps the ladder with both hands, letting her weight bear down on her left foot, which is set firmly on the bottom rung. Above her, Ned Monkton sways precariously as he leans out over the lane. He looks like a bear that's climbed to the top of a maypole and got stuck there. Cursing, he tries to attach the newly made board beside the sign of the Jackdaw. It takes him a few minutes and an excess of profanities, but before long the new banner is in place: the unicorn and the jackdaw swaying side-by-side in the breeze. Southwark now has a tavern *and* an apothecary, all in one. You can forget your tribulations with a quart of knock-down, and get colewort and hartshorn for the resulting hangover, in the same place.

'Don't that look a fine sight?' says Rose, Bianca's maid, as she admires the scene – though whether it's the apothecary's sign or the sight of Ned's hugely muscular legs wrapped around the ladder is somewhat unclear to Bianca.

'I wish I could have seen the faces of the Grocers' Guild when they signed my licence,' Bianca says, sweeping her proud, dark hair from her brow. 'They've been trying to shut me down since the day I arrived. And now I'm legal! Who would have imagined it? Bianca Merton of the Jackdaw, a licensed apothecary!'

Whatever her curative talents, Bianca makes an unlikely tavern-keeper. She's slender, with a narrow, boyish face topped by a trace of widow's peak, and extraordinarily amber eyes that gleam with a mischievous directness. Having been born of an Italian mother and an English father, her skin still boasts a healthy lustre infused by the Veneto sun, despite all that three years in Southwark have contrived against it.

'Shame a *someone* isn't here to see it,' says Rose, a plump, jolly young woman with a mane like tangled knitting. 'How did he manage it? I thought he were out of all regard with them physicians in their pretty college on Knightrider Street.'

'He called in a favour, Rose,' Bianca says wryly. And beyond that she will not go. The memories of the horror she and Nicholas endured together are still too raw. Before he left for Suffolk to make his peace with his family, they'd scarcely spoken of it between themselves, let alone with outsiders. The nightmares still come to her, though less frequently now. When they do, they have a terrifying fidelity about them. Once again she is back in that vile place deep in the earth, feeling her flesh tense as it awaits the draw of the scalpel. She consoles herself with the knowledge that no more bodies will wash up on Bankside. The man who put them in the river has met his just reward, thanks to Dr Nicholas Shelby, who came to her as a talisman from out of that very same river.

She wonders what Nicholas is doing now. Is he reconciled with his family? Do the ghosts of his wife and child haunt him still? Will he return to Bankside, as he promised? And how will she feel about him, if he does?

He's so very different from the men she'd known in Padua. A yeoman's son from the wilds of Suffolk who'd found the intellectual courage to battle the stultifying hand of tradition during his medical studies is as unlike a fashionably clad *libertino* as she can possibly imagine. She scolds herself for the sudden, unexpected surge of jealousy that comes with knowing how capable of love Nicholas is, despite his stolid roots. It would be so much better, she thinks, if he could devote that love to the living, and not the dead.

Her reverie is broken by the sole of Ned's boot on her hand as he descends the ladder.

'God's mercy!' she cries, snatching her hand away and shaking it vigorously. 'Have a care where you're putting your feet, you clumsy buffle-head!' Catching herself using the vocal currency of the London streets, she smiles. She thinks, soon I shall have lost that accent Nicholas says he can hear in my voice whenever I get fractious. Soon I shall be as English as Rose.

Ned Monkton, just turned twenty-one, built like King Henry's great *Mary Rose* – and just as liable to capsize, if too much liquid flows in through an open port – steps back to earth. He scratches his fiery auburn hair and slaps his belly with his great fists. 'There now, Mistress,' he says, looking up at the two signs, 'they can't beat that at the Turk's Head or the Good Husband, eh?'

'You've hung it upside-down,' says Rose.

And for just a moment Ned is taken in.

They're an odd pair. Rose is as ungovernable as a sack of wild martens. Her idea of a day's leisure is a trip to Tyburn to watch a good hanging. Ned used to be the mortuary warden from St Thomas's hospital down by Thieves' Lane. Smiling, Bianca remembers her mother's firm conviction: there's always *someone for someone*.

It's good to see Ned above ground now, she thinks, instead of deep in the hospital crypt, surrounded by the dead. He's even getting some colour back in his face. Since Nicholas set off for Suffolk, Ned has taken his place as the Jackdaw's handyman and thrower-outer-in-chief. There's been not a jug spilt in anger since. And with Rose beside him, he's beginning to recover a little from what befell young Jacob, his younger brother, whose death gave Nicholas his first lead in tracking down the man they all now describe – in lowered voices that still have an echo of dread in them – as the 'Bankside butcher'.

Bianca looks up at the two signs again, satisfaction welling in her breast. A measure of cautious contentment stirs within her. She waves happily at a *fee* of young lawyers – the invented collective noun slips into her head, unbidden. They've come across the bridge for the stews and the cock-fights. They'll be lucky to get back to Lincoln's Inn with the hose they put on this morning. She receives their clumsy, ribald replies as down-payment and ushers them towards the Jackdaw's entrance.

And then her taproom boy, Timothy, comes running down the lane. In the excitement of raising the apothecary's sign, she'd almost forgotten she'd sent him down to Cutler's Yard to pay the sign-maker.

'Mercy, young Timothy, what's the alarm?'

'The watermen say a new barque will drop anchor in the Pool tomorrow,' he tells her breathlessly. 'She's coming up from the

Hope Reach on the morning tide. Four masts!' He raises the appropriate fingers to indicate the wonder of it. 'Imagine it: *four*!'

For the denizens of Southwark, a newly arrived ship is like a freshly killed carcass to a wolf. There are victuals to be replenished at twice the going rate; goose-feather mattresses for men who've spent months sleeping on salty boards; a predictable uncertainty of the legs, which makes lifting a purse that much easier; an outlet for desires that until now have been only solitarily satisfied. It's been this way since the Romans were here, and Bianca Merton isn't about to pass on the opportunity.

'From which state is she? Do they say?' she asks, factoring translation into the equation – French and Spanish mariners take less time to serve than those from Muscovy, and Moors don't take drink at all.

'Venice,' says Timothy eagerly, with not the slightest comprehension of just how much powder he's about to ignite. 'She's the *Sirena di Venezia*.'

✠

It is the day after the story of the whitewash. Being a Wednesday, it is market day and Woodbridge is busier than Nicholas can remember. Well-heeled wool merchants, weavers, tanners and saymakers bellow at each other in the shadow of the session house like sailors in a storm. Stolid, boxy-faced Dutch refugees from the war in the Low Countries greet each other expansively and puff on their long clay pipes. In the stocks on Market Hill, scolds, habitual drunks and other disturbers of the queen's peace look on with sullen resignation.

Once the carts are set up, there is really very little for Nicholas to do. His father, sensing his restlessness, says, 'Away with you, boy! Find your ease where you choose.'

'Are you sure?'

'With a physician in the family, they'll think I'm after robbin' them.' It's meant kindly, but there's a grain of truth in Yeoman Shelby's words.

With no real purpose in his steps, Nicholas heads down to the river.

After years of helping his father scatter seeds on the ploughed fields, he has a mariner's sway in the shoulders when he walks. At Cambridge, the sons of gentlemen took it for upstart arrogance and beat him for it – until the day he forgot his place and broke the wrist of a minor baronet-in-waiting.

He's stopped by people he knows at least half a dozen times before he reaches the foot of Market Hill. They observe that he's put on weight; that he's thinner; that he looks younger without his beard; that he looks older. In truth, he knows exactly what he looks like: a yeoman's son – possessed of all his former rough edges. The man of medicine who spent a summer in Holland serving as surgeon to the Protestant army of the House of Orange, or the London physician, is someone else entirely. None of them ask why he's returned. None of them ask him about Eleanor, though he can see the question clearly enough in their eyes.

Along the quayside the little hoys bound for London are loading up with cheese and butter. Scottish salt-boats and Suffolk herring-drifters disgorge their cargoes by the barrel-load. The smell of pitch and freshly sawn timber reaches him from the small shipyard. It was from this very quay, he remembers, that he departed for Holland, the ink barely dry on his medical diploma. 'The Dons are murdering innocent Protestants in their beds,' he'd explained to Eleanor when he'd told her of his intention, his head brimming with idealistic rage at what the Spanish were doing to good Dutch Protestants across the sea. 'Sir William Havington has raised a company to aid the House of Orange in their just revolt. They need a surgeon.' Her reaction had astounded him.

Instead of admiration, there had been only cold-eyed anger. He'd discovered later that she'd taken his pompous talk of duty and responsibility for a sign that he was having second thoughts about the wedding. He can sense her now, standing beside him on the day the *Good Madelaine* sailed, refusing to weep, accepting his farewell with the pretence of indifference, a determined set to her jaw.

There had been others taking leave of loved ones that day, he recalls. Sir William Havington himself – a gentle white-haired soul who had long since retired from the profession of arms – had come to wish good fortune to the company that bore his name. He had made a point of shaking hands with everyone, from its new commander down to the lowliest recruit. Behind his smile, something in Sir William's face, some sadness he couldn't quite hide, had told Nicholas that a test was coming – a test that would make a bloody mockery of all their boisterous, innocent confidence.

And he'd been proved right. Within a month a dozen of them were dead. By winter, several more had returned to England maimed, condemned to wander the open roads begging for alms, because the House of Orange had somehow neglected to pay their promised bounty. As for those who'd remained in Holland – Nicholas included – all that had kept them from becoming a fleeing mob of desperate, starving fugitives – or, worse still, prisoners of the Spanish – had been the iron will and extraordinary courage of the man who had taken Sir William's place at their head: his son-in-law, Sir Joshua Wylde.

And there had been a third figure on the quayside that day, Nicholas now recalls: Sir Joshua's son, Samuel. He remembers a thin, pale lad with fair hair and a worried face. The boy had wanted so much to follow his father, but his youth and sickliness had made that impossible. *You couldn't have known it, Samuel*, says a voice in Nicholas's head as he gazes out over the leaden flatness of the estuary, *but you were luckier than many of those brave young lads with whom – even though you were still a child – you so fervently longed to trade places.*

On a whim, Nicholas leaves the quayside and follows the track along the bank. He knows where he's heading, though he won't yet admit it to himself.

I'll just take a quick glance from the riverbank, that's all... See if the house fits my memory... It can't hurt...

The grey expanse of the estuary cuts through the flat bleakness on its serpentine journey towards the sea. He catches the familiar fetid reek of tidal mud on the wind. It reminds him of the smell of flooded graves.

And then there it is: a modest but gracious thatched manor house set back from the creek, a well-grazed lawn sloping down to a reed-bed and a private jetty – Sir Joshua Wylde's Suffolk home. The place he prefers over the family seat in Gloucestershire, because here in Suffolk there is no sickly Samuel to remind him that he has no healthy heir to whom he can entrust Sir William Havington's legacy.

For a moment Nicholas thinks he has stepped back in time. The picture is almost exactly as he remembers it, even down to the thirty or so lads – a thin leavening of older men amongst them – who squat in expectation in a semicircle on the grass. And at their centre, standing as though he's just forced a breach in a rampart, is the fiercely bearded resplendence of Sir Joshua himself; a little older perhaps, a few more lines around his eyes from the permanent black scowl, the points of his jerkin stretched somewhat tighter around the belly, but undoubtedly the same mad-gazed hammer of the heretic.

If Nicholas believed in ghosts – as all right-minded people do – he'd think that's what these figures are – wraiths from the past. But he can hear Sir Joshua's voice as clear and as real as the exchanges on Market Hill, and he realizes that he's happened upon another company in preparation for the war in the Netherlands, a war that has been raging now for more than twenty years and shows no apparent sign of ending.

'Your average Don is born with a bloody heart,' Sir Joshua is telling the entranced company. 'He drinks slaughter with his dam's milk. He has no place on a civilized earth. It will be your God-given task to tear that heart out of his filthy, blaspheming body with your bare hands, if needs must!'

A rousing cry goes up in reply, though from what Nicholas can judge from the earnest faces, the nearest these lads have yet come to slaughter is catching coney for the pot.

And then Sir Joshua stiffens, as he spots Nicholas watching him from the path. A slow smile breaks through the great foliage around his face. It reminds Nicholas of an old tree trunk slowly parting after the axe blade has done its work. 'God's blood! As Christ is my saviour – look what the wind has brought!' he booms, beckoning with one leather-clad arm for Nicholas to step forward. 'This, my fine bully-boys, is Dr Nick Shelby. Came with us to Gelderland in '87. Callow as a country maiden when he joined. Best damned surgeon in the whole Orange army when he left. Almost as good as that scoundrel Paré, and he was a Frenchie, so he don't count.'

As Sir Joshua's fist closes around his own proffered hand, pumping his arm alarmingly, Nicholas offers an embarrassed grin to the upturned faces. He has never found Joshua Wylde an easy man to like. But he knows full well that, like every other fellow in Sir William Havington's company who returned, he owes Sir Joshua his life. He wonders how many of these eager fellows he'll bring safely home.

With another barrage of blood-curdling oaths fired at the

Spanish, Wylde instructs his recruits to attend to their preparations, and insists that Nicholas share a jug with him inside the house.

Stepping into the shadows of the hall, Nicholas finds the way almost blocked by a mountain of chests and sacks containing the necessities of comfortable campaigning: crates of malmsey, mattresses and pewter, polished plate armour, stands of matchlock muskets. A servant is dispatched and hurries back with sweet Rhenish in silver cups.

'Surely you're not in practice here in Suffolk,' Sir Joshua says as they drink. 'They still look to magic and wise-women in these parts.'

What can I tell him, Nicholas wonders as he feels his stomach churn; how can I explain what I've been through, to someone who thinks grief can be dispensed with by a quick prayer and a toast raised to the dead?

'After I came back,' he begins tentatively, 'I did set up in practice in London, but—'

Sir Joshua – who conducts conservations the way he assaults heavily defended bastions: relentlessly – doesn't wait for Nicholas to finish his reply. 'Married yet?' he asks bluntly. 'Sons? Healthy sons?'

'Sadly, no.'

'Don't tarry too long, lad. Greatest reverse of my life, not having a healthy son,' Sir Joshua tells him, and for a lingering moment Nicholas wishes he'd stayed beside the session house with his father.

'I thought you were still in the Low Countries,' Nicholas says, hoping Wylde won't notice how moderately he's drinking his wine.

'I took leave for Sir William's funeral, and to muster new volunteers.'

'Sir William – dead?' Nicholas has a vision of the white-haired Sir William Havington shot down in one last, ill-advised foray against the Spanish.

'In his bed. Quatrain fever, or so the physician said.' Sir Joshua raises his cup to toast his late father-in-law. 'Here's to a life honourably lived.'

Nicholas acknowledges the toast and takes a small sip of wine.

'Rhenish not up to scratch?' asks Sir Joshua quizzically.

'It's excellent. It's just that I don't sup so much now, not after...' Nicholas pauses, deciding there are some things Joshua Wylde doesn't need to know. 'And your son? How does Samuel fare?'

Sir Joshua stares into his cup as though expecting to find the answer written in the lees of the wine. 'Don't mistake me, Nick. I hold the boy in the deepest affection, always have.' His mouth twists with ill-disguised guilt. 'But I must confess it: to be long in his presence troubles me deeply. His sickness is an affront to a man like me. A reproach from God.' He spreads his hands as though seeking sympathy. 'The Wylde family won its first honours at Crécy. We've been warriors, every one of us, from that day hence. Why the good Lord chose to reward my services to Him with an heir who suffers from the falling sickness – well, I must have offended in some manner. Perhaps He thinks I haven't slaughtered enough heretics for Him yet.' Wylde takes his deep draught of Rhenish as though it were a medicine. 'I do my best for Samuel. He is not alone. I make sure he has company – companions.'

'Companions?'

'He can't mix with the village lads, you see. They taunt him. They say he's possessed by devils.'

'That's what a lot of ignorant folk say about the falling sickness.'

'Young Tanner Bell is with him. Came across from Havington Manor,' says Wylde. Then he notices the blank look on Nicholas's face. 'Tanner – Dorney's younger brother. You remember Dorney Bell, surely.'

Nicholas remembers Dorney all too well – a beanpole in a dented steel breastplate that made him look like a stand on which to hang plate armour. He remembers Dorney's country-boy ability to have the company laughing, even in the worst of the Dutch rain. But neither breastplate nor humour had saved Dorney Bell. He'd died in Nicholas's arms on his nineteenth birthday, a Spanish ball lodged in his spine.

'I really should be thankful Samuel still lives,' says Wylde, emitting a grunt of guilty laughter. 'There were physicians who told me he'd never see fifteen summers.'

'The falling sickness is indeed a cruel malady, Sir Joshua.'

'He's as weak now as his mother was, and she was scarcely seventeen when she died. Had she been made of hardier stuff, she might have survived the whelping.'

'Then perhaps there's still hope.' Nicholas says, trying not to wince at Wylde's apparent callousness.

'Oh, there's hope aplenty, according to the new doctor my wife has engaged.'

Nicholas's eyes widen. 'You've remarried?'

'*Isabel*,' Wylde explains portentously, seeing the look of surprise on his guest's face. 'We were wed in Utrecht last year.'

'She's Dutch?'

'English to her soul. She's a Lowell.' He frowns, as though the lineage escapes him. 'Don't know them, myself. But she's handsome enough. Young, too. Should breed well.'

'Forgive me,' says Nicholas with a smile, 'but I never thought of you as the wooing kind. I thought there was no space in your heart for anything but killing Spaniards.'

'Nor is there, Nick. But perhaps she might whelp me an heir – one with the proper constitution to take up the work when, like Sir William, I am aged and can no longer wield a sword.'

'How did you meet?' Nicholas asks, only too happy to keep the conversation away from his own marital history.

'She sought me out.'

Wylde has never struck Nicholas as the likely victim of an opportunistic woman, however comely.

'She'd heard of my reputation!' Sir Joshua says, just to make things clear. He leans forward until his beard juts close to Nicholas's face and adds in a conspiratorial whisper, 'Swore she would have no husband other than a Christian knight who knew his duty to the new religion. What was I to do? I can't sire an heir to the Wylde name off any common Hogen-Mogen whore, can I?'

'No. No, of course not,' replies Nicholas, almost lost for words. 'Is Lady Wylde here or still in Holland?'

'She's at Cleevely. Looking after Samuel. She moved him there from the Havingtons'.'

As Sir Joshua takes another swashing gulp of wine, Nicholas notices a sudden cunning gleam enter his deep-set eyes. 'Christ's blood! I swear there was ordination in our meeting today, Nick. I'll be damned if there wasn't. Another hour and I'd have been aboard the *Madelaine*. She's out in the river, taking on provisions at this very moment.' He regards Nicholas in silence a while, then tilts his head in contemplation. 'Busy, are you – at present?'

'Busy?'

'A thriving practice? Lots of patients? I can't believe a man with your skills finds himself underemployed.'

Nicholas shrugs. 'To be honest, I'm at something of a loose end. It's been a difficult year...'

'Then you can do me a service.'

'I can?'

'This new physician Isabel has pressed upon me – for Samuel. She's much taken with him. Says he can work miracles.'

'That's a dangerous claim, Sir Joshua.'

'A modest one, from my experience of physicians, Nick. Saving your presence, of course.'

'What's his name? Perhaps I've heard of him.'

'Arcampora. He's Swiss.'

Nicholas shakes his head and tries not to look too sceptical. 'Not a name I know, I'm afeared.'

'I've only met him once, in Holland – when Isabel brought him to me. Told me he'd studied at Basle. Swore on his life that he could cure Samuel's malady.'

'I don't wish to dash your hopes, Sir Joshua, but from all I've read, the falling sickness is not amenable to any lasting physic. I hope this fellow is not a charlatan. They're as common as weeds, and just as stubborn, I fear.'

'Then set my mind at rest.'

'How?'

'Visit Cleevely. Give me your honest opinion.'

'Me?'

'I've seen you at your chosen toil, Nick. As I told my bully-boys out there, you're the best damned physician I know. You'd be doing me no small service.'

'I fear I have to tell you something, Sir Joshua—' Nicholas begins.

But Wylde cuts him off with a wave of his hand. 'I'll pay your London prices, Nick – don't fear on that score. If this Arcampora fellow is as good as he claims, my mind will be set at ease. And if not, then my purse will be all the heavier for your discovery – the fellow's costing me an earl's ransom.'

Nicholas has no desire to become entrapped in the briars of Joshua Wylde's relationship with his sickly son, who clearly disappoints him so. But he remembers the look on Samuel's face, that day on the Woodbridge quayside: the desperate desire to please an unmatchable father. And, unquestionably, he could do with the money – at present he has no means of income. He thinks it might tide him over while he haggles with the warden at St Thomas's on Bankside; tries to get his old position back as a part-time physician to the poor of Southwark – a shilling a session, and all the sprains, fractures and hernias you can treat. He's good at the practical physic. It's the astrology, the piss-reading and the dogma he has no time for. Besides, were it not for Sir Joshua Wylde, his own bones might even now be mulching some desolate Dutch polder.

So Nicholas accepts the commission – if not exactly gladly. After all, it seems a small price to pay in exchange for the two precious years Wylde's bravery in Holland allowed him to share with Eleanor.

2

Gloucestershire. The next morning

'Slow down, y'daft nigit! What's the hurry? We'll be lucky to catch a single trout this early in the season.'

Against the rush of the wind, Samuel Wylde barely registers the breathless cry from somewhere behind him. Reaching the crest of the hill, high above the little village of Cleevely, he allows himself a moment to imagine that he's the only human soul alive on earth: a new Adam, unmarked by sin. With a single thought, he unpeoples the England laid out before him. His two companions – one a tall lad with delicate, questioning eyes; the other a mischievous overstuffed package of youthful rebellion – are instantly swept away. So too are the village boys who throw stones at him and call him 'Lucifer's familiar'. And he doesn't stop there. A snap of his fingers and there is no Queen Elizabeth, no Pope, no Philip of Spain. No lords and ladies. Not even his father, who anyway prefers far-away Holland to the company of his unsatisfactory son. With a single stroke of his imagination, they are all swept away. There is only him – Samuel Wylde – and the songs God sings to him when the light in his head becomes too bright to bear.

From his high vantage point it is easy for him to imagine this unpeopled world. He can see all the way to the far horizon and the Malvern Hills guarding the way into wild Wales. In the fields below him, oxen draw the first plough-blades of the season through the hard earth, for the sowing of the Lenten crop.

In their wake come wheeling flocks of birds in search of juicy worms. The sheepfolds look like tiny white clouds fallen to earth from a sky of cold, crystalline blue. Sinking to the cold grass to ease the ache in his legs, he sets down the parcel of manchet bread and cheese wrapped in cloth, to be eaten while the trio fish. His fingers, ungloved and now more than a little blue, are long and delicate. Samuel works tirelessly to keep them still. If they begin to tingle, it is a sure sign another of his paroxysms is on the way – a sign that God is about to shame him once again for the sins he doesn't remember committing.

But the world that Samuel has conjured is not quite empty. There is a dark shadow somewhere at the edge of it. He is not too sure what to make of the shadow yet. Does it threaten calamity? Or is it a sign that one day soon he will be the same as his two companions, Finney and Tanner: made afresh, unblemished, like the Adam of his imagination. A son whom a father might love.

The shadow is Professor Arcampora. Arcampora, with his strange accent and hawkish profile, his receding hairline, his savagely knife-like nose, and his jutting chin tipped with a spear-point of close-cut beard as dark as jet and shot through with sparks of silver. Arcampora, always clad in his black physician's gown, which makes him look like a magus straight out of the pages of the Old Testament. Somewhere deep inside Samuel, a last ember of hope begins to glow: perhaps this time it will be different. Perhaps this time, after the procession of stern men of physic that his father has sent to treat him – and to ease his own conscience into the bargain – this one, terrifying though he may appear, might really bring with him a cure.

The extraordinary Dr Arcampora is not working alone, Samuel has discovered. In overheard snatches of conversation between the physician and his stepmother, he has learned that there are others who are concerned for his health. Who these others are was not revealed. All Samuel knows is that they are brothers, and they live beyond the Narrow Sea. Apparently it is safer for them in the Netherlands than in England, though if that's the case, Samuel wonders why his father is so occupied fighting there. But these brothers obviously know of Samuel. And very soon someone will be arriving in England on their behalf, to gauge the efficacy of Dr Arcampora's work.

✠

'Look at him, Tanner – staring out into space like he's expecting to spy the Almighty winking back at him from behind a cloud.'

Finney, the taller lad with wide-set eyes that seem frozen in a permanent stare of puzzlement, sets down the three fishing rods he's carried up the hill, brushes aside the shanks of brown hair that the wind has blown across his brow and turns to his friend. He's the same age as Tanner Bell – sixteen – but he lacks the patience that stops Tanner's rebelliousness from sometimes sinking into youthful minor cruelties. 'I tell you truthfully, Tanner, if he has one of his falling spells up here, he can slither back to Cleevely on his belly like the little arseworm he is.' Finney doesn't find it easy, looking after Samuel Wylde.

'Leave him to his thoughts,' Tanner replies. 'He's not harming anyone.'

'Jesu,' says Finney despondently, 'let me see Southwark and the playhouse again just once more before I die of boredom in this wilderness!'

'I can usually tell when one of his fallings is on the way,' says Tanner Bell. 'He goes all hawk-eyed. At the moment he's just enjoying the view. Trust me.'

Finney and Tanner Bell are looking at a young willow of a lad, about their own age. He's tall, slightly stooped, with milky skin and wide eyes, and a mop of thin hair the colour of early corn.

His neck looks all the thinner for the scarf wrapped around it. He wears a dun-coloured broadcloth coat, defence against the chill wind, and calf-high boots laced tight, to support his ankles on the walk.

'But what if he has one of his fits up here – a bad one?' asks Finney. 'What if the Devil comes into him? Are you comfortable with that notion, Tanner: us, him and the Devil, all on our own out here on a hilltop?'

'It's happened before,' says Tanner Bell with a shrug that tightens the mutton-leg sleeves of his ill-fitting brown worsted coat across his plump shoulders. 'It's scary at first, but you get used to it.'

Given that Finney has been paid in coin to be here, Tanner Bell considers himself the only true friend Samuel has. Probably has *ever* had. While Sir Joshua Wylde has spent much of the last sixteen years in Holland, fighting hand-to-hand with the Pope, Tanner had been his son's companion at Havington Manor, where Samuel had been deposited into the care of his grandparents, Sir William and Lady Mercy Havington.

'I don't know how you bear it,' Finney says dismissively. 'I wouldn't have come if I'd known the truth. Compared to this, the playhouse is like living in Elysium.'

'We Bells have served the Havingtons for three generations,' says Tanner indignantly. 'They've been good to us – better than a fellow could expect from the quality.'

'Marry! The quality will throw you out at the first fart! How d'you think I ended up in the playhouse?'

'Not Sir William and Lady Mercy,' protests Tanner. 'When my father lost what was left of his wits, after Dorney died, Sir William did his best to look after him – right until the end.'

'Who's Dorney? Not another addle-pate the Havingtons took in?'

'My older brother. This is his worsted coat I'm wearing.'

'I wondered why it doesn't fit you.'

Tanner's impish face becomes suddenly serious. 'Dorney was tall, and very thin – more like your build. But he was seven years older than me.' He turns his back on Finney and sticks out his backside. 'See that patch?' he says over his shoulder.

'Yes,' says Finney, looking at the coat where it spreads in broad pleats over Tanner's buttocks. A coarsely stitched square – of a quite different pedigree from the rest of the coat – betrays the hasty repair.

'That's where the Spanish ball struck – the one that killed him,' Tanner says in an awed voice, as if the patch is a holy relic.

'That must have hurt,' observes Finney.

Tanner Bell straightens and turns to face Finney again. 'They sent the coat to my father, afterwards – didn't fit him, either.'

'And that's why your father lost his wits: because of a coat?'

'The coat was the last straw,' says Tanner, wondering if all young players are as dull in the wits as Finney. 'You see, Porter – my father – had gone to the Netherlands with Sir William in '71. But Porter Bell wasn't much of a soldier. He got caught, daft bugger – spent months as a captive of the Spaniards. Dorney's death – June '87 it was – was the very end of him. It was like the Devil just gathered up what the Dons had left of him the first time around and threw them on the midden.'

'So he's dead, is he – your father?' asks Finney in a comradely tone. 'Mine, too. Hanged for thieving a purse.' He shrugs at the fickleness of fortune. 'Would have got away with it, too, if he hadn't chosen to rob the only magistrate in all twenty-six wards of London what could sprint more than ten paces after lunch.'

'He's not dead,' says Tanner indignantly. 'He's in Gravesend.'

'Have you ever *played* Gravesend?' asks Finney.

'It's where he came from.'

'Oh.'

'When he became too ungovernable to stay at Havington Manor, Sir William set him up there, as a waterman. Even bought him his own wherry. That's the sort of man Sir William was. I suppose I should have gone with him, but...' Tanner's voice trails off as he remembers the drunken blows, and the slurred protestations of regret that always followed. 'Well, there was Samuel to look after, and I was always treated more like family than servant.'

'Well, Gravesend or Cleevely – I know where I'd rather be.'

'The theatre?' says Tanner, knowing a little of Finney's former life. 'It might sound exciting. But sleeping on planks, and starving whenever the Lord Mayor chooses to shut the playhouses? At least here you get a mattress and fresh pottage.' The habitual cheeriness returns to his puppyish face. 'So stop griping about Samuel and his fits. Pick up those rods. There's trout to catch – when *he*'s ready.'

Finney looks at Samuel, kneeling in impenetrable contemplation on the grass, and then in the general direction of Cleevely House. 'Alright, Tanner – let's say you're correct and Samuel isn't possessed by the Devil when he has one of his fallings,' he says, sounding unconvinced. 'But now that Dr Arcampora has arrived, Samuel doesn't have very far to crawl if he wants to be. Does he?'

✳

The city Customs House, set back a little from the river to the east of Billingsgate, is built like a castle keep: a stern hexagonal tower on each corner, and a door like the entrance to a prison set menacingly into the façade on the right-hand side. Glancing at its dour brick face in the early-morning light as she hurries along the quayside the next morning, Bianca wonders why the English like to reward an honest merchant's endeavours with such a forbidding welcome. She already knows the answer: because of seditious Catholic pamphlets secreted in sacks of ginger from the Indies; because of forbidden Masses hidden amongst bags of Baltic hemp; because of letters wrapped in oilcloth and hidden in casks of herring – letters from the continental Catholic seminaries to their agents in England.

She can spot the men from the High Court of Admiralty and the Privy Council searchers in the crowd, simply by the way they appear to have no employment except to scan the throng with suspicious eyes.

Bianca comes across the bridge infrequently now. She has little need to. She long ago whittled out the merchants who pass off crushed acorns and rowan berries as genuine spices from the Indies, and the purveyors of hoof-shavings who swear on their mother's grave they're selling real narwhal horn landed from the western ocean. Most of what she uses in her concoctions, distillations and infusions comes from the little patch of ground that is her physic garden, down by the river and known only to herself and Nicholas. The rest – the small measures of frankincense and fenugreek, the cerasee and cardamom – she gets in exchange for her balms and salves from those few importers she trusts.

Since she arrived in the city, little more than two years ago, she has noticed how London's mood has changed. The people are not as tolerant to strangers as they once were. On the heels of the threatened Spanish invasion in '88 has come a deepening wariness of foreigners. They are taxed more, stopped by the watchmen more often, railed against in church sermons and official proclamations. And although she has absorbed the peculiarities of her adopted country as best she can, Bianca – betrayed by her corona of richly dark hair and the warm hue of her skin as one who has grown up beneath the Veneto sun – stands out in a crowd like a falcon amongst a flock of seagulls.

But most of all she puts this hardening of attitude down to the fact that England's queen is almost sixty. She could die soon, though even to suggest such a possibility in public is treason. Now people are beginning to consider the possibility that Philip of Spain – once married to Elizabeth's half-sister Mary – may once again seek to claim his late wife's dowry, this time by conquest rather than marriage.

On Bankside, none of this seems to matter so much. In the liberty of Southwark, where the Lord Mayor's writ does not run, people appear much less concerned by matters of state and faith. The theatre, the bull- and bear-baiting pits, the stews and the taverns seem, to Bianca, a clearer echo of what England might once have been, before the new faith with all its godly rectitude got its hands on the rest of the land.

Her trip across the bridge today has a purely commercial motive. As foretold by Timothy, her taproom lad, the *Sirena di Venezia* has arrived, and Bianca is not about to let the Hanging Sword and other taverns along the wharves grab the profitable trade of thirty or more Venetian mariners with coin to spend – not when there's the Jackdaw just a brief walk away on the other shore. Not when Bianca Merton can flash her vivid amber eyes and extol the attractions of Southwark fluently in her mother's own tongue: Italian. She's even brought with her a leather jug of her best knock-down to sway any doubters.

Making her way around the piles of shining Muscovy pelts, neat stands of ornate panelling from Saxony and ingots of Swedish iron, Bianca sees the *Sirena* lying a little way ahead. Just as Timothy had said, she's the largest ship at the wharf: a fine four-masted carrack. Painted proudly on her high stern-castle is a winged lion: the emblem of Venice. On the quayside, a gang of stevedores is raising a rampart of sacks. Suddenly she hears someone calling to her in a clear, sharp voice that carries the dialect of the central Veneto.

'*In nome dei santi benedetti! Bianca!*'

Turning, Bianca searches for a familiar face amongst the men clustered around the Customs House. And then she sees him, strutting towards her, head held high, all five feet three inches of him. A little Venetian cockerel of a man: Bruno Barrani, her cousin from Padua – champion of the Catholic faith, as handsome as Alexander.

Perhaps not Alexander, she concedes in the moment of recognition. The aquiline nose is softly blunted at the tip, robbing it of patrician force, and the delicately curled black moustache he wears above his bud-like lips – and which in Padua he sported like a knight's banner – might be considered by some (especially the English) as a little preposterous. But still, he's handsome enough. Clad almost entirely in black – black hose, black doublet, black half-cape – his only concessions to colour are the crimson-braided points securing his doublet and the gilt buckles on his shoes. Even his hair, worn extravagantly long, is black. Unnaturally so. Then she remembers: Bruno was always in the habit of applying a dye of sage and indigo to it. She feels the smile spread across her face like the heat from a good fire.

As he reaches her, Bruno bends a knee so extravagantly that she could be Caterina di Medici herself. One arm sweeps across his little body as if he intends to make her a gift of all London. He seizes her right hand to kiss, and she gets a glimpse of black doeskin gloves studded with gemstones – probably glass, knowing Bruno. He launches himself upon a tide of voluble reunion.

Bianca stops him with a laugh. 'Cousin, peace! English, please! Speak English.'

He looks hurt. 'English? Why English? Have you forgotten your mother tongue since you came here?'

'No, of course I haven't. But it's better that way,' she tells him, not wanting to hurt his pride. 'When the English overhear someone speak in a foreign language, they think he's trying to outsmart them at commerce or plotting their downfall.'

'Then it shall be so,' says Barrani with a sigh, adopting the expression of a holy martyr bracing himself for the pagan's arrow. 'If you wish me to be uncouth, then for you I shall forbear all *onore*. I do my best to make myself understood.'

'I'm sure you'll manage,' she says, knowing that he had his lessons for free at the knee of her own father, who was English to his roots. 'What are you doing here, Bruno – in London, of all places?'

A ribbon of that impossibly dark hair has fallen across his brow. He raises one gloved index finger to it. But instead of brushing it aside, he moves it to a more pleasingly rakish angle. Bianca cannot help but laugh. How can such a small vessel hold such a quantity of vanity? she wonders. But she knows it also holds a generous heart of equal measure. 'Rice, Cousin!' he announces proudly. 'I have come to sell the heretic English some fine Lombardy rice.'

'*Rice?* You used to cry at the very sight of it, I seem to remember.'

'I sell it – I don't eat it.' He scans the low ceiling of grey cloud and the choppy river. 'Where it is always winter, it will not grow. So I bring!' He brushes his hands together with a slap of expensive doeskin, as though he's just successfully concluded a difficult transaction. 'Very good profit!'

'You – a merchant, Bruno? Since when?'

'A year or two. These are early days.'

'Well, you seem to be prospering,' she says, taking in the inky braid woven into the ebony silk of his doublet. 'But I'm surprised.

When we were children you wanted to be a captain of pike for the King of Spain.'

'I have unquestionably the heart,' he tells her proudly, before raising one hand to the level of his temple and explaining with a self-deprecating smile, 'but sadly not the *altezza* – the height.'

She smiles at his pronunciation of height: *ayt*; and at the image of the diminutive Bruno Barrani attempting to wield a ten-foot pike-shaft. 'Besides, I thought you were bound for the seminary. Last time I saw you, you were determined to become a chaplain to Cardinal Fiorzi.'

'The cassocks are too big,' he says. 'I would look like a peregrine hidden under a sack. Besides, I dislike celibacy even more than I dislike rice.'

'Well, it gladdens my heart to see you. You're the first proper contact with home I've had since I came here.'

'And now you are an English milady, yes? Like your queen – very rich!'

Bianca laughs. 'Not rich, Bruno. I own a tavern, and I dispense cures. Over there.' She points in the general direction of Bankside, hidden by the buildings that sit on the bridge like a grand boulevard floating above the water. 'I came across because I heard the *Sirena di Venezia* had docked.'

'She is a fine vessel, Cousin, is she not? His Eminence helped mc to purchase her. We are joint owners.'

'So you are Cardinal Fiorzi's man after all.'

He looks at her shrewdly. 'You 'ave a man now? English man, yes?'

'No, Cousin. I do *not* have "English man". Nor do I desire one, if he were to be offered; thank you for asking.'

'Almost thirty and unmarried!' he says in horror. 'How do you expect your dear departed mother to find peace in heaven?'

He has a point, Bianca thinks. At eight years old, like all the girls in her street, she had wanted to marry Christ. By now – she assumes – a goodly proportion of them already have. But her father had protested that it would be a barren bridal bed for a nature as inquisitive as hers. So she'd lowered her sights a little – to Cardinal Santo Fiorzi. Barely coming up to his waist, she'd somehow found the astonishing nerve to march up to that magnificent, scarlet-attired confidant of God, one day after Mass.

'Yes, child? What is it that you want?' he had asked. 'Are you not a little young for confession?'

She had taken a deep breath and asked the question she'd been rehearsing for a month: 'Would you mind awfully being my husband, Your Eminence? Mother says I cook clams very well, and I wouldn't need a throne – not yet.'

She'd sulked for a full week when, to her mortification, Fiorzi had laughed with delight and told her that, sadly, his heart was already taken.

But Cardinal Fiorzi had not forgotten the precocious child who could cook clams. He had found a way to reward her devotion. Although she'd had no comprehension of it at the time, the Sacred College of Cardinals was more a snake-pit clad in crimson cloth than a nexus of piety. Fiorzi had powerful enemies. So he had entrusted her and Bruno with messages that he didn't want carried by servants who could be bribed or threatened. Their reward was a prominent position in the procession when the effigies of the saints were paraded through Padua on feast days. It placed them amongst the most popular youngsters in the city.

Her first great secular *infatuazione* – at sixteen – had been the ne'er-do-well son of the man who painted the shrines in Father Rossi's church. He was as lean as a greyhound, Bianca remembers, with cascades of lustrous curls and a face that looked like she imagined Christ's might look, if it was his cherished desire to be crucified three times a week and twice on Sundays.

As soon as her mother had got to hear of it, Bianca found herself accompanied everywhere by a phalanx of protectors, led by Bruno himself. Most galling of all, the object of her desire had resolutely refused to hurl himself against their ranks in order to reach her. And then she'd discovered that the crucified look was something he put on for any maid foolish enough to buy it.

And now I have feelings for a man married to a ghost.

Where, in all of God's bright dominions, was that thought spawned? she wonders. Startled by the sudden image of Nicholas Shelby, she blushes.

'Cousin?'

Bruno's voice cuts into her embarrassment. 'You must come see my fine crew! All best men of Veneto. Very handsome. Fine teeth. No squints. Maybe not all as perfumed as gentlemen, but a bull is not a bull without his musk. I find you one for a husband.'

Laughing, Bianca takes Bruno by the arm. 'It's a long time, Cousin, since I had an offer like that,' she says. And being a good half-head taller than him, she allows herself to feel positively regal as he leads her towards the *Sirena* while promising her that his fine Venetian bulls will eat, drink and entertain themselves in no tavern in all of London save hers.

✠

On the deck of the *Sirena*, and safe from suspicious ears, Bruno falls back into Italian. A dozen sun-bronzed men are labouring to bring the sacks of rice out of the ship's hold, sweating even in the cool of the English air. Their faces – mostly young – are familiar to her, even though they're the faces of strangers. In their gestures and voices is the edgy vibrancy of the Veneto. Bruno calls them to order. When he explains proudly who she is, the men instantly assume a reverent humility, coming forward in turn to greet her formally, starting with the tall, saturnine sailing master, Luzzi. Then she meets a Piero, and a Luca, and a Francesco, and a Cesare – not one of them less than a palm's width taller than their master – and so on, until the last man is standing before her.

'This is Graziano,' Bruno says proudly. 'He is our lucky charm, our mascot. Graziano is a father to the boys when they are away from home.'

Graziano is the oldest of the crew, almost sixty, she guesses. His weather-beaten face is the colour of expensive leather, his jaw frosted with thick white stubble. He has a power and a dignity about him that would better suit a duke. If he were not a humble sailor, she could imagine him a man accustomed to giving orders and having them obeyed. He regards her with deep, clever eyes that have a familiarity she cannot place; and speaks to her as though she's an old friend, although to her certain knowledge she's never seen him before.

'Signorina, it does my old heart good to see a friendly face in this heathen land,' he says in a rich baritone that wouldn't be out of place delivering Mass in the little church of St Margaret's in Padua, where she'd worshipped as a child. The sound of his voice, the song of her own language, makes her feel suddenly homesick.

And then, as if they'd been waiting for Graziano to give her his blessing, the rest of the crew are bowing and grinning, doffing their caps, fussing their shirts and hoisting their mariner's slops around their waists, as though a duchess had just stumbled upon a poor man's game of dice, and are all eagerly drinking from the leather wine jug she's brought with her.

All, that is, except Graziano, who stands aside as though he's not quite one of them, even though they have appointed him their portafortuna: their lucky charm. And she catches him studying her. Studying her as if – for all the warmth of his greeting – he's trying to decide whether she can be trusted.

Clad in a muddy riding cloak and knee-length boots, the stranger arrives at Barnthorpe the next day.

The first of the family to catch sight of him is Nicholas's sister-in-law, Faith, who's standing by the village well, infant on hip, complaining to Mother Haskett about the increasing number of vagrants troubling decent folk on the Ipswich road. She will say later that he looked just as she imagined the man who brought the Scots queen's death sentence to Fotheringhay might have looked.

Barely ten minutes later, the letter he bears is safely delivered into Nicholas's hands:

To our right worthy and learned friend, Dr Nicholas Shelby of Barnthorpe in the county of Suffolk. Know you that the President of the College of Physicians, William Baronsdale, Esq., has ordered upon this fourteenth day of February anno Domini 1591, the thirty-third of our sovereign majesty Elizabeth, that the said doctor shall present himself on the twenty-fifth day of March before the Censors of this College, to answer truthfully several and diverse charges laid upon his conduct and proficiency.

Reading the summons again, it occurs to Nicholas that any thought of returning to the world of physic might be fatally premature.

3

London, 4th March 1591

As Nicholas Shelby rides beneath the portcullis at Aldgate in the fragile spring sunshine, the city hits him like a fist.

The strident voices of the women traders battle for his attention and his purse. *Comfits by the ounce. Sweet comfits by the ounce! Fine black bullaces, tuppence a box! Damsons, noble damsons!* Labourers in cloth shirts and baggy galligaskins jostle his horse. Apprentice boys, their heads bobbing insolently beneath their caps, dart around him like minnows in a stream. A pair of pigs' trotters wave cheerily at him, as a butcher's lad lumbers by with half a hog's carcass slung across his broad back. On Fenchurch Street, women out shopping for cambric and ribbons fuss each other out of his way, steering their broad farthingales to safety like errant offspring. The air is a pungent mix of ammonia from the tanners' workshops, the waste of horse and oxen, the lanolin of sheep's wool, the beery breath of the King's Head tavern... every scent known to a human nostril. Sleepy Barnthorpe could be on the far side of the planet.

To return feels surprisingly good, better than he'd imagined. In truth, he has been dreading returning to the city that belongs so irrevocably to Eleanor. It is just eight months since his mastery of physic failed them both. How mockingly ineffectual his years of study, all his vaunted knowledge, had proved. None of it had stopped Eleanor and the child in her belly slipping away from him, consigning him to a grief that had then robbed him of what little else of his former life was worth keeping. His medical practice on Grass Street is gone, his friends – mostly fellow physicians – believe he has vanished into a life of vagrancy. What would they think of him now, he wonders, if they knew he had found another existence in Southwark, an existence that even now often feels as alien to him as if he were the sole survivor of a shipwreck, cast up upon some exotic island shore.

Heading down Gracechurch and into New Fish Street, he passes the fine new houses that no ordinary soul can afford to rent. He crosses London Bridge, riding slowly between the shops and houses that cling to it like huge square barnacles made of plaster, brick and wood – a whole city thoroughfare laid across the water on stone pillars. At the far end he passes beneath the great gatehouse that guards the southern approaches to the city. Around its top the skulls of executed traitors set on spikes seem to smile at him: *Welcome home, Dr Shelby! We may be long past curing, but there's work down there for you to do amongst the living.*

It's almost dusk when Nicholas returns his rented horse to the ostler at the sign of the Tabard. He makes the last part of his journey on foot, through the lengthening shadows. Slung almost jauntily over his shoulder is a small leather drawstring sack with his few possessions: clean hose, a day shirt, his ivory comb, his nightshirt. It also contains his purse. He's on Bankside now. True Banksiders don't carry their purses on their belts.

The Jackdaw tavern stands halfway down a narrow alley to the south of the Mutton Lane river stairs, in the liberty of Southwark. Once a hostelry for the pious visiting the nearby monastery of St Saviour's – long since cast down – it has occupied this spot since the reign of the second Richard. Indeed, there are some who will tell you it served its first quart of stitch-back to great Caesar himself, when he found himself suddenly in need of ale and oysters on his way up from the coast. Just as its less judicious patrons sometimes need a little support when they leave, so too does the Jackdaw look to its neighbours to keep it from toppling over. Its old beams sag with inebriated contentment between the houses to left and right. The lodging rooms on the upper floors seem frozen in the act of falling into the street after too much of an indulgent night. When the wind is from the north, you can smell the river mud even above the scents from the new brewhouse that Bianca Merton has installed on the far side of the rear courtyard.

When he sees the apothecary's sign hanging alongside the Jackdaw's own, he allows himself a contented smile. One of his last acts before leaving for Barnthorpe had been to seek the help of his friend, Lord Lumley, the patron of the College of Physicians' chair of anatomy, in procuring the licence from the Grocers' Guild, which manages such things in the city. It would appear Lumley has kept his word.

The flickering candlelight beckons to him through the tiny lozenges of pitted glass that make up the Jackdaw's lopsided windows. For a moment he hesitates. It's an ingrained reticence. It stems from what his father calls 'the evil harvests'. When famine threatens and the pottage bowl only goes so far, you wait your turn; father and elder brother must eat their share first, because they are more use on the land than a ten-year-old.

At Cambridge, during his medical studies, it was reinforced: the sons of yeomen are so far beneath the sons of gentlemen that they must hang back, defer, carry and wait.

But it was mostly knocked out of him in the Low Countries. No one there stood in the way of the physician when the cry for his services went up. Now it is merely an almost unnoticeable pausing, a momentary slowing of the beat. Ducking under the lintel – Nicholas is of average height, but the entrance seems to have sunk a little further into the earth than the last time he was here – he steps inside.

At once the familiar smells of wood-smoke and hops envelop him, followed by a tide of unrestrained chatter: wherrymen arguing over mooring fees, players from the Rose berating the Master of the Queen's Revels for his lack of artistic imagination, chandlers from the waterfront complaining about tight-pursed ships' masters. And there's no mistaking the huge form of Ned Monkton propping up the counter, or Rose's cry of *Anon!* as she calms impatient customers.

He has to strain his ears to catch the familiar sound of a lute. But there it is: the Jackdaw's taproom boy, Timothy, is strumming a ballad to a pair of lovers in the far corner.

There have been times when Nicholas has wanted to tear that lute from Timothy's gentle hands, smash it over his knee and hurl the wreckage into the fire. In his grief, lovers' ballads had been like a virulent poison to him. But he can bear them now; and besides, Bianca had quietly instructed Timothy to drop 'The Gallant's Heart' and 'The Maid and Her Beau' from his repertoire, along with the other tunes that she has somehow discovered were Nicholas and Eleanor's favourites.

At first he can't see Bianca amongst the throng. He casts his gaze over the crowded taproom, searching for that unruly cascade of dark tresses.

He spots her at the centre of a knot of brightly dressed men who look as English as an elephant. She's wearing the emerald-green kirtle that flatters her slim figure, her hair pinned loosely beneath a white linen coif. That darting smile, like the flash of a sunlit kingfisher's wing, lights up the dark interior. Those slender hands, brimming with animation, are doing half her talking for her. The men around her seem enchanted.

And then she sees him.

He feels suddenly foolish – standing there in his plain white yeoman's doublet, the simple bag slung over his shoulder as though he were an itinerant seller of cheap trinkets. He lifts the fingers of his right hand to his head and fusses at the tangle of coarse black hair – then stops self-consciously: what if she mistakes his attempt to make himself presentable for an infestation of lice?

All the way from Barnthorpe he's imagined what he would say to Bianca, how he would greet her. He's rehearsed everything from high courtesy to easy heartiness, from an extravagant bend of the knee to a kiss on the cheek. But all that comes out of his mouth is 'How now, Mistress Merton?'

'Well, hey nonny, nonny, if it isn't Dr Shelby,' she replies languidly, with an almost imperceptible lifting of one finely arched eyebrow.

Ned Monkton turns from the counter. Though he's younger than Nicholas, his huge chest and wiry red hair make him look like a mother bear surprised by the return of a wandering cub. His ruddy face breaks into a grin. On the other side of the taproom, Rose stops in mid-*Anon*. Timothy's fingers hesitate above the strings of his lute. Even the admirers around Bianca fall silent.

Letting his sack fall to the taproom floor, Nicholas spreads his hands, palm upwards, as though mystified by his own arrival. 'I've returned,' he says lamely.

'So you have,' observes Bianca.

She studies the solid, guileless face before her. She notes the jaw is still shaved unfashionably close – hardly a beard at all, more like soot on a hearth-brick. His chin carries its customary upward tilt – to her mind, an oddly belligerent pose for a man she knows to be inherently gentle. She takes in the raised hands: the battered fingers looking as though they should belong to a shipwright rather than a physician; the strong wrists with their filigree of tiny black curls disappearing into the sleeves of his doublet. She thinks he looks shorter than she remembers.

'I said I would.'

'Yes, you did.'

'And here I am.'

'And so you are.'

For a moment they fall silent, regarding each other through the taproom fug.

'Have I offended?' he asks, puzzled by her coolness.

'Mercy, why should you think that?' she asks softly as she bestows a chaste kiss upon his right cheek. 'I was simply wondering: have you not brought your two friends with you?'

'My two friends?'

'Master Mayhem and Mistress Chaos. Or perhaps they're at home, keeping their friends Disruption and Calamity company.'

As she steps back, he searches those astounding amber eyes for a sign of levity. And finds it.

'I see Southwark's new apothecary specializes chiefly in ginger and vinegar,' he ripostes.

And then, without conscious agency, they're embracing – like the lovers they might be, if life (and Eleanor) hadn't got in the way.

'By the way, I think the new sign does very well. Don't you?' says Nicholas when they part.

'And I must thank you for it, Nicholas, however you managed it.' She smooths her green brocade kirtle over her hips. 'You look as though you've had a hard ride. I've kept your lodgings in the attic free, if you need a bed for the night – or longer. There's pottage still, if you're hungry. I'll get Rose to bring you a bowl.'

For a moment she looks deep into his eyes. He can feel her gaze laying out his thoughts like cards on a gaming table, face up – revealed.

'I'd like that.'

'Then welcome back, Dr Shelby,' she says sweetly with a nod of her head. 'Come, there's someone I want you to meet: my cousin Bruno. His ship is moored at Galley Quay.'

She leads him to the group of foreigners and introduces him to the man who appears to be their chief: a diminutive fellow clad all in black, with mustachios the Earl of Leicester and Francis Walsingham might envy, had they still lived.

'This is my cousin, Bruno Barrani,' she says. 'And these *bravi ragazzi* are his crew.'

Barrani immediately appoints Nicholas his long-lost brother, embracing him as though he's just been rescued from a shipwreck. In an instant Nicholas is enveloped in a frenzy of hand-pumping, cheek-kissing and back-slapping as the crew of the *Sirena* greet him expansively. Though by nature a reserved man, he does his best to respond in kind. 'Drink with us, *mio fratellino!*' Bruno insists.

'Oh, Nicholas doesn't sup,' says Bianca.

He knows she's only trying to protect him. Before Timothy found him in the Thames mud last year – one-third drowned, one-third frozen, one-third barely clinging to life – he'd spent months trying to find oblivion in knock-down and stitch-back. But at Barnthorpe, with his family, he'd discovered that he could drink weak small-beer again and not succumb to the old temptation. A milestone, he'd thought at the time, on a road whose end was as yet unknown to him.

'A cup of small-beer will be fine,' he says, accepting Bruno's offer.

'Are you sure?' Bianca whispers in his ear.

'Surer now than when I left,' he replies. In truth, he's surer about quite a lot.

✠

The lad named Finney has never troubled himself much about the judgement of his Maker. The wild licentiousness of the player's life, the delights of Bankside with its taverns, its bear-pits and its dice dens, the companionable weeks on the road when pestilence or the Privy Council shut the London theatres, all these have made him canny; older than his sixteen years might suggest.

But Finney is troubled now.

So troubled, in fact, that he's desperate to put as many miles between himself and Dr Arcampora as he possibly can, before his absence is discovered. For Cleevely House has become a very different place since Dr Arcampora rode out of the dark beech wood.

Take, for example, the once innocently appointed chamber off the great hall – the chamber that the physician has now made his own, and where no one may enter other than by express invitation. Now it almost bursts at the seams with vials of strange liquids, astrolabes and almanacs, pestles and mortars, flasks, syringes, pots of yellow alum and Attic ochre, and all the other marvels that Arcampora has apparently brought with him from fabled Basle.

And what is the casual observer to make of a freshly killed fox, with its dull poisoned eyes and bloody mouth? Or the wooden board with the number 4400 written on it in a dozen different ways, from Greek to Hebrew via Aramaic, and which apparently is the Cabalistic number associated with the archangel Samael?

None of this is what Finney had expected when he arrived.

When offered this new part by the player-manager – this admittedly unorthodox part – for twice the usual wage, he hadn't needed much persuading. *It's easy: all you have to do is play the part of a companion. Smile. Be a friend. You don't even have to learn any lines.*

But the player-manager had said nothing about him becoming Lucifer's apprentice boy. Nothing about sleepy Cleevely being the mouth of the worm, the gateway to the most abominable of sins.

So at dusk, under a rising moon, Finney slips out through a window in the buttery, left unlatched for just that purpose. He considers himself well prepared for the journey. No, not the journey. He will call it as he truly sees it: the *escape*. He's wearing thick woollen hose against the cold evening air, and Tanner Bell's brown worsted half-coat, stolen admittedly, but more use to him now than to Tanner. Besides, it's not strictly Tanner's coat, is it? It's his brother Dorney's, and Dorney is dead. It even fits Finney – with his tall, thin frame, which has always confined him to female roles, every one of them, from a virgin maid to the Queen of Sicily – better than it does Tanner. It troubles him not a jot that Dorney Bell died in this coat. It's warm, and that's all Finney cares about.

Stuffed inside the coat is a small hoard of bread and cheese. Once he's put enough miles under his feet, he'll find a tavern and put on a performance – something from *The Friars* or *Hieronimo* – in exchange for a meal and somewhere to sleep. With his long stride, he reckons he can make Oxford in two days. He'll be back on the boards at the Rose or the Curtain inside a week: a proper 'roaring boy' once more. He'll be done with the smell of damp sheep, the company of country goose-caps, boys with the falling sickness and – most important of all – blaspheming, crazy-eyed Swiss necromancers.

He slips through Cleevely village like an angular wraith, a shadow puppet propelled on invisible strings. The houses are shuttered and dark, the lanterns extinguished; not the meanest glimmer of light to be seen anywhere. Not even the growl of a waking dog marks his passing. Above him, streamers of grey cloud flit across the moon like a ripped shroud drawn across a dead man's face.

He's into his stride now. He reckons he can keep up this pace for hours. Till sunrise, if necessary. An owl calls to him from the beech wood. He welcomes it as an encouragement; certainly not a warning.

Because Finney – in his stolen, dead man's coat – is already beginning to think himself free.

4

ext morning, Nicholas is surprised to see that a small queue has formed in the lane outside the Jackdaw, waiting for the tavern to open. He knows at once they haven't come for the knock-down and the mad-dog, because he's seen the same quietly stoic faces before – when he was the part-time physician at St Thomas's hospital for the poor on Thieves' Lane. He watches with growing admiration as Bianca treats the inflamed eyes of the parish constable's wife with turbith and agaricke juice, and brings ease to a waterman afflicted with a particularly phlegmy cough by mixing a syrup of sanicle and hoarhound. The rest seem content with a wise-woman's advice on maladies various – from inconstant lovers to chilblains. This is physic that Nicholas has sworn to eschew as superstition. But he can't deny the constable's wife when she says her eyes have never felt so refreshed, or the noisy but victorious elimination taking place in the alley – and all achieved without a single horo-scope being cast or a word of Latin spoken, as would happen if it had been a member of the College of Physicians at work and not a half-Italian, half-English tavern-mistress. Which makes what he has to say after a breakfast of sweet eggs, bread and butter all the more an admission of defeat.

'I've been summoned to attend a hearing at the College of Physicians, before the Censors' panel,' he tells Bianca despondently.

She regards him quizzically. 'A hearing? Into what?'

'Into my professional conduct – after Eleanor died.'

What she knows about his fall is only what he's already confessed: the drunken rampages, the public rants against an uncaring god, the flight of patients who no longer cared to be treated by a raving madman, the final desperate attempt at self-destruction in the river...

'But you redeemed yourself, Nicholas. Think of what you *prevented*.'

'I swore an oath to heal, and instead I killed a man.'

'You didn't kill him, Nicholas – the Privy Council killed him. And with just cause. He was a monster.'

A darkness comes into his eyes. 'But they can't know the truth, can they? They must never know.'

'Did you know that, while you were in Suffolk, Ned and Rose went to the execution? They wouldn't believe that man was truly dead unless they saw it with their own eyes.'

'You didn't attend?'

'Oh, I thought about it, believe me. But in the end...' Her voice tails off into silence.

For a moment Nicholas says nothing. Seeing the fear in her eyes, he lays a hand on her wrist. 'It's in the past. Let it remain there. He can't harm either of us any more.'

'They told me he never uttered a sound, not even when they cut out his entrails and burned them before his eyes. Utter silence, as if he wasn't really there.'

'He can't return, Bianca. You're safe.'

'Do you promise? No more madmen offering Satan their souls in exchange for knowledge?'

'I promise.'

She holds his gaze for a while, as though taking the measure of what he's just said. Then she laughs. 'What's the worst they can do to you at this hearing – stop you attending their interminable feasts?'

He knows what she's trying to do. And he's genuinely grateful. But it doesn't make him feel better. 'They could have me imprisoned – condemned to the Bridewell for charlatanism.'

A wave of anger floods across her face. 'Have physicians now become justices of the peace? Are we to be sent to the Tower for falling ill?'

'I'm sure the idea would appeal to more than a few of them.'

'But you're not a charlatan – are you?'

'I don't believe so.'

'Tell them to ask people around here. They'd soon learn the truth.'

'The College Censors tend to avoid Bankside, unless it's for a discreet visit to the stews.'

'Well, whatever they decide, if you want to use your skills, why not here? An apothecary *and* a physician – that would make Bankside as civilized as any ward in the city.'

'There's another reason I've returned.'

'Is that so?' Bianca says, the interest blooming brightly in her eyes as she wonders if his heart is beginning to heal.

'I've made a promise to someone I served with in Holland to visit his son in Gloucestershire.'

Interest turns to disappointment in an instant. 'Oh, I thought you were going to say something else.' She affects indifference. 'When will you leave? Only I have some casks that need moving out of the brew-house.'

'In a few days. I can be there and back in just over a week. If it turns out the roads are bad and I get delayed, well, what's one more blot to the College of Physicians? They've probably already made up their minds. Besides, you'll likely be glad of my absence. I won't be much company, with the hearing on my mind.'

Before she can reply, Rose enters the parlour carrying a stack of mugs and pottles, which she sets down on the table with a clatter. 'I see your Venetians are all still abed, Mistress!' she says in wonderment. 'Do they not rise of a morn, like God-fearing English folk? When am I supposed to air the bedding?'

'They're not *my* Venetians, Rose,' Bianca says. 'Let them have their sleep; they've been good for business.'

'They're all very handsome, I must say,' announces Rose with a grin. 'Even the ugly ones.'

Bianca gives her a warning stare. 'Maybe they are, but if they want to spend their money on more than just ale, you leave them to the stews, my girl!'

Rose looks horrified. 'Fie, mistress! I have my own gallant now. I have my Ned.'

It pleases Bianca that Rose and Ned are close. For all his rough exterior, Ned has a gentle heart. Like Nicholas, he too has lost someone dear to him – his younger brother, taken by the killer who stalked these lanes around the Jackdaw less than a year past, the man whose execution she and Nicholas have just been discussing.

'Master Nicholas, you're looking sore troubled this morning,' Rose observes. She turns back to Bianca. 'Yesterday he seemed so pleased to see you. Now he looks positively dejected. Have you spurned him, Mistress?'

'Rose!'

'I was only asking!'

✠

The desk is hewn from Flemish walnut. It is a very large desk for such a small man: a riot of arabesque panels and chiselled within an inch of its life. It sits in an airy room – equally splendid – in a mansion the queen herself might covet, somewhere between the Strand and the fields of Covent Garden to the west of the city walls.

The man who sits at this desk is Robert Cecil, the crook-backed young son of Lord Burghley, the queen's Lord Treasurer. He has spent the morning dealing with state business. He has signed documents on behalf of his father; read intelligence reports from the small army of agents the Cecils employ to watch for sedition; studied digests from ambassadors and emissaries across the known world. There are princes – kings, even – who know fewer secrets than Robert Cecil.

Yet to look at him – he's not yet thirty – you might think him better suited to studying choral polyphony, or penning a learned treatise on interpretations of church liturgy. He's short. Very short. And his back is an abomination to God's design for the human skeleton. Yet his face is placid, tapering noticeably to a tender mouth and a thin umbrage of beard trimmed to a sharp point. The weight of the face is in the brow – broad and flexed, like a book cracked open at the spine.

At present he is studying a list of foreigners recently arrived in the country. (His men visit the hostelries and boarding houses regularly to record their names.) He notes nothing out of the ordinary. There's a Zealander who's rented rooms at the sign of the Mermaid on Water Gate Lane; a Fleming in lodgings at the Crossed Swords by Porter's Quay... He puts the document aside and picks up another. It's a copy of the returns of the Court of Admiralty and the London Customs House. He's pleased to see that since his father reformed the inefficient and corrupt collection of duties last year, the records are more scrupulously kept.

He already knows of the *Sirena di Venezia*. She was picked up long before she rounded the North Foreland, by a pinnace running into Falmouth from Alderney. Now he reads that she has properly declared her cargo of Lombardy rice, and that the searchers have found her to be a wholly innocent trader. The name of her owner is recorded: one Signor Baron, which he takes to be the English corruption of Baronelli or perhaps Barrani. (Robert Cecil has studied at the Sorbonne, and is thus more familiar with the renderings of foreign names than is a harried London customs clerk.)

Surprisingly, it's Englishmen he's seeking amongst the *Sirena*'s crew. A seemingly innocent Venetian cargo ship making her way up the Narrow Sea could easily put into a French creek and there take aboard a native-born traitor schooled in the Catholic seminaries of Europe; someone who's come to spread the Pope's commandment that all English men and women who wish to save their souls should rise up against their excommunicated queen.

There have been plots aplenty against her these past years. There will undoubtedly be more to come. Not even the vast network of intelligencers and informers that he and his father have established can prevent it. All it will take is a moment's carelessness on his part, a moment's laxity by those he employs. And even the most diligent watchdogs must sleep occasionally.

But the *Sirena di Venezia* appears unimpeachable. Nevertheless, Cecil has already taken precautions. As soon as she had come to his notice, he'd written the letters AF next to the vessel's name – *a faenore* – Latin for 'of interest'. He has dispatched a man to keep an eye on her master and his crew. Consequently he now knows where they sup – at the Jackdaw tavern on Bankside. He gives a thin smile of recognition.

Bianca Merton.

While we may not be at war with Venice, we are at war with her religion; and if watchdogs must sleep, so Robert Cecil likes to think, they should do so lightly.

A discreet double tap on the door tells him it's time for the first audience of the afternoon.

'God give you good day, Robert,' says a slender, handsome woman in her middle fifties, as the livered servant who ushers her in slips away silently, as if he had never existed.

The woman is smartly turned out in a gown of ochre brocade trimmed with green lace. She has a wide elfin mouth and mischievous eyes the colour of summer wheat. Her greying hair is tucked modestly beneath a white linen coif, and though she holds herself with a stern dignity, there's no trace of severity in her smile. Indeed, it is Cecil – leaving his place behind the desk to bend a gracious knee to her – who bears a slight trace of disapproval in his clever green eyes.

'What have I done *now*, Robert?' Mercy Havington asks, as – formalities done – he raises his head to bestow a welcoming kiss on her cheek.

'The sleeves, madam. You do it to tease me. I know you do – and I shall not be provoked.'

Lady Havington glances at her sleeves. They are slashed in the fashionable Spanish style. 'Just because we're at war with the Don,' she says, 'that is no reason for a woman to dress like a milking maid, Robert.'

Cecil shakes his head in good-natured capitulation. 'Then I shall prepare myself to find my own dear wife dressed up like a Castilian duchess when I am done here. And *yours* will be the fault, madam.'

Having scored her point, Mercy Havington returns his kiss. She has come up from Gloucestershire for the christening of Robert's first son. She is related to his wife, Elizabeth. Indeed, were she not kin, she'd still be waiting in the entrance hall along with all the other petitioners.

'It is a joy to see your young boy so bonny, Robert. I confess my heart has needed a little lifting recently.'

Robert Cecil is not given to obvious displays of emotion.

Nevertheless, he makes his best attempt at a show of sadness. 'You must be feeling the loss of your husband severely, madam. I know Lord Burghley was much affected by the news of Sir William's death. He held him in high esteem.'

'I count myself fortunate to have had thirty-three years of mostly happy marriage, Robert. Few enough can call themselves so lucky.'

'Indeed.'

A slight hesitation while he waits for her to come to the point of her visit.

'I know how busy the queen keeps you, Robert, but I wanted a moment of your time – in private. It's about our grandson, Samuel.'

Robert Cecil remembers a thin lad with fair hair and troubled, expectant eyes. 'Has his falling sickness worsened?' he asks.

'No. It is more the care of it that troubles me.'

'If it's a physician you're after, I fear I can recommend none,' Cecil says, fixing Lady Havington with a gaze that seems to dare her to notice the warped fall of his gown where it hangs on his shoulders. 'I'd hang them all, if I were allowed.'

'Oh, he already has a physician, Robert. And that is where my concern lies.'

'Then how may I help?'

'When his mother – our daughter – died some years ago, it fell to Sir William and me to look after the boy. We have done so diligently, and love him dearly. But Samuel's father, Sir Joshua Wylde, has recently remarried – unexpectedly.' She pauses, as though considering carefully how to continue. 'He has passed Samuel's care to his new wife, the Lady Isabel.'

'Surely it is good for a son to be with his father,' says Cecil, who has learned things from Lord Burghley that a man could live three full lifetimes and never acquire.

'My son-in-law has returned to serve in Holland, Robert. Even marriage cannot keep him from his duty, fighting the Spanish tyrant. It is the physician Isabel has persuaded him to appoint who worries me.'

'You fear he may be a charlatan, but you don't want to cause a family rift?'

'I knew you would understand, Robert. You were always such a perceptive boy.'

'Does this physician have a name?'

'He's Swiss, apparently. Dr Angelo Arcampora.'

'Ah, the genius!'

'You know of him?'

Robert Cecil smiles a secret smile, as if to say: no one comes into England without my knowing it. 'I met him at Lord Tyrrell's house, at a dinner, when he came into the country. I assumed he was one of Tyrrell's actors, straight from the playhouse – a preposterous braggart.'

Lady Havington sighs with vindication. 'Unfortunately, Isabel Wylde holds him in high regard.'

'I could have him arrested, if you want. A night or two in one of my cells and he might decide Switzerland isn't so bad after all.'

'But what if Arcampora really can effect a cure for Samuel?' Mercy Havington says. 'Lady Wylde is mightily convinced by him.'

'Then I am at a loss as to how I may be of help, madam.'

'It's really very simple, Robert.' She pats the Lord Treasurer's son lightly on one shoulder, like an indulgent aunt. 'Do what all England thinks it is that you do.'

'And what, pray, might that be?' Cecil says archly.

'Why, have one of your clever fellows spy on him, of course.'

5

Having come so far, having risked high seas and marauding pirates, Bruno Barrani wants to see if London lives up to its reputation. It would be good, Bianca thinks, to show him her city, now that she's managed to wrestle her own little corner of it from the guilds and the aldermen, the parish busybodies and the disapproving Puritans. The day dawns encouragingly bright, the skyline of steeples bathed in the spring light. Bianca musters Nicholas, Ned and Rose in the parlour and makes her dispositions as though she's a captain of pike preparing her band to receive a charge: brew-house floor to be scrubbed – thoroughly, mind; no rats' carcasses left behind the casks; and most important of all: no further credit extended to alderman Miller until he apologizes for calling the Jackdaw's mistress a brazen sorceress.

'I never expected the heretics to have so many churches,' Bruno says as they walk along Bankside.

She offers to show him St Saviour's. At first he refuses to go in, on the grounds that only a madman would step inside a lion's den. But he relents when she convinces him that heresy is not adhesive.

'Cannot the Antichrist afford some gold paint and plaster?' he asks, astounded by the simple plainness of the church.

By the time they reach Whitehall, the sun has vanished and the drizzle has set in. Bianca blames the Puritans. Bruno is inclined to believe her.

She takes him to the public parts of the sprawling site, walks him through the great gate and past the tilt-yard. They turn heads: the slender young woman with the flash of the Veneto sun in her amber eyes, and the black-clad sprite strutting at her side. Bruno doesn't notice. He's too busy trying to catch a glimpse of England's queen – a creature he regards as falling somewhere between a tyrannical sultan from Araby and Mephistopheles. He's disappointed when Bianca explains that Elizabeth is not in the habit of strolling amongst commoners, certainly not since the Prince of Orange was shot by an assassin brandishing a wheel-lock pistol.

At the Royal Exchange she shows him the merchants and financiers haggling. In a shop on Cornhill he insists on buying her a set of white Antwerp stockings. 'I cannot have my sweet cousin dressing herself like a peasant girl from Puglia,' he explains. In return she pays the fare for a tilt-boat. From the river, they view the great houses along the Strand and play a game in which they imagine the impossibly wealthy men who live in them. She doesn't tell him that one of them is Robert Cecil, whose infamy is known even in Padua.

The tilt-boat drops them off at Galley Quay. Bruno wants to tell the Sirena's sailing master Luzzi, and the two crewmen who have drawn straws to remain aboard as watchmen, that they will be relieved later in the day and can then join their shipmates at the Jackdaw, where the first jug will be on the house. While Bruno makes his rounds of the ship with Luzzi, Bianca seeks refuge from the drizzle in his cabin on the stern-castle.

It's the only private accommodation on the vessel, no larger than a prison cell, with planked walls that slope inwards towards a small skylight set into the ceiling. It smells of paint, freshly scrubbed timber, tar and hemp, and of the uneasy intimacy it has forged with the sea. A simple cot protrudes from one wall. The only furniture is a tiny table and two chairs. As Bianca stoops to avoid cracking her head on the beams, she feels the movement of the river through the soles of her feet, as if it's breathing. As if it's alive.

'A chamber fit for a duke!' laughs Bruno proudly as he enters to find her sitting in one of the chairs. 'Though a little stuffy, I will admit.' Leaving the door open behind him, he sits on the edge of the cot.

In this cabin – a fragment of his own world brought with him across the water to a strange shore – he speaks to her in the language they share. The warm vigour of it, so unlike the English she learned at her father's knee in Padua, spills over her like sunlight over the incarcerated.

'We men of the Veneto are great mariners,' he asserts bravely. 'A little discomfort is nothing to us!'

'I don't know how you can bear it, being cooped up in here for weeks on end, while the floor rolls about under your feet.'

'I could ask the same question of you, Cousin, could I not?'

'What do you mean?'

'How can you live in this place?' he says, pointing with his doe-skin-gloved hand in the general direction of the quayside. 'Do you not yearn for the nourishment of the Mass? Your soul must be as parched as an unwatered desert!'

'Oh, we get plenty of water here, Bruno, believe me,' she replies, glancing up at the water trickling over the skylight.

'That's right, laugh at me,' he says, holding up his hands to show he can take a teasing with the best of them. 'But don't they watch you? Don't they know you're a true Catholic?'

'Of course they do.'

'Yet you are still free?'

'Free enough. Free to keep my religion to myself. As long as we don't proselytize, they tolerate us.'

A look of outrage spoils his handsome face. 'Do you call what they do to the brave priests we send amongst them *toleration*? I call it vile butchery. Perhaps you think I hadn't noticed the heads stuck on spikes on *that* thing?' He points through the open doorway to the bridge, barely visible beyond a misty tangle of masts, spars and cordage.

'Are you suggesting that if England were to send her priests into Rome to call upon all Catholics to overthrow the Holy Father, they'd be welcomed with dishes of *cappelletti* and the best Barolo?'

Bruno shakes his head. 'What has become of you, Cousin?' he asks with a sigh, as though she's not the Bianca he once knew. 'Don't you remember when Cardinal Fiorzi came to our little church? He said that, of all the children, it was you who took the wafer and the wine most piously. What was it he told Father Rossi to call you?'

'*Passerotto*,' Bianca answers with a smile. 'Little sparrow.'

'You have a duty, Cousin,' he tells her gravely, 'especially now that you live amongst them.'

'A duty?'

'You must play your part – as must we all, in this battle against the heretic.'

'Are these your words, Bruno? To my ears, they sound as if they come from Cardinal Fiorzi's tongue.'

'You were glad to aid him once, Cousin.'

'The little sparrow grew up, Bruno. She grew wiser.' She stares down at the scrubbed deck planks. 'When I was an innocent child, I thought Cardinal Fiorzi so magnificent I wanted to marry him. When I was a girl, you and I carried secret messages for him. We watched his enemies and reported who they consorted with. I did those things because I believed God spoke to him directly, that he could do no wrong. Then the Holy Office of the Faith charged my father with heresy and left him in a cell to waste away. Fiorzi could have saved him. He chose not to. So I left the city of my birth to come here, to my father's land. Like England, I have no further use for cardinals.'

Bruno gives her a pained look. 'His Eminence is but one cardinal amongst many. His voice is not always in the ascendant.'

'Ascendant or not, I no longer have any wish to hear what he has to say.'

'He has need of you again, Cousin. A private need.'

Bianca stares at her cousin in horror. 'Need? What possible need can Cardinal Fiorzi have in England that he should—' She breaks off, raising a hand to her mouth and staring around the little cabin as though she's found herself trapped in a snare. 'Oh, Bruno. You cannot ask this of me. I have already come to the attention of the Privy Council watchers once before. Do you wish to see my bleached skull hoisted on that bridge?'

Bruno laughs. 'Have no fear, sweet cousin. His Eminence has not sent me to ask you to spy on your new countrymen, or to subvert their vile religion. I told you, it is a privy matter. He needs someone he can trust in this den of disbelievers.'

She's about to challenge him to explain what he means when Graziano pokes his grizzled face around the door.

'Forgive the disturbance, Master. You have a visitor,' he says, tugging the brow of his cap. 'An Englishman.'

Bruno raises a hand in consent, and a stocky figure in a leather jerkin ducks into the cabin.

'I'm told this is where I may find Master Barrani,' he says in a throaty voice.

He has a lazy face, Bianca notices, with slack eyes and an almost lipless mouth that slashes across his jaw like a wound. His sleeves are rolled up over his meaty arms, his hair plastered to his head by the mist. He's a *two-pot*, she decides instinctively: two pots of ale and then he'll start putting the world to rights in an increasingly belligerent manner, until I have to have him thrown out. London is full of two-pots.

'I am he. I am Barrani.'

'I'd rather we spoke in private,' the man says, eyeing Bruno's mustachios with an English distaste for extravagance, and apparently deciding that because he's small and appears to have an inordinate care for his appearance, he poses no threat. He glances at Bianca as though she were something in a shop that he wouldn't dream of buying and adds, 'I don't talk business in the company of riverside whores.'

Bruno puffs himself up like a raven ruffling his feathers dry after a rain shower. He springs from the cot, drawing his dagger, his little face crimson with insulted honour. '*Cane sporco!*' he cries.

'Don't you *sporco* me, you rogue!' the man growls, leaning forward over the table – as much to avoid braining himself on the deck-head as to threaten. 'You're in England now. Speak English!'

'He called you a dirty dog,' Bianca says sweetly, her face barely a foot from his. 'And if he doesn't prick you with that poniard he's just drawn, I'll be only too happy to do it myself.'

'Yes, I call you a dirty dog,' Bruno says with a murderous look in his eyes. 'You insult my cousin!'

'Your *cousin?*' echoes two-pot. 'Why didn't you say so at the start?' He gives Bianca a grudging shrug of contrition. 'A comely woman on a ship – well, it's easy to draw the obvious conclusion, ain't it?'

'Is it really?' says Bianca icily.

'Munt, Tobias Munt – merchant of Petty Wales,' two-pot says, running a fist through his lank wet hair. 'Pleased to meet you, Master Barrani. Sorry if I offended, I'm sure. I take it you were expecting me?'

'Indeed, Signor Munt. And there is no offence taken,' says Bruno grandly.

'Isn't there?' asks Bianca, horrified by how easily he's capitulated – worse than that black-haired, Christ-faced boy in Padua.

Bruno sheathes his dagger. 'How can I be of service, Signor Munt?'

Uninvited, Munt eases his stocky frame into the chair opposite Bianca. He smells of dusty sacks and stale vegetables.

'Can this fair cousin of yours be trusted, Master Barrani?'

The question is directed to Bruno, but it's Bianca's eyes he's holding, with that covetous look she's seen on men's faces before – and still doesn't care for.

'To the grave, Signor Munt,' replies Bruno.

'I should be going,' Bianca says. 'Whatever business you have to discuss, I'm sure you'd prefer to do it without a *woman* present.'

'Peace, Cousin, stay,' says Bruno. 'I wish Signor Munt to know how well you are trusted.'

'Bruno, if this is about what we've been discussing, I really do not wish—'

Her cousin raises one small black-gloved hand to silence her. To her irritation, her innate curiosity gets the better of her. She complies.

'This won't take long. Isn't that so, Signor?'

Munt fishes in his purse and takes out what looks to Bianca like a well-worn coin, an angel or perhaps a ducat. He places it on the table and holds Bruno's gaze with such intensity that Bianca can't help herself staring at the design embossed on the surface of the dull metal. In the centre is a woman standing over a coiled serpent, heavenly rays emanating from her head. Bianca recognizes the figure at once: St Margaret of Antioch, the martyr swallowed by Satan in the form of a serpent; a woman so pious she emerged from the ordeal unscathed, bathed in God's holy light. In the church Bianca had attended in Padua there was a chapel dedicated to the very same saint.

Bruno's expression is impassive as he looks at the medallion, then at Munt. 'Have you perchance brought anything else with you, Signor Munt?' he enquires.

Munt returns the medallion to his purse and wrings his beefy hands. 'There I have to disappoint,' he says. 'I shall need a little more time.'

'There is a problem?'

'Only that you had favourable winds, Master Barrani. We weren't expecting you so soon.'

We, hears Bianca. Not *I*. Backers? Stockholders? Or conspirators? For who else but a conspirator needs to identify himself to another with the aid of a medallion?

'How long?'

'Ten days from today – the sixteenth day of March. But not here.'

'Then where, Signor Munt?'

'At my warehouse on Petty Wales – the sign of the three tuns. Shall we say noon?'

'If that is how it must be, well, we have come a long way, Signore. At least I shall have more time to spend with my beautiful cousin.'

Munt looks at him enviously. 'You're a lucky man, Master Barrani. Until then.'

'Until then, Signor Munt – *la pace di Dio su di te.*'

'And a *patchy day-oh* to you, too.'

And with that, Munt offers Bianca an ill-disguised leer and leaves.

Bianca leans closer to her cousin. 'What, in the name of the saints, was that implausible piece of theatre about?'

'I do not understand what you mean, Cousin,' says Bruno with an airy smile.

'I'm not a fool, Bruno. You made me sit through that exchange

66

so that I would be complicit, didn't you?' The anger blazes in her eyes.

'Complicit in what, Cousin?' asks Bruno in a hurt voice, as though innocence flows in his veins in place of blood. 'I am the part owner of a ship. This is a port. Signor Munt is a merchant.'

'So why does he carry a medallion with a Catholic saint on it and show it to someone he's never met before?'

Bruno throws his arms in the air. 'Cousin, enough! All these questions – they're giving me a headache. Trust is important in commerce. I prefer to deal with men whose faith is not corrupt.'

'So I'm right? Munt is a Catholic.'

'This is a problem, Cousin? You wish me to trade only with heretics?'

'Bruno, you'd trade with a churchful of Lutheran bishops if you thought there was a ducat to be made, despite your love for Cardinal Fiorzi. But I thought I had made myself plain. I'll have nothing to do with treason. It ends in but one way: on the scaffold, in lingering torment. Take my advice: complete your trade, sell your rice, sup in my tavern in well-ordered peace and then sail back home to Venice. *Please*. Anything else, and all the cardinals in Rome will be unable to save you here.'

✠

By dawn a vile wind is prowling up the river from Woolwich, raising spiteful teeth on the grey surface of the river. It slips into the Southwark lanes like the chill of death spreading from the extremities. The twin signs hanging above the entrance to the Jackdaw snap at each other like fighting dogs. Rose has rekindled the fire in the taproom. The chimney whines like a cheap whistle. When Nicholas comes in from the Tabard, where he's been trying to reduce the price of a horse to take him to Cleevely, he finds Bianca in the company of two men. One is a heavyset, jovial fellow in his fifties with a face veined by malmsey. The other is about Nicholas's age. He has a smooth, boyish face framed by a mane that puts even Bruno's to shame. But unlike Bruno's, it's honey-coloured and – as far as Nicholas can tell – a stranger to the barber's skill with dyes. He sports a threadbare line of beard along the rounded jaw, and his limpid eyes – crowned by finely arched eyebrows – contain a hint of venal menace: an angel who'd not think twice about selling his soul. I disliked you when we first met, Nicholas thinks, remembering the bane of the Cambridge divinity professors, the iconoclast, the mercurial sprite with the unpredictable temper who'd matriculated in the same Michaelmas term; and I have no reason to alter my opinion now.

'Come and meet Master Christopher Marlowe,' Bianca says, beckoning Nicholas over. 'He and Master Burridge are going to be visiting us a while.'

The older man extends his hand with a flourish. In a voice that stops Nicholas in his tracks, he announces, 'Walter Burridge, sir! Player-manager of the finest company of actors in all London – Lord Tyrrell's Men.'

Like all of his trade, Burridge has the loudest voice in the building. Clearly handsome enough for a heroic lead in his youth, he now looks more like the owner of a down-at-heel French perfumery. He's squeezed into a green coat of Kendal wool that's seen too many winters, with a bright but tattered knot of ribbons tied to the collar.

'Good morrow, Master Burridge,' says Nicholas, noting that Lord Tyrrell's patronage of the finest company of actors in all London doesn't extend to a new coat.

'And this is Kit,' says Bianca, with an approving smile. 'Kit, this is Dr Nicholas Shelby.'

'A doctor of divinity, Master Shelby? And in a Southwark tavern? How intriguing.'

Nicholas thinks he can detect a trace of the Kentish

shoemaker's son in Marlowe's drawl, a fragment of the original man freeing itself of the playwright's insouciance. 'Of medicine, Master Marlowe,' he replies, irrationally irritated by the fact that Marlowe clearly doesn't remember him – and that somehow he's managed to make the journey in Bianca's estimation from 'Master Christopher' to 'Kit' in so short a time.

'Kit's a playwright,' Bianca says, smiling. 'He's famous.'

'I know,' says Nicholas. '*Tamburlaine*.' He recalls passing the Rose theatre last autumn when it was playing there. It was the day he'd thrown his doctoral gown into the Thames. Where one man falls, another rises, he tells himself dejectedly.

'Kit's writing a new play,' Bianca says admiringly.

'Is Kit really?'

'It's about a doctor, too.'

'Oh, a comedy.'

'Nicholas!'

'In truth, it's a tragedy,' says Marlowe.

'You're telling me.'

Bianca glares at him. 'Did you not sleep well last night? You've a contrary mood upon you this morning, Nicholas.'

He raises his hands, fingers spread, as if to make amends. 'I'm sorry, but if Master Kit here had the slightest experience of the College of Physicians, he'd need to pen a comedy to stop himself taking a torch to the place.'

'It's about a physician named Faustus,' says Marlowe. 'He makes a pact with Lucifer: all the mysteries of the world revealed to him alone – but one day the Devil will come calling for the reckoning.'

Nicholas thinks, I might have made a bargain like that, if it had been offered to me – before Eleanor died.

'These good gentlemen have sought our help, Nicholas,' says Bianca proudly. 'They need somewhere to try out their acts.'

'What's wrong with the Rose theatre?'

'Master Henslowe has the carpenters in,' says Burridge.

Marlowe gives him a laboured smile, as though Nicholas is too much the country greenhorn to comprehend the playwright's art. 'We need to judge if the invocations play well.'

'Invocations are not easy things to present, Dr Shelby,' explains Burridge. 'Ineptly done, they invite ridicule. Too forcefully, and you're a blasphemer. Too *accurately*, and – well, who knows what spiritual dangers will ensue? As the Rose was closed to us, we thought a suitable tavern would suffice.' His purple-veined jowls crease as he smiles. 'And thanks be, we have found one! Mistress Merton has been the very goddess Fortuna herself! Dear madam, you have sped to our aid like Perseus to Andromeda.'

Nicholas wonders if all player-managers speak like this.

'So here we are!' says Marlowe brightly.

'Do you object?' Bianca asks, noticing the look on Nicholas's face. 'Don't tell me you've come over all Puritan.'

'It's not my tavern,' Nicholas says, feeling like a fool. 'But you know how gullible some people around here can be. Look what Ned said about you last summer: that you were a witch and flew around at night in the shape of a bat. Half of Southwark believed him.'

'That was before Ned got to know me,' she says pointedly. 'And he was in his cups. He didn't really mean it.'

Nicholas shrugs. He can hear by her voice that she quite enjoys the notoriety. 'If you think it wise, go ahead. It's just that there are some superstitious souls around here. It doesn't take much—'

Marlowe shakes his head. His eyes gleam. To Nicholas, they are the eyes of a precocious child who's realized he's just got away with deceiving an adult and has thus come to the conclusion that deceit is easy. His voice oozes condescension. 'Mercy, Dr Shelby, don't be afeared. It's only play-acting. We're not planning to conjure up *real* demons! That would be against the law.'

✠

'Why did Finney leave so suddenly?' asks Samuel Wylde, closing the pages of his Ovid.

'I don't think he favoured country living,' replies Tanner Bell, lounging in the corner of the room, carving a stick with his knife. He pauses to brush a rebellious shank of hair away from his right eye, then absent-mindedly pushes it back into the unruly brown mop that overhangs his brow. 'He missed the excitement of London.' He gives the stick a puzzled look. 'Though why the bastard had to steal my coat, I really don't know.' Tanner's face sags with the hurt of loss – and not just for the coat. 'It was my brother's. It was Dorney's. I know it didn't fit me, but I'd have grown into it. Now I have nothing at all to remember him by.'

'Perhaps the Professor scared him off,' says Samuel Wylde. 'I could have put his mind at rest, if he'd asked.'

There's no doubting the Swiss doctor's methods can appear a little alarming, thinks Samuel. All those invocations from books written in a language that only he can decipher; the sulphurous distillations that make the nostrils rebel; the consulting of almanacs that list planets and stars Samuel has never even heard of...

'He had no cause to be afraid,' Samuel continues. 'Dr Arcampora says my falling sickness stems not from any demonic agency, but from a confusion of my own thoughts.'

'I don't think Finney cared much for thoughts – confused or otherwise.'

'But I don't like to think of him being afeared, Tanner.'

'Don't fret. I told him when he arrived that your fallings had nothing to do with the Devil. It's not our fault if he didn't listen.'

'According to Dr Arcampora, my paroxysms come from within my own mind. It's certainly more plausible than the remedies prescribed by the other doctors my father sent: don't eat eels, don't wear black, sleep only on goatskin...'

'I'm sure he's right,' says Tanner. 'Being a physician, he must have read at least a thousand books. Perhaps more. Perhaps he's read every book in Switzerland – maybe even the world. He can read languages I've never even heard of.'

'He says if I'm to have calm thoughts – thoughts that won't lead to seizures – I must become immune to the fearsome ones: the ones that cause other people to have nightmares.'

'Finney's nightmare was being stuck here in the countryside. We'll do without him. Now, back to your Ovid, or Dr Arcampora will be displeased.'

Samuel takes up the poetry book again. Arcampora's methods make perfect sense to him now. And no doubt, when the Professor has time and the inclination, he'll be just as able to solve the mystery of why Finney disappeared without a single word of goodbye.

✠

'I don't like what these players of Marlowe's are up to,' Ned Monkton confides to Nicholas the next day, shortly after the noonday cacophony of the city's church bells. The two men have been manhandling casks in and out of the brew-house most of the morning. Nicholas can feel the sweat cooling in the hollow between his shoulder-blades. Not being of Ned's build, he hasn't had much energy left over to take an interest in Kit Marlowe and his two companions.

'Master Kit says not to worry, Ned. It's just play-acting. Something to do with a fellow who asks the Devil for all the knowledge in the world, and offers his soul in payment. It wouldn't be my idea of an afternoon's entertainment, but then I'm not a *playwright*.'

'Well, there's more than a few people round here would call it blasphemy.' Ned wipes his brow with one huge forearm. 'I saw a couple of the watermen watching from the taproom window a while ago. You should have seen their faces: looked like a brace of bishops who've walked into a bawdy-house by mistake. Imagine that: Southwark watermen turned into Puritans by a couple of actors.'

Marlowe's voice reaches them effortlessly from across the yard. It seems to Nicholas that when he raises his voice, the Canterbury cobbler's son speaks louder than the London playwright: 'You're meant to be summonin' up Mephistopheles, Robbie, not stirrin' pottage! The lines are: "There is no chief but Beelzebub to whom Faustus doth ded'cate 'imself. This word damnation terrifies not 'im." Have you got that? It's "damnation", Robbie. Not "*Dalmatian*". He's tryin' to summon up a demon, not a fucking dog!'

Ned grunts contemptuously. '"No chief but Beelzebub"? That should have the weaker constitutions amongst the audience fainting dead away. It's not right to make light of such matters.'

'He's trying to get a reaction,' says Nicholas. 'He was like that at Cambridge – always a provocateur.'

'Mistress Merton seems to have taken a shine to him.'

'Has she really? I can't say that I've noticed.'

Timothy puts his head around the door, a grave look on his young face. 'Master Nicholas! There are two men asking for you in the taproom.'

'That was quick,' says Ned. 'They'll be the Bishop of London's men, about the play. They've probably come to arraign us for blasphemy.'

Nicholas can tell from the set of his mouth that Ned's not entirely joking.

'Are they wearing gowns?' Nicholas asks, wondering if the Censors have decided to drop by to deliver their verdict in person, before they've even listened to his defence. That would be the very end, he thinks – Censor Beston finding him watching an invocation of Beelzebub!

Timothy shakes his head. 'Not unless physicians need to go about armed. They have swords.'

6

'God give you good morrow, Dr Shelby,' says Robert Cecil, leaning back in a high carved chair that's almost a throne and resting his fingers lightly on the edge of his vast desk. His tone is welcoming, but to Nicholas's mind, Burghley's son can make even a welcome sound like an accusation of treason. His voice, soft and pleasantly modulated, is like his face: you know it masks things you'd rather not dwell upon.

Through the tall windows behind Cecil, Nicholas can see the fields of Covent Garden stretching away towards the spire of St Giles. The last time he was in this chamber, he recalls, Robert Cecil had blackmailed him into spying on the Catholic Lord Lumley, patron of the College of Physician's chair of anatomy. Cecil had used Bianca's life as the incentive – his searchers had found her father's heretical writings hidden at the Jackdaw. On that occasion the journey from Bankside had been made by night – a terrifying voyage in utter darkness, not knowing what awaited him at its end. Today's trip on the turbulent water has been merely stomach-turning.

'And good morrow to you, Master Cecil,' he says cautiously, knowing that Robert Cecil is not in the habit of summoning itinerant doctors solely to catch up on medical gossip.

'And how is Mistress Merton these days?' asks Cecil with a wolf's smile. 'Still cleaving to papist heresy? Should I be thinking of locking her up again, for the realm's protection?'

'She is well, Master Robert, thank you. And unimpeachably law-abiding.'

'I hear the Grocers' Guild have allowed her a licence to practise as an apothecary. How did she manage that – bewitch them?'

'Lord Lumley used his influence.'

Cecil studies him awhile, his pale, elongated face with its little blade of beard tilted slightly. He has the eyes of an innocent, thinks Nicholas: wide, with arched eyebrows as soft as a child's. Yet somehow you're reminded of the bright stare of a hungry fox, stalking its prey in the small hours of the night.

'On the matter of the noble Lord Lumley, I still can't *quite* fathom how you played me such a fast match, Dr Shelby.'

'I, Master Robert – play you a match? Why would I do such a thing?'

'I sent you to Lumley to spy upon him and bring him to justice for treason.'

'And spy upon him is what I did.'

'Yet now, in the queen's estimation, Lord Lumley is the most loyal man in the realm, lauded by her and the entire Privy Council for unmasking a Jesuit traitor! That was not exactly what I had in mind when I engaged you.'

'A wise judge does not decide the verdict before he's heard the evidence,' says Nicholas innocently. 'Isn't that what they say?'

Robert Cecil declines to answer. He makes an elaborate display of nonchalantly inspecting the papers on his desk, easing his crooked shoulders under his gown and sucking at his lower lip, as if he can't decide what crucial matter of state to attend to first.

'Do you have any employment at present, Dr Shelby – other than as a tavern-hand, that is?'

'Not really.'

'You're not still pursuing a glorious medical career, treating the vagrant poor at St Thomas's for a few bartered eggs and a stolen goose?'

'Not at the moment.'

'I heard the College Censors were of a mind to strike you off their roll.'

'Then you heard right, Master Robert.'

'Excellent!' Cecil rubs his hands together. The rubies and emeralds in his many rings wink at Nicholas in the light from the window. 'Then you are free.'

'Free for what?' asks Nicholas with a sense of foreboding.

'Free to do me a small service.'

Nicholas frowns. 'I'm not the betraying kind, Master Robert. I learned that with Lord Lumley. If you want a spy, I'm afraid I'm not really your man.'

Robert Cecil opens a desk drawer and pulls out a small box. It is a very fine box, Nicholas notes, its corners reinforced with beaten silver, the lid embossed with the Cecil crest. With his long feminine fingers, Cecil opens the lid and lifts out a silk purse. Making a play of weighing it, he sets it down on the desktop. The contents make a sharp-edged, expensive rattle.

'There are more gold angels here, Dr Shelby, than a physician might hope to earn in a plague year – if you desire them.'

Nicholas eyes the offering with suspicion. He remembers this morning's conversation with Ned Monkton, about the unholy bargain at the centre of Kit Marlowe's new play. He has no illusions about the consequences of taking Robert Cecil's money. It will be a pact with the Devil.

But the money won't be for himself, he reasons. He could repay his father in some small measure for the cost of his medical studies. If the Censors permit him to continue practising, he could subsidize the penurious part-time position at St Tom's, should he decide to return to it.

'What do I have to do in return? Plant incriminating evidence on the Earl of Essex? Denounce the Bishop of London as a closet papist?'

Cecil seems to enjoy Nicholas's attempt at bravado. He picks up the purse. Jangles it seductively. 'Call it a fee – for professional services rendered. I want your opinion of a physician: one Dr Arcampora. He's treating the grandson of a kinswoman of my wife – Lady Mercy Havington. You served in her husband's company in the Low Countries, I think. Is that not so?'

Nicholas struggles to suppress a laugh. Robert Cecil is offering him more money than he's seen in his life for something he already has every intention of doing. It's a small victory, he thinks. But even small victories against Cecil are worth savouring.

'Have I said something humorous, Dr Shelby?'

'Why not ask one of the Censors of the College?' he asks, his practical nature asserting itself. 'They're far more experienced.'

'You already know my opinion of physicians, Dr Shelby. If it were left to me, I'd hang the lot of you for dissembling rogues – saving your own presence, *of course*.'

Cecil pushes the purse across the desk, and a part of Nicholas hates him for his easy presumption.

'This will be a privy matter between us. I want it done discreetly. And this time I'd prefer that it didn't end with you telling me Dr Angelo Arcampora is the most honest man in Christendom and by rights should be attending our sovereign majesty as her personal doctor. I conceded the last match, Dr Shelby. This one, I expect to win.'

✠

By late afternoon the wind has dropped. Bankside basks in the spring sunshine. The cut-purses and the coney-catchers come out of their holes, in the hope a few rash souls might cross the bridge in search of entertainment. While Marlowe and his players rehearse their parts in the Jackdaw's yard, Nicholas helps Bianca prepare the evening pottage. When they've finished dicing, paring and chopping, he suggests a stroll around the fishponds in the Pike Garden. She agrees, unaware that it's an offer made not entirely without artifice.

In the shade of a broad yew tree he tells her about his meeting with the Lord Treasurer's son.

'Again?' Bianca says in horror. 'You're going to be Cecil's man *again*?'

'It's not like the last time, Bianca. This is different.'

'How? I thought your stomach had had enough of his rotten meat.'

'For a start, he's not asking me to spy on anyone, to betray anyone – he's simply requesting my help. I was going to Cleevely anyway. And he's paying me well for it. Very well.'

'He's a serpent, Nicholas. Robert Cecil crawls around on his belly, sniffing out those who question his queen's religion, with that little serpent's tongue of his.' She wriggles her fingers in front of her mouth, in case his imagination needs a little help.

'He's the son of the most important courtier in the land. Besides, if the Censors stop me practising, how else will I earn a living? I can't be your paid man for ever. My father mortgaged his farm to pay for my doctorate in medicine.'

'And what exactly does Robert Cecil want you to do, for all this money?'

'There's a young lad whose father has cast him away, down in Gloucestershire. He suffers from epilepsy. The grandmother thinks the physician his father has employed to care for him might be a charlatan. She's kin to Robert Cecil's wife.'

'And why should any of this concern you? Save for the money?'

That stings him. 'The boy is the son of someone I served under in the Low Countries. Sir Joshua Wylde probably saved my life. I owe him this, at the very least. All he's asking is that I make a discreet observation.'

'You – discreet?' exclaims Bianca with a snort. 'Last time you worked for Robert Cecil it ended up with a manhunt, me in fear for my life and an execution on Tower Hill! What, in Christ's holy wounds, was *discreet* about any of *that*, Nicholas?'

Provoked, he replies without thinking, 'Bianca Merton is versed in discretion now, is she? There's nothing discreet about the way you cling to Marlowe's every word like a maid dancing around the maypole.'

The explosion is like a charge of black powder set off by a careless match.

'*Coglione! Al diavolo con te!*' she shouts, loudly enough for a couple on the other side of the fishponds to turn their heads. '*Ma che dici?*'

Nicholas knows a few Italian curses, from his time treating the mercenaries in the army of the House of Orange. Even if he didn't, he'd have to be deaf and blind not to know that Bianca is hardly being complimentary. Foolishly he holds his ground.

'Tell me, what do you know of Marlowe? I mean *really* know.'

'What does it matter to you?'

'There's talk about him.'

Bianca rams her fists against her hips. 'Talk? This is Bankside, Nicholas. You can buy talk as easily as you can buy ale and pleasure.'

'Remember, I was at Cambridge with Marlowe. They say he went abroad for the Privy Council: a *real* spy. Spying on Catholics. Apparently he only got his degree because of it – probably as a reward. He's a provocateur, with a dangerous taste for other people's secrets. I also seem to remember that a couple of years ago he stood trial for killing a man in a fight.' He adopts a faux innocence. 'Self-defence apparently. If you believe it.'

'You really don't like him, do you?'

'No, I don't. And now he's planning to put on a play about a summoning-up of demons – in your tavern. How is that going to look, when some superstitious busybody goes to the Master of the Revels' office and cries blasphemy?'

'I know what all this is about. You're jealous!'

'Of Christopher Marlowe? Don't be ridiculous.'

Bianca tilts her jaw at him aggressively. The words fly out of her mouth as if they have a life of their own. 'You have no claim on me, Nicholas Shelby. You're already married!'

Frettoloso, that's what her Italian mother had always called her – hasty. She sees by the look in his eyes how she's opened his still-healing wounds. Worse still, she's just betrayed her inner-most feelings.

'Forgive me,' she says, lowering her head. 'I should never have said that.'

Nicholas does not reply. He stands stoically in the shadow of the yew tree, like an old ox awaiting the slaughterman, too tired, too drained of spirit to think of escape. After what seems like an age he says softly, 'I can't help how I feel. I don't even *know* how I feel.'

Tentatively she touches his arm.

'You loved her, Nicholas. I understand that. I admire the strength of it, I really do. I've told you before that I'd feel myself blessed if a man should have such a love for *me*.'

He opens his mouth to speak, but she raises a finger to stop him.

'Perhaps one day a man will love me that much. And perhaps one day *you* will find a way to allow your love for Eleanor its proper weight in the scales. If you don't, you'll never be able to set the balance evenly. It will always fall to one side. You will have given your whole life over to grief. And that would be a fearful waste.' She turns from him and stares into the depths of the pond. A pike turns lazily in the shallows, the sunlight glinting on its sinewy back. The next instant it has vanished into the depths. 'In the meanwhile, I have my own life to lead,' she says, as though addressing the departed fish. 'And I'll lead it on my own terms. Not yours.'

✠

The lengthening shadows point the way east, back to the Jackdaw. The setting sun strikes petals of fire from the windows of Winchester House. It paints the building on London Bridge with a wash of dirty gold. Nicholas and Bianca walk in silence, each lost in their own thoughts, their own recriminations. Both know there is no escaping what has passed between them.

As they approach the Mutton Lane river stairs, Nicholas is the first to spot a familiar figure running towards them.

Breathless, Timothy bends almost double before his mistress. He looks like he's been in a brawl, even though – with his lute and his songs – he's the most peaceable boy in all Southwark. His jerkin is untied and there's a smear on one shoulder that looks uncomfortably like freshly spilt blood. For a moment Bianca fears he's fallen victim to a cut-purse.

'Mercy! Are you hurt?' she asks, lifting him up. 'Whatever is amiss?'

His eyes dart between her and Nicholas, wide with alarm. When he finds his breath he has but one word to speak.

'Murder!'

The evidence of the fracas is everywhere: overturned tables and benches, spilled plates, clay jugs shattered on the taproom flagstones...

Bruno lies behind an overturned table, a little black raven felled by a hunter's lucky shot. He seems so peaceful that he might almost be taking a nap, dreaming of the Veneto sun, were it not for the blood that spreads like a gentle flood tide against the shores of his unfamiliar world. His companions stand in a defensive semicircle around him. It's taken all Graziano's persuasion to stop them chasing Bruno's assailants across Bankside and putting them to the blade.

Nicholas kneels down to examine his body. Bianca begins to pray for her cousin, lapsing into Italian. She is battling to hold back the tears.

Timothy has already explained what happened. A gang of Bankside hotheads, convinced by Kit Marlowe's play-making that the Jackdaw is staging a real invocation and that the Venetian visitors with their heretic religion are responsible, has come to restore God's one true religion in their preferred manner: by brute force.

'They came in shouting the odds about blasphemers,' Ned Monkton says. 'That spindly little fellow from St Mary's church – sideman Perrot – had them all whipped up.'

'I'll take most low-lifes in this tavern,' Bianca says under her breath, 'but I draw the line at Puritans!'

'He's not dead,' says Nicholas, looking up. 'He's sorely hurt, but he's still alive.'

Tenderly, Rose and Bianca help Nicholas roll Bruno onto his side. With each shallow breath, an alarming pink foam bubbles around his mouth.

Nicholas thinks, if I were back in the Low Countries, I'd be asking if there was a priest amongst the Catholic prisoners to give the *Viaticum*. But this is Protestant England. Apart from Bianca and Bruno's friends, there's no one to care a damn about the welfare of the Venetian's soul.

Marlowe emerges from the ruins, grinning like an ape, his knuckles bloodied, his angelic face bright with excitement. 'Oh, but I do so enjoy a good quarrel,' he says cheerfully.

'Have you any idea what's happened here?' asks Nicholas furiously. 'This isn't some Cambridge student jape.'

'Nicholas, please! You have to help Bruno,' begs Bianca, clutching the sleeve of Nicholas's doublet. 'Please, *please* don't let him die in a foreign land, so far from home. Not like this.'

Ned drags the board away from where Bruno is lying and sets it upright. The Venetians lift their master and set him gently down on his back. His eyes are half-shut. His face, where it's visible between the streaks of blood, has taken on a biliously pale hue. The breast of his black doublet hardly appears to rise and fall. As Bianca unlaces the points to help him breathe, the only sign he's alive is that awful bubbling froth around his mouth.

Nicholas leans forward and peers at Bruno Barrani's ruined head. For a moment that dread sense of inadequacy that he felt when he tried to save Eleanor floods into his thoughts, that mistrust of all he's been taught, that fear that so much of his medical knowledge is built on quicksand. He fights it off. This is physic that he knows and trusts: meat work – the kind of medicine he practised with the army of the House of Orange. This calls for the practical treatment of visible injuries, the setting of bones crushed or broken, the cleansing and stitching of deep lacerations, the extraction of broken blade-tip or cudgel's splinter. This is healing that has no use for casting horoscopes or lengthy expositions in Latin. This is what he can do. This is what he *knows*.

First, he sends Rose hot-foot to fetch clean linen to staunch the bleeding. Then, to Bianca, 'Mistress apothecary, do you have any spirit of turpentine?'

'Yes.'

'Eggs?'

'Laid this morning.'

'Rose water?'

She nods.

'Good. Mix a collation. It's better for cleansing a wound than hot oil, and a lot kinder to the patient.'

Graziano kneels beside his friend and asks in deep, pious Italian, '*Quanto è male ferito? È fatale?*'

Nicholas doesn't need Bianca to translate for him – the meaning of Graziano's question is clear by the tone of his voice. 'You may tell Signor Graziano that it is too early to tell,' he says. 'But I will do what I can. He has my promise.'

He tells Bianca the correct proportions for the collation. She runs – something no one can ever remember seeing her do in the Jackdaw – to her apothecary's store in the cellar. On the way she almost collides with Rose, returning with the clean linen. Yet the tongue-lashing Rose expects does not come; just a mumbled, almost tearful apology.

While Rose tears the cloth into ragged strips, Nicholas sets to work. Soon there's a growing pile of roseate linen on the floor beside the table. Bruno gives no response to Nicholas's touch. His skin feels like cold, wet dough. He's breathing fast, but almost imperceptibly. As Nicholas struggles to stem the blood-flow, he

85

knows both of them could be fighting a battle already lost. He works quickly, but with immense care. If the *pterion* is damaged, any pressure applied could prove fatal.

When Bianca returns with the collation, Nicholas dips the remaining linen into the mixture and has her hold the wet cloth against her cousin's head. 'Did anyone see him struck?' he asks. 'Was it a blade or something heavier?'

Bianca translates, but the Venetians have no answer for Nicholas. It seems Bruno is simply another unlucky victim of a Bankside tavern riot.

Marlowe says languidly, 'Mercy, but they are an excitable lot in Southwark. To lose their wits over mere play-actin'.'

'This is partly *your* doing, Marlowe,' Nicholas snaps. 'Provoking people's passions like that! This man could die because of your stupid play.' He looks at Bianca. 'I tried to warn you.'

She avoids his gaze. Marlowe stays where he is, idly chewing a thumbnail as though none of this concerns him.

Once Nicholas has staunched the blood-flow, he has a better opportunity to examine Bruno's injury.

'They've done him a great hurt,' he says, lifting away a sodden red cloth to reveal a patch of bare skull about the size of a thumb. It's marbled white and pink. A trickle of blood rolls across it, like wine spilt on alabaster.

'Oh, *Jesu!*' whispers Bianca, lifting a hand to her mouth.

'The blow took away a length of scalp, right down to the surface of the parietal bone.' Nicholas makes a slicing motion with his hand, to show how it was struck.

'Will he recover?'

'Too early to tell. I have a number of concerns: for a start, the shock of a blow that fierce can transmit to the *pterion*, just above the ear. It's the weakest part of the skull. It doesn't appear to be splintered, but I can't guarantee it. The good news is that the blow hasn't cut either of the two main vessels that run up the side of the skull.'

'But will he live?' asks Bianca.

Nicholas bites his lip. 'I honestly can't say. If the wound was anywhere else, I'd wash it thoroughly right now – wine would do the trick. Then I'd suture it and wait for the suppuration to expel any internal poison. But on the skull... well, it's not recommended. I don't want to risk paroxysm or palsy.'

Graziano runs a bloodstained hand through the thick white stubble on his head and says something in Italian to Bianca.

'They want to take him back to the *Sirena*, she explains.

Nicholas's answer is unequivocal. 'Impossible. Getting him upstairs to a bed will be danger enough for him.'

'Is there nothing else you can do?'

'I'll put a wad in, for a day and a night – linen strengthened with flour boiled in vinegar. That will keep the wound open.'

'Why do want to keep the wound open?' she asks, a sour look on her face.

'That way I'll be able to inspect the exposed parietal bone for fractures. I can't see any at the moment, but they might be small. If I trouble it further, the bleeding will start up again.' He wipes his hands on the last pristine piece of linen. 'I'll remove the wadding in a day or so and bathe the wound with wine and soot.'

'Soot?' she echoes, horrified.

'When I wash it away, the blackness of the soot will reveal any fractures.'

'Are you sure it will work?'

'As sure as Hippocrates was when he wrote the book. I don't imagine a Greek skull is very different from a Venetian one.'

'So you'll know in a couple of days?'

'If he lives that long. In the meantime, let's get him somewhere more comfortable. You've a lodging chamber free, haven't you?'

Bianca tells the *Sirena*'s crew what Nicholas has said. From men ready to kill at the slightest provocation, they have now become like small boys robbed of a favourite uncle's company.

'And after a couple of days, what then?' asks Bianca.

Nicholas reaches out and gives Bruno's little beard a single, gentle caress. 'That depends. If he lives but shows no sign of recovery, then he may require trepanning.'

Bianca scowls. '*Trepanning?* Whatever is that?'

'It's physic for severe injuries to the head,' Nicholas says. 'Also taught for relieving the falling sickness – epilepsy. I simply bore a large round hole into the other side of his skull, to allow the airs corrupted by the blow to escape. Something like a screw-auger will suffice. Do you know a good carpenter?'

Bianca tries hard to keep her face impassive. Even if I knew the right word in Italian, she thinks, some things are better left un-translated.

✠

How could there be so many things about yourself you did not know? How could one body hold so many wondrous secrets? Why am I no longer who I thought I was?

Samuel Wylde sits before Dr Arcampora in his chamber at Cleevely, a book of Ovid's poetry open but unread on his lap, and ponders these troubling questions.

For example, how could he have imagined that his beloved Grandma Mercy and Grandpa William weren't his real grandparents? That his own mother had been stolen away at birth and dropped into Havington Manor like a cuckoo's egg?

'But *who* stole away my mother, sir?' Samuel asks, trying his best to withstand these thunderclaps. 'Who took her from the birthing bed?'

'Deceivers. Liars and blasphemers,' Arcampora tells him. And just in case Samuel hasn't fully understood, he adds portentously, 'Heretics.'

Samuel struggles to comprehend what Arcampora has told him. But he must be telling the truth. Dr Arcampora has been tutored in a mysterious place called Basle. He can speak in ancient languages and discourse on the stars and the planets, on physic and natural phenomena. He knows more than any man yet born. How then can he be mistaken?

Another of Arcampora's thunderclaps weakens his faltering grip on what – until now – Samuel has assumed were the unshakeable facts of his life: 'You have been schooled all your life not in scripture, Samuel, but in heresy,' Arcampora tells him. 'This is not your fault. You, too, have been deceived. But you must cast away all that has gone before – including your grandam.'

'But *why* was my mother stolen away?' Samuel asks plaintively.

'Because the deceivers, liars and blasphemers feared that when she grew to womanhood, she would bring back the one true faith to England. They wanted to keep the majesty of our holy mother church from her. They wanted to keep her soul in darkness!'

'Then they should be punished, shouldn't they?' asks Samuel, needing to please the Professor – something he finds himself doing more often these days.

'And they will be: those who are still alive. As for the rest, they are surely already suffering everlasting torment in the fires of hell.'

'What will happen to Grandma Mercy?'

'If she was complicit, she will burn – either in this life or the next. She should pray for the former. The torment will be over much quicker. If not, if she was unwitting, then she will be encouraged to recant.'

By 'encouraged', Arcampora seems to be implying a considerable amount of scourging will be involved.

'How do you know all this, sir?'

'Because I have seen written proof, Samuel. And because Arcampora is skilled at deducing what heretics attempt to hide. Do as I instruct. Believe what I tell you. Obey me always. Only then – when you are stronger – will God be revenged on the deceivers, the liars and the blasphemers. And *you* will be the instrument of his wrath.'

✠

Keeping a discreet eye on Bruno, Nicholas spends the next two days preparing for his journey to Gloucestershire. His sudden industry is the result of a letter from Robert Cecil – barely half a page of neat script, listing everything Cecil's intelligencers have managed to unearth about Dr Angelo Arcampora. A theology degree at Fribourg, which means Arcampora has had a papist education. Medical studies at Basle, a Protestant university. Then barely a sniff of the man until he's presented to Sir Joshua Wylde by his new wife, Isabel. Altogether inconclusive. Contradictory. A scribbled footnote in Cecil's hand warned that it might be months before his agents across the Narrow Sea could provide more detail. Nicholas had been required to return the letter after reading it.

But the document had not been the only thing Cecil's man had delivered. He'd brought the purse of golden half-angels, which he required Nicholas to sign for in five separate places on another sheet of paper, this one with a legal seal attached.

With more money to his name than he'd ever had when practising at Grass Street before Eleanor died, Nicholas had bought a pair of thick felt slops from a hosier on Cordwainers' Street, and riding boots to go with them, and a good gaberdine in case of rain. He had not replaced his old white canvas doublet – unexpected wealth can only stretch the ingrained prudence of a Suffolk yeoman's son so far.

At Bianca's insistence, Ned Monkton is to accompany him. Cut-purses are known to frequent the road to Gloucester. For his part, Ned is as eager as a child about to visit his first frost-fair. He's never been out of the city before. Gloucestershire might as well be in the Indies. He asks Nicholas if they'll be able to understand what the natives say, and what wild beasts they might encounter on the journey.

'They speak nothing but Latin in Oxford,' Nicholas teases him, 'and the men all keep their brains inside books. Beyond Oxford – who knows?'

'Don't you be getting yourself into trouble, Ned Monkton,' Rose says sternly as Ned and Nicholas assemble their packs in the Jackdaw's yard, ready for the walk to the livery stables beside the Tabard. 'Don't take a quarrel. And stay away from them village women.' She wags a warning finger at him. 'They mix potions to snare travellers into love. And they have cats with names like Grimalkin and Paddick what scratch like tigers – which is what I will do, if you come back with another maid's favour flying from your coat!'

Ned opens his mouth to protest his fidelity, and then wisely shuts it. He is not the only man on Bankside who's learned that the Jackdaw's women are best left uncontradicted.

Nicholas's last act this morning, before climbing the stairs with Bianca to Bruno's chamber for a final inspection of the patient, had been to purchase a razor-sharp poniard with a blade almost a foot long, and a scabbard to go with it. His experience of working for Robert Cecil has not been without risk, and although he'll have Ned for company, he rather enjoys the notion of looking like a man you wouldn't want to tussle with.

'Your cousin is a game little cockerel,' he says as he leans over the mattress to feel the strength of Bruno's pulse.

'Paduan stock,' replies Bianca. 'We're a hardy breed. What are you going to do now?'

'Current practice is to leave the wound open, so the bad humours may escape.'

'I thought you didn't hold with current practice.'

'I don't.' He searches the exposed bone for the hair-thin soot traces that will betray a fracture. He finds none. 'It's better than I'd expected. Before I leave, I'll get a sail-maker's needle from the chandlery by Bridge House and stitch the scalp.'

'Graziano and the boys want to know when they can carry him back to the Sirena,' Bianca says.

'I'm sorry – it's impossible. Bruno really must remain here if he's to have any hope of recovery.'

'What about St Thomas's? Wouldn't a hospital be best for him?'

'I wouldn't risk moving him even that far. Besides, why would you want to hand him over to sisters who are mostly ex-patients and drunk half the time? I've practised there, remember. I wouldn't trust the warden to tell a head injury from the French gout.'

'I should write to his father in Padua.'

'Why alarm him unnecessarily? If Bruno lives, then by all means write. But at the moment he could be dead before the letter arrives.'

'Are you so without hope for him?' Bianca asks, her eyes suddenly brimming with tears.

'I'm trying not to encourage false expectations, Bianca. Even if he does recover, he might be a very different Bruno from the one you knew. He may be no better than those poor souls in Bedlam.'

'You spoke of trepanning. Will that help him?'

'Drilling a hole in his head? What do you think?'

'If it might save his life—'

'*If.* It's a last resort. If I get it wrong, he'll die anyway.'

She turns away from him, refusing to accept his bleak prognosis. 'Then I'll tend him here – until he recovers.'

'Once I've sutured the wound, let the suppuration run its course and hope for the best. If his senses haven't returned by the end of the week, shave about a hand's width around the wound and apply a wax of mustard seed, castoreum and euphorbium. I can't swear it will have an effect, but it's recommended.'

'And if he declines?'

'If I was a different physician, I'd blame God.'

'But you blame God anyway, Nicholas.'

'Well, it'll be either His fault or mine. There's no one else to blame, is there?' he says, self-consciously rubbing one eyebrow with his fist. 'Do you know what our friend from Bankside told me, in his cell, before his execution? He told me he believed the heart was somehow responsible for propelling the blood through the body. The *heart.* That's contrary to everything the ancients ever wrote, everything our physic believes. Yet when he suggested it, I honestly thought it sounded more plausible than anything Galen and the others have had to say on the subject in the last fifteen hundred years.' He looks into her face, frightened that she'll see the extent of his doubt. 'And what if he was right, Bianca? Do you know what that means?'

She shakes her head, troubled by his intensity.

'It means God reveals His truth not just to the virtuous in this world. He also reveals it to those who would do evil. Maybe your Kit Marlowe should consider *that* next time he has one of his players recite an incantation.'

Rose appears in the doorway, a black doublet tucked under one arm. Beside her is a tall, saturnine man with a face scoured by salt-wind, whom Bianca recognizes as Luzzi, the *Sirena*'s sailing master. He's holding a canvas sack.

'Master Luzzi has brought Master Bruno's possessions from his ship,' Rose announces. 'And I've managed to get most of the mess out of his doublet.' By 'mess' she means his blood.

Luzzi places the sack in the corner of the chamber, kneels by Bruno's side, kisses him gently on the forehead and then makes the sign of the cross over him. Rose looks the other way.

'Does the English doctor think there is hope, Mistress Bianca?' Luzzi asks in Italian, looking from Bruno to Bianca and Nicholas. She hears in his accent the hot, arid anchorages of Messina and Syracuse.

'Dr Shelby here is a fine physician, Master Luzzi. You may assure your shipmates he will do all that can be done.'

'Is he any better, our little Venetian Achilles?' Rose asks when Luzzi has taken his leave. She peers at Bruno with a look of deep compassion on her broad, cheery face. 'Bless him. He looks almost peaceful, don't he? Mind, I always imagined Achilles to be a bit taller. And Greek.'

'We need to wash him,' says Bianca, rolling her eyes. 'Go to my chamber. I've some oil of burdock in a green glass bottle. Bring it to me. And some dampened linen.'

When Rose closes the door behind her, Nicholas says, 'Perhaps I should go to Gloucestershire alone – without Ned. What if sideman Perrot and his Puritan friends come back?'

'Stop worrying. I'll be fine,' Bianca answers, as the sound of Rose's hurrying footsteps on the stairs fades into the murmur from the taproom. 'At least with her man away, I might hope for some actual *work* in return for the money I pay our Mistress Moonbeam. Besides, I have a bodyguard, thank you – or hadn't you noticed?'

'Marlowe?' Nicholas's eyes widen in distaste.

'No! Not Kit – Bruno's boys.' She favours him with a gently mocking smile. 'It's alright, Nicholas. You needn't fear I'll be Mistress Marlowe when you get back. Besides, haven't you noticed the admiring way he looks at Timothy?'

'I thought he was sizing up Timothy for an actor.'

'Nicholas! Sometimes you really are no better than a country green-head.'

So why do I feel jealous whenever you mention Marlowe's name, Nicholas wonders as he leaves the chamber. Especially after what you said to me in the Pike Garden.

You have no claim on me, Nicholas Shelby. You're already married!

PART 2

The Beech Wood

1

Havington Manor lies beneath a steep slope of trees at the head of a small valley studded with ancient thatched barns. It's a rambling, gently sagging stone pile with ivy-covered walls and little windows that peep anxiously out on a world it turned its back on sometime around the reign of the sixth Henry. In the yard, a plump speckled sow suckles her young in the lengthening shadows of early evening. A woman in a plain country kirtle kneels beside her, fussing to ensure every piglet gets its time on a teat. When Nicholas and Ned ride in, the woman rises and greets them with a bright smile.

'Gentlemen, welcome, both. Pray tell me: what service can I do you?'

From the saddle, Nicholas is looking down at a handsome woman in her middle fifties. Her wide, mobile mouth suggests a mischievous impetuosity untamed by the passing years.

'Madam, I seek Lady Mercy Havington. Could you tell me where I might find her?'

'I am Mercy Havington,' says the woman, appraising him with steady eyes the colour of freshly harvested wheat. 'You look as though you have ridden far. What service may I do you?'

'I come at the commission of Master Robert Cecil, madam.'

The woman brushes the yard-dust from her kirtle. 'Would this commission perchance concern my grandson Samuel?'

'It would, madam.'

'Then you must be one of Robert's clever intelligencers.'

'Sadly not, madam. I am Dr Nicholas Shelby.'

'Imagine that, sweet,' says Mercy Havington, addressing the sow. 'He's sent me a *real* physician. How thoughtful of him. It is not often that Robert's generosity exceeds my expectations.'

'My sympathies on your recent bereavement, madam,' says Nicholas. 'I had the honour of serving with your late husband's company in the Low Countries.'

'With William? You look far too young, Dr Shelby.'

'With his successor, madam. With Sir Joshua Wylde. Gelderland – in '87.'

A sudden wariness comes into Mercy Havington's pale eyes. 'You are a friend to my son-in-law?'

'If you fear partisanship, madam, rest assured. I served under Sir Joshua, it is true. He probably saved my life. In many ways I admire him. But not in the matter of his son. My concern is solely for Samuel; you have my word upon it.'

Mercy Havington regards him in silence for some time while she considers his honesty. Then, giving the merest hint of a nod, she turns her attention to Ned, looking up at him the way she might look up at a mountain peak. 'And who is this extraordinary edifice of a man?'

'Master Ned Monkton of Bankside, madam. My friend. You may trust his discretion entirely. As for his manners, I apologize for those in advance.'

Ned makes as much of a bow from the saddle as his huge frame allows. Nicholas is sure he sees a slight buckling in the forelegs of Ned's mount, though it's probably just his imagination.

'Then you are both right welcome, gentlemen,' Mercy Havington says, her generous mouth creasing with pleasure.

She stoops again to shove a squirming piglet back amongst its siblings. 'And this is Isabel,' she says, introducing the sow. 'Say good morrow to Isabel, sirs.'

Nicholas bites his tongue as it occurs to him that Lady Havington has named her sow after her grandson's stepmother. Perhaps this kindly woman has a sharper side to her than he'd first thought.

Ned eases his huge frame out of the saddle and drops to the ground, groaning at the stiffness in his muscles. He kneels down and fusses over the wriggling piglets. Nicholas smiles. It was only a few months ago that Ned spent his days in the company of the dead, at the mortuary crypt at St Thomas's. Now he's like a child let out into the fresh air after a long illness.

Lady Havington summons a servant to take the horses. Then she leads Nicholas and Ned inside. The manor smells of scrubbed stone and dried lavender. A row of stout knee-length leather buskins stands just inside the door, the soles worn at the edges from use. Nicholas assumes Sir William Havington liked his walks in the surrounding hills.

In a pleasant, panelled room overlooking a meadow that slopes down to a winding stream, wine is served. Nicholas comes straight to the point.

'How fares the boy, Lady Havington? Have you had the opportunity to observe him closely since he was taken to Cleevely?'

'I fear I've detected a growing reluctance from Isabel of late. Indeed, she's become quite possessive of Samuel since Dr Arcampora arrived.'

'Perhaps you could tell me when your grandson's malady first revealed itself?'

'Shortly after his birth. The week before our daughter Alice's churching, in fact.'

'And did she suffer from it, too?'

'Yes. At first, Alice's attacks were mild. A few paroxysms, but uncommon sleepiness for the most part. But when she fell with child, the paroxysms grew worse. She died shortly after Samuel's birth, during a particularly violent episode.' Her eyes darken. 'I suppose I should give Joshua credit for the love he bore her. Marrying a maid with such a malady attracted disapproval from many quarters. Yet the physicians assured him it could not be passed to her child. They were wrong.'

'We often are, madam,' Nicholas says. The notion that Joshua Wylde could have loved a woman who was not a perfect example of English breeding stock surprises him.

'This disease is a curse from God, is it not, Dr Shelby?' Mercy Havington says. 'A punishment, perhaps.'

'A curse, certainly. But undeserved, I'm sure. Forgive my bluntness, Lady Havington, but are you also afflicted?'

He's seen the look she gives him before: it's the look of a schoolmaster when a student asks a surprisingly perspicacious question.

'No, sir. I am not,' she says calmly. 'God has reserved His displeasure for my daughter and grandson alone. It was the firstborn who died, was it not? Pharaoh was untouched.'

Puzzled, Nicholas asks as gently as he can, 'Why do you think God would be so displeasured as to visit the falling sickness on your daughter and her son?'

'It is the physician, not the *patient*, who is my particular concern, Dr Shelby,' Lady Havington says, with a tightening of the jaw that tells him to change his line of questioning.

'Have you spoken to Arcampora about the treatment he proposes?'

'Yes. It was incomprehensible to me. But to listen to him, you'd think he was the wisest physician who's ever lived. His bombast is really quite insufferable.'

'You clearly haven't attended many gatherings of the College of Physicians,' Nicholas says.

A little of Lady Havington's humour returns. Her mouth softens again. 'My husband was a magistrate as well as a soldier, Dr Shelby. I can imagine.'

'How was Arcampora engaged? Do you know?'

'Lady Isabel is somewhat evasive about that. But she is most vocal on his qualifications. Apparently he was trained in theology at the College of St Michael, in Fribourg. William said that was a papist establishment.'

'Whether it's practised in London, Rome, Paris or Madrid, madam, physic either works or it doesn't.'

She smiles, accepting his correction. 'Of course. I'm just surprised that my son-in-law, who is at this moment fighting in the Low Countries against the heretics, should choose one of their number to treat his son. Perhaps Isabel hasn't told him.'

It can't hurt, thinks Nicholas, to let Mercy Havington know the little Robert Cecil has managed to discover about the man who claims he can cure her grandson. 'Master Robert told me that Arcampora went on from Fribourg to study medicine at the university at Basle, which is Protestant. However, he didn't finish his doctorate in medicine. After that, there's almost no trace of him.'

'I *knew* he was an imposter!' Lady Havington says, her jaw tightening. 'I told William, but he wouldn't listen.'

Nicholas raises a cautionary hand. 'The fact that Arcampora left Basle is not in and of itself damning, Lady Havington. There are physicians in England who did not complete their studies where they began them. Not all of them are charlatans.'

Lady Havington crosses her arms over her bodice, as though trying to restrain the doubt in her breast. 'The question I need you to answer, Dr Shelby, is this: are his skills real? Or pretence? Are they doing Samuel good, or are they harming him?'

'I don't make casual diagnoses, madam. I won't answer your questions until I've had a chance to see this paragon of physic for myself. Shall we ride together to Cleevely – say, tomorrow?'

'We shall, Dr Shelby. I've already lost a husband and a daughter. I don't want to lose a grandson, too.'

✠

When Nicholas rises the next morning his thighs ache so cruelly from the ride that he climbs out of bed like a man who's survived a racking. He dresses in the unfamiliar surroundings, wincing as he struggles into his slops. He goes downstairs like a greybeard, stretching out tentatively one leg after the other and puffing as the muscles protest.

Ned, who has seldom sat on a horse, can barely walk. He lumbers crab-like into Mercy Havington's parlour, swearing he'll have nothing to do with horses again, even if it means walking back to Southwark. But as he's made the same vow every morning since they left the Jackdaw, Nicholas tells him not to be such an old woman.

Over a simple breakfast they try to make polite conversation with Lady Havington's brother-in-law, to whom Havington Manor has passed upon Sir William's death. He's a sullen, red-faced fellow who seems almost as irritated by Mercy's presence as he does by theirs. Failing miserably, they endure a lengthy lecture about the faults commonly found in sheep's wool.

The plan is for Nicholas and Lady Havington to appear at Cleevely House unannounced. Ned is to remain in nearby Cleevely village and glean whatever he can about the foreign physician.

'How do we explain your presence, Dr Shelby?' Lady Havington asks. 'Will Arcampora not suspect that I have brought you on a pretence?'

'You can tell him I've been sent by Sir Joshua to report at first hand how his son is faring.'

'Do we admit to him that you're a physician?'

Nicholas gives her a self-deprecating smile. 'Perhaps it's better we don't. Besides, Robert Cecil likes to remind me I don't look like one anyway. For my part, I like to think that's a compliment.'

✠

It is less than an hour's ride to Cleevely. They take a narrow track that follows the folds of a little valley, past well-hedged fields and apple orchards. Lady Havington leads, elegantly riding side-saddle. In the spring sunshine it seems to Nicholas the easiest way he can imagine to earn more than a year's income in so short a time. He's even become oblivious to Ned's murmured oaths of discomfort.

'What will you do if I determine Arcampora's a charlatan, madam?'

'I shall write to Sir Joshua – tell him the truth.'

'You do understand that, even if he's not a fraud, there is no known cure for the falling sickness?'

'Then it will be all the better for Samuel not to have his hopes raised. He is not a strong lad, Dr Shelby, either in mind or in body. I've seen how easily he can be influenced.'

They reach a wood where the first of the early bluebells lie amongst the undergrowth like lapis pebbles cast from a careless hand. The soft earth steals away the sound of horseshoe and harness. The trees deaden their voices.

'I take it you have little time for Samuel's stepmother,' Nicholas says cautiously, remembering a sow named Isabel.

'How perceptive of you, Dr Shelby,' says Lady Havington, trying to hide a guilty smile. 'You must understand: I do not hold it against Sir Joshua for marrying again. It's just that Isabel does appear to have stolen his affections rather swiftly.'

'Yesterday, Lady Havington, you told me you were free from the falling sickness. Does it occur in any other member of your family?'

'No, Dr Shelby. It does not.'

'Or in Sir William's? His brother, perhaps?'

'Gilbert? Dr Shelby, a paroxysm in that man would be a welcome sign of animation. I cannot tell you how tedious I find my days, now that I must reside in *his* household. I'd leave – but at the moment I can't bring myself to abandon William's spirit. He loved Havington Manor so very much, you see.'

Nicholas recalls the boots still standing in the hallway. 'I understand, madam. So your daughter was the first to feel its affliction?'

'As I told you when you arrived, Dr Shelby, God has reserved his punishment only for Alice and her son.'

'His punishment for *what*, exactly?'

A tight smile, grudgingly offered. 'I spoke in general terms, Dr Shelby. We are all sinners, are we not? We must all bow our heads to God's judgement.'

It's as clear an invitation to change the subject as Nicholas has ever heard.

✠

'Whyever did you not send word, madam? I would have warned the cooks!'

Isabel Wylde speaks with a smile, though to Nicholas the words sound like a reprimand. She's younger than he'd expected: about thirty, tall and narrow-boned. The round, even face is whitened with ceruse and has the sad, brittle beauty of a Madonna, like the ones he's seen painted on looted Romish altars in the Low Countries.

'Forgive the inconvenience, Lady Isabel, but Master Shelby here must soon return to his place with Sir Joshua's company,' Lady Havington explains apologetically. 'We didn't want to waste time, and my son-in-law is eager for a goodly report of his boy.'

'He did not write to me on the matter,' says Isabel sternly.

'Sir Joshua was much exercised in preparing his recruits for the voyage to Holland, madam,' Nicholas explains. 'I'm sure it simply slipped his mind.' He takes in the expensive gown of cherry-red taffeta with French sleeves, worn beneath a bodice pinked with green silk, the auburn hair parted severely down the centre and pinned beneath a white linen coif. There's a crucifix on a gold chain at her throat, and she has the habit of pressing it against her skin with the fingertips of her right hand. Nicholas can't quite determine if she's devout or a little discomforted by their sudden arrival. He can imagine her walking a dangerous line between devotion and temptation. He remembers what Sir Joshua told him, in the house at Woodbridge: *She'd heard of my reputation! Swore she would have no husband other than a Christian knight who knew his duty to the new religion...*

He looks around at the expensive Flemish hangings; at the polished plate armour; at the portraits of the Wylde lineage, every one of them male. Half a dozen generations of warriors, each with eyes that blaze with martial zeal and beards that you could hide a whole company of archers in. He suspects there is no current plan for a portrait of Samuel.

'I must confess, Master Shelby, in Holland I met most of Joshua's officers. Yet I do not recall seeing you amongst them. How is that?'

'I have been back in England a while, madam. I happened to encounter Sir Joshua in Suffolk, before he departed. He asked me to do him this small favour.'

'Suffolk? That's a long way to travel for a small favour.'

You'd make a good interrogator, thinks Nicholas. Perhaps, when this is over, I should recommend you to Robert Cecil.

Mercy Havington comes to his rescue. 'Master Shelby was also acquainted with my late husband. William took the liberty of asking him if he might bring some Haarlem linen on his next visit. He's been kind enough to oblige. Two birds with one stone, if you like.'

Nicholas thinks he ought to nod, for extra veracity. 'Sir Joshua is most eager for first-hand news of his son, madam. I should not like to disappoint him.'

'I shall have to ask Dr Arcampora if such an audience is possible.'

An audience? Does Isabel Wylde think her stepson so full of grace that he gives audiences? Nicholas casts a glance at Lady Havington. She replies with a look that says *I told you so.*

'Sir Joshua will be most vexed if I return with nothing to tell him,' he persists as firmly as he dares.

Isabel Wylde's shoulders give the merest hint of a shrug. 'Very well,' she says. 'You have come a long way. It would be un-wifely of me to deny my husband news of his son. Follow me.'

She leads them down a long panelled gallery that is as well presented and ordered as its chatelaine. No untidy homeliness here. Not a chair or a cushion out of place. On a sideboard the pewter is stacked neatly by size, as though no one dares use it. A servant vanishes like a wraith the moment his mistress strides into view. The fireplaces are empty, not a made-up hearth to be seen. Over one of them hangs a fine woven arras. It depicts a woman bathed in rays of heavenly light, while in the background a serpent coils itself around a tree. Nicholas assumes the woman is a Christian martyr and the scene is meant to depict some improving allegory, though for the life of him he can't recall which one. He wonders if Isabel Wylde's aloof and icy piety wouldn't be better suited to some cloistered foreign nunnery. What must it have been like for Samuel Wylde to be uprooted so summarily from his grandparents' home and set down in such an austere place?

They emerge onto a small terrace. The spring sunshine lies at bay, between the shadows cast by the house. Then it's down a flight of steps and into a small privy garden trimmed to within an inch of its life.

And there they are, standing beside a sundial set on a stone plinth: a tall aquiline man in a black gown and starched ruff, and a willowy fair-haired youth who looks as though he hasn't slept for weeks. Nicholas is reminded of his first day at petty school: standing bewildered and not a little terrified before a master in just the same sort of gown, who'd addressed him in incomprehensible Latin. Looking at the mop-haired, willowy figure of Samuel Wylde, hc feels a sudden deep sympathy for the boy.

It's a moment before he realizes that Samuel and Arcampora are not the only two figures in this tableau. Two men in leather doublets and woollen slops lounge at a discreet distance, like seconds at a duel. Or perhaps bodyguards.

But what most surprises Nicholas is the sudden change in Isabel Wylde. One instant she is the inscrutable guardian, and the next, adoring stepmother. She presses the crucifix at her throat deep into the flesh, so that when she takes her fingers away, there's a red wheal left imprinted in the white ceruse. Almost fawning, she picks up the hem of her gown and curtseys deeply to Samuel.

'My dearest, most gentle sir: will you give audience to these two visitors? Here is your grandmother – and here an emissary from your father.'

She must think he's royalty, says Nicholas to himself. Yet Samuel looks like the survivor of a catastrophe who can't quite believe he's alive. His eyes dart between Mercy Havington and himself, unsure if he should acknowledge them or run for his life. The slender fingers work themselves like starfish clinging to a rock in a torrent.

'You look tired, Samuel,' observes Mercy Havington. 'Have you been sleeping properly?'

Arcampora answers for his patient – in a strong accent, Nicholas notes.

'He is a diligent boy, madam. He will not give up his studies, even to sleep. I must go into his chamber to tell him: no more candle!'

'And are you as diligent with your prayers?' asks Lady Havington.

Again Arcampora answers. 'He is most exact, in all his devotions.'

'And the paroxysms, Samuel?' asks his grandmother in a voice laden with compassion. 'Do they abate?'

'Is too soon to say,' says Arcampora. 'We have a long journey ahead of us before he is cured.'

It seems the boy has decided his visitors pose no threat. He turns his pallid face to his grandmother and admits sheepishly, 'I have had a few fits, madam. But I *am* trying.'

Nicholas makes his play. 'Perhaps I could speak to you alone, Signor Arcampora.'

'You wish to speak to Arcampora?' the Professor says, as though surprised by a mild impertinence.

'To get a proper account for Samuel's father – so that I understand what I'm telling him.'

'Is most complex,' says Arcampora loftily. He lifts his chin as he speaks, the little black-and-silver blade of beard stabbing at Nicholas as if to warn him not to come closer. 'But Arcampora will explain in simple terms. You have knowledge of physic?'

'No, I fear not,' says Nicholas. It's not *much* of a lie, he thinks. 'But Sir Joshua would very much like to hear about Samuel's progress, if that's possible.'

'Is possible, I suppose. Though you will not understand most of what Arcampora tells you.'

'I'll try,' says Nicholas, gesturing for Arcampora to join him in a stroll around the privy garden – adults' talk, man-to-man.

'This malady, it is very difficult to treat,' confides Arcampora as they walk. 'Many famous men of physic, they try.' His hands wave dismissively. 'They do not succeed. Do you know why?'

'No. Please, do tell me.'

'Only Arcampora has the knowledge!'

'How fortunate for you,' says Nicholas admiringly, 'and for Samuel.' He thinks, you could be president of the College of Physicians with that sort of attitude.

'The ignorant say this disease is the result of possession.'

'Possession?' says Nicholas fearfully, trying hard to sound the most ignorant of country green-pates.

'Possession by demons,' explains the Professor. 'But Arcampora does not believe this. This is tale of old wives.'

'I'm glad to hear it.'

'In the boy's case, the demons are already within,' asserts Arcampora, pressing his fingers against his temple for clarification. The blade of his nose dares Nicholas to disagree.

I've got you, Nicholas thinks. *Possession. Demons.* You're just another Parson Olicott or sideman Perrot. You've read a few medical books that you barely understood, slept through a few lectures. At Basle you probably told your professors about your theory and they – quite sensibly – decided you were beyond instructing and threw you out. Now you're peddling your stupid ideas to anyone gullible enough to pay you.

But then Arcampora surprises him.

'The demons I speak of are agitated human thoughts,' he proclaims. 'The same thoughts that cause us the nightmare. I believe these occur in the ventricles of the brain. This agitation can pass swiftly from one ventricle to another, via the *corpus callosum*.'

Nicholas tries to look suitably mystified.

'This disturbance can pool in the thalamus,' Arcampora continues, tapping the top of his head vigorously to suggest some place deep inside. 'When the thalamus is full, the disturbance overflows into the brainstem, and thus into the nerves.' He pronounces it *nerv-es*.

'Nerv-*es*?' repeats Nicholas, again trying his best to sound mule-headed. 'I've never heard of a nerv-es.'

'These are vessels which carry animated spirit from the brain to the limbs,' Arcampora explains. 'If this spirit is contaminated, the limbs become oppressed. This is the cause of paroxysm.'

Nicholas does not question this explanation, lest he betray a competence he's not supposed to possess. But it's as plausible as anything else he's been taught. An awful memory seizes him. He recalls the moment he came face-to-face with the Bankside killer in the death cell, hearing a man no less armoured than Arcampora in his own self-belief telling him about discoveries built not upon books and lectures, but upon living flesh. If disturbed thoughts cause paroxysms, he thinks, why aren't I having one now? He forces the image from his mind. 'And how do you subdue these agitated thoughts?' he asks Arcampora. 'How do you stop the paroxysms?'

'We must discipline the mind,' Arcampora replies, clenching a fist for dramatic effect. 'Make it strong. Ordered. Samael is weak. We must make him *robusto*!'

'But can you cure him?' Nicholas asks disingenuously, trying not to smile at Arcampora's pronunciation: *Samael* instead of Samuel.

'I must cure him! He is no ordinary boy. Very special. The rarest flower must always be saved from the blight, yes?'

'Special?' asks Nicholas. 'In what way is he special?'

For an instant the conviction in Arcampora's deep-set eyes

falters. It's as if he's committed a serious indiscretion. 'Special to his papa, of course.'

'Of course,' says Nicholas, nodding wisely. 'It all makes perfect sense. Thank you.'

They walk on, Arcampora expostulating, Nicholas nodding in the appropriate places and asking the occasional inane question.

It all makes perfect sense. Samuel Wylde is special. He's the rarest of flowers. He's so rare, in fact, that his father has cast him adrift in an echoing house that he does not visit, under the protection of an icicle of a stepmother, watched over by two burly men who look like bodyguards, and treated by a cadaverous Swiss physician who believes rebellious thoughts cause epilepsy. And while we're on the subject, Dr Arcampora, would you care to explain why your patient – whom you insist is red-eyed through diligent academic study by candlelight – looks as though he's recently emerged from a particularly difficult exorcism?

When he tries to catch a moment with Samuel, Nicholas finds himself deftly manoeuvred aside by Isabel Wylde. The boy is tired, she says. The boy must rest. The boy cannot be overexcited, lest his sickness returns.

'Then perhaps I might speak with young Tanner Bell,' says Nicholas, remembering his conversation with Joshua Wylde. 'I was told by Sir Joshua that Tanner had accompanied Samuel from Havington Manor. Is he here?'

Mercy Havington's face lights up. 'Yes, that would be most agreeable, madam. I would like to see young Tanner again. We miss his presence at the Manor.'

The ceruse on Isabel Wylde's face almost cracks like an old portrait as the muscles in her jaw tighten. She lifts a hand to the crucifix again, though this time the fingertips don't quite make it. They fall away to brush absent-mindedly at the side of her cherry-red taffeta gown, as if she's suddenly become conscious of an unsightly stain. 'How sad for both of you,' she says. Nicholas waits for the accompanying apologetic smile, but it doesn't come. 'I fear I am compelled to disappoint, Lady Havington. Tanner went with the other boy, Finney. They left for London some weeks ago.'

2

Bianca kneels beside Bruno Barrani's recumbent body. A sheen of sweat gleams on his brow. Along the hairline runs a thin violet tracery that she can't quite identify. She dabs at it gently, fearing his wound has begun to bleed again. Then she realizes the sage-and-indigo dye he applies to his now-lank tresses has leached out a little. She almost weeps at this insult to Bruno's cherished vanity. Worse still, his once-fine mustachios have wilted across his cheeks like dead ferns in a vase.

She remembers how, when she was a little girl, she would place the dolls that her mother made for her in a line, pretending they were in a ward at Padua's great hospital and she was their nurse. In her young mind, they were not inanimate collections of straw and cloth with painted faces, but brave warriors wounded in battle; intrepid explorers, rescued at the last moment before starvation, or from the cannibal's cooking-pot; poets driven to prostration by courtly love. And always male. Women, her Italian mother used to tell her, were by far the stronger sex. A good one never required so much as a moment's rescuing. Indeed, a woman who got herself into a condition where she required rescuing was as much use to anybody as a cloth thimble.

Inevitably, when her mother died, Bianca had turned her restorative instincts upon her father, Simon Merton, himself a seeker of cures for the sick and troubled of Padua. They had lived a strange, precarious life. Bianca's mother already possessed a dangerous fame for her skill at mixing balms and distilling curative potions from the herbs and flowers that grew in the warm soil of the Veneto. Her father, too, was coming to the attention of the Holy Office of the Faith. Though not a qualified physician, he would write books and pamphlets on such weighty matters as the workings of the cosmos – he was convinced the stars were prevented from falling to earth by the collective exhalation of all human breath – and the flow of blood through the body, which he was sure was controlled by the movement of the sun and moon around the earth. Listening to his angry polemic, she had understood from an early age the danger he was attracting by writing such things.

To deflect attention, she had tried to convince the Church that she was the most pious of all its flock: Signorina Bianca, Simon Merton's little girl – the perfect Catholic. That way, she thought the Church might not look too closely at him.

And for a while her ploy had succeeded. Cardinal Fiorzi had thought her a little saint in the making – his *Passerotto*, his little sparrow. But in the end her father's books had led to nothing but a cold death in a prison cell.

Bianca had carried those books with her to England, where Robert Cecil's men had found them in her possession. Cecil had used them to coerce Nicholas into spying on John Lumley: *Work for me, or Bianca Merton hangs for a papist witch.* Cecil has them still. She suspects they're on display somewhere in Cecil House, like the quarters of executed traitors they nail up in public places to deter sedition.

She knows, if she's honest, that her instinct to save, to protect, to successfully resurrect in the face of overwhelming odds found a new purpose that October day last year, when Timothy discovered Nicholas Shelby lying in the Thames mud. *And here I am again*, she thinks, *tending another of my mute heroes. Not a rag doll this time, but a corpse that doesn't know it's dead.*

The chamber door opens and Rose returns, carrying a wicker basket full of clean linen. When the two women have washed Bruno, Bianca says, 'I suppose we'd better take a look in that bag Signor Luzzi brought him from the *Sirena*. It might have a clean shirt in it. Or at least some favourite thing we can place beside the mattress as a comfort, in case he wakes up.'

Laid out on the floor, the contents are not an overly rich haul for an ambitious young merchant venturer. There's a pewter bowl for his meals; a knife; two neatly folded shirts, one for daywear, the other for night; a purse – Bianca resists the temptation to open it, in search of a medallion with St Margaret of Antioch embossed on it, like the one Munt offered Bruno aboard the *Sirena*; a small book of what she assumes is poetry; the pair of fine black doeskin gloves she'd seen him wearing that first day at Galley Quay; a small brass astrolabe; and a neat pocket-compass of the same metal, folded and latched.

Out of pure curiosity, Bianca puts a thumbnail under the catch of the compass lid and springs it open. A little triangular fin pops up over the lodestone – a miniature sundial.

How clever, she thinks, as she folds it away and shuts the lid. But it's of no use to Bruno now. He is following a course quite unmarked on any map, and no compass can help him find a safe landfall.

Next she picks up the book of verse, wishing she could read it to Bruno – soothe him somehow, aid his recovery. But it's printed in Latin, a language she does not know, beyond the Mass – though it takes no effort to translate the author's name, Jacopo Sannazaro.

But it's the gloves that bring her closest to tears. They seem to her a symbol of the man himself, an elegant expression of his character: small but gloriously exuberant. She holds them up to inspect the fine embroidery that lies on the calfskin like a tracery of black veins.

'Aren't they beautiful?' she says to Rose. 'If I were not a tavern-mistress and an apothecary, I think I should like to be a glover.'

Rose pushes back the curls that have slipped over her eyes. 'Marry, mistress! Have you not quarrelled enough with the Grocers' Guild? Now you want to pick a fight with the Worshipful Company of Glovers as well!'

'Why shouldn't a woman make gloves for a living?' Bianca asks, with a stiffening of her jaw.

'Because we'd all forget to eat and sleep,' says Rose. 'And we'd make far more of them than we have hands to fit them on! Look at the queen – I hear tell she has more gloves than subjects.'

Bianca shakes her head and laughs. Whenever her flights of fancy soar too high, there's always Rose waiting with her bow, ready to bring them plummeting to earth. But she wouldn't have it any other way.

She admires the gloves for a while longer. Then she twists her mouth to one side and says, 'Rose, have you noticed anything about these gloves? They're different sizes. The right glove is bigger.'

'Perhaps God made Venetians with one hand larger than the other – for all that waving-about they do.'

'It's thicker on the back. It's been overstuffed.'

'Maybe it's been repaired.'

Bianca returns her cousin's possessions to the sack, placing the gloves in last, gently, like an offering.

'You're probably right, Rose dear. You'd best find a chest with a lock that we can put all this in. This is Southwark after all, and I can't keep watch *all* the time.'

Pulling the drawstring tight, she tells herself, Bruno *will* need them again. I'm certain of it. Just like when Nicholas went into the river to drown his grief, it's not yet his time to die.

✠

'Your verdict, please, Dr Shelby,' says Mercy Havington as they ride away from Cleevely. 'Is the man a mountebank or not?'

Nicholas considers her question carefully before answering. 'At first, I thought so. Now I'm not so sure.'

'You believe him to be genuine?'

'He was knowledgeable – as far as anyone can be, about the falling sickness. As for the treatment, I've heard wilder suggestions made in all seriousness.'

Lady Havington sighs. 'I'd hoped you'd find him a fraud. At least then I could have asked Sir Joshua to dismiss him.'

'Arcampora seemed utterly convinced he could find a cure for your grandson's malady.'

'But look how sickly Samuel appeared. The treatment cannot be in his best interests.'

'I confess that did cause me worry. So did Arcampora's talk about Samuel being somehow unusual – apart from the ordinary.'

'He is. He's my grandson.'

'Of course. But once or twice I felt as though he and Isabel Wylde were speaking about a quite different Samuel. Something is not right, but I can't put my finger on it.'

They ride on to the little drover's inn at Cleevely village, where Ned Monkton is waiting for them. He is not alone. He has company.

'God's blood! What's that?' asks Nicholas as they join him at a table in a dark corner.

'What's it look like, Master Nick?' says Ned proudly, grinning at the creature nestling contentedly in his huge lap.

'It's a dog!'

'I promised Rose I'd bring her something pretty.'

Nicholas runs a hand through his hair, perplexed. 'If I remember only one thing about the ride here from Southwark, Ned, it is that you don't *have* a dog. Please don't tell me you've stolen it. They won't have stocks here big enough to fit you.'

'Course I ain't stolen it,' protests Ned, stroking the beast's pink belly. 'I won Buffle fair and square, in a game of *primero*.'

'Buffle?'

'On account of the bufflehead what let me win her off him.'

The beast gazes adoringly up at Ned with a spaniel's grin on its face, though the provenance of the rest of the animal is anyone's guess. It puts a paw up into Ned's great auburn beard, as though it intends to make itself a nest.

'Well, I think she's a very fine little dog,' says Lady Havington.

Ned gently takes the dog's paws from his beard and waves it. 'Say good morrow to Lady Havington and Master Nicholas, Buffle,' he says in a child's voice, utterly at odds with his size and scowling red face.

Jesu, they're both at it now, thinks Nicholas, remembering the sow Isabel and rolling his eyes heavenwards. But he can't resist a smile. It's barely five months since Ned Monkton lost his young brother Jacob to the Bankside killer. He deserves a little joy. 'So you were gaming at cards?' he says, trying to patch his thread-bare authority.

'You wanted me to spy out the lie of the land, Master Nick. Cards is a great way of getting a fellow to natter.'

'Aside from the dog...'

'*Buffle.*'

'Aside from Buffle, what else did you manage to prise out of the honest folk of Cleevely?'

'For a start, they all have an opinion about what's going on, up at Cleevely House.'

'And what would that be?'

'The boy is possessed by demons; he's an addle-pate without enough brains to stop himself falling in a heap; he ate a surfeit of eels and that's what's made him moon-struck. Take your pick. It's naught I haven't heard people say about my little brother Jacob, when he were alive,' says Ned despondently. 'Warms your 'art, don't it – some folk's consideration for their fellow man.' He gives the dog a sliver of cold mutton from his trencher. Buffle repays him with a look of bottomless devotion.

'And what of Arcampora or Isabel Wylde?'

'Apparently Lady Wylde awards herself more airs than the Queen of Spain.'

'We noticed.'

Ned bows his head towards Mercy Havington. 'Then, if you'll excuse me, m'lady, there was the uproar with your servant. They all knew about that.'

'That would be Porter Bell,' Lady Havington explains with a regretful smile. 'It was the moment William and I realized we could no longer keep him in the household.'

'What happened?' Nicholas asks.

'It was the day Porter finally lost all command of his anger – around Shrovetide last. He was in this very tavern, swearing the Duke of Alba and the Devil were at Cleevely. He was ranting that he would hasten there at once, to murder them both. I had to come down here myself to calm him. He was so in his cups it took all my wits to stop him attempting it.'

'Alba was dead by the time I went to Holland with Sir Joshua,' says Nicholas. 'But I never met man nor woman of the Orange faction who didn't tremble at the mention of his name.' He thinks for a minute. 'I seem to recall Porter served in the Netherlands, didn't he – during Alba's time in command of the Spanish forces?'

'Yes, Porter went with my husband. He was returning from foraging for the company when he was taken prisoner, poor fellow. He spent a harsh time in a Spanish cell. It changed him utterly. He sought solace in ale. When his son Dorney was killed – well, that was the last straw.' She looks at Nicholas with a tearful gleam in her eyes. 'You must have known Dorney, Dr Shelby. He was with Sir Joshua around your time.'

'I did, madam.'

'Dear, *dear* Dorney. We miss him greatly. My husband was heartbroken at the news. Dorney was more friend to him than groom, despite the years between them. How well did you know him?'

'At the end, madam, I think better than any man. He died in my arms, a Spanish ball in his back.'

'*Oh*,' whispers Mercy Havington, placing a hand in front of her mouth.

'He didn't suffer,' says Nicholas quickly, trying to spare her further pain. 'He was beyond physic. I thought he'd simply fallen asleep.' He adds this to the list of all the other lies he's told to the grieving.

She reaches out and softly touches his arm. 'To know that you were with Dorney at the end is a comfort. My husband blamed himself for letting the lad go with Sir Joshua.'

'Rest assured, madam, Sir William would have had to fetter Dorney by the ankles to prevent him going.'

She smiles. 'You have a generous heart, Dr Shelby. Your patients must have great confidence in you.'

'May I speak with Porter Bell, madam?'

'Not unless you search him out. And that may take quite some doing.'

'He's no longer at Havington Manor?'

'Sadly, not.' Mercy Havington's mouth gives a little twist of regret. 'We had to let him go. Those drunken rages... the violence... After Dorney's death they got steadily worse. Eventually it became impossible to keep him in the household, if only to protect Tanner. My brother-in-law was all for casting him into a cell at the Gloucester assizes.'

'Do you know where he is now?'

'Gravesend, I hope.'

'Why there, of all places?' asks Nicholas, puzzled.

'It's where Porter was born. He spoke of the river often. My husband gave him enough money to set himself up as a waterman. It was his father's trade. I just hope Porter hasn't drunk it all away. Or worse.' She shakes her head despondently. 'And now Tanner has gone, too. No more Bells at Havington Manor. William would be *so* sad.'

'Your son-in-law told me Tanner was serving as a companion to Samuel,' says Nicholas, remembering his conversation with Joshua Wylde in his Woodbridge house. 'Why would he suddenly leave – for London?'

'I don't understand that, either, Dr Shelby. Tanner was raised in our household. He defended Samuel from the cruelty of the village boys – sometimes with his fists. He would never willingly have abandoned him. And even if he had, he would have returned to Havington Manor. He knew he always had a place there.'

'Perhaps he thought your brother-in-law would refuse to take him in, now that Sir William is no longer master.'

Mercy Havington answers with a dismissive snort. 'You mean because of Tanner not having four legs and being clad in wool?'

Nicholas smiles at her spirited dismissal of her brother-in-law. 'It's a reason, madam.'

'Nonsense! I would have insisted. I still have *some* standing in the Havington household.'

'Then perhaps Tanner has gone to find his father, in Gravesend.'

'I doubt that very much. The boy had become greatly afeared of his father's unpredictable violence. No, Dr Shelby, Tanner would never have gone to Gravesend.'

'Does he have any friends in London? Any cousins? Any reason at all to go there, apart from to accompany this Finney?'

'That's what troubles me, Dr Shelby,' says Mercy Havington. 'To my certain knowledge, Tanner Bell hasn't been within fifty miles of London in his life.'

3

When Bianca and Rose return from fetching the evening's water from the public well on Scrope Alley, Kit Marlowe is waiting in the lane, leaning against the wall of the Jackdaw as nonchalantly as a court poet. His full, honeyed locks are pushed back over his ears, and his left leg is bent at an acute angle, the heel of his boot pushed flat against the plaster. He's wearing a grey damask doublet pinked with crimson and looks almost worn down by his own beauty. Bianca has learned from Nicholas of his humble parentage, but today he looks and sounds the very essence of the latest success to hit the London playhouses. Beside him, the plump, malmsey-mottled figure of Walter Burridge toys with the bright ribbons of the Lord Tyrrell's Men stitched into his coat.

'How *now*, Mistress Bianca?' Marlowe oozes as she stops beneath the twin signs and puts down her pail. Something about the way the two men are standing there so boldly makes her stiffen, though she can't explain why. Customers are customers, after all. Marlowe's money is as good as anyone's. And there is something dangerously appealing about him. Perhaps it's the contradiction, she thinks: the cultured wordsmith inhabiting the same body as the Canterbury street-fighter. Behind her, she can sense Rose brushing her kirtle self-consciously.

'Does Master Henslowe at the Rose still have the carpenters in, Master Kit?' Bianca asks with a tight-lipped smile. 'Have you come to my tavern to practise a full rendering of the Day of Judgement, perhaps? One riot not enough for you?'

Marlowe places a hand over his mortally wounded heart. 'Was this the face that launched a thousand ships, and burnt the topless towers of Ilium?'

'I've no idea what you're talking about, Master Kit,' Bianca replies loftily.

'Just a verse I composed – in praise of beauty.'

'I'm flattered,' Bianca says. 'But you'll have to do better than that. I was raised in Padua, remember. I've been paid court to by experts.' She hoists her pail again. 'Now, if you'll excuse, I really do have labours to attend to.'

Rose follows her with a flounce, brushing her curls from her eyes with her free hands. 'You can burn my topless towers if you like, Master Marlowe,' she says coquettishly, earning herself a hissed 'Rose!' from Bianca.

'How is your little Venetian gamecock today?' Marlowe asks, following them inside.

'He still languishes, Master Kit,' Bianca says, without altering her expression.

Marlowe has asked the same question in one form or another every day since Nicholas left. Surely, she thinks, he can't be suffering pangs of guilt. Then she remembers Nicholas's warning: *They say he went abroad for the Privy Council... Spying on Catholics...*

'A most terrible violence,' says Burridge sadly. 'And to think we are partly to blame. I pray for him, honestly I do – even if he is a foreigner.'

'The only blame lies with those superstitious Puritan fools who came here looking for trouble,' Bianca says curtly.

The taproom is beginning to fill with evening customers. Timothy is flitting from table to table like a worried swallow.

Bianca goes to the parlour, lays down her pail next to Rose's. 'When you take Master Kit and Master Burridge their ale, give them a pack of *primero* cards,' she tells her maid. 'I want them occupied, not upsetting the other customers with their wild nonsense. I've had to do enough, bobbing and curtseying to the constable over that riot, as it is.'

'You could just ban them, Mistress.'

'Yes, I could, Rose.'

'But Venetians and Master Kit together – well, they do rather pretty the place up a bit, don't they?'

'Rose, dear – *customers!*'

It is four days since Nicholas left for Gloucestershire. On each one of them Bianca has carried out his instructions to the letter. Every evening at about this time, no matter how busy the taproom, she has slipped away and climbed the stairs to Bruno's chamber, carrying freshly washed linen, a jug of hot water and a fresh cataplasm – made of lavender, garlic, camomile and clematis, crushed in a mortar and mixed with oil – for his wound. Today, with both Rose and Timothy occupied, she will have to attend to her cousin alone. But it won't take her more than ten minutes, if she's quick about it. She gathers up what she needs and sets off for Bruno's chamber. As she approaches the stairs, she almost collides with Graziano, coming down.

'How now, Master Graziano?' she says, falling automatically into the language they share. 'Have you been keeping my cousin company awhile?'

'I've been regaling him with tales of the Veneto, Mistress Bianca,' Graziano says in that deep, cultured voice that somehow doesn't fit a grizzled mariner. 'I like to believe he can hear them. Also, I pray for him. I ask our Lord to make him well again.'

'As do we all, Master Graziano. And I hope He is paying attention,' she says, allowing him to pass.

He makes a formal bow and joins Luzzi, the sailing master, and a few others of the *Sirena*'s crew at their *trappola*, a card game she herself plays, but which her English customers have found incomprehensible.

Bruno's chamber is deep in shadow. The air is heavy, pungent with the sourness of old sweat and the reek of the butcher's block. It is the scent of a weakening body struggling against its own failing. Bianca throws open the window. From the alley below, she catches fragments of a slurred but good-natured argument.

She washes her cousin's body, using a cloth and water from the urn in the corner of the chamber. Bruno's skin, though tanned, feels like marble after a rain shower. She takes off the old dressing from his wound, bathes it carefully, then gently applies the cataplasm. Throughout he makes no sound, gives no indication that he is aware of what is happening. If it were not for his slow, measured breathing and the warmth in his flesh, she would think him dead. She offers up a prayer for him and kisses his forehead.

Gazing at him, she recalls how her mother used to recite incantations when mixing her healing potions – meaningless phrases handed down over generations, carried along the old Gypsy routes from ancient Araby. They've stuck in her mind like children's nonsense rhymes. She wonders if they might be efficacious now.

Requiring something of Bruno's, some item of clothing or possession, to act as a focus, Bianca notices the small iron-bound chest she had asked Rose to bring to the chamber. She searches through the keys on her chatelaine belt. It takes a while, but eventually she finds the one that fits the lock.

And then she sees it: one edge of the iron faceplate is slightly bowed out from the side of the chest, as if an attempt has been made to lever it off. For an instant she wonders if Graziano had another motive for his visit to Bruno's room this evening. Has he tried to force the lock?

She dismisses the idea. If the crew's *portafortuna* had wanted something from his master's possessions, all he would have to do is ask. The attempt must have been made by someone else, before Rose brought the chest here. Bianca shakes her head. Paduans can thieve like few others, she thinks; but given half a chance, the English would steal Christ's nails off the holy cross.

Opening the chest, she takes out the canvas sack that Luzzi brought from the *Sirena* and returns to her cousin's side.

She discounts the astrolabe and the compass – too irregular, too hard, too resistant. She discounts the Sannazaro poetry. Too many words. For all she knows, even though they're in indecipherable Latin, they might somehow compete with the rhymes and weaken their power, the way echoes in a church blur the crispness of the Holy Mass.

Then her fingers touch the softness of Bruno's black doeskin gloves.

She takes them out, admires them in the candlelight, then pulls them over her own fingers. She at once feels a greater contact with him, as if it's his own skin against hers, rather than smooth leather. Softly she begins to chant her incomprehensible lullaby, all the while running the fingers of her left hand gently up and down the edge of her right, from the top of her little finger to the wrist, in a soothing motion.

After a few moments she stops.

A coarse unevenness in the stitching of the right glove has wormed its way into her consciousness. There's no denying it. The finish of the seam on the right glove is markedly inferior to the one on the left. And yet these exquisite black gloves have clearly been made by a craftsman who cares greatly for his work.

And then she recalls her brief comment to Rose, a few days ago: *They're different sizes. The right glove is bigger... It's thicker on the back.*

Crossing to the candle, Bianca holds her right hand close to the flame. Now visible to her, the seam of the glove is clearly not as skilful as the rest of the needlework. She pushes down on the back of her hand, feeling the pleasure of the doeskin against her fingertips.

And as she does so, she feels the faintest trace of regular edges beneath the leather. This isn't careless overstuffing by some inattentive glover, she tells herself – there's something inside.

Muttering an apology to the unconscious Bruno, she takes up the candle and slips from the chamber. She is still wearing the gloves.

Why do I imagine danger, with these gloves in my possession and Kit Marlowe downstairs in the taproom? she asks herself as she enters her own chamber.

She hears Nicholas's answer in her head.

They say he went abroad for the Privy Council... Spying on Catholics...

Closing the door as quietly as she can, Bianca searches out her sewing box. She slips off the gloves, opens the box and takes out a bodkin and a small pair of spring-scissors – her mother's, she recalls with a smile. Sitting on her bed, she begins to worry away at the stitching of the right-hand glove, twisting the bodkin through the thread.

It takes her some time to unpick enough to get the blades of the spring-scissors in place. But eventually she's prised loose enough thread to cut. A little more work with the bodkin and she's made a long enough breach in the leather to insert the tips of a thumb and finger. She worms around between the two layers of material, searching.

With the breath frozen in her throat, slowly – very slowly – she draws out a tightly folded wad of fine silk.

Opening it out, she sees it's about seven inches by four. The candlelight shines through it as if it were of the finest gossamer. It seems to glow with a translucent beauty, like the extended wing of an angel.

There is nothing written upon it. Yet cut into the silk and, miraculously edged in some manner she can't yet ascertain, are a series of small random apertures – a score or more of them, like little windows made for her to see through into another world.

As to what it is, Bianca has not the faintest idea. She knows only that it was never meant to be found.

4

'A free man and his dog on the open road, with no Pope to tell him how to pray – that's the sort of freedom we're fighting the Spanish for,' says Ned Monkton contentedly as he and Nicholas coax their horses across a sloping meadow dotted with grazing sheep.

'I'm sure you're right, Ned.'

'All that talk of the Duke of Alba yesterday made my blood run cold. I remember my father frightening me and Jacob with tales of the Don when we were little. He was right. Look how close they came in ' 88 when they sent their Armada against us.'

'Don't worry, Ned. Alba's been dead for years.'

'Yes, but the Don bull has sired plenty more like him, hasn't it? Give 'em half a chance and we'll be paying our taxes to Madrid and crowning our next king in the Escorial, you mark my words, Master Nick.'

The wind is making streamers in the long grass. Fixed against the sky, a kestrel hovers above the hillside as though painted there.

'You're not expecting that dog to walk all the way back to Southwark, are you?' Nicholas asks, glancing down from the saddle to where Buffle is following her nose down the slope.

'Course not. When she gets weary she can sit up here with me.' He whistles to the dog to come closer. Buffle takes no notice. 'So come on then, tell me about this Arcampora fellow.'

Nicholas shrugs. 'You heard everything I told Lady Havington.'

'I know you, Master Nicholas. You can be a secretive bugger when you want to. I think you're suspicious of him.'

'Whatever Arcampora is doing, Ned, I don't think it's intended to cure the boy – even if that were possible. There's something else going on. But what that is, I really have no idea.'

'And what about those two big rogues who mind his back?'

'I've been asking myself the same question. I don't think they're there to protect Arcampora. I think they're for Samuel.'

'And why in the name of Christ's nails would *he* need protecting? The greatest danger he faces around here – apart from the village boys who throw stones at him – is accidentally treading in sheep shit.'

'I don't know, Ned. I truly do not know.'

Ned takes one hand from the reins and scratches his fiery red beard. 'When I was working in the mortuary at St Tom's, there was people who would come across the bridge from the city and pay me money, just so they could look at the stiffs. Not my idea of entertainment, I grant you – but a man 'as to make a living, and as we both know, 'ospitals pay fuck-all. If I 'ad a particularly messy arrival, I could double what I charged. Now if this fellow could cure the falling sickness, well, he'd be able to charge whatever he wanted, wouldn't he?'

'Yes. He would, Ned.'

'So maybe that's what he's about.'

Nicholas shakes his head. 'Arcampora has a high regard for his reputation, I'll grant. But that's not it. It's as if he's trying to *prepare* Samuel for something.'

'Perhaps his father wants him by his side in the Low Countries. Perhaps he's trying to toughen Samuel up.'

Nicholas pictures the line of portraits at Cleevely House, every single one a stern Christian warrior. 'Samuel will never be the son Joshua Wylde wanted, whatever Arcampora tries to make him. No, it has to be for a different purpose.'

They round a hummock carpeted with dogrose and corncockle. Ahead of them the ground slopes towards the little bridge across the stream and the drovers' track leading to the Oxford road. Beyond it, the beech wood on the other side of Cleevely village.

Then, at the very edge of his vision, Nicholas spots a sudden movement in the grass. A hare breaks away down the slope. Buffle gives one high yelp of delight and tears off in pursuit.

'Come back here, you little rascal!' shouts Ned. He tries to spur his pony forward, but the creature seems to know it has three days of bearing Ned's weight ahead of it and stubbornly refuses to break into anything more vigorous than a reluctant trot.

And so it is left to Nicholas to save Rose's present before it disappears from sight. He puts his spurs to his horse's flanks and sets off in pursuit.

But Buffle's head is full of canine desires quite unknown to man. She pays Nicholas not the slightest attention. She crosses the bridge, nose down, at a determined gallop. Cursing, Nicholas follows.

Now they are in the beech wood. The trees crowd over the track. The wind moans in the branches. Buffle, *damn her*, has left the track and is heading into the undergrowth, nose still barely an inch from the ground. Her tail thrashes in ecstasy. And then she swerves and plunges into a particularly dense patch of undergrowth.

Shit! I'll never get her back now, Nicholas curses under his breath. Ned will have to find another present to melt Rose's heart.

He dismounts, calling to the dog with increasing frustration. For long minutes he can hear a disturbance amid the ferns and bracken, but catches not one glimpse of Buffle.

He's about to give up when she suddenly emerges from the thicket a short way off and trots proudly towards him.

At first glance, Nicholas thinks she's found part of a deer's carcass. But when she gets closer, her tail a blur of self-satisfaction, he sees it's the remains of an old coat, covered in mud and leaves. An old brown worsted coat, with broad pleats around the hem.

And from the torn material hangs the fan of a human ribcage. Not yet fully whitened, but well feasted upon by worms, rats, beetles, crows and foxes – all the unwelcome dinner guests that dine on a corpse dumped in a beech wood.

5

'Not much of a way to take your leave of the world – picked over by foxes, scattered about like leftovers. Probably not even shriven, poor sod,' says Ned darkly, sitting on a broken bough while he regards the pitiful collection of filthy bones, flesh and cloth they have managed to collect from the thicket.

It's been a grim task, but they've completed it as best they can. Using broken branches and the sharp poniard Nicholas bought before he left Bankside, they've assembled enough of the remains to establish the corpse is that of a young male. With Buffle's assistance, they even have a gnawed skull with half the grey flesh attached, recovered together with a soiled jerkin from a clump of ferns. The lingering stench almost makes Nicholas gag, but the find tells him all he needs to know.

'I'd wager a golden half-angel against a button that it's Tanner Bell.'

Ned stares at him. 'I knew physicians was clever sods, but that takes the prize, that does. 'Ow d'you know?'

'Because this is his brother's coat.'

A scowl of doubt on his face, Ned says, 'A tattered old thing like that, and you can name its owner at one glance? I want you on my side next time I play *primero*. With second sight like that, we'd win a fortune.'

'First of all, by what's left of this body, I'd say it belongs to a lad around Tanner Bell's age. Then we have Isabel Wylde's claim that Tanner Bell and his friend Finney just upped and left for London – which Mercy Havington refuses to believe. But the damning proof is this.' Nicholas holds up the ruined garment, to reveal a patch stitched low down at the back. 'That's where the ball that killed Dorney struck. I was there when it happened. He died in my arms. Sir Joshua Wylde insisted that we send his belongings back to his father, but we couldn't let him receive his son's coat with bloodstains all over the back and a hole shot through it, could we? So we had one of the washerwomen clean and patch it. I checked it myself, to see if she'd managed a half-decent job.'

'So why was Tanner Bell wearing it?'

'From what Dorney used to say, I got the impression Tanner idolized him. He probably wore it as a memento.'

'According to Mercy Havington, this Tanner lad was on his way to London. What's he doing in pieces in a wood barely a mile outside Cleevely?'

'That's where my second sight fails. You'll have to trust your own, next time you play at cards.'

'What do we do with him?'

'We put him back where Buffle found him.'

'What?'

'Think on it, Ned. If we inform the local magistrate, he'll send word to the coroner at Gloucester. That will take at least a day. Then the coroner will empanel a jury. Before the week is out, it will be common knowledge in every hamlet, village and town for miles. Arcampora will be long gone before the ink is dry on the arraignment. And anyway, Lady Wylde will tell the jury exactly what she told Mercy Havington and me: the boy left of his own volition – last seen heading for London.'

'Except that you can prove someone with medical knowledge killed him. An' the only one round here with that is your Swissy.'

'I could,' Nicholas admits. 'But I'm not going to. Not yet.'

'Why not?'

'I want Arcampora to think I'm on my way back to report to Sir Joshua Wylde, without a suspicion in the world.'

'But if Arcampora did this, isn't Samuel Wylde in great danger?'

'You didn't see how Lady Isabel behaved with her stepson, Ned. Whatever it is that she and Arcampora are doing to Samuel, killing him is the very last thing they intend.'

'What I can't understand,' says Ned, jabbing a finger in the direction of the skull, 'is why anyone would carve a hole in his head like that. What did they use – a fucking carpenter's auger? God's blood, I could stick two fingers in there and pick his nose from the *inside*!'

'It's called *trepanning*, Ned. It's the drilling of a hole through the frontal or the parietal bones. And whether you believe me or not, it's not intended to kill.'

Ned stares at him in astonishment, his eyes wide in his broad, fiery face. 'Well, it can't have been meant to cure a fucking head-ache, can it?'

Nicholas gets up from the bough and stands over the sundered corpse. He stares down at the skull. 'I've seen a lot of damaged bone on the battlefield, Ned,' he says reflectively. 'I've treated skulls struck by lead ball, penetrated by pike-head, pierced by arrow and slashed by sword and axe. And just occasionally I've seen them heal. I can't be sure with the skull in this state, but by the look of the scraps of flesh left around the hole and the granulation of the bone, Tanner Bell – if that's who this really is – may have survived the drilling by a few days. What killed him came afterwards: someone has broken his neck.'

6

Since Ned Monkton left with Nicholas, there has been only Rose and Timothy to help Bianca at the Jackdaw. The tavern, the demand for her apothecary's skills and her nursing of Bruno Barrani has left her weary. But then, on one particularly cold March morning, help arrives out of the blue.

The paid-off crew of an Indies trader enter the tavern, boisterously intent on spending some of their wages. With them is a boy of about Timothy's age. He's a wiry, olive-skinned lad with a shock of jet-black hair and eyes the colour of scorched butter. As Bianca helps Rose take the jugs of knock-down to their table, she notices him politely refuse his companions' invitation to drink. She realizes the lad must be a Mohammedan. He's not the first she's seen on Bankside, but rare enough. And she notices that he has the habit of putting a hand to his forehead and wincing.

'Is your young fellow in need of something for a headache?' she asks.

'Farzad's from Persia,' explains one of the sailors. 'We rescued him from Barbary pirates off the Ethiope shore. Doesn't take to the cold, though. It's given him a cruel ache in the brains.'

'I know the very thing,' says Bianca.

Within moments she has mixed leaves of camomile, marjoram, sage and laurel with oil of pepper to make an inhalation.

'What do you say to the kind lady, Farzad?' the sailor asks, pushing the boy forward to take the bowl.

'I say the Pope is the arse-end of a flea-bitten dog!' announces Farzad with a wide grin that shows a set of gleaming white teeth quite unknown in Southwark.

'He's a good lad, for a Mussulman,' the sailor says, before Bianca can put voice to her astonishment. 'Knowledgeable, too. Specially about foreign countries. Tell the good mistress what you know about Spain, Farzad.'

'The Spanish king has breath that stinks like bad goat-meat! He is womanly!'

'And what about France?'

'The French king has very small pizzle. Can only mate with a snail!'

Further investigation reveals that Farzad, an orphan, has learned all his English in the close confines of the barque *Rachel*, at the hands of her determinedly Protestant crew. He can roundly insult every nation yet discovered. The sailors consider him an honorary Englishman.

'What will happen to him, now that the *Rachel* is paid off?' Bianca asks, shaking her head in disbelief.

'He'll soon sign on with another ship. They'll be glad of him. He's a fine cook – for a heathen. Dances a jig mightily, too.'

And thus a new face joins the Jackdaw's company – someone to help Rose with the pottage and the brawn, the baked sprats and the coney pie. Within three days there even appears the occasional strange and fiery dish that Farzad cooks as if he's mixing some sort of secret elixir, and which Rose proclaims tastes like eating the Devil's own flesh, but which several of the Jackdaw's customers consume eagerly. Bianca, for her part, knowing what it is like to have your faith traduced, allows Farzad quiet moments in which to practise his solitary observances.

And waits for Bruno to wake. And for Nicholas to return.

✠

At Cleevely, it is Dr Arcampora's habit to confide in Samuel Wylde many of the great secrets of physic. This, he says, is in order that Samuel may be knowledgeable far above the level of ordinary men. Today, his subject is virgin birth.

'It is the manner by which a man-child may be brought forth into life, without woman, without womb. By a miracle. You understand?'

'Not really, sir,' says Samuel, a frown of doubt clouding his unblemished face.

'Inside the seed of the man – in the very tip – is a perfectly formed human infant,' explains Arcampora. 'Is called *homunculus*. Very tiny. Very small.' He pinches together the thumb and forefinger of his right hand to illustrate. 'God makes perfect this little man, inside the seed. Like in a bubble.'

That's me and Cleevely, thinks Samuel: a tiny little human being encased in a bubble. But God hasn't made me perfect – which is why my father has sent Dr Angelo Arcampora.

'The ancients describe this. So too does the famous Paracelsus – a genius also from Switzerland.'

Samuel wonders how many geniuses Switzerland can hold.

'Now, the secret,' announces Arcampora grandly. 'The seed must be left to putrefy for forty days, in *venter equinus*.' He searches for the correct English. '*Venter equinus* – in the shit of the horse. In the dung: you follow?'

Samuel follows, if tentatively.

'Then, when it shows movement' – Arcampora wiggles his fingers – 'it must be nourished for forty days in human blood. After that it must be boiled. The result is a perfect human boy infant – no womb necessary. This is a known miracle.'

'Perhaps if I'd been grown in horse dung, I might have flowered better than I have,' Samuel says. 'Grandma Mercy puts it on the roses at Havington Manor and they grow very well.'

Arcampora's raptorial face darkens. 'I tell you before, Lady 'Avington, she is not your grandam. You must forget her. Mercy 'Avington was a heretic whore.'

'That cannot be,' protests Samuel. 'Grandma Mercy is a goodly woman.'

'You must learn the truth,' Arcampora continues in a sort of extended spit. 'When, by her intemperate lusts, this woman fell with child, the infant was taken from her. It was probably cast out to die. Your true mother was put in her place, to be raised in ignorance of her destiny.'

In a rare moment of defiance, Samuel almost shouts, 'Then if Grandma Mercy wasn't my true grandmother, who was?'

'This you shall learn when you are stronger,' says Arcampora. 'For now, know only that she, too, was a miracle sent by God.'

Which, to Samuel, sounds as implausible as a tiny, perfectly formed man in the head of the seed he expends when the loneliness at Cleevely becomes too unbearable.

✠

It is not yet dawn. In the lanes around the Jackdaw the silence is broken by a watchman's dog barking at a shadow. Bianca stretches her limbs beneath the covers. On the truckle beside her bed, Rose burbles in contented oblivion. It is in these early hours, before the Jackdaw wakes, before the streets echo to the rumbling of carts and the shouts of the street vendors, that Bianca marshals her thoughts for the day to come. Like every day that's passed since her discovery, today she wakes to thoughts of the little sheet of silk that has been calling to her like a banner on the eve of battle.

But today she has decided to act.

She slips her fingers under the bolster to retrieve the silk from its new hiding place. Then, taking care not to spoil Rose's dreams of Ned, or Bruno's Venetians, or Kit Marlowe, or – for all she knows – the Earl of Essex, Sir Philip Sidney and every actor in London under forty with his own hair and teeth and who can still fill his hose in a pleasing manner, she climbs out of bed, goes to her clothes chest and takes her keys from her chatelaine belt, eases the latch of the chamber door as quietly as the slight tremble in her fingertips will allow and steps silently across the passage to Bruno's room.

The candle that Rose has placed on the chest in the corner has burned almost to the sconce. It might just last till dawn, she thinks. For a while she contents herself with merely watching her cousin by its guttering light. Watching how its flame paints slow brushstrokes of colour on his otherwise grey face. Watching the sheen of sweat on his brow. Watching the slow rise and fall of his chest. Just watching.

What manner of conspiracy are you caught up in, Cousin? What other secrets are you hiding from me?

A flurry of raindrops against the window breaks her reverie. She goes to the chest, moves the candle sconce to the floor, unlocks the lid and lays out the contents on the floor: the purse, the astrolabe, the pocket compass, Bruno's pewter bowl...

Bianca has no idea what she's looking for. She knows only that her curiosity will not let her discovery lie. If the little sheet of silk is a banner, then who – or what – is it calling to action?

First, she takes up the purse and empties out the ducats. A quick inspection reveals a medallion similar to the one Munt pushed across the table in Bruno's cabin aboard the *Sirena*. She studies the image embossed on its face: St Margaret of Antioch standing triumphant over the serpent. And around the circumference, twelve random letters – some repeated. They mean nothing to her.

She replaces the coins and the medallion in the purse. Then she inspects the compass for a hidden compartment, without success. She does the same for the astrolabe, with the same result. Finally there is only the book of verse left to examine.

It is a fine, leather-bound volume, about fifty leaves of thick parchment. It has that fusty smell of ancient books, like an old leather cloak left too long in the rain. The print is large, perhaps only twenty well-spaced lines to the page. And despite the Latin, Bianca understands most of what is printed on the elaborately illustrated frontispiece. She can work out that the book was printed in Rome in 1545, by Pietro Bembo. She even knows who it's dedicated to: Gian Carafa – Pope Paul IV. There he is, in miniature, sitting on his papal throne, while behind him a jaunty skeleton blows a trumpet to signify that even the Holy Father is not to be spared death and the end of days.

The image brings a childhood memory back to her. She is in the little church of St Margaret in Padua. She is eight years old. Father Rossi has ordered the maids of the district to scrub the flagstones until they gleam with a halo of devotion. For Cardinal Santo Fiorzi, the most august of all the Fiorzi family, the man who calls her his *Passerotto* – little sparrow – is coming from Rome to visit them. He is bringing with him a portrait of Gian Carafa to hang prominently in the church he once attended, because the great man himself is now in heaven, advising God on how to be a good Catholic.

What must such a man look like, the young Bianca wonders as she scrubs away, caught in a delicious moment of religious terror?

In fact, as she now remembers, this hammer of the heretics had turned out to be a lonely-looking old man with a big white beard. When the picture was finally hung, Bianca's response was not pious devotion, but a profound desire to take him home and have her mother feed him a hearty dish of *caparosoli*.

'I'll get you home to Padua, Cousin,' she whispers to Bruno, a wistful curve to her mouth. 'No matter what it takes, I'll get you home.'

Thinking the book might be a good place to hide the silk, she lays it flat between the frontispiece and the first page.

It fits perfectly.

The little windows no longer look out upon a landscape she can't see, but upon the lines of print. They do not reveal a pattern. Some fall between two characters, or in places where there are no letters at all. A jolt of comprehension makes her sit bolt upright. Her heart thuds – the way it did when Father Rossi caught her reading chivalric tales of troubadour knights and captive maidens instead of the Bible.

She turns the silk upside-down. The view through the little windows remains random. Nothing fits.

She tries another page – with the same result. And then another. And another. Each time the windows refuse to let her see the landscape clearly, precisely. But now she knows what she's looking for.

She *could* try every page. But she doesn't know which is the top or the bottom of the silk. She can't tell the front from the back. Given the number of pages of verse, there could be hundreds of combinations.

Bruno, give me an anchor to hold the ship steady in this gale.

And perhaps it's him guiding her, or just her own imagination, but her thoughts clarify, become as sharp as diamonds.

Cardinal Carafa – *Pope Paul IV.*

She tries page four: front, back, up and down. Nothing.

The year of his enthronement.

She has no idea when that was. She looks again at the frontispiece, at Carafa sitting on his throne, at the skeleton behind him. The revelation lands like a slap, sharp and loud in the quiet chamber. *The year of his death.*

This she does know: 1559.

Thanking Father Rossi for making his young flock recite the

years in which every Pope of the modern age gained his reward in heaven, she searches for page fifty-nine. There isn't one. The book ends at page forty-eight.

She tries page fifteen, going through the same sequence of positioning the silk. Again the little windows reveal nothing but fog.

On a whim, she decides to subtract fifteen from fifty-nine. She places the silk on page forty-four as if it were a winning card.

Somewhere in the back of her mind she can hear the angels singing. The landscape has suddenly come into clear view.

In each aperture sit two letters. The very first window falls neatly over the *a* and the *s* in the Latin word *astra*. The next window is a little broader than the first. It falls upon the third line, bracketing *ab annis*, to reveal the *b* and the second *a*. Another frames the *c* and the *u* in the Latin word *cupio*. And so it goes on, covering every letter of the alphabet: an *a* matched with an *s*, a *c* with a *u*, an *e* with a *d*. Bianca realizes she's looking at a transposition cipher, a code with which she could unlock a secret message. A message that would reveal to her the nature of Bruno's conspiracy.

Were it not for one inconvenient fact: she has no message to decipher.

And then she remembers the exchange between Bruno and Tobias Munt, that day aboard the *Sirena*.

Have you perchance brought anything else with you, Signor Munt? her cousin is saying.

Munt's voice forces its way to the forefront of her racing thoughts.

Ten days from today... At my warehouse on Petty Wales – the sign of the three tuns.

'Oh, Bruno,' she whispers to her sleeping cousin. 'What in the name of our all-merciful Lord have you done?'

But his answering silence only seems more deafening than ever.

✠

Dr Arcampora has brought Samuel to the beech wood beyond the little bridge. It is almost dark, a pale scythe-blade of moon rising in a turbulent sky. Samuel can hear the wind rustling the leaves, as if the trees are beginning to wake. By the dancing light from the tallow torches that Florin and Dunstan carry, he can see the physician is sweating, wrapped in the heavy black doctor's gown that makes him look like a magus from antiquity.

Despite Dr Arcampora's extraordinary revelations about Samuel's mother, Alice, and about Grandma Mercy, the boy has come to trust in the physician of late. He knows that men of physic are prone to incomprehensible pronouncements and Cabalistic practices. Indeed, a doctor who did not behave in such a manner would betray his lack of profound wisdom. If physic were simple, anyone could learn its secrets. But the beech wood is eerie and unsettling. He wishes Tanner were with him.

'Why must Tanner remain in the house, sir?' he asks. 'I would wish him present.'

'Because tonight we embark upon the most difficult phase of your cure. Tanner Bell is not of your sort. He would not understand.'

'Is that why you made him hide away when Grandma Mercy brought my father's friend, Master Shelby, to the house?'

'We cannot risk unguarded talk. This physic is *very* secret. It must not be witnessed by ignorant people who do not understand. Perhaps they call the authorities. Then no more treatment!' He looks intently at Samuel. 'Do you wish no more treatment, *Samael?*'

147

Samuel tries not to laugh at the way Dr Arcampora has pronounced his name: Sam-*ael*. 'No! I mean *yes* – I do wish for treatment. But my name is Samuel, not Sam*ael*.'

'It is no matter. You must do everything I tell. You must believe!'

They walk deep into the wood until the old abbey lodge looms out of the gathering darkness. Up close, Samuel can see it's been long abandoned, probably since the track to Oxford was improved back in Mary's reign. Dunstan produces a heavy key. The lock is turned. The physician guides Samuel inside.

By the flickering tallow-light they enter the main hall. It is empty, save for an old bench in the far corner and a chair placed squarely in the centre. The air has a fusty smell of dereliction about it, close and strangely warm, though outside it's cold enough to make the hunting foxes shiver. And another scent tugs at Samuel's throat: a hard, ferrous smell. Looking down, he sees several dark stains standing out on the flagstones.

'Is that blood?' he asks timorously.

'It may be,' says Arcampora with a dismissive pout. 'Vagabonds. They poach. Kill a deer or two. They have to eat, don't they? – even vagabonds.'

He doesn't trouble himself to explain how vagabonds managed to get through the locked door. But what really catches Samuel's attention are the chalk marks on the floor – a series of circles, which he takes to be the orbits of the celestial spheres, the chair standing forlornly at their centre like an anchoring earth at the heart of its own cosmos. He sees the signs of the zodiac drawn around the outer ring; then – moving inwards – other strange images: a hanged man; a creature that looks like a bear, though it's been decapitated; a mouth without a face to go with it; a serpent coiled about the crudely drawn image of a woman; rays flowing from a fiery sun. He sees a flock of sheep with horns and forked tails. Two crudely drawn men stand beside the sheep.

One of them has a halo drawn about his head. Samuel guesses the image is meant to depict the miracle of the Gadarene swine – when Jesus cast out the demons from a man possessed. In the remaining spheres are symbols that make no sense to him at all.

'What are all these marks, Dr Arcampora?'

'To guide us, Samael.'

'And the words – I don't recognize the language they're written in.'

'Is very ancient language: Hebrew and Aramaic. Also Greek.'

'But what do the words say?'

'These are incantations: for your cure.'

'Incantations? Aren't they spells?'

'They are like the Holy Mass – they must be made correctly. Absolutely correctly. If the words of the Mass are spoken with error, then they are of no use. God does not hear them. That is why so often our prayers do not work. They are not told properly.'

'You mean "said"—'

'Exactly. Only when all is said properly, then God hears.'

'But it is forbidden to hear the Mass in England. My father says the Mass is the sound of the Devil singing.'

'Your father is a heretic,' Arcampora says dismissively. 'But your grandmother, she died for the Mass. And before she died, she burned all the heretics out of this land! That is why it is most important to make the invocations correctly.'

This must be the grandmother he has yet to learn about, the one whose daughter was stolen away at birth by the deceivers, Samuel thinks. Because to his certain knowledge Grandam Mercy is not dead. She was at Cleevely only a few days ago – when Dr Arcampora and Lady Wylde had Tanner Bell locked away in the cellar for some infringement they would not reveal. And as for burning heretics, why, Grandam Mercy doesn't even trust the servants to put out all the candles at night!

7

Ten days from today – the sixteenth day of March... At my ware-house on Petty Wales – the sign of the three tuns. Shall we say noon?

Munt's voice wakes her like a cock's crow.

Not that Bianca has slept much. The faintest groan of the Jackdaw's old timbers, the slightest noise from the alley and, within an instant, she has heard in her mind a frenzied hammering on the front door, swiftly followed by plate-clad men-at-arms rampaging through the tavern to arrest everyone within and transport them to the cells, where the Privy Council's interrogators await with white-hot irons and thumb-screws.

She takes no breakfast; there's no room in her stomach, due to all the moths seemingly fluttering there. When Rose comes to her with a disapproving scowl on her face that would make a Puritan envious, it is all Bianca can do to rein in her temper.

'It's Farzad,' Rose complains. 'He won't do what he's told. He says it's not dignified for him to obey the commands of a woman!'

Bianca seeks out the lad and steers him into an alcove where she may speak to him privately.

'I presume you have sorcery in Persia, Farzad,' she says sternly.

'Of course, Mistress. Very powerful *sirh*. But Allah – may He be exalted – forbids us to employ it.'

'But you believe in it?'

'Most assuredly.'

'Good. Well, we have sirh in Southwark, too. And if you don't do what Rose tells you, I – not being forbidden to employ it – will turn you into a very small worm. There are big fishes in the river out there, Farzad' – a hand stretched in the general direction of the Thames – 'and Banksiders like to catch them. They use worms to bait their hooks. Especially little worms. Do we understand each other?'

Farzad, who by now has heard enough from the Jackdaw's customers to know the rumours about his new employer, nods his head in silence, his eyes the size of ducats.

'And I know most of our Venetian guests have little English, if at all – but they do venerate the Holy Father. So no more references to the Pope and dogs' backsides within their hearing, yes?'

'Yes, Mistress.'

'And Farzad...'

'Yes, Mistress?'

'Promise to come and speak with me if you feel homesick.'

'I will, Mistress.'

'Good. Now you may tell Rose I'm going across the bridge – to see a new merchant on Petty Wales. Apparently he deals in rice. If it's any good, I might bring back some for your pot.'

✠

A malevolent bank of leaden cloud hangs low over New Fish Street as Bianca emerges from the north end of London Bridge a little before noon. The fluttering moths are still having their sport with her stomach. In fact she thinks they've been joined by a family of dragonflies.

Munt's warehouse is all but identical to the others in the lane. The bottom storey is a solid ragstone barn with a pair of heavy wooden doors large enough to admit a loaded waggon. Shut and bolted, they are sturdy enough to keep a small army at bay. The peeling sign – three barrels in the shape of a pyramid – over-hangs the street, the rusting hinges screeching a faint chorus of protest in the wind. A hundred yards to the east, the brooding Bulwark Gate of the Tower casts its corrosive shadow.

Bianca looks up, hoping to find an open window, perhaps even Munt himself leaning out in expectation of Bruno's arrival. But the windows, opaque with accumulated grime, look as though they haven't been opened for years.

She hammers on the right-hand door three times in quick succession. The old timbers soak up the sound and bury it. Her hand begins to throb. The first shots in a barrage of sleet begin to land noisily in the street.

She toys with the idea of making a run for the Bulwark Gate. Maybe the guards will let her shelter there. But the guards at the Tower must see traitors' faces every day. Surely they can tell, just by looking into your eyes, that you have secrets to hide – even if you don't actually know what those secrets are.

And then she sees it: a gap barely wide enough for the span of a pair of shoulders, between the end of Munt's warehouse and the lime-store next door. She slips into the little passageway just as the heavens open.

The narrow space smells of cat's piss and damp hemp sacks. At the far end is a flight of rickety wooden stairs leading to a landing and a door. Halfway up, painted on the ragstone wall, she can just make out three casks painted on the wall. Munt's invitation to do business. To sell. To trade. To *conspire*. She begins to climb.

Reaching the top, Bianca takes a steadying breath and raps on the door with a determined rhythm that says: *I'm here – ignore me at your cost.*

Silence – save for the sound of her own breathing.

I misheard. I got the day wrong. I misunderstood the whole exchange.

My cousin sells nothing but rice, and you don't buy secrets. I'm here on a fool's errand. And I'm the fool.

But then if there's no conspiracy, how do I explain the silk cipher?

She hears a heavy latch being raised. The door opens inwards. To her relief, there are no armed men waiting beyond the sill to arrest her for crimes she doesn't know she's committed. There's only Tobias Munt, merchant of this parish, standing before her in the same day-labourer's shirt and woollen hose he was wearing that day aboard the *Sirena*.

'God's grace! Do you think I'm dead and need resurrecting?' he demands to know. 'I can *hear* you.'

Bianca stands before him, the melted sleet sheening her brow. The parish-church bells begin to strike noon. Now that they're face-to-face, she doesn't know what to say.

He's a big man, with a roll of fat that lies around the base of his neck like a noose. His eyes range over her with an interest she does not care for, as he tries to make out her features in the gloom. Then he recognizes her.

'Well, how now, Mistress? If it isn't the maid with the sharp tongue – from the *Sirena*.' He looks over her shoulder into the shadows of the landing, presumably expecting to see Bruno. At the bottom step the hailstones ricochet in from the street, like water spilt on hot fat.

'I've come in my cousin's place, Master Munt.'

'Come for what?'

'It is the agreed time and place, isn't it?'

'I don't know what you're talking about, Mistress.'

Bianca fears he's going to slam the door in her face. She thinks of putting one foot over the sill to stop him, but the combined impact of Munt and the door would crush it easily.

'I was *there*, Master Munt – in the cabin on the *Sirena*. Remember?'

She holds up the medallion of St Margaret that she found in Bruno's purse. Munt eyes it like a dog waiting for a titbit. 'Signor Barrani is indisposed. He sent me in his stead.'

'I'd heard he's had what we might call "a tumble". Mending, is he?'

How does he know? Bianca wonders. Who told him? 'Bruno is a good man, Master Munt. God will look to his recovery,' she says, with more confidence than she feels.

'Well, if I were asked who I'd prefer as an emissary, I could think of no one comelier,' he says, looking deep into her eyes with an intensity that makes her skin crawl. 'You'd best enter, hadn't you?'

She doesn't need the brooding presence of the nearby Tower to help her imagine how someone may pass through a doorway, never to be heard from again. But she's come too far to turn back now. As she steps inside, she hears Munt turn the key behind her, even above the drumming of the hail and the pounding of her own heart.

✠

'I've just come from Master Samuel's chamber. I could not raise him, and the door was locked. Is there aught ill with him, my lady?' Tanner Bell says to Isabel Wylde when he comes across her in the privy garden at Cleevely. His usual puckish good-heartedness is today dulled by worry, a worry not at all soothed by Lady Wylde's coldly dismissive response.

'Do not trouble yourself over Samuel. He is not to be disturbed. He is resting.'

'But if he's had one of his paroxysms, I should be there to comfort him.'

'Samuel is merely sleeping, Tanner. Nothing more.'

'But it's gone noon.'

Lady Wylde looks around the privy garden, as though searching for a servant to remove something unpleasant that she's stumbled upon during her otherwise untroubled walk. Finding no aid amongst the bushes, she sighs, clasps the crucifix that hangs at her throat and resigns herself to dealing alone with distasteful necessities. 'Dr Arcampora has begun a new regime for Master Samuel – to strengthen his body. It requires from him much physical exertion. That is why he is resting. Now, if you—'

Tanner's concern for his friend gives him the courage to persist, even in the presence of a woman he thinks of as being a terrifying amalgam of the Holy Madonna and a hanging judge. 'But he was outside in the middle of the night: out beyond the house...'

'You *followed* them?'

'I wasn't spying, honestly. I was just looking out of my window and saw them heading in the direction of the beech wood. It was a cold evening. I would have lent Samuel my coat for warmth, if that thieving rogue Finney hadn't stolen it. It's not good for Samuel to risk a chill.'

In Tanner's mind, Lady Wylde's eyes seem to narrow in the pale ceruse globe of her face. Her long body stiffens. She's like a beautiful white owl sitting atop a post, he thinks, watching an unsuspecting mouse wander past below; and I'm the poor mouse.

'Who are you to question a physician such as Dr Arcampora, sirrah?'

'I wasn't questioning, madam, I swear it.'

She traps him in that unnerving gaze a while longer. 'You have served the Havingtons since you were old enough to fetch and carry, have you not, Tanner?'

'Aye, madam. My father was Sir William's man. So was my brother, Dorney. But he's dead now.'

'Do you have a good memory, young Tanner Bell? Do you remember things well?'

'I think so, my lady.'

'Then tell me, did Lady Mercy ever say anything in your hearing that made you question Samuel's lineage?'

'Lineage? I don't know what you mean, madam.'

'In a careless moment perhaps – when she believed herself unobserved...'

'I still don't—'

'His *mother*, Tanner! Did Mercy Havington ever speak in your hearing about Samuel's mother?'

Tanner stares at her, transfixed with fright. 'I know she and Sir William were inconsolable when Samuel's mother died. My f-f-father told me so. But I never heard them speak of their daughter in my presence, other than with affection.'

'Your father then. Did he ever mention having heard anything?'

'My father?' Why is she putting me through this unnerving interrogation? Tanner Bell wonders. What does she want me to say?

The cheeks of the white ceruse mask give a little shudder as Isabel Wylde expels an impatient breath. 'Did Porter Bell ever mention anything to you – anything at all – that might suggest Lady Mercy knew Alice Havington wasn't her child?'

Bianca looks around the chamber, hoping to spot some evidence of humanity to tell her that Munt is a man like any other, with normal human sympathies, perhaps even with a family. But there's not a piece of plate, not an ornament, not a personal possession anywhere. Just a plain table and a few chairs. Compounding her unease, she notices a doorway set into the far wall, the arched lintel embossed with ships under sail. The door is ajar, leading to heaven knows where. Or what.

Munt gestures for her to sit. He wrings his big hands. 'Forgive my omission, Mistress. I'm a poor host indeed. Wait here, I'll fetch us some sack. I won't be long. Then we can be about our *business*.'

Take an hour if you want, Bianca thinks with revulsion, as Munt disappears through the little doorway. Take all the time in the world. Because, for the life of me, I have no idea why I'm here. And I can hardly ask you, can I?

She looks at the little medallion cradled in her hand. At the figure of St Margaret of Antioch in the centre. At the random letters around its edge.

What could possibly tie these to Tobias Munt, merchant of Petty Wales in London? she asks herself.

She tries to picture the little chapel dedicated to the saint in Father Rossi's church in Padua, searching her memory for something – *anything* – that might come to her aid. She lets her senses wander over the image in her mind. She can smell the heady fragrance of the incense. She gazes in her thoughts at the brightly painted statue of the saint: the one she has watched being paraded through the streets every feast day for as long as she can remember. She sees the pink plaster face suffused with candlelight, like the light of God into which St Margaret herself stepped after her miraculous passage through the belly of the serpent. St Margaret the martyr: swallowed by Satan, yet so holy that she emerged unharmed. Living proof that devotion to God can protect the pure in spirit from such an intimate entanglement with the Devil. St Margaret of Antioch.

Antioch. The city where the Apostles first agreed to call themselves Christians.

Now Bianca realizes what the random letters engraved around the edge of the medallion are. P... J... S... Peter... John... Simon... They're the initials of the twelve disciples.

'Mistress Merton.'

Munt's voice shocks her out of her reverie. A volley of hailstones batters at the windows. She looks up. Munt has returned.

But there's no glass in his hand. He hasn't brought the promised drink. Just a tall, bearded man whose eyes look ready to produce a hailstorm of their own.

8

'I think you and I need to have an honest talk, Mistress Merton,' says the stranger. In his voice Bianca can hear the echo of great houses and grassy deer parks, of liveried servants and rolling English acres. He's as unlike Munt as a biscuit is to a broom-handle. The alarming beard and the deep, ferocious eyes may appear piratical on the surface, but his brown doublet is pointed with gilded laces and dagged with yellow satin. His knee-high boots are made of the best leather. The sword he wears on his hip has jewels set into the guard and quillion.

'My name is Thomas Tyrrell,' he tells her. 'You may have heard of me – I have some minor reputation, or so I like to think.'

Yes, I've heard of you, Bianca replies silently. It was your players whose antics got my tavern smashed up and put my cousin close to death.

'A reputation?' she says innocently, firming her jaw to disguise the fear in her voice. 'If you have one, I'm afraid it has passed me by, Master Tyrrell.'

There's no sudden flare of anger, no outrage at her nerve, just a cold chuckle at her boldness. 'I'll be content with "Your Lordship", Mistress Merton,' he says. 'Let's not add insolence towards your betters to your list of crimes.'

'Crimes, Lord Tyrrell? I wasn't aware I'd committed any.'

To help her, he counts them on one upraised hand. 'Firstly,

entering Master Munt's warehouse with the intention to steal from him.'

'I had an appointment,' she protests. 'Or at least my cousin did. And, as you can see, I haven't stolen anything.'

'Secondly, encouraging this loyal and devoted subject of the queen, Master Munt, towards treason.'

'Treason? Since when was trading in rice considered treason?' She wonders if he's noticed the sudden busyness in her throat.

'Thirdly – and this is the one I think you should consider *very* carefully, Mistress Merton – attacking him so violently that I was forced to run you through with my sword, lest he lose his life to your wild and unprovoked assault.'

She can see by his eyes that he'll do it. And get away with it, too – a man of his station. He even has a tame witness who'll lie through his teeth and claim she came at him like a wildcat. Now she understands the nature of the pit she's fallen into. Only I didn't fall, she thinks; I came here of my own will.

What is Bruno to this man? she wonders. Is he friend or enemy? And what does Lord Pricey-Boots think I am? His friend's friend? His friend's enemy? Or his enemy's friend? If there's one thing I've learned in the three years I've been in London, it's that a body may be all three in a single hour. We're like two people blind-folded in a dark room, trying to find each other. Except that one of us has a sword.

'What is it you want of me, Lord Tyrrell?' she asks.

'Mistress Merton, *where* is Bruno Barrani?'

'I think you both know that, don't you? He's at my tavern, the Jackdaw on Bankside.'

'But does he *recover*?' Tyrrell asks. 'You see, it's the measure of his incapacity that I'm have a little trouble in establishing.'

'Under my protection, yes, he recovers. But it's early days. That's why I'm here.'

'Protection? You're *protecting* him?' says Tyrrell warily.

'Of course I am. He's my cousin.'

Munt coughs apologetically. 'She has the token, my lord. Barrani would not have entrusted it to her if he thought she intended to deceive the Brothers.'

The brothers. The words echo in her head like a peal of bells.

Who does he mean, she wonders: siblings? Or is Munt referring to a fraternity of some sort, a religious order perhaps. If by 'token' he means Bruno's medallion, then the answer is clear: *The Brothers of St Margaret of Antioch.*

You've just offered me the first of your secrets, Bianca thinks. You've made me a gift of it, without even realizing. A sense of dangerous elation surges through her.

'Your cousin, Mistress Merton – he is a learned man, is he not?' says Tyrrell, studying her intently. 'Merchant venturing is not his only passion, I assume.'

How is she supposed to answer? What other passions of Bruno's can he be talking about? Dice? The cock-fight? Dancing a volta with a pretty maid? She feels the way she felt when Father Rossi or Cardinal Fiorzi called her out to recite some religious litany she had forgotten to learn.

And then a flash of inspiration. A moment of revelation – as though Bruno has just woken up, raised himself effortlessly on his elegant elbows, told her he's never felt better and handed her the book of poetry that now contains his secret cipher.

'Poetry,' she says as casually as she can manage. 'His particular love is Sannazaro. He'll read Boccaccio, but when he's in a reflective mood it's Sannazaro every time. Especially the 1545 edition, printed by Pietro Bembo for His Holiness, Paul IV.'

Less than five minutes later Bianca is striding down Petty Wales, oblivious to the last efforts of the dying storm to soak her. Her heart pounds with relief, and more than a little terror at what the small parcel wrapped in sailcloth that she's tucked inside her gown might contain. For Tyrrell has not seen fit to tell her.

Have you perchance brought anything else with you, Signor Munt? she can hear Bruno asking. And Munt's reply: *I shall need a little more time... favourable winds... We weren't expecting you so soon.*

As Bianca approaches the shelter of the bridge, something – some hint of the wise-woman buried deep inside her – makes her look back over her shoulder.

The scene is no different from any other she might expect to see in this city: urchins and vagabonds on the lookout for an unguarded purse, citizens of every shade and humour going about their business, lawful or otherwise. Everything as she would expect to see it.

Save for one man in a weather-worn cloak who seems taken by an unaccountable desire to turn his face from her and inspect the finer points of an utterly random doorway.

9

When the Jackdaw closes its doors for the night and Rose, Timothy and Farzad are asleep, Bianca steals into Bruno's chamber. By candlelight she unwraps Tyrrell's parcel. Inside is a slim wooden box, banded with straps of metal, one lengthways, one across. She turns it over, searching for the catch. Where the bands meet, she discovers a small keyhole. She shakes the sailcloth, expecting a key to fall out. Nothing does.

She shakes it again. Still no key.

'Where is it, Cousin?' she asks the unconscious Bruno. 'If Tyrrell hasn't placed one in the parcel, then you must have a key of your own.'

The slow rise and fall of his chest keeps the same steady rhythm.

Fetching the sack with Bruno's possessions in it from the chest, Bianca spreads the contents out beside his mattress. For a while she just stares at them.

She's sure it's not in his purse – she'd emptied that when she'd retrieved the medallion of St Margaret to take to Petty Wales. She can discount, too, the Sannazaro. She's well acquainted with that now, and there's definitely no key secreted in the cover or between the pages.

She checks the gloves, working them vigorously between her fingers. No more secrets hidden there, either. The astrolabe she can also discard – there's nowhere amongst its thin metal rings to hide a key.

'You must have it *somewhere*, Cousin,' she tells Bruno in a whisper. 'I can hardly ask Lord Tyrrell – I'm supposed to be your accomplice. I'm supposed to know everything.'

The slow rise and fall of his chest keeps the same steady rhythm.

A terrible thought strikes her. Perhaps he keeps the key aboard the *Sirena*. If that's the case, it is lost to her.

Only the compass remains now. Thumbing the brass catch, Bianca opens the lid. The lodestone gives a quiver of excitement, swinging wildly in the compass rose, before settling to the north. The blade of the sundial clicks up into place, standing proud like a little brass fin. Bianca peers at it more closely.

At the apex of the blade she sees a small decorative finial, a flat curlicue of metal about half the size of the nail on her little finger, a miniature dash of exuberance by the craftsman to show off his skill.

Bianca takes Tyrrell's box in her other hand and matches the keyhole with the finial. The little brass ornament is a perfect fit. She turns it. A satisfying *click* and the metal bands release. With her heart beating wildly, Bianca opens the box.

Inside are several sheets of parchment, neatly folded. She takes them out and spreads them on the floor. On each one is a meaningless collection of apparently random letters, laid out in neat lines of secretary hand. She knows at once that all she needs, in order to reveal their contents, is the transposition code revealed to her by the little silk banner.

With her heart pounding, Bianca puts the documents back in the box and goes to her apothecary's room in the cellar as quietly as the Jackdaw's ancient timbers will allow.

She's already taken the precaution of writing the code into the book she uses to record her patients and the treatments she's prescribed, set down in a way that would be meaningless to a casual observer. She sets the candle close to her chair, takes up paper and pen and – fighting the instinct to hurry – goes methodically to work. The letter *a* replaced by an *s*...; *c* replaced by *u*...; *e* by *d*...

Bianca gets through only three lines on the first sheet before she lays it aside. She tries again on the second sheet. This time it takes only one line before she abandons it and moves on to the third piece of parchment. Only two words before she moves on to the fourth. Then she gives up. Not one group of letters has yielded its meaning. The words are all in Latin.

A wave of frustration breaks over her. Her disappointment, the tension of her visit to Petty Wales, her cousin's injuries, all bring Bianca close to tears.

She remembers what Bruno had said to her the day Munt came aboard the *Sirena*: *... it is a privy matter. He needs someone he can trust in this den of disbelievers...*

The thought that her cousin is a conduit for secret messages passing between Cardinal Fiorzi and an English lord who is somehow connected to a secret cabal calling itself the Brothers of Antioch can mean only one thing: treason.

She's almost glad she can't read the letters. Whatever these conspirators are saying to each other will have to wait for the return of the one person she would dare to trust with their translation: Nicholas Shelby.

And God alone knows where he is at this moment.

✠

'Rose, dear, I'm going for a walk, down to the river,' Bianca says the following morning after breakfast. The guest's trenchers have been cleared away and Rose is upstairs, hanging the bed sheets out of the windows to air. Farzad is eagerly assisting her, as though it's all he was created for. 'Can you manage without me?'

A walk, down to the river. It's not exactly a lie. It's just not the whole truth.

From the Jackdaw, it's less than five minutes to the river bank. Bianca strides through the lanes towards the Thames. At the narrow foot of Black Bull Alley the great watery-brown serpent slides endlessly across her vision. She can smell fecund river mud, rotten fish and the stink of wet hide and fresh blood from the Mutton Lane shambles.

To her right, about fifty yards from the river, is a patch of open ground between two houses. It's a small wasteland of weeds, burnt timbers and shattered masonry, where a tenement once stood. At the back is an ancient wall of flint and brick about ten feet high, pierced by a door. Hoisting the hem of her kirtle, Bianca steps carefully across the rubble. She takes a key from her girdle and slips it into the lock. The door swings open easily on greased hinges. She steps through into her secret world.

She purchased this little plot from the parish, using what was left of her father's money, after she'd taken the Jackdaw. It's a rectangle of ground between the still-standing garden wall of the long-demolished tenement and perimeter wall of the Southwark Lazar House. No one had wanted to buy it, because of the grim shadow cast by the derelict leper hospital, even though there's not been a case of the malady reported since Elizabeth ascended the throne. Old stories, old fears have deep roots on Bankside.

But now it's no longer a wasteland. Hidden away between two high brick walls and the gable ends of the adjoining houses are her herb beds, neatly ordered, the climbers trained fastidiously, the shrubs trimmed to within an inch of their lives. She stands for a while, eyes closed, just taking in the scents of horehound and anagallis, of pennyroyal, and wood-sorrel, all her flowery familiars working their magic on her senses. A contented smile spreads across her face. As far as she knows, this is the only physic garden in the city. Possibly in all England.

When she arrived in London, it had taken her a while to realize that she could not treat this patch of waste ground in the same manner as she'd tended her mother's physic garden in Padua. English soil and Protestant weather were enemies she hadn't expected. She smiles as she recalls how she tried to deal with the caterpillars by the old method that her mother had always espoused: walking barefoot through the patch when she was in her menses time. It was about the only spell of her mother's that hadn't worked.

But she persevered with more practical methods of cultivation. Now she often comes here just to revel in the scents, to walk between the beds and rub the leaves between her fingers, releasing their fragrant charms. And when she does, she thinks not just of the healing balms and infusions she will prepare, but also of her Italian mother and her English father, sleeping their everlasting sleep in the sunny graveyard a mile beyond the city walls of Padua.

I am the daughter of magicians, she thinks: a sire who believed he could uncover the secrets of the natural world by study, and a mother who'd been using those same secrets all her life to concoct her potions – some to heal, others to poison. When she looks at it plainly, she's the child of a heretic and a witch. No wonder dear Ned Monkton once thought her capable of flying down Long Southwark in the dead of night in the shape of a bat. No wonder the customers of the Jackdaw still feel a little less than bold when they run up a tally. They're still not *quite* sure that she can't curdle their pottage on a whim, or bring their children out in shingles.

Bianca walks carefully along the back wall until she finds the spot she is searching for, a distinctively twisted root of holly. Beside it lies a large lump of old plaster, mossy-green with age. She rolls it away from the wall, revealing a deep cavity. She buries the sailcloth parcel containing Tyrrell's box of documents and heaves the masonry back into place. Then she gathers up a selection of leaves for Bruno's cataplasm, so that on her return Rose won't badger her about where she's been.

Oh, Bruno, whatever are you up to? she says to the sleeping ranks of lavender just before she leaves. *Have you forgotten what these people do to their enemies if they catch them – how merciless they can be?*

She's almost reached the top of Black Bull Alley when something makes her turn her head and look back over her shoulder: a sensation, a feeling, nothing more. Or perhaps that intangible sense of something being not quite right.

A shadow – *there* – flitting beneath the overhang of a house.

Her heart begins to race. She stares intently down the lane.

It's nothing. Just a shadow. A window being closed, perhaps. Certainly not a man in a dark winter cloak, like the figure she thought she glimpsed when she left Munt's warehouse. A nothing shadow.

You're losing your wits, she tells herself. You're turning into a scared mouse. She curses her foolishness and continues on her way, satisfied that Tyrrell's parcel is safely hidden where no one can possibly find it.

✠

When Bianca returns to the taproom, she finds Kit Marlowe sprawled at a table, one booted foot on the bench, the other draped over the corner of the board, as though he owns the place. Walter Burridge sits beside him, like an undergroom who's been drinking too much of his master's malmsey.

Until Lord Tyrrell had stepped through that door at Munt's warehouse, she'd thought Kit Marlowe an innocent party in the riot that had left Bruno close to death. She'd put the blame squarely on the shoulders of sideman Perrot and his Puritan friends. Kit, the gifted playwright, would inevitably provoke people with small minds. But now she wonders if he might not frequent the Jackdaw for a different reason. After all, he hasn't actually done any rehearsing for days now. He lodges somewhere across the river, she's learned; so why does he come here almost every day? Is he Tyrrell's man? Or – as Nicholas had warned her – is he the Privy Council's? Where, she wonders, do Kit Marlowe's true loyalties lie?

But she cannot deny there is something about his dangerous disregard for convention that she finds appealing. And as Rose is only to eager to point out, as a male, Kit really is exceptionally enticing – if perhaps just a little *too* beautiful for her own tastes. (She distrusts such polished edges, especially ones so clearly borrowed.) Maybe if he could rediscover a little more of the Kentish brawler in him... She knows it's there – she's seen it peep round those oh-so-smooth corners more than once. That's what I like so much about Nicholas, she thinks. No pretence. No playing the gallant. After all, how can you trust a man who so easily deceives even himself?

'Why, Mistress Bianca,' Marlowe cries theatrically as he spots her, 'bright Phoebus himself could not grace Bankside with half so divine a crown of light! The darkness is extinguished by your return!'

Before she can stop herself, Bianca realizes she's running her fingers through her hair to subdue any waywardness. 'I haven't the faintest notion what you're talking about, Master Kit,' she says, cursing the weakness of her resolve.

'Rejected!' guffaws Burridge in delight. 'Careful, Mistress Bianca, you have the gift of my friend's contentment in your hands. Be gentle, I implore you.'

'The only thing I have for Master Kit is his reckoning,' she says, regaining her composure. 'He owes me a week's worth of ale and sustenance. And that doesn't cover the damage done in the riot that harmed my cousin. Any time will be fine.'

Burridge bangs his ale-pot heartily on the table to show how much he appreciates her spirit.

'If you find yourself a little short, Master Kit,' she says, raising her chin, 'I'm sure Lord Tyrrell would help you out.'

She waits for the response. Will a faint hardening of his expression tell her what she needs to know? Will the merest flicker of those oh-so-fine eyebrows betray him?

'Lord Tyrrell?' he says innocently. 'Why would Thomas Tyrrell give *me* gelt?'

'Because you're with his company of actors: Lord Tyrrell's Men.'

'Actually, he's not,' says Burridge, toying with his pot as though he's been caught hiding a guilty secret.

'But I thought—'

'Mercy, no!' Marlowe laughs, interrupting her. 'If I am retained, it's either by the Earl of Nottingham or the Lord Strange. I had *The Jew* on at the Rose in January with Strange's Men. I merely use Tyrrell's fellows when I'm working up a play. Saving Master Burridge's presence, I'd trust Sackerson the bear to deliver lines better. Didn't you hear them in the yard, clubbing my verse to death with their doltish delivery?'

Burridge gives a weak smile to show he can take an insult on the chin with the best of them. Then, with just a hint of bile in his voice, he confides to Bianca, 'Actually, we're all Master Kit can afford.'

'If I didn't have to keep standing you malmsey, Walter, I could keep the great Ned Alleyn on a retainer for the rest of my career. And buy him silk Venetian hose every month.'

'Have you ever actually met Lord Tyrrell, Master Kit?' Bianca asks Marlowe innocently.

'Once or twice. Dreadful fellow, if you ask me. If ever I need inspiration for a well-bred murderer, I can think of no one better.'

Bianca doesn't respond immediately. She considers the possibility that if Marlowe isn't Tyrrell's eyes in the Jackdaw, then perhaps he's Robert Cecil's or that of some other member of the Privy Council. Or perhaps Nicholas was wrong – perhaps Kit really is just a jobbing playwright with an insufferable self-assurance. She decides there's only one way to find out.

She draws herself up to her full height, which she knows accentuates her neck and her waist, runs her fingers through her hair – willing it to attain an impossible lustre – gives him her best coquettish smile and invites him to take her to the Royal Exchange tomorrow to hear the musicians play.

✠

Out in the beech wood, the door of the lodge flies open, shattering the pre-dawn silence like a cannon shot.

Florin stumbles out into the clearing. He bends double, like someone exhausted after running a great distance. His woollen breeches cling to his legs as the sweat sucks the cold out of the departing night. All across the wood the birds shriek a wild chorus of alarm.

'Quiet, Florin!' hisses Arcampora to his assistant as he follows him out of the lodge. 'What if there are poachers?'

But Florin wouldn't care if the queen's Privy Council was waiting for him with a letter of arraignment bearing his name on it. He thinks he'd almost prefer the prospect of the scaffold to another night like this. He fills his lungs with air and stares pleadingly at Arcampora. 'We are damned!' he rasps. 'All of us! We're going straight to Purgatory! We'll burn there for all eternity. There'll be no redemption. This cannot be right, not even for so godly a cause.'

Arcampora regards his assistant with a sigh of disappointment. To discover weakness at such a crucial moment troubles him.

'I picked you, Florin, because you are no frail woman,' he says, laying a hand on the man's shoulder. The deep black sleeve of his physician's gown hangs between them like a rallying banner on a battlefield. 'I picked you because I believed your mind was not given to superstitious imaginings. If you saw something, if you *felt* something, then perhaps it is real. Perhaps the words are coming together as they must. Perhaps the invocation is beginning to work. But you cannot run from it like a scared little boy! God insists that you must have *forza* – strength.'

In the chill darkness Florin tries to make sense of the night that has passed. The stolid part of him, the part for which he was chosen, makes its case against the irrational: this is the first time they have attempted a summoning to its conclusion. They are exhausted, confused. Perhaps the heady vapours of bearberry, juniper and monkshood issuing from the sconces and chafing dishes that Arcampora has set around the chalk circles have overpowered his senses. Perhaps they have all entered into some transforming religious mania. Florin has seen such a thing happen before, felt it himself when hearing the Mass at the English College in Rome, where they'd trained him and Dunstan with no less rigour to become soldiers of God – soldiers who could return to their native land and save it from the depredations of the heretics.

But what if I'm wrong, thinks Florin. What if the things I experienced tonight inside this little shrine to Arcampora's extraordinary self-belief weren't brought about simply by overheated emotion and a lack of sleep? What if it really is beginning to happen: the return?

Dunstan joins him in the clearing. He takes a deep breath, slow and settling. Then he marks the stations of the cross on his head and chest. 'What did you see?' he asks Florin.

'I thought I saw shapes in the air,' Florin says in a voice fractured by uncertainty. 'I thought I saw a face, too.'

'But was it *her* face? Was it the queen's face?' Arcampora demands to know.

Neither Florin nor Dunstan dares to answer.

'We must continue,' says Arcampora, suddenly animated. 'Like the Mass, we must discover the exact words God desires to hear. Only *those* words. None other. Otherwise we waste our time. We waste God's time.' He looks back at the open door of the lodge. Lit by the flickering candlelight within, he glimpses Samuel's feet lying still on the boards. 'When the *principe* has recovered, we will begin the incantation anew,' he says. And for a moment he imagines the body that he can partly see is not the body of Samuel Wylde, but of Jesus brought down from the cross.

10

Sunday dawns to a sudden flurry of brisk showers. London's pelt gleams as it dries in the spring sunshine. Across the city, the faithful dress themselves in sober worsted and temperate linen. With pious hearts aglow, they sit on unyielding pews and lose themselves to Thomas Cranmer's liturgy: the words of God unblemished by Romish heresy, the words that earned Cranmer his martyrdom in Mary Tudor's regressive fires.

At the Jackdaw – in the liberty of Southwark, where the parish authorities are somewhat less condemnatory of non-attendance at sermon – Bianca sits beside the insensate Bruno and engages in a one-sided conversation about what they'd be doing if they were in Padua: making confession... contemplating the sixteen holy mysteries while listening to the Mass... reciting their Pater Nosters and Ave Marias... watching the parades... feasting to celebrate the end of Lent... All in all, she thinks they'd be having more fun.

As the worshippers spill out of the churches, Marlowe arrives for their assignation. By the redness of his eyes, Bianca suspects he hasn't been within a hundred yards of a pulpit – or a bed. She feels herself starting to blush. I've spent so long cooling the overheated ardour of beery wherrymen, uncouth cordwainers and morose mariners, she tells herself, that I've almost forgotten what it's like to be the subject of a cultured man's attention – even if he is one who's unbearably full of himself.

With a guilty start, she thinks of Nicholas, which is odd, she decides, seeing as how, not so very long ago, she'd lectured him on having her own life to lead. She cannot deny there have been moments when something has passed between the two of them. She admires his decency, his courage and his honesty, and there's a wit beneath his stoic yeoman's exterior that can make her laugh unexpectedly. His desire to heal is unquenchable. And he is handsome, though not in the manner of the traditional gallant. Earthier. Which she likes.

But the moments have been fleeting. They've never stood a chance against the towering shadow that is his dead wife. The flame that banishes that darkness has yet to be lit, and she's not even sure she's the spark to light it. So why shouldn't she enjoy a mild flirtation with Kit Marlowe – purely to determine how much of a threat he is, of course.

She allows herself an amused but wistful smile. In Padua her mother had always despaired of her stubborn rejection of the city's young gallants. 'Who are you waiting for – a Medici or a Farnese?' she'd demanded to know, when once again Bianca had turned up her nose at a prospect. 'What's wrong with the magistrate's son, Giacomo? I've heard him sing poetry to you from across the street.'

'It's not the poetry I mind,' Bianca had replied. 'It's the voice. He squawks like a crow being eaten by a cat!'

'Don't fret, you'll find a good match one day,' her father had said with a fond sideways glance at her mother.

But how can you find something if you have no idea what it is you're looking for? Or if you stubbornly refuse to look, because the discovery might force you to accept that your dreams are just that – dreams?

In the courtyard of the Royal Exchange on Cornhill the liveried musicians come out from under the awnings to play 'The Hunt Is Up' and 'This Sweet and Merry Month of May'. A band of militiamen parade, to the accompaniment of the crowd's bloodcurdling threats against Spain and her king. A sergeant in breastplate and crested *burgonet* discharges his matchlock musket into the air. Its deafening roar echoes around the boarded shop fronts, setting the women shrieking and the pigeons careening into the air. While the smoke billows and their victims are distracted, urchin cut-purses make a killing and are off scampering down Cornhill before anyone notices.

'Bravo!' shouts Marlowe, clapping his hands. 'A sudden noise and a little smoke, and the groundlings flutter like doves in the presence of an eagle. A riot! What fun!'

'Fun?' Bianca says, her ears still ringing. 'Was the riot at my tavern just a game to you then, Master Kit?'

'You give me too much credit, Mistress Bianca. I incited no one to riot.'

'You staged an incantation with such fidelity that several people thought it was real.'

'Then blame *them*. Don't hold *me* guilty, if the people of Bankside are so superstitious they see demons hiding under their beds when they kneel to pray. How is Signor Barrani, by the way?' he asks, brushing his locks back over his ears so that she can get a better view of his profile.

'Oh, he mends.'

'Mends? Is that all?'

It hasn't escaped her notice that he's asked the very same question every day he's been in the Jackdaw. On whose behalf does he pose it? Could it have been Kit Marlowe who'd sneaked into Bruno's room and tried to force the lock on the chest containing his possessions? she wonders. 'Nicholas has done all he can, Master Kit. We hope Bruno will soon be fully restored to health.'

'No word of when the *Sirena* sails?'

'He hasn't told me.'

'So he's conscious?'

'Why all the questions, Master Kit?'

Marlowe grins. 'I like your cousin. He was roaring good company. And all those handsome Venetians of his – surely they raise just a little blush, at the very least.'

'You sound like Rose.'

'Beauty, strength and danger, all on one trencher. An alluring feast for a hungry woman. Or man.'

'Where's the danger?' she asks. 'Graziano and the others wouldn't hurt a fly, as long as no one threatens their peace.'

'Foreign entanglements,' says Marlowe with mock menace.

'I'd have thought that you, as a loyal subject of the queen, would think twice about consorting with Catholics,' she says, hoping to lead him into indiscretion.

'Ah, all that dark holy sorcery. That guilty desire to confess. I'd rather share my board with a fellow of those appetites than a Puritan killjoy any day.' A direct look. The hint of a dangerous smile.

'And what are your appetites, Master Kit?' she says, her amber eyes flashing the challenge at him.

'Haven't you heard by now? Pretty girls, pretty boys, but mostly tobacco.'

'So Nicholas was right. You are a provocateur.'

'Dr Shelby? Now there's a man whose heart is ripe for the purchase.'

'Whatever do you mean?'

'I was told by someone at the Jackdaw that you plucked him from the river, like a discarded puppy in a sack.'

'We didn't pluck him, we rescued him – all of us. Timothy found him. Rose and I nursed him.'

'He seems the sort of fellow looking for somewhere to sell his heart. Have you not thought of buying it? I've seen how he looks at you.'

'He doesn't *look* at me,' Bianca says firmly. 'He's still in love with his wife. She's dead.'

How did he make the words slip out of her mouth like that? It's *his* secrets she's brought Kit here to reveal, not hers. She stares at her hands while she wonders if it's possible to make him unhear what she's just said.

'Oh, a *double* trade!'

'What do you mean?'

'He would sell his soul to bring her back. You would sell yours to stop him. My, but the Devil has such an easy living!'

'You're going to hell, Christopher Marlowe,' she says, feeling the anger rise in her cheeks. 'You *do* know that, don't you?'

'And when I get there, I shall sell Satan a conduit and a cistern to bring the heat down. I'll make it a lush green garden within a week, you see if I don't.'

'Then I shall pray for your soul. I doubt anyone else will.'

'Prayers for the soul? So I was right! You *are* of the old faith, Bianca Merton! Mercy, but I'm strolling in the March sunshine with the fairest heretic in Southwark!'

'Don't jest. The safety of one's immortal soul is a serious thing.'

'Listen to me,' he says, suddenly very close to her, beguiling her with his eyes. 'Save your prayers. There is no God. Jesus was a fool. Mary was a whore. There's no point in making a trade if there's nothing worth the barter.'

Bianca's mouth gapes at his blasphemy. Appalled, she glances round to see if anyone has overheard. 'How can you *say* such things? Do you really hold damnation to be such a small matter?'

With a sweep of his hand he encompasses the lane, the buildings, the people passing by. 'Look, no thunderbolt. I'm still here. You're still here. If God's vengeance is really so impotent, why should I fear Him *or* the Devil?'

Is it his blasphemy that makes her shiver? she wonders. Or is it because she finds his utter contempt for convention – his *daring* – more exciting than she cares to admit?

'So may I take it your soul is already purchased?' she says, regaining her composure.

'Several times over,' he says with a carefree laugh.

'And the buyers?'

'Ah, that would be telling.'

'The Brothers of St Margaret of Antioch perhaps?' she says casually.

Silence. Then a lazy frown. Nothing in the eyes.

'The Brothers of who?'

'St Margaret of Antioch,' she whispers like a sigh of endearment. Or the prelude to a poisoned kiss. Two can play at provocation, she thinks.

'Never heard of them. Who are they – a new supping club I haven't heard of? Sounds too biblical for my tastes.'

He looks genuine, she thinks. But then he's a writer of conceits and inventions. A provocateur. He's probably told more lies than he has truths.

'It's just a name I heard somewhere,' she says. 'It's of no account.'

✠

In the afternoon, Southwark opens its arms to those seeking respite from the self-denial of Lent. The Tabard, the Jackdaw, the Good Husband, the Turk's Head – every hostelry between the Lambeth marshes and Battle creek – throws open its doors to the tide of eager citizens crossing the bridge in search of the pleasures that the new faith frowns upon. Waiting for them are the fakers, the dancers, the tumblers, the swordsmen, the dice-kings, the card-sharps, the whole purse-diving, eye-for-an-opportunity crew. Fire-jugglers light their way. Street musicians serenade them with sackbut and tambour. Master Heathercrop, the bear-warden, leads old Sackerson by a chain through his nose all the way down Long Southwark. The beast ambles obediently, as though he's thinking that if he can just get through this, they might let him go home to his German forest, to grub for fruit and play with his grandcubs. Behind him, leashed in by their handlers, come the mastiffs, eyeing Sackerson hungrily with their yellow eyes – waiting for the bear-pit to open and the bloody business to begin again.

Outside the Jackdaw, under an old sheet painted with imitation scales, squats Timothy. He has one arm thrust out through a tear, an approximation of a dragon's head fashioned out of painted cloth and paper set upon his fist. The mouth opens quite realistically to the motion of his fingers. Only the flame is missing, which Timothy tries to replace with a roaring noise from beneath his scaly cloth. 'See the dragon! See the dragon! A farthing a go!' shouts Farzad, who's in charge of the money. 'See the fiery dragon that burned the Pope's arse black!' They make three shillings before Bianca calls them in to help her serve the customers.

As she works, she lets her mind return to the time spent in Kit Marlowe's company. She's as certain as she can be that her mention of the Brothers of St Margaret of Antioch meant nothing to him.

He's in the taproom now, she notices – sitting with Walter Burridge and a young lad she hasn't seen before. Burridge looks as though he's trying to convince the lad to agree to a business proposition, while Marlowe watches with languid interest. The three of them leave a short while later. Something Marlowe had said to her earlier echoes in her mind as she watches them go: *Pretty girls, pretty boys, but mostly tobacco...* She wonders which particular appetite Marlowe is thinking of satisfying this time.

Nicholas arrives at dusk, weary after the ride from Gloucestershire. The Jackdaw is busy when he enters. Timothy is playing one of his newly learned Venetian *spagnoletti*, his dragon-companion Farzad beating out the rhythm on a tambour.

'Mistress Bianca!' Nicholas calls out across the taproom.

She turns and sees him standing inside the doorway, his gaberdine riding cloak mud-stained, his wiry black hair unruly beneath his leather hat. He's smiling. Remembering another of Kit Marlowe's provocations – *He seems the sort of fellow looking for somewhere to sell his heart. Have you not thought of buying it? I've seen how he looks at you* – she finds herself blushing.

'How long have you been standing there?'

'Not long.'

But his answer serves only to make her blush a deeper crimson.

Behind him, Ned fills the doorway, a bundle of fur cradled in his huge arms.

'And what is *that*, pray?' Bianca asks, recovering her composure.

'Say good morrow to Mistress Buffle, Mistress Bianca,' Ned says, holding out the dog for inspection. 'I told Rose I'd bring her back a present. And Ned Monkton is a man of his word.'

Rose lets out a shriek of delight. Bianca looks from the dog to Ned, to Nicholas, across to Rose and back to the dog again. Defeated, she gives a weary sigh. 'Well, I can only recommend that you keep Buffle away from the bellmen's hounds or she'll get eaten alive.' She shakes her head. 'A *dog*! God give me fortitude! Don't I have enough dumb creatures to look after, as it is?'

She stalks off towards the parlour. Rose scoops up Buffle and starts to fuss over her. And as she does so, she leans closer to Nicholas and whispers into his ear, '*See* what happens, Master Nicholas, if a gallant don't bring his woman a favour when he returns from a jaunt?'

'Have you done all as I instructed?' Nicholas asks later in Bruno's chamber.

'To the letter.'

'With the ingredients I prescribed? Lavender, crushed garlic, camomile, clematis...'

Bianca nods.

'And in the correct measures?'

'Nicholas! I'm an apothecary! I know how to mix medicines.'

He removes the cloth bandage from Bruno's head and inspects the wound, sniffing for the telltale stink of putrefaction. He places two fingers against the carotid artery on the left side of Bruno's neck and gauges the strength of the pulse. Then, beckoning to Bianca to bring a candle nearer, he gently lifts Bruno's eyelids and peers into his eyes.

'Well?' she asks fearfully.

He sighs, though whether through satisfaction or resignation, Bianca cannot tell.

'Your cousin really is a game little cockerel. To be honest, I hadn't expected him to survive this long.'

'But does he *mend*? Tell me, Nicholas – I need to know. Graziano comes every day to seek after his condition. His crew want to take him home.'

'There's little suppuration. To my mind, he does seem stronger. But whether he will live – whether he will ever recover to his former self – that is still in God's hands.'

'Ah, the physician's old alibi!' she says derisively. 'I thought you'd decided not to believe in God any more, like Kit Marlowe.'

He stands up, frowning. 'Marlowe? Please don't tell me *he's* still hanging around.'

Bianca puts a fresh dressing over Bruno's wound, then says as nonchalantly as she can manage, 'Nicholas, I have to tell you about something that happened while you were away. I'm not sure you're going to approve.'

An expression of jealous foreboding enters his eyes. 'Don't tell me: you've fallen in love with Master Provocateur—'

Her angry cry of 'Nicholas!' is even heard by Timothy, who's at the foot of the stairs, fixing a broken string on his lute.

✳

'What in the name of Jesu possessed you to do it?' Nicholas asks Bianca later, when she's told him about the little rectangle of silk hidden in Bruno's glove, and of her meeting with Munt and Tyrrell.

'Curiosity, I suppose. I needed to know what Bruno had got himself mixed up in.'

'But to go to Petty Wales – to walk into this Munt fellow's warehouse – alone. What were you thinking?'

'I was thinking that you weren't there to come with me,' she replies, her voice sounding unusually defensive.

'And if I had been, I'd have told you to burn the silk and the Sannazaro on the nearest fire, and stay well away from these Brothers of St Margaret, or whoever they are.'

'And still I wouldn't have listened to you,' she says, pulling a face.

'So instead you've managed to become a courier between an English traitor and a cardinal of Rome,' he says, exasperated. 'Christ's wounds! God alone knows what you could have achieved if I'd been gone a couple of days longer.'

Bianca folds her arms. Her mouth tightens. A hint of menace enters her eyes. 'You're only behaving like this because you're jealous of Kit Marlowe.'

'Nonsense! I'm "behaving like this" because you've put yourself in grave danger. Anyway you're only behaving like this because I haven't brought you a dog back from Gloucestershire.'

'Now you're being absurd.'

'What happens if the Jackdaw gets raided? Have you thought of that? It's happened before. Imagine if Robert Cecil were to get his hands on those letters. You, Bruno, me – we'd all be facing an appointment with the Duke of Exeter's daughter!'

'What has *she* got to do with anything?' Bianca asks with a scowl.

'It's what they call the rack!'

Her mouth tightens. Though she's loath to admit it, the same fear has haunted her since the day she opened Bruno's glove.

'Well, Robert Cecil won't find them. They're hidden in my physic garden.'

'I still say burn them.'

She studies his face, but he's wearing his physician's mask: inscrutable, any number of unwelcome diagnoses behind the eyes.

'Well, that's my week in a nutshell,' she says flippantly. 'Now tell me about yours. Feet up at Cleevely, supping ale with Ned, I shouldn't wonder.'

✠

'Dead? With a hole drilled in his head?' Bianca's hands are clamped over her mouth. She's just listened with mounting horror to Nicholas's story. 'And you think this Arcampora killed the poor lad?'

'Either him or his two bully-boy assistants. Perhaps it was physic that went wrong. Or maybe he was killed to keep him from telling anyone what Arcampora is up to at Cleevely.'

'And what *is* he up to, Nicholas?'

'I wish I knew.'

Bianca shudders. 'What did you call it – the thing you said might help Bruno? The thing they did to this poor Tanner Bell.'

'Trepanation. It's been practised since the time of the ancients. It can help ease the falling sickness, or the effects of wounds to the head or of madness and delirium. Believe it or not, it's not as rare as you'd think. I've heard of physicians in Europe attempting it in their studies on the functioning of the human brain. But never in England.'

'And the patients *survive*?'

'Some do. Some make a complete recovery. I can't say I'd risk it on a patient of mine, not if there was any other treatment available. I think Arcampora is practising on these companions that Samuel's father provides him with. I think he means to use it to cure Samuel Wylde of the falling sickness.'

'What is this Samuel Wylde to you, anyway?' Bianca asks. 'Why do you care about him?'

'I explained to you before I left. His father saved my life in Holland. And now that I've seen how Samuel is, my heart aches for the poor boy.' Nicholas shakes his head in sorrow. 'You should have seen him, Bianca. He couldn't have been lonelier if he'd been living in a cave on Mount Ararat! His father has cast him off – pays people to pretend they're his friends. His stepmother is as warm as a winter blizzard.'

'Do you think the father knows what's happening?'

'No, this is Arcampora's and Isabel Wylde's work.' He begins helping Bianca to gather the balms and cloths from around Bruno's mattress. 'Arcampora is everything I despise in physic. He puts me in mind of the charlatan Ned Monkton's father gave his last farthing to, the one who'd told them he could cure their little Jacob of his slow wits. I don't much care for people who sell false hopes to the desperate.'

Bianca remembers with a chill the second victim of the Bankside butcher – Jacob Monkton, Ned's younger brother. She turns to Nicholas, her face clouded. 'What are you going to do?'

'Go to Robert Cecil first thing tomorrow and tell him what I've discovered. He can send some of his men to Cleevely and rescue the boy from Arcampora's grasp.'

Bianca brushes her hair from her temples, as though making space for her thoughts. Instinctively Nicholas reaches out and pushes back a rebellious strand that her fingers have missed. She makes no attempt to avoid his touch, but her eyes are bright with half-formed tears.

'Remember what you told me the day you returned from Suffolk?' she says. 'You told me there would be no more madmen offering Satan their souls in exchange for knowledge. That's what you promised me. Kit Marlowe's theatricals I can bear. But not the real thing. Not again.'

11

The bell at St Olave's chimes midnight as Nicholas and Bianca return from the physic garden with Tyrrell's box of letters, flitting silently through the empty lanes.

Rose is already asleep on the truckle bed in Bianca's room, Buffle curled up beside her. Timothy and Farzad have settled down on their mattresses beside the taproom hearth, and Ned has returned to his father's house on Scrope Alley. Tonight Bianca is glad no one is lodging at the Jackdaw. She makes a final check on Bruno, then goes down to her apothecary's room in the cellar, with Nicholas close behind.

As he lights the candles with a taper, Bianca's secret world takes shape out of the darkness: ceiling beams festooned with dense sprigs of peony and knapweed, gilliflower and galangal, fleabane and featherfew; sloughed snakes' skins, as brittle and translucent as spun sugar hanging from pegs; shelves crammed with pots and jars full of spices and herbs she's gathered from her physic garden, or from the few merchants along the wharves whom she trusts – a leafy arbour of mysteries that he thinks should, by rights, belong to a magical forest rather than a Bankside tavern. The multitude of scents swarm about him like hiving bees, some with sharp, acidic stings, others so warm and soft they feel like honey in the back of his throat. If some of the more impressionable of the Jackdaw's customers could peek inside here, they'd have their suspicions about Mistress Merton's darker skills confirmed in full measure.

Bianca takes the sailcloth package and unwraps it on the table. 'You'd better hurry,' she says. 'These can't stay here a moment longer than necessary.'

'I'll do my best, but I wasn't exactly the finest Latin scholar,' Nicholas tells her. 'Have you written down the code you deciphered?'

'I've done better than that,' she says, fetching him the book containing the record of her patients and the cures she's mixed for them. She opens it to what appears to be a random page. Nicholas sees a column of letters. They mean nothing obvious to him. They might be customers' initials, the first letter of a herb or plant, a distillation, a syrup... anything. 'Look at the top left corner of the page,' she tells him.

Nicholas sees an F written there.

'Instead of page numbers, I've put letters. Page six is marked F, which is also the sixth letter of the alphabet.' She places a finger-tip to guide him. 'Now, if you look at this column of letters I've written, the sixth one down is a T.'

'So when I come across a T in Tyrrell's papers, it's really an F?'

'Exactly.'

'How very devious of you, Mistress Bianca,' he says admiringly.

'If the Privy Council searchers had come, I would have told them it's just my way of listing the pages. The last time Robert Cecil sent them here, they behaved like rampaging vandals. I don't think they'd be sharp enough to spot this.' She gives him a proud smile. 'You see – I've thought of everything.'

'Have you got any paper? I'll need it for the translations.'

'Oh.' She bites her lip.

'And nib and ink.'

As she climbs the stairs, he finds himself noticing the

serpentine weaving of her slender back, sees the way the thick fold of her dark hair sways across the olive skin of her neck, just above the laces of her bodice. And for one guilty moment he remembers a time before he knew Eleanor.

✠

Bianca returns with paper, ink and nib. Then she sits quietly while Nicholas sets to work.

He'd first studied Latin at petty school. By the time he was a fresh-faced lad attending Woodbridge Grammar, he was translating Ovid and Livy from Latin to English and back to Latin again. But even by his own admission, he'd never been amongst the better students. At Cambridge, while the sons of the aristocracy flaunted their expensively tutored ability, the professors had looked down their noses at him, damning him for a country clod-pate. And despite often having to use Latin in his medical career, he's still not as fluent as the College of Physicians would like. But as he works, the task becomes easier.

After half a page, he can match each one of the transposed letters to its original, without referring to Bianca's book. But the mental labour is taxing. Increasingly he finds he must guard against errors. St Olave's bell rings the passing of another hour before he approaches the completion of his task.

'They seem to be a collection of letters and reports,' he tells her. 'Evidence of some sort.'

'Evidence of what?'

'The true identity of someone.'

'Who?'

He pauses before answering, trying to dull the sharp edge that's entered his voice.

'Samuel Wylde.'

'Your boy from Gloucestershire?' She stares at him, astonished.

'It seems you and I have come across the same conspiracy, but from opposite ends. You with Tyrrell, me with Samuel.'

'What do the letters say?'

'Tyrrell appears to be writing on behalf of some religious order or fraternity.'

'The Brothers of Antioch.'

'You *know* of them?' They are standing so close, he can smell the scent of Bianca's skin.

'It was something Munt let slip, at Petty Wales. He and Bruno each have a medallion that bears the image of St Margaret of Antioch. They're a sort of proof of identity.'

'The new faith has little truck with saints,' Nicholas says. 'I've never heard of her. You'll have to tell me who she was, this Margaret of Antioch.'

'A Christian martyr. Before the Romans killed her, she underwent a miraculous transformation: she was swallowed by the Devil in the guise of a serpent. But she was so pious he couldn't digest her. She emerged from his gut bathed in holy light.'

Even in the candle glow she can see his eyes widen.

'There was a tapestry at Cleevely,' he says. 'It was of a woman standing in front of a serpent!'

Bianca points to the papers on the table. 'Who are these addressed to – Bruno?'

'Not named. But he's someone of considerable position in the Catholic Church. They begin: *Your Most Reverend Eminence.*'

'It could be Cardinal Santo Fiorzi. Bruno told me he's come here on a privy commission for him.'

'He *told* you?'

'Bruno and I ran privy errands for the cardinal when we were younger,' she tells him, watching the expression of mounting horror spread across Nicholas's face. 'Bruno is still his man. The day we were together on the *Sirena*, he tried to enlist me again.'

'You're party to this?'

'Of course not! I refused him.' She squirms like a guilty child. 'It's just that my refusal doesn't seem to have worked, does it?'

Nicholas leans forward, retrieves his written translations from the table and hands it to her. 'It's probably best if you read these for yourself.'

In the candlelight it's not easy for Bianca to follow Nicholas's handwriting. It's certainly not secretary-style. She wonders if all physicians have such poor control of a nib. But once accustomed to his lopsided script, her eyes fly over the words.

The first document is clearly a letter from Tyrrell:

Your Most Reverend Eminence, be so gracious as to receive by the hand of your chosen and faithful emissary these diverse proofs regarding the matter of the Revenger. I have sent secret word to JL and PK, who were with me at the drawing-up of Her Majesty's Will and testament, so that they may also confirm the statements herein provided and send news of them to Md. The physician A has told me he is in full measure satisfied with the method of his physic and its progress. The boy strengthens in both health and resolve. He will, with God's grace, be soon full disposed unto the matter's ultimate resolution: the saving of this Realm. The Brothers await Your Eminence's commands and willingly submit ourselves to the direction of your ambassador, Signor B.

The other pages appear to contain digests and reports taken from other documents. With growing unease, Bianca reads on:

The following was intercepted by agents of the Holy Office of the Faith in the rebellious province of Zeeland and passed to His Excellency the Duke of Alba without alteration:

Rejoice in the knowledge that a girl child was safely delivered to M at St James's, this third day of March, in the sixth year of our Sovereign Majesty's reign. The mother sends her heart's felicity unto you and assures you of her devotion. The child is safely delivered unto a place of protection against the malevolent designs of the ungodly.

Another appears to be a physician's report, written in a broken, rangy scrawl, the ink faded to a pale brown:

I, Charles Pelham, physician in the parish of St Martin-in-the-Fields, so attest that the infant born unto M on the third of March last is afflicted by the sacred disease. I have witnessed the several and diverse paroxysms and have advised accordingly. The child should be purged regularly with a weak tincture of white hellebore. Foods tending to loose stools should be her diet. Bleeding the child must not be countenanced until she is of eight years, no younger. Other than this affliction, the infant is in sound health and prospering.

The last is written in a newer, more recent hand:

Our man has been given sight of the queen's will. He has repeated under oath that the codicil dated the twenty-eighth of October was written in a hand contrary to the original, expressly to deceive. He states under fear of extreme duress that he was informed of this by one present in the privy chamber at the time of its making. This deceit was purposed solely to deny the original of the thirtieth of March, namely her attested statement that the Queen's Majesty believed herself to be with child.

Bianca stares at Nicholas, her amber eyes dancing with reflected candlelight. 'The queen? With child? Even I know there has been no issue from that womb. What does all this mean?'

'Well, the first letter is presumably from Lord Tyrrell and the Brothers of Antioch, to – I assume – Cardinal Fiorzi. "Signor B" is clearly Bruno. It mentions Arcampora and Samuel by inference. The second letter can't be about Samuel, because it mentions the mother as "M". Samuel's mother was Alice.' He scratches his hairline. 'The last document appears to refer to a statement in the queen's will.' He finds the place. 'Look: "*namely her attested statement that the Queen's Majesty believed herself to be with child...*" Apparently there was a codicil added to the will later, in which the queen states that she was mistaken. But according to someone Tyrrell trusts, this codicil was a fake, designed expressly to deceive.'

'So the queen *was*, in fact, pregnant,' whispers Bianca, laying the translations between them on the table.

'Apparently.'

'But why would the child have been taken to – what does it say?' Bianca retrieves document and finds the line. '"*A place of protection against the malevolent designs of the ungodly?*"'

'That's where I started to become really worried,' Nicholas says, his brow creasing. 'Samuel is about sixteen, which means his mother must have been born around the time Mary Tudor died.'

'How do you know that?'

'Sir Joshua Wylde told me, at Woodbridge. He said Alice Wylde was scarcely seventeen when she died, just after Samuel was born.'

'So when the letters talk about the Queen's Majesty...'

'Exactly. It's not Elizabeth's majesty, it's her predecessor's – Mary Tudor.'

Almost too afraid to speak, Bianca mouths the letter M.

'I thought perhaps M might mean Mercy Havington. The time would be about right. But so far as I know, when she was an infant Alice was always with Mercy. She didn't need taking into protection, least of all from the ungodly.'

Nicholas squares away the papers, like a lawyer coming to the end of his argument – an argument he'd do almost anything not to have to prosecute.

'These papers infer that Mary bore a child. A daughter with the falling sickness. A daughter spirited away at birth, so as not to fall into the hands of the ungodly – in Mary's eyes, the new faith.'

'And that daughter gave birth to a son,' whispers Bianca. 'Samuel Wylde.'

'If these letters are authentic, Samuel has a rightful claim to the English crown. A *Catholic* claim.'

Bianca raises a hand to her mouth. 'Which means this conspiracy could reach as far as the Holy Father in Rome.'

'But according to the new faith, he's not the Holy Father, is he? To England, he's the Antichrist.'

Bianca stares at Nicholas, ashen-faced. '*Jesu!*' she breathes. 'What have I got us into?

✠

The lanes are empty when Nicholas and Bianca slip quietly out of the Jackdaw. The night threatens rain. They can smell it in the air. Beneath a fractured moon glimpsed through a wind-blown tattered grey veil, they hurry towards Bianca's physic garden to cache away Tyrrell's papers.

Nicholas had wanted to carry them, but Bianca had refused, consigning the slim package to the depths of her bodice. 'I got us into this,' she'd said. 'I'll get us out of it.' Their greatest fear now is not of running into cut-purses, but of the Southwark bellmen. The watch is known to vary its rounds, the better to catch house-divers and footpads. Or possessors of dangerous secrets.

'I can't go to Robert Cecil. Not now,' Nicholas says in a low voice as they hug the walls beneath the overhanging buildings to stay hidden. 'We're on our own.'

'Whyever not?'

'Because these letters connect you to Arcampora and Tyrrell, and to a Romish cardinal and a credible plot to put a Catholic heir to Mary Tudor on the throne of England.'

'You can tell him that Bruno and I are innocent – that we didn't know anything about it.'

'Bianca, you went to Munt's warehouse. You came back with Tyrrell's papers. On top of that, the cardinal's emissary is unconscious in your tavern, and you've made yourself his go-between.'

'I suppose that does look bad, doesn't it?'

He rolls his eyes to the heavens. 'Have you *heard* the tale of Perkin Warbeck?'

'No, Nicholas. I haven't. I don't recall any Warbecks in Padua. Is this going to be one of your morality lectures?'

'You may mock me, Bianca, but it might just make you understand the danger you've got yourself involved in.'

'If you must, then...'

'Over a century ago England was riven by the Wars of the Cousins – a civil strife between two great houses, York and Lancaster. Each house took a different-coloured rose as its emblem – you can see them today, combined as the Tudor rose, symbol of Elizabeth's descent from the victor, her grandfather...'

'Roses?' Bianca snorts. 'Only the English could have a war over gardening.'

'Do you want to hear about him, or not?'

'I'm sorry. Go on.'

'During that conflict, the two young heirs of the Yorkist King Edward were confined in the Tower. They disappeared – never to be seen again.'

'What happened to them?'

'Murdered, or so it is said.'

'By who? This Warbeck?'

'No, by their Uncle Richard. It was Richard whom the queen's grandfather – the seventh Henry – vanquished.'

'So who was Warbeck?'

'He appeared later, during Henry's reign. He claimed to be one of those missing princes.'

'The rightful heir to the throne – in place of Elizabeth's grandfather?'

'Exactly.'

'Was he telling the truth?'

'He was well schooled enough to make some people think so – including men of high position. But truth wasn't the issue. Henry was never going to let him live long enough to contest the issue. In the end, Perkin Warbeck hanged.'

Bianca considers this for a moment. 'And you think Samuel Wylde could be the Warbeck of Elizabeth's reign?'

'Can you imagine what would happen today, if the Brothers of Antioch were to prove Samuel Wylde has a legitimate claim to Elizabeth's crown? And not merely her crown, but the very souls of her subjects? It would herald a war not of roses, but of faiths.'

He describes to her how he sees it: brother set against brother, father against son. The Catholic clans, so long subdued and humbled, rising in arms. The Spanish and French joining to raise a vast host that England could not possibly repel. 'Under Mary Tudor, three hundred Protestant souls were burned away in just five years. I believe these Brothers of Antioch want the fires lit again. Samuel is not yet a man. Fires lit in his name could burn for decades. To stop that happening, Robert Cecil – or his friends on the Privy Council – will kill everyone remotely connected with Tyrrell's papers. You, me, Bruno, Samuel Wylde...'

'Then we destroy the papers,' Bianca says brightly. 'Get rid of them.'

'And wait for Tyrrell and his people to come calling? Presumably the Brothers of Antioch expect *some* form of response from your Cardinal Fiorzi. What happens when they realize that you're an imposter? They've already killed Tanner Bell. And his friend Finney, for all I know.'

They walk on, unable to speak, silenced by the enormity of what Nicholas has said. And then Bianca does something that's become a habit recently – she stops suddenly and turns, looking back down the lane.

'What is it?' he asks. 'What have you seen?'

Should I tell Nicholas about the man in the brown cloak? she wonders. What good would it do? It would only add to his fears. Besides, the lane is empty – no matter how hard I peer into the darkness, trying to people it with watching eyes.

'It's nothing,' she says. 'Just my imagination.'

And then their luck runs out.

Turning down Black Bull Alley beneath the overhang of a chandler's house, they run slap into the night-watch.

12

In Southwark the bellmen go about in pairs, for security – one to hold the lantern, the other in charge of the mastiff. Unusually for this time of night, they're both sober, and no more than ten yards away. And the mastiff is the size of a well-fed ram.

Nicholas can observe all this because the moon has just emerged from behind the tattered clouds to illuminate the alley in a cold, accusing light.

It is Bianca who seizes the moment. Before Nicholas can react, she throws her arms around his shoulders and presses into him, pushing him against the wall, her head buried in his neck. He can smell lavender in her hair. He's not been this proximate to a woman since Eleanor fell with their child. It feels at once both achingly familiar and impossibly alien. Desired, yet feared. Right, yet wrong, in equally disturbing measure.

'*What are you doing?*' he whispers into her hair.

'Why else would two people be out in the streets at this time of night?' she says through gritted teeth. Then, after a contemplative pause, 'You're *really* not at all like an Italian, are you, Nicholas?'

'What do you mean?' He can hear the footfalls of the watch very close, and the heavy panting of the mastiff.

'You're as taut as a Puritan in a jumping-house! *Relax.*'

'I'm trying to relax,' he hisses.

'Am I *really* that much of an antidote to desire, Nicholas?' she asks wearily, her voice liquid, her body melded against his.

'There's something in this wall. I think it's an eye-bolt. You're impaling me on it.'

She eases her grasp a little. They cling together in the darkness like the lost souls they can't admit they are.

The mastiff is so close now it's sniffing Nicholas's boots. It glowers at him as if it can't quite decide which course of the meal he should be.

And then a friendly voice breaks the night. 'God's red wounds! It's Dr Shelby!'

Nicholas stares, horrified, over Bianca's shoulder at the dog's master. 'Do I know you, sir?'

'It's me, Doctor, Jed Boley!'

'Of course, Master Boley...'

Hearing the confusion in Nicholas's voice, the man says, 'You cured my little Mary when I brought her to St Thomas's last year. She had the tenesmus.'

'Yes, I remember now.'

'She wants to be a physician, bless her. Of course I told her God hasn't given females the capacity.'

'Evening, Mistress Merton,' says the other man, tipping his cap.

'Good evening, Ralph Dingle,' Bianca replies in a monotone, recognizing the man as a regular at the Jackdaw and wishing the ground would open up beneath her feet.

'A fine night for the season, is it not?' says Dingle with a lascivious wink.

'Very fine,' says Bianca through her teeth.

'All's well?' enquires Dingle.

'Very well, thank you.'

A long, painful silence. Then, suppressing a smirk, Boley says, 'Well, rogues and vagabonds won't be a-catching of themselves! God's good night to you both.'

As the watch departs in the direction of the Rose playhouse, Nicholas and Bianca clearly hear Dingle say cheerily to his companion, 'The Jackdaw's clearly doing well, Master Boley – not a bed to be had, by the look of it.'

Waiting until the bellmen are out of hearing, Bianca says in a long, slow release of breath, 'Well, that's decided then.'

'What's decided?'

'My future on Bankside. It is now officially impossible. When Bruno is up and about, I'm going back to Padua.'

But the watch is almost out of sight before they release each other.

✠

At Havington Manor, alone over a breakfast of sweet eggs, Mercy Havington reviews the accounts that Ralph Wilson, the head husbandman, has prepared for her. She does so diligently. William would expect no less, were he still alive:

> ...thatching for the long barn – ten shillings... a team of horses to haul felled lumber from Furze Wood – three shillings and sixpence...

From where she sits, she can hear her brother-in-law in the great hall, lecturing his hawking friends on the wisdom of keeping sheep out of the barley stubble until the hogs have had their fill of the waste. She tries to tame a growing sense of despair.

There was a time, Mercy Havington remembers, when the conversations she might expect to overhear would be somewhat more elevated: discourses on who was the better poet – Ovid or Horace? The better painter – Holbein or Hornebolte? If she was of a mind to thieve snatches of other people's conversations, it would have been from scholars and archbishops, ambassadors and emissaries.

She hears her brother-in-law's ponderous oration move on to his pet topic: blain-worm in cattle. Is it possible, she wonders, to be more distant from the palaces of Whitehall or Greenwich than this Gloucestershire farm?

Until William's death, life in the countryside hadn't been the sentence of banishment she'd feared. She had loved William enough to follow him to deepest Muscovy or the furthest Indies, and she'd found the life of a country squire's wife fulfilling enough. Besides, her niece Elizabeth was married to Robert Cecil, Lord Burghley's son – so there was always the opportunity to travel to London and enjoy a little of her former life.

But all that had changed last Christmas, when William died.

Now she feels besieged, the virtual prisoner of a Puritan bore who can speak about little else but loose bowels in cattle. And she fears for Samuel and how lonely he must be, himself almost a prisoner of Arcampora and Isabel Wylde.

Laying aside the account rolls, she goes out into the yard, a shawl around her shoulders to ward off the morning chill. She fetches a pail of feed from the barn and walks to the wattle pen, where the other Isabel – the one she likes – is lying stoically on her side in the mud, surrounded by her squirming pink litter.

Mercy Havington has almost reached her when she sees a rider on a mud-streaked grey courser appear through the open gate. He's wrapped in a dark leather riding cloak, his face almost hidden beneath a scarf and a woollen bonnet – as though he'd rather no one got a clear view of him.

'Sir Gilbert is indoors, with his friends,' Mercy says pleasantly, assuming it's her brother-in-law he's come to see. 'I hope you're interested in sheep.'

The man shakes his head. 'I bear a letter,' he says. 'Privy, for Mistress Mercy Brooke.'

Mercy almost drops the pail on the spot. She stares at the letter the man is holding out to her. Why has he come? Is he playing some cruel sport with her? Some jape whose purpose she cannot fathom? Because no one has addressed her by her maiden name – Brooke – in over thirty years.

✠

'I could seek out Boley and Dingle – make a plea for their discretion,' says Nicholas around noontime as he and Bianca walk down Borough High Street. They've employed a trip to the cutler's shop by the sign of the Horse's Head to allow themselves the chance to talk. 'After all, I did treat Boley's daughter. And you could give Ralph Dingle a little ease on his account. That might buy his silence.'

Bianca is wearing her emerald-green kirtle and her carnelian bodice. She's turned heads all the way from the Jackdaw. And not just because her Mediterranean complexion marks her out as exotic. Ever since Ned Monkton hoisted the sign of the unicorn beside that of the jackdaw, every tavern between the Falcon Inn and the Horse's Head has been trying to sign up its own wise-woman. The Southwark aldermen's office has stopped accepting requests for an apothecary's licence.

As for Nicholas, he's only just noticed that the bellmen's mastiff has left a banner of dried snot over one thigh of his hose. But he can still feel the warm pressure of Bianca's body against him, even though many hours have passed since they ran into the watch at the top of Black Bull Alley. It's seared into his mind like a brand. And there's no doubt about it: the responsive flesh he can still feel against his hands is not Eleanor's. It's definitely Bianca Merton's.

'There's no way out of this,' she says with a quick shake of her head. 'No way at all. I'm ruined.'

'Really? It wasn't *me* who pinned someone to a wall in the dead of night.'

'I was *trying* to protect us!'

'I could have told them we were out for a breath of air.'

'After the curfew bell?'

'I could have said I'd been attending a patient. I could have said you'd come along to help.'

'You *do* know what's going to result, don't you? Tonight, or very soon, Dingle or Boley is going to let slip that they just happened to come across you and me playing *gallant-and-his-mistress* up against a wall. And knowing my luck, it will be just as Rose serves them their ale. At which point the Spanish fleet could arrive in the Thames, the Pope could appear on East Cheap, and the Privy Council could announce Elizabeth is to marry the King of Ethiopia – and I'd *still* know for certain what the topic of conversation was going to be!'

He waits for the tempest to calm.

'That's the least of our worries, I'd have thought.'

'Then you've had a *very* untroubled life, Nicholas Shelby.'

As soon as she says it, she wishes she'd held her tongue. No man who's tried to block out the memory of his dead wife by walking into the Thames could be called untroubled.

'I'm sorry. That's not what I meant.'

If she's hurt him, he doesn't show it. 'The fact remains: we've found ourselves involved in a conspiracy,' he says. 'And you know what that can lead to in this city.'

'But is any of it true? Is Samuel Wylde really Mary's grandson?'

'As I said before, it only matters that enough powerful people believe it to be true. Of course there is *one* person who might be able to tell us.'

'Not Robert Cecil, surely. You said it would be too dangerous to confess to him.'

'I'm thinking of Lord Lumley. He was a young courtier during Mary's reign.'

'John Lumley – the man Robert Cecil tried to get you to destroy? Why would *he* help you?'

'Because I saved him from the scaffold, that's why. So far the only favour I've asked of him in return is your apothecary's licence.'

They walk on a little way, passing a public well with a pillory beside it. A miscreant is being unshackled by the constable, his sentence served. He slinks away into the crowd, massaging his wrists, his left ear already carved close to his head, a punishment from some previous offence. Nicholas thinks, if we're caught out in this, either by Tyrrell or the authorities, an ear-trimming is the very least we can expect. The queen's Privy Council doesn't take kindly to her subjects hiding, let alone deciphering, letters conspiring to replace her.

'I don't know how much time we have on our side,' he says. 'Tyrrell must be expecting a reply of some sort. He won't wait for ever.'

'If only Bruno would wake up.'

'Even if he does, he may not be the Bruno you knew before. Let's just pray he strengthens quickly enough to get him back aboard the *Sirena* and out of the realm before he can cause any more mayhem. Or before the Privy Council comes banging on the door.'

'And in the meanwhile?'

'In the meanwhile I need to come up with a stratagem to prise Samuel Wylde out of the clutches of the Brothers of Antioch.'

✠

To the north of Tower Hill, in a neighbourhood of handsome town houses with neat gardens and orchards, lies Woodroffe Lane. One of the finer homes belongs to John Lumley, Baron Lumley of the County of Durham, a man who has spent most of his adult life living under a faith he rejects and a monarch who still favours him, despite it. It is John Lumley whom Robert Cecil had sent Nicholas to destroy less than a year past. Now both men share a trust and a friendship born of their bruising collision with the Lord Treasurer's crook-backed son.

A servant ushers Nicholas through the great hall and out into a pretty apple orchard, where a well-dressed gathering, around fifty strong, is taking its collective ease amongst the trees. It's a mixed crowd, notes Nicholas: gallants and grey-beards in subdued but expensive silks and brocades, young women dressed in French gowns spread over wide farthingales, soberly dressed matrons, and well-fed children playing hide-and-seek amongst the trees. Discreet servants bear plates of candies and comfits, jugs of sack and hippocras. Musicians stroll through the orchard, entertaining with pipe and tambour. Nicholas feels utterly out of place. But he can't help imagining himself amongst the crowd, his wife on his arm, their children piping excitedly as they frolic with the others.

This is what the lies that our physic tells have stolen from me, he thinks.

And then a thought rocks him like an unexpected blow. What if this vision is *not* beyond his grasp?

For a moment the idea confuses rather than comforts. Eleanor and her child are dead. So the notion is impossible. It cannot be.

But what if it were possible to love *two* women, he asks himself – one a memory, one very much alive. Then the vision might not be so fantastical. There is even the possibility it might become a reality. As much of a reality, say, as the sensation of Bianca's body pressed against him on Black Bull Alley – a sensation so real that it has not yet faded from his senses.

To his surprise, the idea that the future course of his life might not be set in stone by Eleanor's death is not followed by the customary pang of guilt. In fact it brings the first surge of hope that he's felt for as long as he dares recall.

'Nicholas, it does my heart good to see you again. I trust you are enjoying God's good grace. Is all well with you?'

The soft Northumbrian burr breaks into his thoughts. A tall, mournful-looking man in an ankle-length gown of dark broadcloth is grasping him firmly by the hand. He wears a green velvet cap on his head and a greying spade-cut beard on his jaw.

'It is, my lord,' replies Nicholas with a smile.

'I want you to know that I brought to bear what little influence I possess with the College of Physicians on your behalf,' John Lumley says. 'Apparently the fact that I endow them with forty pounds per annum for a chair of anatomy doesn't entitle me to demand they stop persecuting you. When is your hearing before the Censors?'

'At the end of the week, my lord.'

Lumley lets out a bark of derision. 'Pah! If they knew the truth about what your actions prevented, they'd make you a senior Fellow overnight. There's not a man amongst them brave enough to confront evil such as you and Mistress Merton uncovered.' Lumley waves to a servant. 'Will you take a glass of sack – or are you still a Puritan in that regard?'

'A small glass, thank you.'

'And Mistress Merton?' Lumley enquires as he raises his glass to Nicholas. 'Is she fully recovered from her ordeal?'

Her ordeal. The events that simple phrase conceals seem to have happened an age ago, Nicholas thinks; yet it has been barely two months.

'I believe she is, my lord. And again, I must thank you for her apothecary's licence.' Nicholas smiles self-consciously. '*We* must thank you.'

'*We*?' echoes Lumley with a raise of his wintry brows. He smiles. 'Good! I favour the sound of *we*. You deserve happiness, after all you've been through.'

'I didn't mean it in that manner, my lord,' says Nicholas, blushing. 'At least, I—'

Lumley spares him further agony. 'What brings you here? It's a fair walk from Southwark.'

'I thought you might be able to help me in a case I'm involved in: a young lad with the falling sickness.'

'My library at Nonsuch is always open to you. You know that.'

'That is kind of you, my lord. But what I'm searching for is not to be found in medical books. And I hesitate to speak of it where we may be overheard.'

Without asking why, Lumley says, 'Come with me – my guests can bear my absence for a while.'

He leads Nicholas back into the house, along a panelled gallery and out into a small inner courtyard. Gravel paths cut geometrically through flowerbeds bordered by neatly trimmed box hedges. At the centre is a small statue of a leaping horse, a miniature of the original Nicholas has seen in the great inner courtyard at Nonsuch Palace, Lumley's magnificent mansion in the Surrey countryside. He wonders if John Lumley comes here privately to hear the Catholic Mass, away from prying eyes and ears.

'Is *here* privy enough for your needs?' Lumley asks. 'Or must we find ourselves a deep cave where Robert Cecil may not overhear us?'

Nicholas looks sheepishly at the gravel. From the moment they first met, Lumley has been able to see through his artifice.

'He has not sent me to you, my lord, not this time. But in the matter of the boy with the falling sickness, he does have – shall we say – an interest. The boy's grandmother is kinswoman to his wife.'

'Then you'd better tell me how I may help you.'

Nicholas gives Lumley a brief account of his visit to Cleevely and his meeting with Arcampora. He makes no mention of Tanner Bell's body, or the apparent evidence of trepanning he'd seen on it, even though Lumley has such an interest in anatomy that he endows the College of Physicians with an annuity to provide a reader in the discipline. And he says nothing about Bianca's cousin or Lord Tyrrell's letters. For the time being, he thinks, such secrets are best kept between himself and Bianca alone.

'Being a patron of the College of Physicians and close to its president and senior Fellows, I wondered if perhaps you were familiar with Arcampora's reputation, my lord. Even Robert Cecil has been able to discover little about him.'

Lumley appears to choose his words carefully. 'I've heard him spoken of. Little more than hearsay, really. But it's hearsay from men who in the past have not lied to me. Sir Joshua Wylde must be paying him handsomely.'

'Why so, my lord?'

'Because nothing but a significant amount of money would bring him into a realm whose religion he holds to be an abomination.'

Is it money – or something far more precious to the old religion? Nicholas wonders. 'Is there a way I might meet with these gentlemen, my lord?'

'Sadly, Nicholas, that will not be possible. They are men presently living beyond our shores for their own safety.'

Nicholas understands immediately. 'Is that because Robert Cecil might call them traitors?'

'Cecil may call them what he likes – they have hides tough enough to bear it. I would prefer to call them men who desire the re-establishment of a properly pious England.'

'Are you in touch with these men, my lord?'

Lumley smiles and raises a finger in gentle caution. 'That would be treason, Nicholas, wouldn't it? Let me say simply that while I approve of their aim, I do not approve of their methods.'

'And what exactly is it these men have to say about Arcampora?'

'That he was expelled from Basle, for pursuing studies the professors found heretical and dangerously provocative.'

'I knew he left. I didn't know why.'

'Are you also aware he's sold his services to some of the great Catholic households in Europe? Including that of Fernando Álvarez de Toledo, the Duke of Alba?'

At once Nicholas hears Mercy Havington's voice in his head, speaking of Porter Bell's drunken outburst. *He was in this very tavern, swearing the Duke of Alba and the Devil were at Cleevely...* And he recalls his translation of Tyrrell's second letter: *The following was intercepted by agents of the Holy Office of the Faith in the rebellious province of Zeeland, and passed to His Excellency the Duke of Alba without alteration...*

'Alba, the Iron Duke,' whispers Nicholas to himself. The garden suddenly seems colder, as the recollection floods back like a silent wraith rising in a churchyard.

Alba had been dead almost five years by the time Nicholas arrived in the Netherlands, but just the mention of his name still put the fear of God into people. Memories were still raw – memories of whole towns butchered to the last newborn babe by Alba's soldiers. The Dutch had even coined a name for the brutality: 'Spanish fury'. If even a fragment of Alba's hatred for the new faith survives in Arcampora, then perhaps *he* is the force behind the Brothers of Antioch. 'So it wasn't a drunken fancy, after all,' Nicholas whispers, realizing Porter Bell must have seen Arcampora in Holland, during his captivity there – must somehow have learned of the physician's connection to Alba.

Lumley's voice breaks into his consciousness. 'Nicholas? You seem distracted.'

'Forgive me, my lord. I was thinking out loud. It was something the boy's grandmother told me.'

'I hope I have been of help, Nicholas.'

'You have, my lord.'

'Then come and meet some of my guests. They have healthy purses, but like so many of their station they tend to melancholia, as far as their health is concerned. You might come away with the kernel of a new, prosperous practice.'

'That's kind of you, my lord. But I wonder if I might trouble you just a little further...'

'Of course.'

'How well do you know Lord Tyrrell?'

Lumley looks at him askance. 'Thomas Tyrrell? We haven't spoken more than half a dozen times in thirty years. Why do you ask?'

'I thought that both of you being staunch defenders of the old faith, you might be closer.'

Lumley fixes him with his mournful eyes. 'Nicholas, I'm glad to see you once more, I truly am, but this is beginning to sound like an interrogation. Are you *sure* Robert Cecil hasn't sent you?'

'Forgive me, my lord, if I sound uncivil, but this is a matter of great consequence. I promise you I have not come to waste your time.'

Lumley maintains his gaze a moment, then gives an almost imperceptible nod. 'I was growing weary of all that chatter in the orchard anyway.'

'So you do know him?'

'We met during the preparations for Mary's wedding to Philip of Spain. To speak truly, I was surprised Tyrrell did not flee abroad when Mary died and Elizabeth restored the Protestant Church.'

'Why do think that might have been, my lord?'

'Perhaps, like me, he can't abandon England, even though England has abandoned him – and his faith.'

Or Tyrrell could just be waiting for the tide to turn, thinks Nicholas. He remembers the line from one of Tyrrell's papers: *I have sent secret word to JL and PK, who were with me at the drawing-up of Her Majesty's Will and testament...*

'Do the initials JL or PK mean anything to you, my lord?'

'In connection with Tyrrell? Of course,' Lumley says without hesitating. 'John Lowell and Peter Kirkbie. They were both gentlemen of Queen Mary's privy chamber – part of a cabal at court.'

'What manner of cabal?'

'Zealots. Young fellows fired with the desire to preserve the one true faith.'

'Trusted by Mary?'

'More than trusted, Nicholas. They helped draw up the lists of those to be burned for the blasphemies that had gone before. They counselled Mary against mercy. They gave her strength. To be honest, I thought they were insufferably sanctimonious. They seemed to think God spoke only to them, and always in words of fire.'

'And Tyrrell was part of this cabal?'

'On the fringes, never at its heart. Otherwise he'd never have risked staying after Mary's death.'

'And I take it that Lowell and Kirkbie are, as you put it, "presently living beyond our shores for their own safety"?'

'The Brothers were abroad when Mary died, on an embassy to Philip of Spain. Given their history, it will not surprise you that they dared not return when Elizabeth ascended the throne.'

'Brothers? Lowell and Kirkbie are brothers?'

Lumley laughs at Nicholas's misinterpretation. 'Brothers in Christ, Nicholas. At Mary's court they called themselves "The Brothers of Antioch". Antioch was where Christ's disciples were first named Christians.'

Nicholas's heart begins to beat faster. He almost dreads where his next question will lead.

'Did you ever have sight of Mary's Will, my lord?'

Lumley gives him a quizzical look. 'Yes, I was with my father-in-law, the Earl of Arundel, when the Will was read before the ministers of her council, a few months before she died.'

'Then you know Mary believed herself to be with child?'

'I have an uncomfortable feeling about where this is leading, Nicholas.'

'The question I need answering, my lord, is this: Was it true? Was there a child?'

For a moment Lumley does not reply. He looks around the courtyard to ensure he cannot be overheard. Then he speaks softly, as if he's frightened even the birds might bear witness to his words.

'You must understand, Nicholas, it was a time of great uproar and jeopardy. Mary had married a Spanish prince. That prince had become King. But Mary's ministers refused to allow him to rule in England. Once he'd accepted that, Philip became an absent husband...'

'But could there have been issue?'

Lumley raises a hand to calm Nicholas's impatience. 'Philip came to England for a brief while in the year before Mary died. He could have sired a child on her then. It's certainly what she believed in early '58. After he left, Mary declined with each passing day. She became ever more dispirited. We all knew it was just a matter of time. And so did she.'

'She knew she was dying?'

'That's why she made her Will. But she would not give up hope that a child might yet be born. And nor would the more zealous of her advisors. Not until almost the very end.'

'But you yourself witnessed no visible sign that she was carrying a child?'

'We saw but little of her in those last months. I heard from those close to her that there *was* a swollen belly. But her first – in '55 – had turned out to be nothing but a deceit of the body. We assumed the same malady was afflicting her then.'

Nicholas stares at the sky, marshalling his thoughts. 'When did Philip depart England for the last time?'

'July 1557.'

'So if there *was* a child, it would have been born before the end of April '58.'

'Yes,' says Lumley. 'But in her Will, Mary denied the pregnancy. No infant was ever brought before her ministers.'

'My lord, I've seen papers that suggest that denial was forged. They suggest that a daughter was born.'

Lumley's long face is customarily pale. Now it looks to Nicholas like the face of a corpse. 'Do you have these papers, Nicholas?'

'I have access to them.'

'Then I advise you to burn them at the earliest opportunity! On *that* matter, you are treading on thin ice, Nicholas. Keep walking and you'll likely discover there's *very* deep water beneath.' Lumley takes his arm in a warning grip. 'That's my counsel. Burn them. Unless, of course, you're content to be remembered as the man who opened the way to a civil war.'

13

The guildhall of the College of Physicians is a fine tim-
bered building on Knightrider Street to the south-west
of St Paul's. Though modest in size, it exudes an air of
almost Puritan rectitude. The learned Fellows who pass through
its door are no less sober in dress and character. A bright ribbon
tied around the knee, too extravagant a feather in your cap, and
you'll be taken for a dangerous renegade. Nicholas remembers
how Eleanor used to tease him that one day she would wake up
to find herself the wife of just such a staid and stern physician.

Eleanor had been the very antithesis of conventional: a lithe-
limbed, freckled meadow-sprite daughter of a neighbouring
Barnthorpe yeoman, as hard to hold in one place as gossamer
caught on a summer breeze. How could she ever have loved such
a country dullard as I? he wonders. She'd had time enough, after
all, to see his many faults – they'd known each other since childhood. Yet when he'd asked her to marry him – barely three years
ago now, at the Barnthorpe May Fair – she'd coolly asked him why
it had taken him so long to pluck up the courage.

Wondering if his imaginings in John Lumley's orchard might
have been somewhat premature, Nicholas rubs a precautionary
hand across his eyes. He cannot enter this stolid place unmanned
by tears.

Shown into a stuffy, low-ceilinged chamber on the first floor,
Nicholas is allowed a moment's enjoyment of the noise of carts

passing by in the street and the smell of the wet-fish stalls, before a clerk in formal gown closes the window. The physicians would have the Lord Mayor expel the fishmongers from Knightrider Street, but the Fishmongers' Guild was incorporated first – by a good two hundred years. So the physicians must either sweat or smell fish. The impasse does not bode well for Nicholas.

Behind a long polished table, their backs to the window, four Censors sit like hanging judges, resplendent in formal gowns and starched ruffs. Led by Arnold Beston, a wiry little man with a squint in his left eye that gives him a permanently doubting expression, they are charged with maintaining the College's professional standards. It's clear to Nicholas from the start that they consider him lacking in every single one.

'Mr Shelby, where is your doctor's gown?' asks Beston.

'I don't have one,' says Nicholas bravely.

'You don't own one – or you were never awarded one?'

From the other end of the line, Censor Frowicke stabs at a sheet of paper with a finger. 'It says here – Michaelmas '86, under Professor Lorkin.'

'Then where is the gown, Mr Shelby?' asks Beston.

'I threw it away. Into the Thames. October last, if I recall. My memory of that time can be unreliable.'

Silence, save for the low rumble from the street. Thank God they can't smell the fish, thinks Nicholas.

'You *threw* your gown away?' asks Frowicke in disbelief. 'Whatever for?'

'I had no want of it any more. I do remember regretting that.'

Beston's face softens. He likes contrition. 'You regret a moment of foolish rebellion?'

'I regretted not being sober enough to think of selling it.'

Beston coughs behind his hand. He leans back to exchange whispers with his colleagues. Then he says, with a gentleness that surprises Nicholas, 'This was because of your wife and unborn child, I presume. In a distempered rage?'

'You could call it that.'

'Because you couldn't save them?'

'Yes.'

'Do you expect to save *all* your patients, Mr Shelby?'

'Of course not.'

'Then why should you have expected – of all whom you treat – to have saved *her*?'

'You weren't married to her, Mr Beston.'

A veritable outbreak of august coughing.

'And from thence you fell into a decline,' suggests Frowicke. 'We have a report here, from about that time, of you being taken up by the watch for brawling drunkenly in Blackfriars churchyard.' He passes the papers from which he's gleaned this information to Beston, who studies them intently.

'Cut-purses,' explains Nicholas wearily. 'They tried to rob me while I was too cup-shot to resist.'

'When Mr Frowicke says "a" report, he means several – on differing occasions, that is,' says Beston sadly.

'They're a quarrelsome lot around Blackfriars.'

Beston sucks his teeth. 'So it would appear, Mr Shelby.' He smooths over the papers with the palm of his hand. 'You come to our attention again a while later, as a temporary physician at St Thomas's on Bankside.'

'Dispensing physic to the poor,' observes another of the Censors, a portly man named Hedgecoe, whose jowly expression of self-contentment hasn't altered by so much as a twitch since Nicholas sat down. 'From what we can make out, you appear to have been performing the functions of a barber-surgeon there, without being a member of that Company. *And* without seeking payment from your patients.'

'As you've pointed out, Mr Hedgecoe, they were the *poor*.'

'And what exactly was it that you were offering them so generously?' Beston enquires.

'Only what I could be sure actually worked: setting bones, mixing plasters, stitching wounds, that sort of thing. Meat work.'

'What do you mean by "worked"?' asks Hedgecoe, still almost completely immobile.

'Anything that had a visible, lasting and repeatable effect. I didn't consult a patient's horoscope before treatment, and I didn't regale them with lengthy diagnoses in Latin they couldn't understand. And I didn't charge them money they didn't have.'

'No astrolabe? No horoscope?' asks the fourth Censor, McLaren, a thin Scot with a narrow collar of pimpled red skin between his beard and his ruff. 'How then would you know if the treatment you were prescribing was propitious?'

Nicholas shrugs. 'Do you really think casting his stars is going to help mend a Bankside labourer's broken hand before he has to seek parish charity because he can't pay his rent?'

'Are you claiming you have no need of astrology when making a diagnosis?' McLaren asks, with apparently genuine puzzlement. 'Did you not listen to your professors at Cambridge, Mr Shelby?'

'I don't believe that if a night-soil man is suffering from melancholia, it can only be because Saturn is in the ascendant. Or that he needs to give you a bowlful of his blood to have his humours balanced. For all I know, he's just sick to death of hauling away other people's shit.'

'You'll be telling us next that uroscopy is a waste of time, too – that the colour of a man's water is no guide to the condition of his health!' says Beston, astounded.

'Ah, the ancient art of studying urine,' says Nicholas, rolling his eyes at the ceiling. 'Paracelsus calls that "mere gazing at piss".'

McLaren appears to be attempting to eat his ruff. 'The late Paracelsus of Switzerland?' he growls between bites. 'Are you one of his ranting disbelievers, Mr Shelby?'

'No, but I've read some of his writings. If you want to know, I think he was right about one thing at least: theory alone, no matter how ancient, cannot by itself cure. It has to be tested. Proven. Otherwise it's worthless.'

'I think we should determine what else Mr Shelby has so rashly chosen to question,' says McLaren, eyeing Nicholas as though he were a dangerous madman.

And so the examination proper begins. As is customary, it's conducted in Latin. Nicholas does his best, but it's soon clear that if they hold him to it, they might be here all day. So Beston admits defeat and reverts to English. Another mark set down against Nicholas.

'How does the physician determine the extent of damage to the ventricles of the brain, following apoplexia?' Beston asks, as though he were standing in a pulpit.

'The taught method is by the strength of the breathing,' Nicholas replies. 'The heavier the breathing, the worse the damage.'

'From where would you drain the blood in order to ease the symptoms of epilepsy, Mr Shelby?' asks Frowicke.

'From the cephalic vein.'

'In the human eye, how many types of cataracts may be found?' Hedgecoe asks, still almost motionless.

'Seven – only four are curable.'

'How would you remove them?'

'With a needle, of course. Then apply a plaster of turbith, aloe-hepatica, mace and quibbes.'

The questions continue relentlessly for an hour. Nicholas answers them concisely and with humility. As for the cures and procedures that he has not observed working with his own eyes, he qualifies each answer with "It is taught..." He is even able to let his mind wander a little. He recalls that it was in this very building, less than a year ago, that he attended the dissection of a crippled vagrant boy – then without so much as a name – that began a journey that led Bianca into the hands of a killer. He wonders if Beston and the others truly understand how their vaunted theories can be so easily put to dark purposes.

When the sound of a loud argument in the street forces its way to the Censors' attention, Beston calls an end to the hearing. He stands up and gathers his gown around him, a judge considering a capital sentence.

'Mr Shelby, it is clear to us you are no charlatan. You appear to be uncommonly proficient in your knowledge.'

Nicholas braces himself for the inevitable *but*.

'Nevertheless, your recent conduct has been at best... shall we say, *erratic*?' Beston gives him a vicar's look of sympathy. 'We are by no measure indifferent to your recent loss, Mr Shelby. But you are a young man. You will surely marry again.'

That's your diagnosis, is it? thinks Nicholas.

'And we cannot have members of this great College behaving like drunken vagabonds. I might add that answering our questions with the phrase "It is taught..." implies to me that you consider yourself above many of your more learned colleagues. The Censors will consider this matter further. We will summon you again to hear our findings. God give you peace, Mr Shelby.'

✳

Returning to the Jackdaw after delivering a syrup of mustard, honey and pellitory for Aggie Wyatt, wife of a Rotherhithe waterman, whose stubborn head-cold has resisted all other attempts at a cure, Bianca pauses at the top of the lane. Ahead of her, the twin signs sway gently in the breeze on their iron brackets: the jackdaw and the unicorn. Until this morning, catching sight of them has caused her heart to swell with pride.

Until this morning.

Now they beckon her towards catastrophe. This, she thinks, is how Anne Boleyn, Jane Grey and Mary Stuart went to their deaths: a procession of brave but hopeless steps on the slow walk to the block. Ordained. Inevitable.

The procession to her own nemesis had begun early this morning, shortly after Nicholas had left for his hearing before the Censors. Edward, the hop merchant's boy, had made his weekly delivery. Young Edward: barely seventeen, possessed of a handsome face punctured with the carmine eruptions of youth and – for as long as she's known him – brimming with puppyish devotion directed solely at her. But today he had stayed silent. Painfully distant, his eyes brimming with the hurt of the unrequited.

Next had been Aggie Wyatt herself.

''S'appened then, has it?' Aggie had sniffled.

'Happened? What's happened?'

'You and your physician.'

'I don't know what you're talking about, Aggie.'

'You deserve it, my dove. Don't worry, the secret's safe with me.'

But this is Bankside – where there's no such thing as a secret.

Now I've arrived at the steps to the scaffold, Bianca thinks. Face-to-face with my executioner. The block awaits. Time only for a brief valedictory word before I lower my neck to the inevitable judgement. She takes a deep, resigned breath and continues the walk to her destiny.

'Can I be a maid of honour, Mistress?' Rose asks chirpily as she enters the taproom. 'I do so love a wedding!'

✠

Nicholas returns to the Jackdaw as the bell at St Saviour's rings for Evensong. The taproom is almost empty. A quartet of tired watermen are taking their ease at one table; at another, Graziano and two sailors from the *Sirena* are enjoying a meal before returning with news of their master – the exact same news they carried yesterday and the day before: our master still lingers close to death.

Bianca is with them, deep in conversation. Nicholas watches her from the doorway, as if seeing her for the first time. Her fluent Italian and her animated gestures seem to belong to a stranger. She has never looked more beautiful to him. He again recalls the vision he had of them together, strolling in John Lumley's little orchard. And again – to his surprise – he feels no guilt, hears no reproach from Eleanor.

Turning her head as she laughs at something Graziano has said, Bianca catches sight of him. She jumps up and leads him into the little passage between the taproom and the parlour. It's a squeeze for two people. They are almost as close to each other as they were when the watch found them.

'There's something I want to tell you,' he begins.

'I know.'

'You *know*?' he says, caught by surprise. How can she know what has been in his mind all the way back from Knightrider Street? How can she possibly know what he's decided to do?

'Yes, I've heard it. I've had to suffer it all day!'

'I don't think we're talking about—'

'Everyone knows! From Edward, the hop merchant's lad, to Aggie Wyatt, the waterman's wife. Dingle and Boley must have been shouting the news from the bridge gatehouse. It's all over Southwark! Worse still, Rose wants to be a bridesmaid.'

Nicholas lets his head fall back against the plaster and laughs with relief. 'Oh, *that*.'

Bianca rams her fists into her hips. Her amber eyes blaze. 'It's not funny, Nicholas!'

'Is it so *very* terrible? Am I such a poor catch that I should be thrown back as displeasing?'

'Of course not. That's not the issue.'

Is he really the most obtuse rogue on Bankside? she wonders. Do *all* the sons of Suffolk yeomen have turnip-mash between their ears?

'Then ignore the gossip.'

'It's alright for you, Nicholas,' she says, almost snarling. 'You won't have to answer for it. No one is going ask *you* in an irritating sing-song, "*Nicholas*, when are banns to be read?" ... "*Nicholas*, shall it be rosemary or daisies for your bride-lace?" It's a *calamity*!'

'I'll tell them it was a mistake. A foolish error. I'll say I'd drunk too much mad-dog.'

She glares at him. 'What are you implying – that a man must be *drunk* before he'll consider embracing me?'

'That's *not* what I said!'

Rose pushes past, her arms full of dirty trenchers. She contrives the merest hint of a bob. 'Mistress. Master Nicholas. Time enough for disputes when you're wed.' She disappears into the kitchen with a happy flounce.

'Do you *see* what I mean?'

Nicholas allows Bianca a moment to calm herself. Then he says, 'Perhaps this might not be the best moment to ask, but I've been thinking about what to do next, all the way back from the College.'

'*And?*'

'How would you care to come to Gravesend with me tomorrow? To see Porter Bell?'

In the courtyard of Cleevely House the servants have set the rush-lights burning in the dusk. Professor Arcampora has announced to Samuel that it's time to return to the lodge in the beech wood. And this time Tanner Bell is being allowed to accompany him.

As they ride out into the approaching night, Samuel tells Tanner of the fantastical things he will see. Things that only a man with more wisdom and knowledge in his soul than all the ancients put together could summon out of the air. 'There will be wondrous alchemy, Tanner. What you or I might take to be nothing but rock and dirt will transform itself into brilliantly coloured clouds of smoke and sparks that almost blind you, if you look at them too long. And if you breathe upon their exotic vapours you will have astonishing dreams, even though you're really still awake. You must not be afraid, Tanner,' he says, understanding now how much of Arcampora's physic might seem frightening to those with less enlightened minds. 'No harm can come to us. God will protect us – the Professor has made sure of it.'

'I wish my brother Dorney was here,' says Tanner Bell, by no means convinced. 'Somehow he always managed to give me courage.'

'It will be alright, I promise. Besides, I wouldn't want to share this with anyone else.'

'But what if you have one of your falling spells out here tonight?'

Even in the light from Florin's burning torch, Samuel's face is as pale as an owl's wing in the darkness.

'It won't matter,' he says, grasping Tanner's arm to encourage him. 'Soon my sickness will be gone. I shall be like you. I shall be cured.' He raises his eyes to the night sky at the wonder of it. 'I shall be cured, Tanner. And then my father will kneel down at my feet. He will have to love me then, won't he?'

14

Billingsgate quayside is thronged with people in the breezy April sunshine, barely twenty of them actual passengers. The rest are friends, servants, street-vendors, message-carriers and more than a few whose greedy, inquisitive eyes mark them as purse-divers and tricksters. The ferry master cries, 'Eastward ho!' to announce the imminent departure of the Long Ferry on the afternoon tide. His voice is almost drowned by the shrieks of the gulls wheeling overhead.

Nicholas and Bianca make their way around a gang of stevedores unloading salted fish from a Dutch turbot boat, descend the slimy, weed-festooned steps and climb aboard the pitching barge. Nicholas finds space on the bench nearest the prow, away from the other passengers and the six live goats being manhandled into the stern. He fishes in his purse for coins. The tide is in their favour, he notices – the fare is always cheaper if the oarsmen don't have to row against it. Bianca steadies herself as the small vessel lifts and falls alarmingly.

At first she had been ready to refuse Nicholas's suggestion, knowing how much of a feast Bankside will make of them spending so many hours in each other's company. And what would Cousin Bruno say, if he were able? Even now, after three years in London, the Paduan part of her finds it scandalous that English women are allowed to mix so freely with the opposite sex: dancing on feast days and at Christmas, parading in couples around the Paris Garden utterly unchaperoned, playing hood-man-blind amongst the trees on Moorfields. Her mother would spin in her grave at the thought of Bianca spending a night in a tavern with a man who wasn't her husband.

'And where, pray, do we sleep?' she'd asked him.

'At an inn, of course. Gravesend has plenty of them – it's where the bigger argosies anchor. I've hardly touched the money Robert Cecil gave me. He can treat us to a couple of handsome rooms with feather-down beds.'

'But why do you need me to come with you?'

'It will go better if there are the two of us. Porter Bell might need the gentling a woman can provide.'

'You mean someone sympathetic to tell him his son is dead?'

The words were no sooner out of her mouth than she'd wished a mighty wave would come and wash her away. Could she possibly have uttered anything more likely to puncture Nicholas's heart?

His response had surprised her. He hadn't flinched. Grief had not misted his eyes. She had wondered then if perhaps he might have turned some small corner on his long road out of despair.

It was Buffle who had changed her mind about going. Rose – to Bianca's horror – had garlanded the poor creature in some dreadful approximation of a bride, with daisies she'd plucked from the gardens of Winchester House, and a scrap of lace tied around the dog's neck. She'd then paraded Buffle around the taproom on a leash made of ribbon, singing 'The Heaven-made Match' at the full extent of her lungs, to the rapturous applause of the customers. Compared to that humiliation, several gruelling hours spent on the Long Ferry to Gravesend in the company of goats and passengers in the throes of mal-de-mer had seemed positively enticing.

Now she wonders why she hadn't trusted her instincts more. And it has nothing to do with her modesty. The barge is almost completely open to the elements. There is only a simple canvas awning for shelter. Its corners are already beginning to snap tetchily in the strengthening wind.

The last chime of the bell, the last 'Eastward ho!' and the oarsmen are edging them out between the Muscovy traders, the Hansa argosies, the flyboats and the estuary hoys. The single sail fills, the ebbing tide lifts them and Bianca steels herself for the ordeal ahead. She takes one last glance at the security of dry land, at the crowd on the Billingsgate stairs.

And she sees – if only fleetingly – a figure watching her. A figure in a dark-brown cloak.

✠

With the wind and the noise of the ferry's passage through the water masking his voice, Nicholas risks speaking freely. He looks around, just to be sure. The other passengers have their backs to him, playing dice or warming themselves from flasks of arak and bingo. The goats have given up fighting the unnatural motion of the barge and have sunk into a resigned huddle. Nevertheless, Nicholas leans close to Bianca to be certain they are not overheard.

'John Lumley thinks it might just be possible Mary Tudor bore a child. He said we should burn the letters. He says public knowledge of their content could lead to a war in England between the faiths.'

'Did you tell him about Samuel?'

'Not in detail. Nor about much else that was in Tyrrell's papers. But I now know who the Brothers of Antioch are: a group of Mary's counsellors, living somewhere across the Narrow Sea. As for Arcampora, he was once the creature of this realm's most implacable enemy – the Duke of Alba.'

'All the more reason to go to your friend Robert Cecil and tell him. Offer him this information, in return for his promise to protect Samuel and my cousin.'

'Firstly, he's not *my* friend. Secondly, Cecil has enemies. It's common knowledge the Earl of Essex would happily see him discredited. If word gets out about this conspiracy, the Privy Council will likely hand everyone involved – including you, me, Samuel and Bruno – to Robert Topcliffe, the queen's inquisitor. And we both already know how efficient *he* is at extracting confessions, be they true or false. The sooner we get Bruno back onto the *Sirena* and out of England, and Samuel Wylde away from Arcampora and the Brothers of Antioch, the smaller the chance of us ending our days on the scaffold.'

Bianca digests his warning in silence, staring out across the heaving surface of the brown river towards the Limehouse shore, where faint smudges of smoke rise over the kilns into the desolate sky. Moving closer to him, like a lover about to declare her heart, she says in a voice he can barely hear above the wind, 'I think I'm being followed.'

✠

The landscape on either bank flattens out into empty marshland. At Woolwich, they catch a glimpse of the gibbets at the Hole and of the sea-rovers rotting in their cages. Some looked newly hanged, others nothing but a dangling collection of bone, scraps of cloth, water-weed and kelp. The sight does not lighten their mood.

Sometimes they doze; sometimes they talk. Sometimes the river and the rest of the world seem to run to two different clocks.

The light is fading. Dusk is coming on. Flights of teal and widgeon skim low over the water like spirits fleeing from opened graves. The barge is close inshore now, the bank rising into low, grey bastions built to house the batteries of cannon that King Henry set up to guard the seaward approaches to London. The wind has dropped, but the air has turned bitterly cold. A cry goes up, and the great chalk spur that pushes out from the southern shore and gives Gravesend its safe anchorage looms out of the river ahead. The barge stands off a while to allow the last ferry of the day to clear the Hythe on its journey across the river to Tilbury. And then the oarsmen port their oars and nimble watermen make fast the lines.

They have reached their destination.

15

The narrow lanes of Gravesend are almost deserted. A damp mist sulks around the huddled houses. The masts of the fishing boats and trading barques puncture the night sky like the spines of the mythical porpentine. It reminds Nicholas of the estuary at Barnthorpe.

The first inn they enter is the Black Bear. Bianca gives it her professional eye and decides it's little better than a mariners' six-penny stew, a haunt of watermen and whores. Nicholas asks the owner if he knows of Porter Bell. The man says, 'Try the Mitre. He's too rough for our palate.'

When they reach the Mitre, they find a cock-fight is about to begin. The two birds glower murderously at each other from inside their cages, the spurs buckled to their legs so keenly sharpened that just one strike will cut flesh to the bone. Two men in leather jerkins and sailors' slops move amongst the customers, each shaking a pewter pot into which flows a cascade of rattling coins.

'On reflection, I think I preferred the Black Bear,' Bianca says.

The landlord is a well-salted fellow in his fifties, with the sea in his eyes and shoulders rounded like a tautly strung bow. He has a mane of lank grey hair, tied back to show the gnarled remains of a left ear burned by the sheriff's brand. Whatever his offence, Nicholas assumes it probably involved violence. But the man greets them civilly enough. In answer to Nicholas's enquiry, he raises a fist – each finger like a well-stuffed bolster – and points to a dark corner of the tavern beyond the improvised cockpit. 'Have you come on the Long Ferry?' he asks.

Nicholas stares at the size of the man's hands. 'Yes.'

'Does Porter Bell owe you money?'

'No.'

'Then count yourself in profit.'

'We just want to speak with him awhile.'

The landlord puts one great arm around Nicholas's shoulder. The pressure makes his knees bend. 'Go gently with him, Master,' he says, with a compassion that catches Nicholas off-guard. 'Porter Bell has been a guest of the Dons, if you understand me. That tends to leave a mark on a man.'

Apart from Nicholas and Bianca, Porter Bell is the only customer in the inn whose eyes aren't glued to the cock-fight. For a moment Nicholas thinks they've got the wrong man. Compared to the landlord, this one looks as temporary as gossamer on a hedge at sunrise. He sits alone in the deepest recess of the tavern, a half-filled jug of mad-monk before him, picking at a plate of brawn. He's staring into his jug as though it's a window through which he yearns to catch a glimpse of the man he once was – before he learned the futility of hope and dignity. He seems to fill almost no space at all. Perhaps it's a trick he's learned in captivity, Nicholas thinks: to become small. To appear insignificant. To disappear. But then Porter Bell looks up at their approach, and Nicholas knows where he's seen that look before: it's the stare that only comes when a man has seen the Devil in all his manifestations, up close on the field of battle.

Nicholas eases onto the opposite bench, Bianca beside him. He whispers in Dutch, '*God geeft u vrede, soldat*' – God give you peace, soldier.

Porter Bell's deep-sunk eyes range slowly over his face. He's like a man trying to catch the strains of a half-forgotten song. When he answers, his voice has a rasp of suspicion in it.

'Do I know you?'

'You do not, friend,' says Nicholas.

'I don't drink with strangers.'

'Would you drink with someone who knew your boy Dorney?'

Porter Bell studies him suspiciously through rheumy eyes. 'Dorney's dead. The Dons killed him.'

'I know. I was there.'

'In Holland? With Dorney?'

'I was surgeon to Sir William Havington's company – though his son-in-law, Sir Joshua Wylde, was our captain then.'

'You don't *look* like a physician.'

'I try not to. It makes treating patients easier.'

Porter Bell peers once more into his ale. 'But you couldn't treat my boy, could you? So you can't be much of a doctor.'

'You don't need to be a doctor to comfort a man when he's dying. Dorney was beyond my help, the moment that ball struck him. But I can tell you he was at peace. I know that, because he was in my arms.'

Bell's distrust seems to ease a little. But he still can't quite bring himself to believe Nicholas hasn't come to gull him for some reason of his own.

'If you're a physician – prove it,' he says. 'Tell me something in physic.'

'What do you want to know?'

'If I was burned by a powder flash, how would you treat my wounds?'

'A balm of salt and crushed onions.'

Bell's thin brows lift a little. In the gloom, Bianca smiles.

'And scalding oil to save them from putrefying, I suppose?' he grunts.

'Not unless you'd stolen my rations. I favour Monsieur Paré's method: a compress of turpentine and egg-yolk. It's more effective – and far kinder. But then you would know that, because you've served in the Netherlands, too.'

Bell's slow smile reveals almost no front teeth in his upper jaw. 'I have, *broer*,' he says, using the Dutch for 'brother'. 'And scant reward it brought me.'

Nicholas nods in sympathy. 'There's many a good man starving on the road because his services are required no longer. Sailors from the squadrons, too, after the Dons' fleet was scattered in '88. It's a poor settling of the account.'

With surprising strength, Bell slams his tankard down on the table. 'How can it be called justice, when the captains live richly on their bounties and the rest of us must go hang for stealing bread?' He glares at Nicholas. 'I'll tell you this, *broer*: the rich man would think twice about kicking us aside if he'd seen how the Don plans to treat this realm, should he ever come into it.'

'Then drink with us, Master Bell, and we'll raise a toast to the rich man's proper education.'

Porter Bell seems pleased with the suggestion. He glances at Bianca. 'And is this your woman?'

'I'm a friend,' Bianca says as Nicholas struggles for an answer. 'Bianca Merton, mistress of the Jackdaw on Bankside.'

'A Bankside bawdy-house? God's blood, the doxies must be a sight, if the bawd herself is so fair!'

'It's a *tavern*,' she says firmly.

'Bianca is also an apothecary,' says Nicholas.

'A *licensed* apothecary,' Bianca adds, irritated by the lifting of Bell's eyebrows.

'Can you mix something for aching bones?' Bell asks her. 'Six months fettered in a Don cell has put the cold of the grave in my joints.'

'I'll send something down on the first available ferry,' she promises. 'My gift to you.'

Nicholas calls to a potboy for ale. While he waits for it to come, he continues his careful enticement of Porter Bell.

Though their memories are separated by almost twenty years, they are shared nonetheless: places they'd slept in, so exhausted from the march that hard earth and flagstones had felt like feather beds; how the greatest loot a captured town could give up was its store of imported English ale; how the Dutch never quite managed to pay them on time; warming themselves around the fire with mercenaries from half the princely states of Europe; and trying hard not to let anyone see in their eyes the visceral terror of falling into the hands of the Spaniard. It's a side to Nicholas that Bianca has never seen revealed before.

'And you tell me Dorney was at peace?'

'More so than any of us there, Master Bell. God's peace.'

The cock-fight begins. The noise of the spectators fills the tavern with a brutal, cloying fog of bloodlust. But Nicholas and Bianca are oblivious to it.

'Have you ever met a man called Angelo Arcampora, Master Bell?' Nicholas asks, praying he's done enough to win Porter Bell's confidence.

'You ask me if I know the Devil's doctor?' Bell's voice is a dry whisper of surprise. 'Aye, I know him. I know him all too well. He should be in hell, but the Devil forgot to bolt the door.'

And as Nicholas and Bianca lean in across the table, Porter Bell's words transport them to another place. Not Gloucestershire, but the Low Countries. And to another time.

The year is 1572. Porter Bell has returned to Naarden.

✠

Imagine a fair town near the Zuider Zee. A town of fine houses, rich burghers and industrious citizenry, set around with ramparts and grassy banks upon which the tulips sway in the soft breeze. Imagine it before the Spanish came.

Now imagine it as I saw it in winter, Porter Bell invites them – a Calvinist town besieged by the Catholic forces of the Duke of Alba.

There is strangely little noise. Just the wind and the intermittent, mournful tolling of the Spanish canon. Their sulphurous yellow smoke is the only colour on the bleak canvas Porter Bell is painting. The inundated fields, flooded to deny close access to the town walls, are a dirty white and frozen over. Snowflakes the size of guilders settle on little islands that thrust up through the ice, where the carcasses of abandoned cattle have become part of the desolation. From the walls and from the tower of the great church of St Vitus, the defenders regard these mounds covetously, for there has been almost nothing to eat for weeks. Not even a rat. The truly desperate have taken to melting snow over a fire and boiling tree-bark in it. Tomorrow will be the first day of December – the day Naarden learns the true meaning of the term Spanish Fury.

The men of the town council, their comfortable burghers' robes now tattered and loose against their famished bellies, have already met to discuss a Spanish offer of mercy, Bell recounts. All are in agreement: when Matins is over, the burghers will make as bold a progress as they can manage to the town gates and throw them open to the enemy.

'It was still snowing when the Spanish rode in,' Bell says, making a fluttering gesture with his fingers, though whether it is intended to convey the snowfall or is rather an anxious trembling for what is to follow, neither Nicholas nor Bianca can be sure.

The Spanish commander is Alba's son, come to do his father's dirty work – a pisspot-sized Caesar in a burnished breastplate, as Bell now paints him. A gloriously waxed moustache astride a horse. A pointed beard in a Castilian comb-morion helmet with a gleaming silver crest on top, impervious to the damp that bedraggles everyone else.

And beside him rides a tall young man with receding hair and a thin, hard nose like a hawk's beak, who wears not armour, but the black gown of a doctor of medicine.

What is the young Arcampora doing in Naarden? Nicholas wants to ask. But he's transfixed by the grim need to hear out Porter Bell's story – however awful he knows it is going to be.

Even as he speaks the word 'doctor', Bell shakes his head vigorously. 'Dressed as a doctor,' he says, correcting himself, 'but he's really the Devil himself, disguised as a man of healing.'

During the parley, Porter explains, Arcampora had assured them that Alba and his son were good Christians. Merciful men. And because he was a physician, they had trusted his word.

'"You will all be spared – helped to recant your heresy," is what he'd said,' Bell recounts. 'So we let them in. We stood around and watched them eat their provisions and drink their wine in the Markstraat. They even threw the scraps to the children who gathered to gawp at them. So we believed what this man of medicine had told us. That was the day I learned how well the Devil lies,' Bell says, his eyes beginning to glisten.

Now his voice has to tear the words out of his memory. 'They were still drunk the next morning – when the killing began. They used anything they could put their hands to: shot and club, rope, stones, blade and pike, sometimes just their fists. Anything that would speed the slaughter of Naarden.' He stares down at the table as if it's a mirror glass, though Bianca cannot bear to imagine what he's seeing in it. 'They almost managed it, too. Eight hundred souls, or thereabouts. The spared not even those babes-in-arms who'd survived the famine. Then they set the town alight.'

The last sight he'd witnessed, Porter Bell tells them – before the random shot that laid him bloodied and senseless on the ground – was of Arcampora casually observing the slaughter, singing papist hymns in Latin, rejoicing that he was witnessing God's holy work.

'I shouldn't even have been there,' says Bell miserably. 'I'd slipped in, carrying secret dispatches from the Orange forces, as a favour to Sir William Havington. Then I'd gone and broken an ankle, trying to sneak back out again.'

'How did you come to survive?' asks Bianca, moved almost to tears.

'I must have lain beneath the corpses for a day or more, bloodied by the passing of that Spanish ball, but otherwise unhurt. Alba's son and his devils had gone. Arcampora had gone, too. A week later, a farmer found me hobbling along the snowy banks of the IJsselmeer, all but frozen to death and raving about the Devil.'

Behind them, the spectators are cheering the combatants in the cock-fight. Bell glances over his shoulder.

'Look at them: they see two birds ripping each other to bits and think they know what death looks like. Well, let them wait till the Spanish come here. Then they'll know what real fury is.'

Nicholas refills Bell's tankard from the jug. His own, Bianca notices, is barely touched.

'But that's not the last I saw of the Devil's physician,' says Bell weakly, like a child recounting a nightmare. 'The farmer sold me to the Spanish. I can't blame him: famine was everywhere and the Dons were offering a bounty on mercenaries. They threw me in a stinking hole in Haarlem while they decided whether to hang me or not.'

'And that was where you encountered Arcampora again?' Nicholas asks warily.

'I recognized him at once – put the fear of damnation into me. He would come into the cells and speak to us, as if he were seeking to find out what manner of men we were. Whether we were pious or blasphemers, clever or lacking in wits. Whether we prayed to our Maker or cursed him. Then he'd go and select one of us.'

'*Select?* For what?'

'At first I thought it was for interrogation, perhaps even execution, for none he chose ever returned. Then one of the guards told me what he was about.'

Porter Bell falls silent for a moment. Nicholas opens his mouth to prompt him, but a sense of mounting dread stops his tongue.

'He was choosing men to take part in his obscene blasphemies,' Bell continues, making a broad, circular sweep of the stubble on his head with the gnarled fingers of his right hand. Nicholas sees in his mind's eye the skull that Buffle unearthed in the beech wood beyond Cleevely, the hole bored so carefully through the bone. And although he understands at once what Porter Bell means by the gesture, he also knows he can never tell this man what fate he believes has befallen his youngest son.

'Surgery? On the skull?' he suggests, praying Bell cannot read what is in his eyes.

'Arcampora became quite open about it, boastful even. He was performing great and wondrous physic, he said. One day he would prove to all mankind that the seats of reason and emotion are to be found in the brain, not in the heart or the blood.' Bell stares into his tankard, as though peering through a window into his memory. 'Can you imagine what it was like to be there – waiting in the piss-stinking straw, half-starved – wondering if the next time Arcampora came, his eyes would fall upon *you*?'

'How did you manage to escape?' asks Bianca in a cracked voice.

'I didn't. I was just lucky. The Hollanders caught a brace of Spanish caballeros and traded them for golden guilders and fifty prisoners. I was one of them.'

The story of Porter Bell's return to England – and to a new imprisonment in a cell built of his own terrors, invisible but no less inescapable – is swiftly told. As Mercy Havington had said, it is a story of ever-steepening decline. Of one son who died in Holland and another who stayed with him, to wipe the shit and piss off Porter when he crawled home from the alehouse, until he, too, could endure his father's tormented flailing no longer and turned his back.

'Do you know where Tanner is now?' Nicholas asks cautiously.

'Safe at Havington Manor, thank the Lord. Safe from *me*.'

'Tanner hasn't come to visit you recently?'

Porter Bell looks shamefaced. He shakes his head. 'Why would he – after what I put him through?' He holds up his tankard, as though to make a toast. 'He's made more of himself than his father ever did, I'll give him that.'

'Is there any reason you can think of why Tanner might come to London?'

'Not while Havington Manor still stands. Sir William's the best master a fellow could have. And Lady Mercy, well, she's an angel, that woman.' He gives them a look of utter defeat. 'Still, maybe my boy will happen by one day, dressed in a fine silk doublet and possessed of a full purse. Perhaps he'll doff his cap and say, "Good morrow, sir – how are things with my old father?" I'd like that. I'd take him out on the river in the wherry Sir William's money bought me. Show him how beautiful it can be, when it's in a kind mood.'

Nicholas wants to press him further. But he dares not.

Besides, Porter Bell seems already to be drifting away into a world where, with a little luck, what he has just imagined might even be possible.

'Yes,' he says dreamily. 'I'd like that. I'd like that *very* much.'

16

The Mitre has no lodgings, and the Long Ferry won't return to London until the morning tide. The night is too cold to wait upon the exposed Hythe. Nicholas and Bianca wander the lanes of Gravesend, huddled together, their breath keeping ghostly company, searching fruitlessly for an inn with vacant rooms. Skeins of frost glisten on the walls of the houses and crackle underfoot. And it's not just the night that chills: Porter Bell's story has sucked away whatever warmth was left in their bones.

'Robert Cecil knows Arcampora is in England, doesn't he?' Bianca asks.

'Yes.'

'Then why has he not already been arrested – after what we've heard from that poor man?'

'Because Cecil doesn't know Arcampora's history. His intelligencers were unable to find out much in the short time before I went to Cleevely.'

'I thought he knew everything.'

'We're speaking of events that happened long ago. Robert Cecil was just a child then. Naarden is simply one more horror in the war between the faiths that's been going on for over twenty years. Anyway, the queen's ministers had other things on their mind that year: in Paris alone, the papists were killing Protestants by the thousand.'

Even in the darkness he can detect the flash of anger in her eyes. 'You mean papists like *me*?'

'Of course not!'

'But that is my faith you're speaking of, Nicholas. And I've never wanted to murder anyone.'

'I'm speaking of the zealots. The men in power. The men in the dark robes and beards. The men who think they have the right to tell God who He should love and who He should despise.'

She relents a little. 'When Cardinal Fiorzi was telling us the English were heretics who must be burned in order to be saved, I asked him why God couldn't simply open their eyes.'

He smiles at the thought of a ten-year-old Bianca wagging her finger at a cardinal. 'What did he say?'

'He said to me, "*Passerotto*" – that was his nickname for me; it means "little sparrow" – he said, "England is so very distant from heaven that even God cannot reach that far. That's why He needs a Pope."'

'Your cardinal was right about one thing,' Nicholas says. 'England is certainly distant enough for Arcampora to have painted himself afresh in the passing of twenty years. Now he's an eminent man of physic. The great healer.'

'But he's not healing Samuel Wylde, is he? From what you've told me, it sounds more as though he's preparing him, strengthening him. He's trying to give him the fortitude to make his claim upon the throne of England.'

A chalky incline rises into the darkness and the Dover Road. They are almost at the edge of the town. Ahead is an inn that looks as though it might still be open. The painted sign shows a swan about to take flight. Firelight flickers in the windows. Nicholas lifts the latch and opens the door, hoping against hope that the inn will have lodgings.

Inside, the warm fug makes his frozen cheeks sting. He smells wood-smoke and unwashed wool that's lain too long against human flesh. But to his joy, the Swan has lodgings. Or, rather, *a* lodging.

One chamber unoccupied. One bed. One shilling.

Or if you prefer, says the landlord, you can sleep on the floor by the hearth.

'I thought you said there were plenty of lodgings in Gravesend?' Bianca hisses, when the landlord is out of hearing.

'I thought there would be.'

'Have you ever actually *been* to Gravesend before?'

He gives her a sheepish look. 'No.'

She does her best to look ill-tempered, but inside she's trying not to laugh at the look of embarrassment on his face.

When they've warmed themselves with a cup or two of hippocras and picked at a meal of cold meat and bread, the landlord leads them upstairs to their room. Nicholas can see by the man's face what he's thinking. He suspects Bianca may be a *crossbiter*. He thinks that as soon as she's got her victim – Nicholas – half-undressed, her pretend husband will arrive, demanding money from the poor sap not to have him arraigned before the church courts, for attempting to seduce an honest man's wife. It's one of the staple ways Southwark has of relieving innocents of their money.

Nicholas decides it's best not to tell her. The response is likely to be unpredictable. After all, this is the only room left in Gravesend. And he doesn't much fancy the hard flagstones downstairs.

✷

It is a surprisingly well-appointed chamber. The tester bed is furnished with a feather mattress. There's a clean sheet of Flanders linen, and a bolster. Nicholas and Bianca remove their boots and lay themselves out side-by-side – like effigies of a crusader knight and his lady on a tomb.

Apart from their embrace on Black Bull Alley, Nicholas hasn't been this intimate with a woman since Eleanor went into her fateful confinement. And unless the landlord really did think him the imminent victim of a cross-biter and decides to do something about it – which in this town is highly unlikely – they are in no danger this time of being interrupted by the local Dingle and Boley. It feels at once comforting and yet utterly alarming.

The memory deep in the muscles of his arms urges him to reach out for her. But something, some tangle in his mind he cannot yet unravel, prevents him. He considers trying to make light conversation. But what if – through long-suppressed habit – he utters some endearment or other? She'll think him a mooncalf. I'm made of glass, he thinks. If she turns her head, she'll be able to see all the conflicted emotions swirling inside me, like smoke in a draughty hearth.

And yet the comfort, the balm of her proximity, is undeniable.

'Does it give you ease?' he asks uncertainly.

She thinks he means their closeness. Her eyes open wide with interest.

'The bed,' he says hurriedly, lest she thinks him forward. 'Is it comfortable?'

'Oh, yes.' Bianca rolls her neck on the bolster. 'Not as comfortable as the Jackdaw. But better than expected, thank you.'

'Do you mind if I unlace the points of my doublet, only they're a little tight for sleep?'

'Not at all.'

A moment's silence.

'Nicholas?'

'Yes?'

'Would you object if I loosened my kirtle a little? Only I'm getting warmer now.'

'Please...'

They roll away from each other. They tug modestly at points and lacings. When they roll back again, they are – unaccountably – closer. He turns his head towards her.

'Better?'

'Much.'

In the candlelight he observes her profile, the arch of her neck as she leans back against the bolster. Her skin has a sheen of liquid amber to it.

She turns her face to him. Her breath slides off his cheek like silk drawn lazily over marble.

'I lied,' Bianca says.

Does she mean the words she spoke in the Jackdaw, when she'd learned what everyone was saying about them? Why am I so hot, he wonders, when there's frost outside? 'You did? When?'

'Out in the lane. When I said I'd never wanted to murder anyone. I lied.'

He stares into her eyes. She doesn't look murderous. But with Bianca Merton, he thinks, you never can tell.

'I wanted to murder Antonia Addonato.'

'Did you?'

'I was twelve. She was fifteen. All the boys in the streets around my father's house in Padua fought over her. She had breasts, you see.'

'And did you murder her?'

'Only a little. I asked my mother to make a potion.'

'And did she?'

'Yes. But it was made of marchpane, and Antonia loved every bite.'

'I accept your confession. That is forgivable.'

'Is it?'

'Completely.'

'And who did you fight over, Nicholas, when you were that age?'

'At Barnthorpe we fought over who got to drive the plough.'

Her laughter has a throaty echo to it that carries the warmth of the Veneto sun.

'When I first came to England,' she tells him, 'I thought I would find gallants who would recite poetry to me. Men whose souls were moved by art and music. Men who would know the courtly ways. I ended up in Southwark.'

'You didn't look hard enough,' he tells her. 'If you'd wanted to see an Englishman with his soul swept by passion, I could have told you exactly where to look.'

A whisper, so close he imagines he can feel the impact of it on his cheek.

'You can? Where?'

'Every Shrovetide. When the apprentice boys are playing football.'

She strikes his upper arm with her hand so hard it hurts.

They lie in silence for a while, listening to the unfamiliar sounds of the inn: the creak of a floorboard, the gurgling grunts of drunken sleep coming from another room. The sound of their own breathing.

'I think we have to talk,' he says at last.

'Yes, we do.' She turns to him again, her eyes locked with his. 'You first...'

For a long while he stares at the filigree of light reflected in the pupils of her eyes. He seems unable to speak. The urge to kiss her, to bury his face in the warmth of her neck, has come out of nowhere. It's almost overpowering. But the bridge ahead of him is just a little too steep to climb – yet. 'Lord Tyrrell's letters,' he says croakily.

Bianca lets out a long, slow breath. 'Oh, *those*.'

Catching the disappointment in her voice, he curses himself for his temerity. But it's too late; the moment has passed. The mention of Tyrrell's name has killed it.

'John Lumley confirmed everything I feared about their importance,' he says. 'If Samuel Wylde really is Mary's grandson, the danger is beyond imagination. This realm could be riven by the most brutal of civil wars. If Robert Cecil or the Privy Council learns of their content, they'll pass the sentence of death on everyone involved, to prevent that happening.'

'But Mary never had a child,' Bianca counters. 'I remember my parents telling me Father Rossi would have everyone pray and light a candle that Mary Tudor and her Spanish prince might beget a child. He said if they did, England would remain under the protection of the one true faith. If not, every English man and woman would spend eternity in Purgatory.'

His face seems gaunt in the meagre light. She finds it a little frightening.

'Well, *some* people believe there was a child,' he says vehemently. 'And *some* people believed in Perkin Warbeck. Look where it got him: the scaffold.'

As though her cousin were not thirty miles away, senseless and unable to speak, Bianca whispers into the night, 'Oh, *Bruno*, whatever madness have you become entangled in?'

'If he could answer you, I think he'd tell us he came here to see the proof for himself – the proof that Samuel Wylde is the true heir to the English crown. That was the intent of the privy commission for Cardinal Fiorzi that Bruno spoke of.'

'But *we* have no part in this, Nicholas,' she protests. 'Our consciences are clear. Go to Robert Cecil. Tell him the truth.'

'The *truth* will be whatever Cecil and the Privy Council believe it to be. It will be whatever the men with the white-hot irons and the ropes have been told it is. And all they have to do is wait until the pain becomes so unbearable that – finally – you *agree* with them.'

Watching him intently, Bianca sees there is a look almost of self-loathing on his face.

'That is how it works,' he says. 'We both know that. But Samuel Wylde? A young lad with the falling sickness, cast aside by his father, used by others for their own end – does *he* deserve to face such an end?'

'Do you truly believe Samuel is Mary Tudor's grandson?'

'I don't know. It's possible. The only thing that matters is that enough people believe it to be true.' Nicholas stares into the darkness. Now he sees nothing but hopelessness staring back at him. 'For myself, I care not a jot if the wafer and the wine are the flesh and blood of Jesus Christ. But I can tell you this: if the Brothers of Antioch use Samuel Wylde to start a holy war in England, this realm will see a thousand Naardens.'

✠

Did Nicholas ever really consider abandoning Samuel Wylde and Bruno Barrani to their fates? Did he consider returning from Gravesend and telling Robert Cecil everything he had discovered, in exchange for immunity for Bianca, Bruno and Samuel, as she had twice suggested? In the darker places of the mind where raw self-preservation lies, he most certainly did – though he never admitted it to Bianca, either on the Long Ferry back to London or, indeed, later.

It would have been by far the easiest course of action. He might conceivably have secured their safety, in exchange for Tyrrell, Arcampora and the others. But he knew he could not rely on the mercy of Robert Cecil alone. It was public knowledge that factions on the Privy Council would happily see Burghley's son humbled. He could almost hear the cruel voice of Richard Topcliffe, the queen's torturer-in-chief, as he set about his interrogation of Thomas Tyrrell: *Tell me, traitor, who carried the messages between you and the foreign agent Barrani?* And Tyrrell, in a voice half-choked by pain, would tell him: *It was Mistress Merton!*

Nicholas already knew that Bianca's welfare was far too precious to him to jeopardize. For it is a truth that love is not confined to its object alone, but to all that is precious to that object – even a love as yet unacknowledged.

He had, however, managed to answer one question that had been troubling him. By the time the barge slipped away from the Hythe that morning on its journey upstream to London, he was certain that there is space in the heart for two loves – one a memory, the other very much alive.

For almost six long hours he sat in the prow of the barge, staring out into the opaque emptiness while Bianca slept fitfully beside him on the plank seat, her head resting on her folded arms. To the other passengers, he was merely searching for something – anything – to break the monotony of the river. In truth, he was struggling to make sense of a dilemma that would have astounded them, a puzzle that he and Bianca had tried to answer from the testimony of Porter Bell, from Tyrrell's deciphered letters, from his conversation with John Lumley; a puzzle they had sought to resolve as they lay close together, close as nearly-lovers, in the little chamber at the Swan Inn.

Was Samuel Wylde *really* the grandson of Mary Tudor? If he was, why had the Brothers of Antioch waited so long? How had the boy remained undetected all these years? If Samuel's mother was the child that Mary had claimed to be carrying in the year of her death, why had not the birth of a royal daughter been loudly proclaimed throughout England?

It took several miles of river, unnumbered echoless strokes of the oars, before a resolution came to Nicholas, in the form of one of Tyrrell's letters: *I, Charles Pelham, physician... so attest that the infant born unto M on the third of March last is afflicted by the sacred disease. I have witnessed the several and diverse paroxysms...*

A female claimant to the throne afflicted by the falling sickness, he reasoned as he watched the interminable passing of the riverbank, would be a banner to which few would dare to rally. Even if Mary herself had acknowledged the child, those around her would have known the risks of placing a sickly infant upon the throne.

Then he remembered another of Tyrrell's letters: *The child is safely delivered unto a place of protection against the malevolent designs of the ungodly...*

In Mary Tudor's mind, he reasoned, the ungodly could only have meant her half-sister, the Protestant Elizabeth. John Lumley had said Mary knew she was dying. Perhaps she and the Catholic zealots around her had feared that the child would be murdered the moment Mary was no longer alive to protect it. Had they carried the infant away to a place where she would be safe, somewhere far from London, remote, unremarkable – a pretty manor house in Gloucestershire, for instance?

And what of Lady Mercy Havington and her late husband? Have they been complicit all these years, harbouring a cuckoo and its chick in their nest? If so, Robert Cecil's retribution will surely be particularly vengeful.

His thoughts were interrupted when the passengers shifted noisily to get a better glimpse of the palace of Greenwich looming out of the river's glassy sheen, the towers and cupolas rising into the milky morning like ancient temples from a desert mist. It was here, Nicholas knew, that Elizabeth had been born. He imagined her now, looking out over the river and catching a glimpse of the passing barge, reaching imperiously into his secrets. The image only made him more convinced how dangerous it was even to have *knowledge* of such a threat to her crown as Samuel Wylde.

By then Nicholas had become resolved upon a course of action. He understood that it was all just a matter of time. That the sand was already flowing in the hourglass.

Somehow Samuel must be prised from the talons of the Brothers of Antioch before they could use him for their purpose. It would be far from easy, he knew that. But he knew that whatever hurt Samuel Wylde might suffer in the execution of his plan, it would be as nothing compared to what would befall him if the Brothers of Antioch were allowed to raise him up as Mary Tudor's grandson.

It had been Porter Bell's testimony that had made up Nicholas's mind for him. He had seen many sights in the Low Countries that would live in the darker recesses of his mind for the rest of his life. But never had he witnessed something on the scale of Naarden, and though he had seen men used cruelly by their captors, he had never seen them used like living beasts tied down for an anatomy lesson. He was filled with a rage against Angelo Arcampora that felt like a burning coal lodged in his gut.

Between that pale dawn and their arrival at the Billingsgate stairs, Nicholas Shelby had what felt, to him, like an age of watery captivity during which to reflect on all this – and on his propensity to shoulder other people's burdens. But without doubt, the strongest hand guiding his thoughts that morning was Eleanor's. He had one last question to ask of her – before he let go of her. What would *she* expect of him?

When he felt Bianca stir beside him, woken by the cries of the bargemen as they approached the Billingsgate stairs, he waited until she had yawned, stretched and made her peace with the ache in her bones, and then quietly and carefully explained to her what she must do.

✠

It is fortunate that Tanner Bell cannot look into a mirror glass and see his face. Fortunate that he wouldn't recognize it, even if he could. More than fortunate. Tanner could only be luckier if he was dead.

His face is no longer smooth and puckish, the eyes brimming with good-natured rebellion. The mop of hair no longer slips down over his right eye. Instead, it is stained red and slick across his brow, as if Tanner Bell has been caught in a crimson rain shower. His face is that of a crazed, blood-smeared apparition.

Where once his limbs, always tending to plumpness, had strength in them, now they are as weak as those of a newborn infant. So weak, in fact, that Dunstan and Florin have tied him to the chair to stop him sliding out of his seat and onto the floor.

A short while ago he was conscious that Arcampora had brought him to the lodge in the beech wood alone, without Samuel. Now he comprehends little – except the pain. He cannot ask Dr Arcampora why he has done him this terrible hurt; Tanner no longer has the power of coherent speech. He sits in the chair, making agitated guttural shrieks, like a goose having its neck wrung. With each squawk a trickle of drool runs down over his chin. On the bench beside him lies a carpenter's auger, the circular cutting blade at the end of the screw-shaft bloodied and wreathed in shreds of Tanner Bell's scalp.

'God's nails! Can't you put an end to this noise, Professor?' asks Dunstan irritably. 'The little sod is giving me the dreads.'

'Is easy,' says Arcampora dismissively. He opens Tanner's blood-soaked shirt, tilts the boy's head back and, with his knife, deftly cuts through the laryngeal nerves, taking care not to puncture the carotid arteries as he does so. He doesn't want his patient bleeding to death. Tanner's mouth keeps moving, but his shrieks of torment instantly fall silent.

'That's more to my liking,' says Dunstan.

Arcampora leans over Tanner's shaved head and inspects the watery pink mass visible beneath the circular hole in the boy's skull.

Florin and Dunstan regard the hole blankly. They are a poor audience. Arcampora would rather have an admiring collection of physicians to address, but the pair are all he has, and so they will have to do. Besides, they are good men, he thinks. They have shown great devotion to his cause. When he had chosen them from amongst the English agents being trained at the Douai seminary in Spanish Flanders to run secret missions into Elizabeth's heretical realm, he had chosen well. But they have scant understanding of physic.

'It is not easy to know if all the foul airs are properly released through the aperture,' he declares. 'But without the expulsion of disturbed thoughts, there will be no space for the inflow of any animation from outside.' He waves one hand airily to indicate what he means by 'outside'.

'How do you know they come out, if you can't see them?' asks Florin reasonably.

'The ancients know this – since many years. Is well understood. But I, Arcampora, make a new discovery! It was believed the vital spirit – what is called in physic *pneuma* – was found here,' he taps the back of Tanner's head, 'in vessels called in Latin the *rete mirabile*. In English, is called the net of wonders.'

Dunstan and Florin peer at the spot indicated by Arcampora's gloved hand, as if they expect to see these miraculous blood vessels through the white skin.

'Is not there!' says Arcampora, confounding them.

Florin looks at his master like a man who's been gulled by a street trickster's sleight of hand. 'Where is it, then?'

'The ancients were wrong!' Arcampora exclaims. 'The *rete*

mirabile is not found in man, only in beasts. This was their mistake. But I, Arcampora, I discover the error – through experiment!' His chest swells with self-congratulation. 'I, Arcampora, believe the well of *pneuma* is to be found deep under here.' He moves his hand from Tanner's neck to his head. He prods the slippery tissue exposed by the hole he has bored in Tanner's skull. A rivulet of blood flows around his fingertip. Tanner squirms weakly, like a dying worm. 'This I call the *cisterna mirabile*: the well of wonders. From this well, the spirit of what we are – our very being – flows into the dark tissue of the brain. From there, it spreads to the *corpus callosum*. Finally it reaches the cerebral cortex as memory and thought.'

His audience of two receives the little lecture in silence. It is quite beyond their understanding. But that, they tell themselves, is only to be expected when men find themselves in the presence of genius. So they simply nod and thank providence that, in the fight against the heretics, God has sent them a champion like Professor Arcampora.

Arcampora regards Tanner Bell's slumped form with a measure of contentment. The boy has survived the trepanation. How long he lives now will be partly a matter of guarding against putrefaction, and partly of staving off a breakdown in the lad's will to survive. It is a pity, he thinks, that Florin was forced to break Finney's neck after they had recaptured him. If Finney had not tried to fight his way free after he'd awoken from the procedure, there would be another subject against which to compare Tanner's progress. Subjects are scarce. Isabel Wylde has had no word from Lord Tyrrell on the matter of when a replacement might arrive.

Florin and Dunstan are watching him intently, like hounds waiting for the signal to feed on a carcass. They are anticipating his signal to fill the chalices, put the lantern's flame to the tinder and set the herbs smouldering. Waiting for him to begin the incantation. Waiting for him to call up the spirits. Arcampora can see the strain on their faces, the struggle to hold in the fear. He admires them. They may be simple men, but they are godly. And extraordinarily brave. It cannot be easy for them, he thinks, to embrace the things they have witnessed in this place. Weaker men, men less committed to their faith, would have run screaming into the beech wood in fear for their souls. But not these two. They are sustained by the example of Our Lady of Antioch, just as it sustains him. It is proof, he tells himself, that as long as a man is pious enough, faithful enough to God, he can withstand anything in the battle for righteousness – even close proximity to the spirits of the dead.

17

Less than an hour after disembarking from the Long Ferry at Billingsgate, Bianca Merton summons Rose, Farzad, Timothy and Ned to join her in the empty taproom. 'Master Nicholas is leaving the Jackdaw,' she tells them.

They stare at her in appalled silence.

It is not the last they will see of him, she hastens to assure them. He is a dear friend and is welcome to drop by whenever he cares to. To Rose's wail of protest, she explains that neither of them wishes to be the focus of mirth and speculation. Any intimacy that some think may have been observed between them has been wildly misinterpreted. They are not lovers. They never have been, and they never will be. But as her mistress speaks these words, Rose notices she isn't looking her straight in the eye.

'And, Rose dear, take that silly marriage garland off Buffle. He looks ridiculous.'

'They've argued over his late wife,' Rose tells Ned confidently, when Bianca is out of earshot. 'But I don't think she really means it – the bit about *never*.'

'Not true,' says Ned. 'His heart has mended. Now he wants to play the goat for a while. He can't do that if he's sleeping in the attic and Mistress Bianca is one floor down, can he?'

This brief exchange, of itself, causes a cooling-off between Ned and Rose that lasts almost a week.

Timothy finds solace in his store of lover's laments, until

Bianca threatens to burn his lute on the taproom fire if he doesn't play something people can drum their feet to.

Only Farzad does not express an opinion. Because Farzad has been entrusted with the smallest sliver of the truth, and can be relied upon to keep his mouth shut – especially as Bianca has explained to him the consequences of him telling *anyone* that he is to be their secret conduit. He takes this warning so much to heart that it is some time before he stops having bad dreams, in which his mistress turns him into a particularly plump and warty toad.

✠

At its narrowest point, Poynes Alley is barely wide enough for two people to pass without rubbing shoulders. It cuts through to the river between St Olave's church and Bridge House, on the eastern side of London Bridge. At the far end, on the left side, lies the property Nicholas has come to see. It is timber-framed, and the spaces between the beams are filled with mud and daub that look as though it would crumble away if you dared to hammer on it with your fist. It is two storeys high, barely ten feet across and already well on the way to dereliction. The landlord, a fellow with the long, wiry body of a bent poker, seems to think it a rival to Hampton Court.

He shows Nicholas the single chamber downstairs that serves as hall, parlour and kitchen combined, and follows him up the flight of narrow stairs that gives access to the sleeping chamber above. The sparse furnishings – a tester bed that must have been built *in situ*, for its dimensions defy the stairway by a considerable margin, and a parlour table – look ancient. Their age and paucity do not trouble Nicholas. He will buy what is needed at the St Saviour's market.

On the way back down from the upper floor, Nicholas says nothing. The landlord takes it as indifference and drops the rent by a penny.

There is a window and a door at the far end of the ground floor. Beyond it, Nicholas can see a narrow balcony and a flight of precarious steps leading down to the mud of the riverbank. A half-feral cat has taken up residence there, but at least it will keep the rats down.

He goes outside and looks back at the river frontage before making his decision. On the upper part of the wall he can just make out the image of a swan, the paint peeling off the plaster. The house, he realizes, must once have been a Bankside stew, the sign calling to mariners from the ships moored across the water at the customs quay.

Some two hundred yards to the left, the great stone starlings of the bridge's foundations march out towards the other bank. In the arches closest to the bank, huge water wheels turn slowly in the current. Nicholas studies with passing interest the buildings perched along the span of the bridge. They are tall enough to shut out half the sky. Little human figures cross in the gaps between them. As he looks, a window glints in the sunlight as someone opens it to pour the contents of a slop bucket or a pisspot – he cannot tell which at this distance – into the water below. He turns and walks back to the house, the mud sucking covetously at his boots and the stink of decay rising out of the ooze.

All in all, he thinks, the place is ideal.

His last action before leaving Poynes Alley is to walk back to the foreshore and look out across the river to the far bank, where the *Sirena di Venezia* lays moored alongside Galley Quay.

✠

The following day, 3rd April, Nicholas Shelby starts to make the lodgings on Poynes Alley an approximation of a home, though he has no intention of staying a moment longer than necessary. Rose arrives, bearing clean sheets, a coverlet and a bolster all tied up with string. She's tearful. She puts the linen down on the table, pulls a kerchief from her sleeve and blows her nose mightily.

'It's not fair,' she sniffles. 'Some bodies are born for each other.'

'People invent things, Rose, even when there's nothing there to invent,' he tells her gently.

'Well, it's not right. The Jackdaw's not right. And if you care for my opinion, Mistress Bianca is not right, either – even though she says she is. Which she always does. And isn't.'

Smiling, he tells her it's all for the best. Good friends can't be expected to live like songbirds in a cage – especially if everyone around them keeps expecting them to sing a song of other people's invention. Rose leaves, unconvinced.

Nicholas, of course, has not left the Jackdaw because of what people think. He has not left in order to save Bianca's blushes. He has moved out because he knows he must distance the Jackdaw and its mistress from what he intends to do.

An hour later, Farzad arrives with a travelling chest containing Nicholas's few possessions.

'Mistress had three offers of marriage since you left, Master Nicholas,' he says, grinning.

'Not that rogue Marlowe?' Nicholas asks, feeling suddenly very lonely.

'Walter Pemmel for one. And Will Slater.'

Nicholas smiles. Pemmel and Slater have barely three teeth between them.

'Old Gryndall the rat-catcher went down on one knee, though Mistress had to help him get back up again afterwards. I like very much in England now – you all crazier than anyone in Persia!'

'Tell her my advice is to make them wait,' Nicholas says. 'Then to choose *very* carefully.'

From the candle-maker on Thieves' Lane he buys tallow wicks to bring a little light to the evenings. He purchases a new mattress at the St Saviour's market and spreads Bianca's clean linen sheet over it. The old one he cuts up with the poniard he purchased for his journey to Gloucestershire, burning the straw and the stained canvas in the single hearth. The stuffing is mouldy. The smoke almost chokes him out into the lane before the flames finally take hold. But by next morning the air in the tenement is almost breathable, tainted only by the smell of the river and the countless unknown lives that have leached into the old timbers of the house.

He eats at the public ordinary on the corner of Poynes Alley and St Olave's Street: eel or coney, oysters occasionally. Sack and ale he takes sparingly – not like the first time he came across the bridge after Eleanor's death, when he would seize every offered opportunity to drink himself into oblivion in his increasingly desperate efforts to get her to stop talking to him from inside his head.

At night he lies alone in the little bed, listening to the unfamiliar sounds of his new surroundings: the lap of the tide against the beams of the balcony outside, the tolling of a different church bell, the cries and shouts of customers leaving a different tavern – the Walnut Tree, by the old abbey ruins on the south side of St Olave's.

He cannot entirely escape the old pain of desolation, but now he can bear it, consign it to its proper place. He knows it is the pain of wounds healing, not of wounds mortal. And he finds he can think of Eleanor and Bianca increasingly as separate entities, and think of each without guilt.

Increasingly, he has visitors. His name is known in this part of Southwark: St Thomas's hospital for the sick poor is barely ten minutes' walk away. Word soon goes round that the physician who worked there in the cloisters for a while last year has returned. A small but steady trickle of visitors appears. He treats without complaint a procession of scalds and sprains, crushed fingers and sundered skin. If balms and salves are required, he directs the patient to Bianca at the Jackdaw, giving each a ha'penny of Robert Cecil's money to offer as payment.

Four days after his arrival at Poynes Alley he rises early, takes a wherry across the river and returns to Knightrider Street. At the College guildhall he seeks out old Wotton, the clerk to the Fellows, a corpulent man – sixty if a day – with large, startled eyes that remind Nicholas of a freshly caught salmon. Wotton has been at the College for as long as anyone can remember. The president, Baronsdale, likes to joke that Wotton folded the great Galen's togas for him. Wotton has the grace to say nothing about Nicholas's appearance before the Censors, though he must know of it.

'I'm trying to trace a Dr Charles Pelham,' Nicholas says. 'He practised in St Martin-in-the-Fields – around 1558.'

While Wotton searches a shelf for the appropriate roll, Nicholas pictures the physician's loose, disjoined scrawl: I, *Charles Pelham... attest that the infant born unto M on the third of March last is afflicted by the sacred disease. I have witnessed the several and diverse paroxysms...*

Don't lead, Nicholas tells himself as Wotton returns. You're just seeking word of a long-lost family friend – a friend who's never been anywhere near the court of Mary Tudor, let alone diagnosed her secret infant daughter as an epileptic.

Wotton fussily opens the roll and scans the lines of neat secretary hand. Stooping closer, he stabs an entry with his index finger. 'Here he is, Mr Shelby: New College, Oxford... licensed by the Bishop of London... became a licentiate of this college in 1543.' He steps back from the roll, a look of surprise in his round, moist eyes. 'But no ordinary physician, by the look of it.'

Nicholas leans over the roll and sees the entry *vicarium regiis medicus*.

'Pelham was a deputy physician to the royal household?' he says, trying to keep the tremor out of his voice.

'So it would seem, sir. But as far as our most sovereign lady Elizabeth is concerned, Pelham is not a name I recall, and I've known all her medical men, from Thomas Bill to old Dr Lopez.'

'Is it possible he could have been physician to the late Queen Mary's household?' Nicholas asks, now barely daring to breathe.

'I can't see why it shouldn't be. The dates would be correct.'

'Is he still alive?'

Wotton fetches the latest roll. 'Apparently he is, Mr Shelby. We have him entered as dwelling by St Mary Rounceval. Whether he still practises, I cannot say – he must be over eighty.'

Nicholas struggles to keep his composure. St Mary Rounceval is barely a stone's throw from the royal palace of St James.

From the doorway, a new voice breaks into Nicholas's thoughts.

'Is that old Mr Pelham you're enquiring after?'

Looking up, Nicholas sees Wotton's assistant, Oldbridge, watching him, his round pink face infused with a desire to please.

'Marry, not a whisper of him for years, and then two gentlemen seek him out within a few months of each other.'

'Who was the other?' Nicholas asks.

'A most striking fellow. Came around Christmastime last. Tall. Very angular in the features. A foreign physician; apparently most eminent. From Basle, I think he said.'

18

Nicholas considers taking a wherry, but the wind is from the west and the tide is ebbing. It will be faster to walk. He heads up Creed Lane, through Ludgate and down Fleet Hill towards the Strand. His mind is in turmoil. Is it conceivable, he wonders, that Charles Pelham was the physician who attended the birth of Mary Tudor's secret child? And if he was, will he dare admit it to a stranger?

An hour later he stands before the site of the old religious hospital of St Mary Rounceval, once home to an order of French nuns long since suppressed by the queen's late father and now converted into private dwellings. At his back is the broad open space around the Charing Cross. Beyond that, the great royal deer park north of Whitehall. His mouth is dry with anticipation.

Giving Pelham's name to the porter, Nicholas is directed to a modest house at the far end of the main courtyard. There he is welcomed cordially by a plump woman of about fifty. She wears a grey kirtle and a white cloth bonnet. Her pale eyes are dulled by travail and disappointment, but her smile remains resolute.

'What is your business with my father, Dr Shelby?'

'I believe he may once have had a patient – a woman – whose son I have recently encountered,' he says, reciting the explanation he's come up with on the walk from Knightrider Street. 'The boy has the falling sickness, and I wondered if perhaps Dr Pelham might give me some insight into the mother's health.'

'Then I fear you've had a wasted journey, sir. Conversation is very trying for my father these days. His wits aren't what they were.'

Nicholas tries to disguise his disappointment. 'I really would be grateful for the opportunity. I've walked a long way – from Bankside.'

Mistress Pelham's '*Oh*' implies that Bankside might be on the far side of the Alps. 'You'd best come in, then. But, please, don't hope for much.'

She leads him to a small room at the back of the house. It smells of unwashed linen and stale breath, though the rest of the house is spotless. A window opens onto a small patch of barren ground bordered by the tall hedges of a grand formal garden running down to the river. In a chair in front of the window sits an old man, as translucently grey as a dead moth caught in a spider's web. His skin is mottled with blemishes the colour of old plums left out in the rain.

'Father, say good morrow to Dr Shelby. He's come all the way from across the river to speak with you. Isn't that nice of him?'

Charles Pelham studies Nicholas for a while, his left foot hammering ineffectively at the floorboards. Slowly his eyes narrow with suspicion. 'I know *you*, young man,' he says at length.

'You do?' says Nicholas, surprised but hopeful.

'You're the Lord Mayor. You've brought me my money!' Pelham twists the wick of his neck towards his daughter and says viciously, 'I told you he would come. You're naught but a lying souse-head, Meg Pelham!'

'Meg was my mother,' the woman explains wearily, as though it's a correction she has to make all too frequently. She kneels beside the chair. 'It's me, Abigail, your daughter – remember? And this is not the Lord Mayor, Father; he's another doctor: Dr Shelby.'

'If he's not the Lord Mayor, then he's a cut-purse come to steal my pension!'

'I did warn you,' says Abigail, looking up apologetically.

'May I at least try?'

'If you can. But please do not tax his wits unnecessarily.'

Nicholas squats down on the other side of the chair. He says as gently as his mounting frustration will allow, 'I was hoping you might advise me, in a professional matter, Dr Pelham. I wondered if you might remember an old patient of yours, from the past...'

'I was the queen's personal physician, you know,' Pelham announces proudly. 'I don't talk to anyone except the president of the College of Physicians.'

I'm not surprised, Nicholas thinks dispiritedly – you'd both get on like a house on fire.

'Don't exaggerate, Father,' says Abigail. She looks at Nicholas through eyes that brim with the hopelessness of a prisoner who knows there can be no end to their incarceration. 'My father was never the queen's physician, Dr Shelby – just as you were never the Lord Mayor. As I said, it's his wits.'

Nicholas struggles to keep the disappointment from his voice. 'Is there no truth to his words? None at all?'

'Oh, he had ambition aplenty. And for a while he *was* assistant physician to the household of the late queen. But he was confined to treating the grooms, maidservants, chamberers – that manner of person.'

'Never the queen herself?'

'Heavens, no.'

'Was he at court when Mary died?'

'No, Dr Shelby. The papists finally managed to have him dismissed early in '58. I remember it well. I was sixteen. It was snowing the day we left our lodgings at court. I thought it was beautiful. I didn't know it then, but it was the day the marriage interests ended.'

'Then you're quite sure your father was never admitted to the queen's privy chambers? I'm thinking around the time of her second false pregnancy.'

'Quite sure. That Romish persecutor of God's children would never have allowed him in intimate contact with her body – he was not of her superstition. My father was only tolerated in the queen's household because of his skill.'

Nicholas is caught off-guard by the vehemence in her voice. 'Then I am sorry to have troubled you, Mistress Pelham.'

'And I am sorry you've had a wasted journey, Dr Shelby.'

Nicholas resigns himself to the wherry ride back to Southwark. It will be early evening by the time he reaches Poynes Alley. The Banksiders will be strolling in the Paris Garden, taking the air around St Saviour's, ambling up and down St Olave's Street, filling the taverns and the ordinaries with their boisterous chatter. He thinks he might drop by the Jackdaw, because the solitude of his Poynes Alley lodgings does not appeal to his mood. He makes one last effort to gain something from his visit to St Mary Rounceval.

'I happen to have seen a brief note from your father, written a few months before the late queen's death – about the time you left her court,' he tells Abigail Pelham. 'It referred to his treatment of a patient he named only as "M". Have you any idea who that might be?'

'I cannot help you, Dr Shelby. I'm sorry.'

'I came by this note in a rather unconventional way. Can you recall your father losing any of his papers?'

'You've seen how he is, Dr Shelby. He loses things all the time.'

'Might it have been stolen?'

'I'm sure I wouldn't know.'

'Has anyone asked to see any of his papers recently?'

A flash of anger gleams in Abigail Pelham's embittered eyes. 'Why are you asking all these questions, Dr Shelby? You said you'd come here about a patient of his. Now you're talking of stolen papers.'

'Mistress Pelham, I don't wish to pry, but the young lad I spoke of earlier – the son of one of your father's patients – is in grave danger. Your answers could help him.'

She considers this a while, and he knows she's wondering if it's time to close the curtain, to shut out the world beyond the barren cell she now inhabits. To his relief, she decides to keep it open a little longer.

'It was just before Christmas last. A woman came here asking to speak with Father, just as you have today. I saw them together, going through his documents. She was raising her voice with him because he couldn't tell her what she wanted to know. I asked her to leave. She could have taken something – I couldn't tell you for certain.'

'Do you remember her name?'

'Yes, she was a striking woman. She said her name was Isabel Lowell.'

Isabel Lowell... English to her soul... Sir Joshua Wylde's voice echoes in Nicholas's head. And then John Lumley's: *John Lowell and Peter Kirkbie... part of a cabal at court...*

'Tell me, Mistress Pelham,' he says, sensing the knots beginning to unravel, 'where did your father go after he left the court?'

'To a household of quality, Dr Shelby – as their personal physician. A God-fearing family. One that has no truck with vile Romish practices.'

'May I ask the name of this household?'

'It was the Havingtons of Gloucestershire,' she says proudly, as though speaking of the Dudleys or the Devereux.

Nicholas battles to keep his voice steady. 'Did you go with him?'

'No. My mother insisted I remain in London, with an aunt, to better my marriage prospects. I barely saw him again until he returned. By then Father was all but a stranger to me. Nevertheless, I have performed my filial duty as God would wish me to.' She doesn't add, *and besides, the marriage prospects came to naught*, but it's written in her eyes.

'Could the "M" I saw mentioned in your father's note have referred to Mercy Havington?'

Abigail Pelham frowns, as though unable to retrieve the name from her memory. Then she smiles, the lifelong disappointment in her face banished in an instant. 'Oh, you mean dearest Mercy Brooke.'

'Yes. Lady Havington – Sir William's wife.'

'Wife?' she echoes with just the faintest lift of a disapproving eyebrow. 'Oh, Mercy wasn't married at the time of the b—'

Abigail Pelham thrusts a hand in front of her mouth to stop the words escaping. She turns her head from him.

'I assure you, Mistress Pelham,' says Nicholas as diplomatically as he can, desperate to stop her retreating into her solitude, 'nothing you say to me will reach hostile ears. I have already spoken with Mercy Havington at some length. It's her grandson I'm enquiring about. She has enlisted my help.'

She studies him, as though trustworthiness might show itself in the pores of his skin.

'Well, Dr Shelby, I'm sure the birth of a bastard child is not an unfamiliar notion to a physician. It's not as if it hasn't occurred before.'

'Was the birthing at St James's Palace, Mistress Pelham?'

'Of course. Mercy was a chamberer. She helped maintain the queen's presence chamber in its proper state of cleanliness. At court, even those menial tasks are performed by women of good quality.'

'But like your father, Mercy Brooke was also of the new faith, wasn't she? How is it that she was accepted?'

'Dr Shelby, when a storm is raging, it is a wise tree that bends with the wind. And besides, Mercy was beautiful. I may have been young, but even then I'd realized men prefer a court to be prettily decorated.'

'You've been of great assistance, Mistress Pelham. I need detain you no longer.'

'Dr Shelby, you said just now that Mercy's grandson is in danger. What manner of danger?'

'That I cannot tell you. But if you are open with me, it could go a long way towards ensuring his safety.' Or it could mean his death, Nicholas thinks. It all depends on you, Abigail Pelham. 'Do you consider it possible that Mercy's child could have been taken from her, and another infant put in its place?'

Abigail Pelham shakes her head. 'No, Dr Shelby. My father was all too cognizant of the dangers that attended the queen's false pregnancies. There were rumours the Spanish faction might attempt to smuggle an infant into Mary's laying-in chamber, if her belly should once again prove empty. I remember he was most diligent in ensuring that Mercy could not be used in such a fashion. But Mercy's child *was* taken from St James's almost as soon as it was delivered.'

'How do you know that?'

'Because it was I who took her, Dr Shelby. I and my father, together.'

'Why?'

'Because Mercy insisted upon it. She and Sir William had no wish to incur Mary's jealousy if – as my father suspected – the queen's pregnancy came to naught. Nor did they want their own child's soul put at risk by remaining a moment longer than necessary in a papist court.'

The mother sends her heart's felicity... The child is safely delivered unto a place of protection against the malevolent designs of the ungodly... The words seem to float before Nicholas's eyes like spirits released from Purgatory.

'May I ask where the child was taken to, Mistress Pelham?'

'Why, to the Havingtons' home in Gloucestershire, of course – into the care of Sir William's parents.' Abigail Pelham says, as if to a child. She frowns. 'Dr Shelby, is the grandson now in danger because Sir William has finally learned of the questions about his lineage? Is that why you came here seeking my father's help?'

Nicholas feels the ground rock beneath his feet. Surely Abigail Pelham cannot know of the Brothers' belief that Samuel is Mary's grandson.

'Questions? What manner of questions?' he asks, stumbling over the words.

'I mean the gossip. The scandal – about Mercy's other lover.'

'Her *other* lover?' Nicholas repeats, staring at her like the victim of a Bankside gulling.

'I was only sixteen, Dr Shelby,' she says with a sudden smile that transforms her face, 'but I was almost in love with him myself. Every maid in the royal household was.'

'Who?' asks Nicholas a little too loudly, as if he's afraid he'll lose Abigail Pelham to her memories.

'He was one of Philip's young chaplains. An Italian. It was all so long ago, his name escapes me. It began with an F. Fierra... Fortese...' She rests the spread fingers of one hand against her brow. Then she smiles. The years release their cold grip on her face, softening it. 'I have it now! Fiorzi. That was it. Santo Fiorzi.'

19

A fine rain begins to mist the lanes around the Jackdaw as Bianca returns from delivering a salve of liquorice and eyebright to old Mother Sawyer, who lives behind St Saviour's churchyard. The chill makes her realize how ravenous she is. To her delight, when she steps across the taproom threshold she finds the air filled with scents found nowhere else on Bankside. Farzad has cooked one of his spicy concoctions from Araby.

In a corner, three travellers who had turned up an hour ago from Kent, wanting to lodge the night before going across the river to do business in the city, are eagerly emptying their bowls. Nearby, four wherrymen from the Mutton Lane stairs are taking their ease after a day labouring on the river. Bianca notices the ale jugs on each table are almost empty. She looks around for Rose. There's no sign of her. Or Timothy, for that matter.

In the kitchen, Farzad is stirring the cauldron with the concentration of an alchemist. 'Have you seen Rose, Farzad?' she asks.

'They're all upstairs: in Master Barrani's chamber, Mistress,' he says. 'Rose said I was to stay here. I did as she told me, Mistress – without complaint.'

A sudden sense of dread grips her. She takes the stairs two at a time. Reaching the landing, she sees the door to Bruno's chamber is open. Graziano is kneeling by the mattress. Rose is standing beside him.

He's dead, Bianca thinks in a moment of utter desolation. *I've lost him, and it was my fault, because I let Marlowe come here with his stupid play.*

And then Rose looks up and sees her. 'Mistress, come in, quickly!' she cries, the words tumbling out of her mouth. 'It's Master Bruno! His eyes are open! He's awake.'

And as confirmation that she's not making reality out of wishing, Bianca hears Graziano announce, '*Grazie a Dio! È un miracolo!*' in a reverential voice that sounds as if it's come straight from the altar of the little church of St Margaret in Padua.

✠

'You've worked a miracle,' Bianca says, the words spilling out of her when Nicholas arrives, summoned from Poynes Alley by Timothy barely ten minutes after returning from St Mary Rounceval. 'You've saved him!' And for a moment Nicholas thinks she's about to throw herself into his arms. In fact he's somewhat disappointed when she doesn't.

Bruno is lying on his mattress, propped up on the pillow, his eyes open, a slow, measured rhythm to his breathing. Nicholas makes his examination.

'The wound seems clean, no smell of putrefaction. The flesh is a little red, but otherwise healthy.'

Bruno's eyes flicker over Nicholas's face, unquestioning as an infant's. 'I understand I have you to thank for my life, Signor Nicholas,' he says in a voice that falls as lightly as winter leaves.

'Wait until I've removed the sutures before you thank me,' Nicholas says, with a man-to-man smile.

'What's a little hurt after so comfortable a sleep?' Bruno asks, bravely trying to smile back.

'Graziano wants to know if he can be moved to the *Sirena*?' says Bianca when they've left Bruno to rest.

'I think so.' He looks at her with narrowed eyes. 'Does he know what you've discovered?'

'Not yet.'

'Best to keep it that way.'

'Did you learn anything new from your visit to Dr Pelham?'

'Yes. Would you walk with me to Poynes Alley?'

'Why?'

'We need to talk, privily.'

'You said something similar to me at Gravesend,' she says with an ironic laugh. 'It turned out not to be what I was expecting.'

'Did I?'

'Yes, Nicholas – when we were abed at the Swan, remember?' Is that the faintest of blushes she sees on his cheeks?

'Strictly speaking, we weren't actually abed, Mistress Bianca. We were *on* the bed. Talking. I assure you, your modesty was never in danger.'

She sighs sweetly, lifts her farthingale an inch or two off the floor and balances on her toes as if about to break into a measure. 'Hey nonny, nonny, what a fortunate maid am I!' she trills.

If he notices the sarcasm in her voice, he doesn't show it.

✠

The rain has stopped. Tendrils of mist are forming on the water, and from the eves of the houses along the riverbank the bats are darting out to sweep the evening air. A tilt-boat emerges from the piers of London Bridge like a beetle crawling on glass.

'So the young Mercy Brooke was in love with *two* men,' says Bianca as they stand together on the little balcony at Poynes Alley, looking out over the river.

Nicholas has just completed his account of his visit to Charles Pelham's house. 'Did you know Fiorzi had ever come into England?' he asks.

'Of course I didn't.'

'He never spoke of it?'

'Yes, Nicholas, all the time. The cardinal was in the habit of telling me his every secret, down to the last detail of his privy conversations with the Pope. Is there anything else I can tell you? What the queen had for supper last night, perhaps?'

'Foolish of me to ask,' says Nicholas, rolling his eyes.

For a while they stand side-by-side, staring out at the skyline of the north bank – at the wharves around Billingsgate and the houses rising towards Thames Street – saying nothing. Then Bianca asks, 'There's something I don't understand. Why are the Brothers of Antioch so sure that the "M" in Dr Pelham's letter is Mary Tudor and not Mercy Havington?'

'Because Arcampora has convinced Thomas Tyrrell of it.'

'And Tyrrell has convinced Lowell and Kirkbie?'

'Exactly. It's a conspiracy they were already predisposed to believe. All it took was Arcampora to confirm it for them. When we *want* to believe something is true, we're only too happy to lay aside our critical faculties.'

'So Arcampora manufactured proof enough to convince them,' Bianca says, shaking her head in wonder.

'He's keeping Alba's dream alive. He'd do anything to bring down the new faith in England.' Nicholas raises his left hand and taps his right index finger against the ball of the thumb. 'First, there's the letter that was intercepted by Alba's men in Zeeland, which mentions a girl child being born to "M" at St James's Palace. It was probably intended for the young William Havington – who, I imagine, was away from his pregnant betrothed, serving in the Netherlands. I don't know who sent it. Perhaps it was Dr Pelham. Perhaps it was William's father. Either way, it ended up in Spanish hands. Alba's men took the "M" to mean Mary. Arcampora probably found it amongst Alba's records.' Another tap, middle finger against open palm. 'Then there's Dr Pelham's letter – a letter written by a man who had been a physician in Mary's household. That was taken from Pelham's house by Isabel Lowell, around Christmas last.'

'How did she know about Pelham?'

'Arcampora told her. Last Christmas he went to the College of Physicians and spun them a tale about an old acquaintance he wanted to trace. In truth, he was after one of Mary's physicians. Pelham was the only one left alive who'd served in her household.'

'And Isabel Wylde found the letter amongst Pelham's papers?'

'Stole it from under his nose – which wouldn't have been difficult, in the circumstances. It gave credibility to that first letter, written thirty years earlier.' Nicholas brushes his fourth finger against the tip of his left thumb. 'Finally, there's Mary's Will, and the letter about the codicil that was added at the close of her life.'

'The codicil where she admits she wasn't pregnant...'

'Exactly. Arcampora helpfully furnishes the Brothers with a supposed secret testament that it's a forgery. That's what the letter we deciphered claimed: that the codicil was written in a different hand from the rest of the Will. That it had been added *expressly to deceive*. In other words, it claimed Mary had made no such retraction. I'd lay odds it was written recently – probably by Arcampora himself.'

'And you think Isabel Wylde – Isabel Lowell – is John Lowell's daughter?'

'I think she deliberately set about seducing Sir Joshua to get close to Samuel.'

'That's monstrous, Nicholas.'

'They're playing for very high stakes, remember.'

Bianca stares out at the driftwood carried on the current, swept along by forces it is too powerless to resist. 'But *was* there a child?' she whispers. 'And if there was, did she grow up to become Samuel Wylde's mother?'

'The Brothers of Antioch believe so.'

'But Lowell and Kirkbie were part of Mary's inner circle. Surely they must know.'

'They were out of the realm at the time, on an embassy to Philip of Spain. And Tyrrell was not close enough to the queen to know the truth. But both John Lumley and Abigail Pelham told me of the febrile atmosphere at Mary's court. Wild rumours were rife. Those of the new faith feared that even if the pregnancy should prove false, the Spanish faction would attempt to insinuate an infant into the birthing chamber – claim it as Mary's heir. On the other side there were zealots of the old religion who believed that a child *had* been born, and that Protestant agents had stolen it away.'

'So that the throne would pass undisputed to Elizabeth?'

'Yes. The truth may well end up being what the victors in a civil war between the faiths decide it is.'

'And what of Mercy Havington? Do the Brothers of Antioch hold her guilty of being complicit in the stealing-away of this supposed child?'

'If they do, her life is in great danger. Even if they think she was merely an unwitting surrogate, they may still want her dead.'

'Why?'

'To prevent her testifying on oath that the child was hers.'

Bianca turns to him. Even in the dusk he can see her eyes are brimful of fear, the way she looked the night he'd found her in the crypt beneath the Lazar House. And he hates himself for being the agent of its return.

'There's only one person who *really* knows the truth,' he says.

'Mercy Havington.'

'Which is why I have to go back to Gloucestershire.'

'Why should she tell you the truth, Nicholas?'

'Because her life depends upon it; Samuel's, too.'

'But what if someone from Cleevely sees you? Aren't you supposed to be back in the Netherlands, with Sir Joshua Wylde?'

'I promise you I'll stay well away from Cleevely House.'

'And Samuel? What of him, the poor child?'

The little balcony has become Nicholas's confessional. 'The fact that Perkin Warbeck wasn't really the heir of the fourth Edward didn't save him from the scaffold. Samuel Wylde is still in immense danger, whatever the truth. Even more so than Mercy Havington. I need to prise him away from Arcampora and the Brothers of Antioch – before it's too late.'

Bianca's eyes widen as she realizes what he intends to do. 'You're going to *kidnap* him?'

He gives her his best physician's smile.

'I prefer to think of it as changing his doctor.'

✠

Farzad arrives at Poynes Alley within an hour of Bianca's departure. He brings with him a bowl of pottage for Nicholas to heat in the hearth.

'Mistress Bianca had me make it specially,' he says, as though it might be a peace offering. 'She says she will call tomorrow morning, for the bowl. That's what she told me I must say: *Tomorrow. For the bowl.*'

Nicholas gives the lad one of Robert Cecil's silver testers as a reward and sends him on his way.

With the tallow candles lit the room is like a monastery cell, and Nicholas the monkish scribe. He sits down at the table, lays out paper, pen and inkpot, and begins scratching careful lines with the nib. The river murmurs to him through the open window. He pauses occasionally to brush an unruly curl of black hair from his temple, leaving an inky smudge between his right eyebrow and the hairline. The only witnesses to what he writes are the moths attracted by the candlelight.

He composes in Latin, for greater authenticity, though it slows him down. It's what he thinks 'His Eminence' would write, or at least his emissary, Bruno Barrani.

Time, or the lack of it, is his major concern. How long Bruno will remain too weak to pursue Fiorzi's mission – whatever that may be – he cannot say. Despite his small stature, the man has a stout heart. It might be mere days.

It takes several attempts before Nicholas has the letter exactly as he desires, the tone authoritative and conspiratorial in the proper measure. When he's finished, he takes Bianca's bowl of pottage from the table where Farzad left it. He unties the string that secures the cloth cover. Taking off the linen, he turns the cover over and removes the little fold of paper Bianca has pinned there. Opening it up, he sees the line of random letters written on the fabric: Bruno's cipher. Bianca's neat, confident hand encourages him. It speaks of her belief in what he is doing, a shared determination to be careful, yet bold. He goes to work encoding what he has written.

When he's finished, he collects the abandoned drafts and the sheet with the cipher written on it, ready to take them to the hearth and burn them. He lays out the cloth cover to the pottage bowl, and beside it the string that held it in place. As he'd instructed, Bianca has allowed enough cloth for him to cut off a piece in which to wrap the letter, ready for her collection in the morning. He smiles appreciatively. She won't even need to come inside the tenement. They can make the exchange in the street, confident that, should they be observed, all anyone will see is him returning an empty pottage bowl.

Nicholas takes up the tinder box by the grate, flints the tinder aglow and sets a fire burning in the hearth. He places the pottage bowl close by, to heat up. While he's waiting he goes out onto the little narrow balcony to gather his thoughts.

The night is cool. The bridge is a black brooding presence to his left, a few lighted windows in the buildings piercing the darkness like a torchlit procession frozen against the sky. Across the river, lanterns burn on the vessels moored along Galley Quay. Off to his right, across the dark expanse of water, the great Tower squats behind its flinty ramparts like a dark and malevolent hunter come out of its lair in search of prey, a monstrous black toad waiting in the night. He recalls how – not so long ago – he stood in one of its chambers watching a man plead for his life. Who will it be this time? Tyrrell? Arcampora? Samuel Wylde himself? *I've fed you once already*, he thinks, *yet still you're hungry*.

And then, as the smell of warming pottage comes to him through the open door, an idea strikes him out of the darkness, carried on the wind like Tanner Bell's murdered soul crying out for vengeance. He thinks upon it for a while, then returns to the solitude of his cell.

Where he writes – and then enciphers – a second letter.

20

'Do you hear that, Tanner Bell? The Professor says you're a monstrous disappointment to physic.'

Dunstan kicks the heavy chair, sending it skewing sideways. Only Tanner's weight stops it from toppling over.

Florin bends down to Tanner's blood-streaked ear. 'Here we are, risking our immortal souls in His work, and all you can do is dribble! I call you a wicked dissembler, a heretic, a resister against God.'

'Leave him be. The boy is not at fault,' says Arcampora wearily, placing his book of incantations on the table. His face is lined with exhaustion, his eyes streaming with the smoke from the roots and leaves smouldering in the chafing dishes: vervain and barberry to help St Margaret protect them all from the demons he has sought to conjure during the night; culverwort to strengthen the courage of the mute boy into whose body he is attempting to drive them. 'It can be done!' he says, wiping the stinging tears from his eyes with the sleeve of his gown. 'I, Arcampora, know this! Did not our Lord drive a host of demons out of a poor madman and into the Gadarene swine? Every good Christian soul knows this!' He slams his palm down onto the book in frustration.

Taking up the lantern from the table, Arcampora crosses to where Tanner is sitting, his head slumped forward, chin on chest. The physician's boots scuff the chalk circle and the symbols drawn on the floor. No matter – they can be redrawn. He reaches out a gloved hand and tilts Tanner's head back. The boy's eyes look like those of a corpse. The two wounds on his neck, where Arcampora cut the laryngeal nerves, are still raw. That was a mistake, the physician thinks. Robbed of his voice, how will Tanner indicate that a spirit has taken possession of him? Perhaps Lord Tyrrell can be persuaded to send another boy to Cleevely.

Arcampora lowers Tanner's head and regards the aperture drilled into his skull, the surface of the brain quivering like the milky breast of a paramour.

'Deep within this tissue is the *vermis*,' Arcampora begins – though whether he's addressing Dunstan and Florin or a wider, unseen audience is unclear. 'According to the great Galen of antiquity, it is by means of the *vermis* that the flow of sensations to the seat of reason may be controlled. But Galen does not suggest by what mechanism the flow may be altered.' He moves Tanner's head from left to right, as though admiring an ornament. He studies the white forehead glistening with sweat. Somewhere behind it, if the Moor physician Avicenna is right, is the *imaginatio*, the spring from which flows all that a human being might envision. 'Perhaps there is some restriction in the *vermis*, preventing the inflow of the alien spirit,' he suggests, though mostly to himself. 'Or there may be emanations escaping from the brain's ventricles that push against the *pneuma*, preventing it from entering.' He refuses to countenance the other possibility: that he has made an error in the invocation.

Angelo Arcampora has never believed his task would be easy. But he has always known he is the man to do it: to summon the spirits of the dead and make them compliant to his will, ready to do his bidding, controlled and made obedient by his immense knowledge.

There is no other physician in all history, he believes, better skilled to achieve it – even if they did hound him out of Basle for daring to study such mysteries. His knowledge of the ancient texts is unmatched. He has taught himself Hebrew in order to read the *Liber Razielis Archangeli* in its original form. He can recite almost verbatim Weyer's *De Praestigiis Daemonum*; quote at length from the *De Occulta Philosophia* and the *Picatrix*. If an invocation or a spell is written in Aramaic, Chaldean or Ethiop, he alone of any physician known to him can comprehend it. And he knows that accuracy is essential. Just as the Mass must be said faultlessly for it to reach God's ears, so must a spell be recited without error in order to reach the ears of a spirit wandering lost in Purgatory.

No, the fault must lie somewhere inside this boy's brain, somewhere deep, where the corruption of sin bubbles away darkly.

Dunstan and Florin watch their master like infants searching the face of a parent for meaning. It is almost dawn. Surely Dr Arcampora cannot intend to begin the ritual all over again?

All they know for certain, looking at the boy in the chair – everything human, everything lifelike stolen away from him – is that they will have to endure more nights like this before the Professor is ready to attempt his physic on Samuel Wylde.

The *Sirena*'s pinnace has crossed the river every day since Bruno Barrani was attacked. Each morning it has tied up at the Mutton Lane stairs, carrying at least two of her crew on their now-customary pilgrimage to enquire after their master's progress.

At first they had attracted suspicious glances. Thames wherrymen, by their nature, consider every new barge or skiff they see as a rival for the customer's penny. But now it is not unusual to find them drinking together in the Jackdaw, laughing uproariously at their almost complete inability to speak one another's language.

They have even agreed upon a lingua franca: the ale-pot and the dice. So today when Graziano makes the pinnace fast to an eye-bolt on the stairs, no one pays him much heed. Or his three companions. Carrying two long poles and enough canvas and rope to make a serviceable litter, they make their way through the lanes to the Jackdaw.

Nicholas is waiting for them. In the little chamber above the taproom, he makes a final inspection of Bruno's wound. He pronounces himself cautiously satisfied.

Bianca and Rose have washed the patient and dressed him in clean slops and shirt. Ned Monkton and Graziano lift him from the mattress and hold him upright while Bianca wraps him in his mariner's thick twill jerkin. Outside it is a pleasant spring morning, but she doesn't want him catching a chill on the river.

Ned Monkton – larger by far than any man present – hoists Bruno over one shoulder like a bolt of cloth and bears him effortlessly downstairs. Bianca entrusts the balms and salves she has prepared to Graziano's care. She gives him precise instructions for their application: exactly so much of the mullein seeds boiled in wine to be massaged into the scalp around the wound; just this much fluellin to be taken by mouth for its general restorative properties. The crewmen lay Bruno gently on the litter. Then the little procession sets off on the return journey.

At first Bruno peers around at his surroundings in a bemused manner. But then, to Bianca's joy, she notes a growing comprehension in his eyes. As for Bankside in general, it takes no notice whatsoever – prostrate mariners being carried back to their ship after a night's carousing are as common a sight here as the doxies waiting for business in the doorways of the stews.

The pinnace makes its way out through the traffic on the water, turns in the current and heads towards the bridge. For a while Nicholas and Bianca linger on the jetty. They watch the departing figure of Bruno Barrani sitting in the stern, propped against Graziano like an old woman sightseeing on the river in the pleasant company of her family.

'Tell me once again,' Nicholas says, casting a glance around the river stairs to make sure they're alone. 'I must be sure you have it right. Everything depends on the timing.'

'Nicholas, your instructions were simple. I'm not a child – there's nothing amiss with my memory,' Bianca tells him with just a trace of irritation in her voice. 'I'm to deliver the first letter to Munt next Monday. Then, on the day you return, I give him the second letter. Satisfied?'

'That second letter: when you hand it over, make all alarm. Give Munt the impression you've come in haste. Hammer on the door, appear breathless – frightened even.'

'I'll be sure to make him think the Furies are on my tail. Perhaps I'll swoon on his doorstep.'

Nicholas is oblivious to her waspish tone. He's too busy testing the robustness of his plan. He knows it will take a while for Tyrrell to act on the first letter. It will have to be deciphered and its contents read. Then the instructions it contains must be sent to Cleevely. At first Tyrrell will not be unduly alarmed, so the journey is likely to take three days at the very least. Arcampora will then have to make arrangements for the journey to London. He will not ride fast – Samuel's health will not allow it. Ten days at the outside.

For his own part, Nicholas has judged that he can make the round trip to Havington Manor in under seven if he doesn't linger. He'll be back in London long before Arcampora and Samuel Wylde arrive there. If his plan works, Arcampora won't learn of the second letter until he reaches Tyrrell's house in Holborn. It will come as a thunderbolt. And that – if Nicholas has it right – will force Arcampora to act precipitously.

'I wish you'd take Ned with you,' Bianca says, steeling herself for his protests. 'I'd be happier if you weren't going alone.' But when he replies, there's a gentleness in his voice that she isn't expecting.

'You've only just made your peace with Buffle. Given the effect she had on Rose, if Ned comes with me, he's likely to round up every stray dog in the county. Besides, I can travel faster alone. Ned on a horse is not the fleetest thing on the road.'

The laughter lights her face like a glass catching the morning sun. 'Will you tarry a while before you leave?' she asks as they head away from the river. Without thinking, she slips her arm through his. 'The weather's fine. It's not cold. We could walk in the Paris Garden.'

He would like nothing more. Poynes Alley is a bleak and solitary place in which to languish. And when he's in her company he finds he smiles more than he has of late. But it is not possible.

'When I return, I would like nothing better,' he says. 'But I cannot tarry here. Time will not allow it. I must be on my way.'

And though it lasts but a brief moment before Bianca masters it, he sees in her amber eyes a flash of disappointment.

Or there again, perhaps he's mistaken. Perhaps it's fear.

At the livery yard by the Tabard, Nicholas sees to his delight that the chestnut palfrey is back. He pays a week's hire in advance. He leaves instructions that the mare be saddled and ready for collection the day after tomorrow. And he asks, or so the Tabard's ostler will affirm later, for an empty hemp sack, purpose unknown.

Less than an hour later, according to Robert Cecil's man, he's at Billingsgate water-stairs, buying himself a seat on the Long Ferry to Gravesend.

The only other sighting of him, before he returns to London

the next morning, will be made by the Gravesend night-watch. They think they have him on the Hythe a little after midnight, in the company of a man known to them: Porter Bell. When called upon to do so by the Kent coroner, the watch will be unable to describe him in much detail, due to the darkness.

But from the description Cecil's man gives them, they're pretty sure it's him – standing by the water's edge, deep in conversation, they will say in their evidence. Only occasionally looking out at the dark shapes of the ships moored in the Hope Reach. Just two men reliving some past shared experience. Or perhaps a common loss. Causing no hurt to the Queen's Peace. No reason to approach them. Nothing out of the ordinary.

Except that, for the first time the watchmen can remember, Porter Bell appeared not to be drunk.

PART 3

✠

Tilbury

1

Nicholas reaches Havington Manor early in the morning of Easter Eve. The little valley is deep in shadow, darkening clouds dragging misty tendrils of rain across the western sky. He has ridden as hard as he dares, slept little and rested the mare just enough to keep her sound. In the time it has taken him, he has come to a conclusion about Mercy Havington.

To his immense relief, he finds her brother-in-law is out visiting tenants. It makes him wonder what his own father would be doing now at Barnthorpe. Probably checking the barley wasn't growing knee-bent, or searching for signs of locust and caterpillar.

A servant escorts Nicholas to the dairy, where Lady Havington is skimming fat off the milk in the cheese-pans, assisted by two maids. A line of swollen muslin sacks full of broken curds hang from a beam. The liquid drains into a row of pails beneath, making a noise like the aftermath of a heavy shower.

'Why, Dr Shelby! What a joyous surprise,' she says upon seeing him. 'You're lucky I'm still here. I leave tomorrow for London.' She pushes a strand of straw-coloured hair back into place beneath her simple linen coif. 'Forgive me for receiving you in so uncivil a place, but I seem to be fighting a futile campaign against broad-clover. If the cows graze it, we're lucky to get one good cheese in three.'

'My mother swears by a high ceiling, madam,' Nicholas says, smiling in sympathy. 'She keeps our cheeses in the rafters – less heat from the cattle when they're milked.' It's a far better opening play, he thinks, than *I heard you might have had a child by a handsome Catholic chaplain – but your husband always believed it was his.*

'I've never met a physician who could opine on cheese,' she says coquettishly, her wide, generous mouth arcing into an inviting smile. And in that smile Nicholas sees precisely how Santo Fiorzi and William Havington were captured all those years ago.

'My family farms in Suffolk, madam,' he explains. 'When I wasn't studying Galen, Hippocrates and Vesalius at Cambridge, I was pulling turnips or carting truckles of cheese.'

'It is a blessing to have happy memories, is it not?'

He replies with some platitude or other, forgotten before the words are out of his mouth. But he's really wondering if she still thinks of Santo Fiorzi. Or is he now just a hazy ghost to look back upon with a fond smile when thoughts of times past come stealing up unannounced?

'I would be grateful if we could speak privily, madam,' he says.

Mercy Havington wipes her hands on her kirtle. 'Privily? Is this about Samuel?'

'In a manner of speaking.'

On the surface, her look of mild surprise seems genuine enough, but to Nicholas – now that he knows her secret – it seems just a little too practised. She leads him out into the yard, into the shadow of an empty cattle byre.

'Well, Dr Shelby. Is this privy enough for what you have to say?'

He begins almost apologetically. 'Lady Havington, I am the son of a Suffolk yeoman; I have no skill for dissembling. I must speak plainly, even at the risk of causing grave offence. Will you hear me out?'

'It would be unkind of me not to, Dr Shelby. After all, I'm sure you didn't come all this way just to watch a country lady fussing in her dairy.'

'I want to ask you about your daughter, Alice.'

'My Alice is dead, Dr Shelby – in God's peace these past sixteen years. What is she to you, that requires that we disturb her now?'

'It is for the sake of her son – your grandchild – that I ask.'

Mercy Havington considers this for a long time. Her gaze is fixed somewhere in the dark interior of the byre. She seems to be struggling with a dilemma that has no favourable answer.

'Is it important to Samuel that I answer your questions, Dr Shelby?' she says at length. 'Will it help him in his sickness?'

'Madam, the question I need answered is perhaps even more important to Samuel's welfare than the matter of his health.'

There is no mistaking the sudden look of alarm in Mercy Havington's eyes. 'What do you wish to know, Dr Shelby?'

'The true identity of Alice Havington's father.'

She returns his questioning look with silence. He searches her eyes for anger. All he sees is a courage he cannot help but admire. Answer one way, he thinks, and Samuel will be the innocent pawn of other men's ambitions – forgivable, no threat to the state, its queen or its religion. But answer in another, and the comfortable world of Havington Manor will be hurled into the fire of a war between the faiths, closely followed by every house, hearth and family in England.

A long, slow breath, exhaled like someone who's just had a close shave with death. A disturbing stillness. Hands tightened suddenly into fists. All the telltale signs that Mercy Havington has been expecting this moment, in one form or another, for more than thirty years.

'Are you suggesting I betrayed my late husband?' she says evenly. 'Have you come to our house only to call me a whore?'

For a moment Nicholas fears he's lost her.

'On the contrary, madam,' he says, surprised by the huskiness in his own voice. 'The picture I have in my mind is of a young maid who finds herself very much in love with two men. A young woman not afraid to permit herself joy. At this point there is no need to give this young woman a name. Agreed?'

A slow, sad smile.

'How extraordinarily adroit of you, Dr Shelby. Agreed. What else do you see in this wild imagination of yours?'

'I see a young chamberer at the court of Mary Tudor. Pretty, vivacious, with a maid's love of life. A young woman who knows her heart too well to allow it to be imprisoned by certain stern male courtiers. Is it possible you also can see her?'

'Is this a medical diagnosis, Dr Shelby?'

'No, madam. Nothing so ordinary.'

'Then pray continue.'

'I imagine this maid setting her eye upon a handsome young chaplain to the newly crowned King of Spain. An Italian chaplain, serving his most Catholic majesty.'

'Is he *very* handsome, this chaplain?' she asks, a hint of wistfulness in her voice.

'So I am led to believe, madam.'

Lady Havington folds her arms and looks directly into his eyes. 'And does he love her in return – despite his priestly calling?'

'How could he possibly not?'

She seems to find his thesis agreeable. 'Pray continue, Dr Shelby,' she says, folding her arms across her chest. 'This is all most intriguing.'

'There is a problem,' Nicholas announces sadly, clouding the idyllic scene he has created. 'A priest enamoured of a maid is no great marvel. But this maid is of a conflicting faith. Indeed, if it were to be discovered that she was secretly a Protestant, it would go very badly for her, would it not? Given the nature of the times?'

Lady Havington nods her head. Slowly, reflectively. Then, to his immense relief, she takes the narrative from him. Makes it her own.

'But that, Dr Shelby, is the least of our maid's concerns. All too soon the subject of her ardour must return to Spain, with his master, the king.' She stares into the gloom of the byre, remembering. When she turns back to him, he sees her eyes are welling with tears. 'I ask you: what were they supposed to do? How could they deny the love that God had so inconveniently sent them? You are a young man; I am sure you can put yourself in their place. Could you deny your passions, if you knew the object of your desire was about to be torn from you?' She dabs at her eyes with the sleeve of her gown. 'Could you not discover that your heart had the capacity to love two people at once?'

Nicholas bites his lip. It is her story that he has come all this way to hear, not his own. 'No, madam, I could not,' he says, lowering his gaze.

Mercy Havington drops her arms to her sides and smiles. 'In this tale you have spun me, Dr Shelby, does the handsome chaplain have a name, perchance?'

'He does, madam. Santo Fiorzi.'

'And the outcome of this liaison?'

'A child – a girl. I believe she was spirited away soon after birth. Was that because of the mother's faith?'

'You must imagine the atmosphere at court then, Dr Shelby,' Mercy Havington says. 'It was not the first time the queen had erroneously believed herself to be with child. On the previous occasion the royal nursery had been prepared, the celebrations already begun. When it became clear that once again there was to be no heir, well – to bear a child when the queen herself could not...'

'I understand the problem.'

'Then there was the issue of the mother's secret faith – *and* the inconvenient fact that she was, at the time, betrothed to another man. A *good* man.'

'You have been most helpful, Lady Havington.'

'And you, Dr Shelby, have woven an extraordinary tapestry. Engaging, I admit.' A long, exaggerated intake of breath, like someone drawing in the luscious scent of an exotic flower. 'But utterly fictitious, of course.'

'Utterly.'

'And told for no one's ears but ours.'

'You may rely upon it.'

Mercy Havington takes his arm and walks him away from the byre towards the manor house, like a mother with a son she hasn't seen for a while, a lot of catching-up to do. And though it takes him by surprise, he allows himself to be led.

'And the other object of the maid's love,' she says. 'Have you considered *him*?'

'I suspect I would picture him as a young gallant of her own faith, about to depart for the Low Countries, to fight against the religion that prevailed in England at that time. For all our maid knew, he was going to his death. Shall we name him William, just as a convenience?'

'We shall, Dr Shelby. A fine name for such a man.'

'And shall we allow him a safe return from battle? A marriage to the maid? A long and happy life shared together, until his recent death?'

'A most fitting ending to the story, Dr Shelby. Most fitting indeed.'

'Is it possible our William could have been the father of the child, and not the priest?'

She fixes him with a sad smile. 'No, Dr Shelby. It is not. And where would be the profit in him ever having learned the truth?'

They have almost reached the house. Through the open door into the hall, Nicholas can hear voices – Lady Havington's brother-in-law has arrived home. He must hurry if he is to put the last brushstrokes to the canvas. He pictures in his mind the lines deciphered from Tyrrell's papers: *The following was intercepted by agents of the Holy Office of the Faith in the rebellious province of Zeeland... Rejoice in the knowledge that a girl child was safely delivered...*

'Can you tell me, Lady Havington, was there ever a letter written – a letter sent abroad to William – telling him of the birth?'

She looks at Nicholas with a hint of surprised admiration. 'Indeed there was, Dr Shelby, though I cannot imagine how you would know. The letter was intended to warm his heart and give him courage. Remember, at the time he was a young man battling the enemies of Christ in a foreign land. And he believed the child was his.'

'Does the letter still exist?'

'I doubt it. The courier into whose hands it was entrusted never returned. His fate is unknown, either to the author of the letter or to its intended recipient. Perhaps he fell into an ambush. The Low Countries were as dangerous then as they are today, Dr Shelby.'

He nods. 'A final enquiry, madam; then I will trouble you no further. Has the maid heard from the child's real father since that time – perhaps recently?'

But Mercy Havington has already let go of his arm. She strides into the house to greet her brother-in-law. She doesn't look back at Nicholas, even though he's certain she heard every word of his question.

✠

An hour later Nicholas is riding down the grassy slope outside Cleevely, past the ruins of an old abbey and on towards the beech wood. Since leaving Havington Manor the weather has broken, black clouds heavy with rain hugging the hilltops. And his thoughts have turned from Mercy Havington's long-ago romantic entanglements to something much grimmer. He can hear Bianca's warning in his head: *What if someone from Cleevely sees you?*

But this is something he knows he must do. I owe this to Tanner Bell, he tells himself. I owe it to his father, Porter – not least because I didn't have the courage to tell him I found his son's bones lying in a pitiful pile under the leaves in this little Gloucestershire wood; that there is no possibility he will ever see either of his boys again, this side of the final resurrection.

He's thought it through carefully. It won't delay him long – an hour or two at the most. He will gather up as much of the remains as he can. He will put them in the hemp sack that he brought with him from the Tabard's livery yard. Then, taking care to ensure he is unobserved, he will leave the sack at the first suitable country church he comes across on the ride back to London. Knowing the snail-like progress of officialdom in the countryside, it will be many days before the county coroner empanels a jury to investigate the bones. With no certain indication as to whose remains they are, no witnesses and no suspects, a verdict of death by assault and ambush will most likely be recorded. Possibly even a verdict of misfortune – he wouldn't put it past a county coroner's jury to miss completely the clear evidence of trepanning. But most important, Tanner Bell will finally be laid to rest in consecrated ground.

He has entered the beech wood now, the track winding like a narrow ravine through the trees. He can hear the rooks calling in alarm at his approach.

He finds the old broken tree-trunk almost exactly where he'd expected it to be, torn out of the ground as though by some giant hand, the rotting bark tuberous with scalycap and black-tooth. He dismounts and ties the mare's reins around a young birch that's grown in the space cleared by the fallen tree. Taking the hemp sack from his saddle pack, he strikes out confidently to where he and Ned temporarily re-interred Tanner Bell's bones under a covering of rocks. He swiftly finds the spot, beneath a tangle of roots projecting from an over-hang. To his relief, the temporary grave hasn't been disturbed by foxes. Tugging his gloves tighter over his hands, Nicholas begins to move the rocks aside. The lingering stench of putre-faction turns his stomach.

As he uncovers the pitiful remains of what he assumes is Tanner Bell, Nicholas thinks of Angelo Arcampora with mount-ing rage. Only a man possessed of a colossal self-regard could dare do what he has done: enter an enemy's kingdom with an enemy's blood already on his hands, utterly confident that no one will find out who he is or what he's done – and then engage in a conspiracy to overthrow its established religion, using an innocent sixteen-year-old boy stricken by the falling sickness. What manner of devil is he?

As he places the bones in the hemp sack, Nicholas ima-gines the unknown faces of John Lowell and Peter Kirkbie. They are puppet masters, dressed in the finery of self-pro-fessed piety, playing with other people's lives from the safety of their seminaries and their foreign courts, unshakeable in their conviction that there is no suffering too great to inflict on others in the pursuit of their own certainties. Without them, he thinks, Angelo Arcampora would be just another wandering mountebank.

With a surge of angry resolve in his heart, Nicholas remem-bers today is the day Bianca will deliver the first letter to Lord Tyrrell's man, Munt. If his plan works as he hopes, the letter will set in motion a chain of events that will free Samuel Wylde from the Brothers of Antioch. Now that he's certain the boy cannot be Mary Tudor's grandson, the battle to come seems to him even more just.

He wonders what role Bruno Barrani is playing in this conspiracy. In the short time before the riot at the Jackdaw, he had come to like Bianca's cousin. He tries to put aside the thought that Bruno could well be a part of the Brothers' plan. Even if he's simply a courier for Santo Fiorzi, that still makes him an enemy to England. It would be better for everyone, now that he is safely aboard, that the *Sirena* sails on the first favourable tide.

The wind has quickened, roiling the darkening clouds. The leaves make a sound like grain flowing through a colander. Or sand through an hourglass. Nicholas is so intent on his task and his thoughts that he barely registers the skittish sound of the palfrey pulling on her tether.

And then, from somewhere close by, comes the sudden sharp report of a dead branch cracking underfoot.

✠

In her physic garden by the river, Bianca Merton trails a hand across the leaves to catch their scents: wild marjoram for relieving maladies of the ears; lovage for the ague; heart's-ease for treating the falling sickness in children... She thinks, if only there was something here to settle a heart that threatens to beat itself off its peg.

Curiosità – that's what her mother had always warned would be her undoing. If only she had put Bruno's black doeskin gloves straight back into the sack that day in his chamber with Rose. Then she would be party to none of this. Oblivious. Innocent.

But still it wouldn't matter. Because Nicholas went to Cleevely and unravelled the conspiracy from the other end. He went because he owed his life to Joshua Wylde, and his purse to Robert Cecil. And, innocent or not, she is irrevocably tied to him.

Yesterday, after the crowds had dispersed from the sermon, she went across the bridge to see Munt at Petty Wales – a day earlier than Nicholas had instructed. It had felt like walking into the bear-pit. But she wasn't going to risk discovering that he'd chosen today to visit his sick mother or an aunt in the country. Be ready, she'd warned him in a serious voice that did not come naturally to her. I will have news for you on the morrow.

'Master Barrani is recovered?' Munt had asked hopefully, as though he'd rather deal with Bruno than a woman.

'He is still unable to leave his bed,' she had told him with what she hoped was convincing sadness. 'I fear Lord Tyrrell will have to deal with *me* a while longer.'

She's hidden the two letters Nicholas wrote, along with Tyrrell's, here in her physic garden. Though she's had no glimpse of her cloaked follower over the past few days, she is taking no chances.

She locates the distinctive holly branch. She drops down, tugging her gown away from her shins, and rolls away the heavy lump of plaster. With her face just inches from the old wall, she reaches inside the cavity in the brickwork.

Her fingers stub against nothing but masonry.

She moves her hand around. Searching.

Still nothing.

Bianca begins to scratch at the walls of the cavity with increasing desperation, like someone who's been buried alive. But the package containing the deciphered papers has gone.

For a moment she tells herself she's made a stupid mistake. She's picked the wrong place. There's another stone, another cavity in the wall, just a foot or so from this one.

But she knows there is not.

Bianca jumps to her feet. She stares wildly around the physic garden, her mind filled with a dread a thousand fathoms deep.

And then she sees him.

From the doorway to the lane a tall, well-built figure is watching her. A figure in a brownish-black cloak.

2

In the beech wood there is no echo to the snapping of the branch, just the flat *crack* of a neck breaking at a hanging. But it's enough to set the rooks cawing in the treetops. Enough of a surprise for Nicholas to let go of the half-filled sack and turn his head, searching for the source of the noise.

Further down the slope, perhaps fifty yards away, he catches a fragmented glimpse of something moving amongst the trees.

Let it be nothing but a hind or a stag, he prays. He crouches to make himself less visible. Steadying his breathing, he scans the tangle of ferns and bracken.

There – between those two gnarled old trunks and the sapling, fighting them for a share of the light: a thickset figure in a stained leather tabard, trunk-hose and boots. Nicholas worms his way deeper into the undergrowth, frightened that the slightest noise will attract the man's attention. Is he a poacher? A villager out collecting kindling? Or something more dangerous: a cut-purse perhaps? Whoever he is, he's coming this way.

The man stops barely twenty feet off. He looks around, unpoints his hose and relieves himself against a tree. With mounting dread, Nicholas recognizes the momentarily beatific face. It's one of Arcampora's two companions. Has he seen the tethered palfrey? Nicholas wonders. Does he know I'm here?

Silently Nicholas lies flat amongst the undergrowth. The earthy tang of the woodland floor is sharp in his nostrils. A small beetle crawls from under one of Tanner Bell's half-scoured ribs, which are lying close by, and makes an unhurried excursion over Nicholas's wrist between his glove and the sleeve of his doublet. He forces himself to resist the urge to brush it away.

The man re-laces his hose and continues his journey into the beech wood. Nicholas clings to the earth for what seems an age, until certain he is out of hearing. Then he hurriedly completes his macabre task and carries the sack containing Tanner Bell's remains back to where the palfrey is tethered. He ties the sack to the saddlebag, hoists himself into the saddle and rides down to re-join the track out of the beech wood.

He can smell rain in the air now. The wind has picked up, dragging the black clouds closer to the treetops. He brings the mare to a halt, twists in the saddle to pull his riding gaberdine from his pack and struggles into it.

As he rounds the next bend, a horseman blocks the way ahead.

It's the second of Arcampora's companions. And on his face is a grim smile of recognition.

A hunter's smile.

3

Bianca stands with her back to the physic garden wall. On either side the gable ends of the two adjacent houses confine her like guards waiting at the steps of a scaffold. The only way out is ahead of her, through the door that leads to the derelict plot of mud and rubble and the alleyway beyond. And to reach *that*, she must pass the man in the cloak.

She knows he hasn't wandered in by chance; she'd closed the door behind her on entering. Besides, in his right hand is the sailcloth parcel containing Tyrrell's papers and Nicholas's two letters.

Is he one of Tyrrell's men, come to kill her for meddling? Or is he one of Robert Cecil's, come to arrest her for treason? Her mouth has suddenly become as dry as ash. Deep in her stomach, a large spider seems to be scuttling around. Cornered, Bianca looks for something to use as a weapon. Her garden hoe is propped against the wall to her right. With its iron blade it would make a handy pike. But it's too far away to reach. Her garden tools – including a sharp pruning knife – are neatly set away in a box a yard further on.

Use your nails, she thinks. Use your feet, knees, elbows; fight him the way a maid born in Padua would fight: like a wildcat.

But what would be the point? He already has the letters and Tyrrell's papers. Besides, the lethargy of utter defeat has robbed her limbs of their strength. All Bianca can do is stand and wait for the *coup de grâce*.

And then, with his free hand, the stranger pulls aside the hood of his cloak. Bianca is staring like a deranged woman at the grizzled face of Graziano, the *Sirena*'s mascot, her cousin's lucky charm, his *portafortuna*.

Suddenly she remembers the day she met him coming down the stairs from Bruno's chamber, the day she noticed the lock on her cousin's clothes chest had survived an attempt to prise it open.

'What are you about, Graziano?' she demands, no longer afraid, but angrier than she can ever remember. 'This is my private sanctuary. How dare you follow me here, giving me the fright of my life!'

But he has one shock left in store for her. And it's greater by far than any that has preceded it in the last few moments.

In their shared Italian of the Veneto, and in the voice that she has so often thought was somehow familiar, he says, 'Do not fear me, *Passerotto* – show me you are God's obedient child.'

And with that, he holds out his right hand for her to kiss, despite the fact he's not wearing his cardinal's ring, or his cardinal's scarlet cassock, and looks less like the Santo Fiorzi she remembers of old than she could ever have imagined possible.

4

Nicholas brings the mare to a halt barely two paces from where the rider blocks his way.

'We've all been wondering if you'd come back,' the man says, his voice hard and accusing. 'The Professor told us you might.'

Nicholas assesses his chances of talking his way out of the situation. If the rider finds Tanner Bell's bones in the sack tied to his saddle, those chances are non-existent. 'I don't know what you're talking about,' he says, his words sounding lame and unconvincing. 'I think you've mistaken me for someone else. Please, stand aside and let me be on my way.'

The rider sets his jaw like a man squaring up for a fight. 'Dr Arcampora said you weren't who you claimed to be. "Dunstan," he said to me, "that rogue was too clever by half to be a soldier of the heretics." Looks like he was right.'

Nicholas hears the sound of hooves approaching on the track behind him. He glances over his shoulder. A second rider is coming up at a fast trot. It's the man in the leather tabard.

'Look what we've caught ourselves, Florin,' the first rider calls out.

'It can't be him, Dunstan,' the second replies with a sneer. 'That fellow told our master he was going straight back to Flanders.' He gives Nicholas a hard look. 'What happened – miss the tide, did you?'

No way forward. No way back. Only the darkness of the wood on either side. Nicholas takes his right hand from the reins and tries to ease it under the gaberdine to find the hilt of his poniard. He's never been in a knife fight before. He doesn't think much of his chances. Not against these two.

'That will do, fellow,' Dunstan warns, drawing an inch or two of steel from the sheath of his own weapon. 'No call to be hasty, now.'

Florin brings his horse closer. 'And what do we have here, then?' he asks, glancing at the sack tied to Nicholas's pack. 'Been hunting coney, have we?' He sniffs the air. 'Smells too ripe for coney.' He leans forward to take a closer look, balancing himself on one stirrup, his body half out of the saddle.

At that moment the black clouds break overhead. A sudden torrent of rain crashes into the beech wood. In an instant, a cold vapour has washed the colour from the trees, turning everything a misty white.

The sudden squall brings Florin's horse close to panic. Nicholas seizes his moment. He grabs Florin by his tabard and slams him down with all his strength onto his own saddle pommel, leaving a long, thin smear of blood on the leather. Florin rolls off the mare's shoulder and onto the path, stunned. At the same time Nicholas rams his spurs into the mare's sides. She rears wildly, her forelegs flailing. Dunstan wheels his horse out of reach.

Nicholas wrenches his mount's head to the right, again sinking his heels deep into her ribs. She turns faultlessly on her hind-quarters. Then she plunges into the shelter of the trees, giving Nicholas barely an instant to thank the nameless horse-master who schooled her.

✠

Now the beech wood closes around him, as much enemy as friend. A leafy serpent coiling itself around its prey. Squeezing. Smothering.

Green scales tumble before Nicholas's eyes as the smaller branches shatter to his plunging flight. Dunstan's curses fall away behind. Soon there is only the sound of his own breathing and the wild song of the mare's flight. It sounds to him much like the roaring of the dark river, when he went into it to drown out Eleanor's voice. But the voice urging him on is clearly Bianca's.

He has no idea where he's going. All he can do is give the mare her head, trust to her fleetness. And she, in return, seems to know the danger they are in. She flies through the undergrowth, leaping fallen boughs, turning so abruptly that Nicholas is sure they'll both be pitched into the stout trunks and dashed all to pieces.

Then, as suddenly as it had swallowed him, the beech wood expels him into a small glade. He brings the mare to a halt. Her flanks heave; clouds of vaporous exertion billow from her tossing head.

At the centre of the clearing, derelict amongst the scrub and meadow grass, stands an abandoned lodge. The walls are covered in moss and ivy.

The windows, long ago put out, are black and empty, blind eye-sockets in a dead face. Nicholas guesses the place must have served Cleevely Abbey, before the religious houses were cast down by the queen's father, fifty years or more ago. Something about the place instantly makes him understand that it is here, not Cleevely, where Arcampora's corrupt physic is practised. It is Porter Bell's prison transferred from Holland, and from down the years. A sense of deep unease pools in his stomach.

He lets the mare draw breath. She's no use to him exhausted. The rain rattles against his gaberdine. Only now does he have the time to realize it's found its way inside, through the points of his canvas doublet and into his shirt, soaking him, mixing with his sweat in a cold embrace that makes him wonder if Tanner Bell's bones haven't reassembled themselves and are now clinging to him for the ride. This damp misery is deepened by an overwhelming sense of despair. His plan is in ruins. Warned of his presence, Arcampora will spirit Samuel Wylde away to somewhere Nicholas can't find him. It has all been for nothing.

For an instant he considers taking shelter in the abandoned lodge. But he daren't risk it. Florin and Dunstan are bound to be combing the wood for him. Wiser, he thinks, to get as far away from Cleevely as he can. Morose, defeated, he takes up the reins again.

He has almost reached the cover of the trees again when he hears the whinnying of a horse put to the spur. Looking back over his shoulder, he sees the two riders burst out of the wood barely fifty yards away. Florin, with his bloody face, looks like one of Kit Marlowe's imaginary demons. With a muttered apology to the mare for what he must ask of her again, Nicholas slams in his heels and, in less than ten strides, she carries him into the trees.

Now the beech wood has truly become his enemy. Low branches rush at him, threatening to sweep him from the saddle, senseless or dead. He crouches low over the mare's plunging neck. Rainwater flies off the leaves and into his eyes as though he's thrust his face into a torrent. The ride has become an insane galloping *volta*, with no pause for breath and no end – other than escape or capture.

A branch slams into his left thigh so hard he thinks for a moment he's been impaled. He glances back and sees the bag containing the mortal remains of Tanner Bell tumbling into the undergrowth. It's as though his last chance to do something decent in the face of Arcampora's monstrous scheme has been stolen from him – a betrayal of everything he had promised Porter Bell that cold night on the Hythe at Gravesend.

The ground appears to be rising now, though Nicholas wonders if it's an illusion brought on by the blur of the undergrowth rushing past. The trees seem less densely packed here. More glimpses of the thunderous sky through the canopy.

Only in the last few yards before the edge of the beech wood does he see that his senses have not deceived him. The ground *has* been rising. The horse is carrying him blindly towards the edge of a cliff. Nicholas cries out a warning and hauls on the reins.

Legs flailing, the mare stops barely a stride from the drop. Her flanks heave with exertion. Plumes of vapour spill from her spume-flecked nostrils. Had he checked her a second later, they would both now be tumbling to destruction.

Looking over the mare's neck, Nicholas can see the ground falls away precipitously to a stream some fifty feet below. The rim cascades with muddy rainwater and debris from their sudden stop. It's not quite a waterfall, but it might as well be.

Now he can hear the noise of Florin and Dunstan approaching at speed through the wood behind him. There is nowhere for him to go but forward.

To ask the mare to attempt the drop is more than he has any right to demand. But he has no choice. Filling his heaving lungs with air, Nicholas urges her on.

She resists, her body tensing with fear. Her stamping hooves send a miniature avalanche of earth tumbling down the slope. He cannot blame her. She has carried him this far without complaint. Hating himself for what he is about to ask, he once again slams his heels into her flanks.

For one extraordinary moment Nicholas has the sensation they are flying. And then their plunging journey begins.

At one point he feels her body sinking, thinks her legs are smashed. That she's sliding on her belly to destruction. At another, he's staring in horror almost vertically down over her head, about to tumble forward into the path of half a ton of falling horseflesh. Together they are making a descent into hell, swept down in a hail of flying stones and earth.

It feels like an age. In reality it lasts only a few heartbeats. And then, to his astonishment, the world rights itself. Horse and rider are standing beside the stream. Dazed, bruised, breathing in violent spasms, but alive.

Looking up at the rim of the drop, Nicholas can only wonder how they have managed it without catastrophe. He allows himself a grim smile of satisfaction. Across the stream lie open fields and safety. He begins to shorten the reins in preparation.

And then a shout makes him look up again.

At the edge of the precipice stands a dismounted Dunstan. He's holding something in his hand. Even at a distance, Nicholas recognizes it as a wheel-lock pistol.

Instinctively he gauges the chances of an accurate shot. High, but not certain. Far less if he's not a sitting target. Still looking back and up, Nicholas sets his spurs once more to the mare's sides. And as he does so, time itself seems to slow again.

Given the luxury of reflection, he would say that what he saw was impossible, that in reality a human eye is not fast enough to record the sequence of events. So it must be his imagination alone that sees the pistol so clearly. The primed dog-head turning on its spring, driving the flint into the pan. The brief flare of the priming charge igniting. The flash from the muzzle.

Nicholas senses the breath of the ball as it passes close by his head. The sound of the shot roars around the slope and out into the open fields beyond.

Dunstan has missed.

And then the mare begins to sink to the ground, as though she's had enough of galloping. As though she can give him no more of her heart.

Nicholas feels the splash of her brave blood on his face. By the way she goes down, he would know she's already dead – were it not for the fact that he's already tumbling over her back and into the stream.

5

It cannot be him.

It cannot possibly be him.

But it has always been him. It's just that she couldn't see it: Santo Fiorzi, in the flesh. Even if it is flesh considerably less magnificent than the last time she'd been in his presence.

As the little craft makes for Galley Quay, Bianca finally accepts that, despite the familiarity of that deep, pious voice, there was never a chance she could have guessed the true identity of the man with the lined face and white stubble who now watches her so intently through grey, contemplative eyes.

She had stopped carrying his secret messages when her father was arrested, still not out of her teens. She can't have seen him more than a handful of times since then. Not at all in the last six years. And until today, she'd never witnessed him in anything other than his immaculate vestments, a scarlet silk biretta on his head, an imposing beard upon his chin. She consoles herself with the knowledge that not even Father Rossi would recognize him now.

This realization does not comfort her. She remembers only too well that Santo Fiorzi was one of the members of the Holy Office of the Faith who had condemned her father to a lingering end in a cold cell, for the heretical books he had written. Just because he once called her his *Passerotto* doesn't mean he's a friend.

The pinnace slams against the *Sirena*'s hull, buffeted by the swell. The crew make fast to a trailing line and help Bianca to the bottom rung of a swaying rope ladder. She begins to climb the slick wet side of the ship. When she risks a glance down at the heaving water below, her stomach lurches. She feels the bile rise in her throat. If her hands slip on the rope, if she falls between the pinnace and the ship, there is but one certain end: crushed into paste, like a handful of seeds in her apothecary's mortar.

Looking up doesn't offer a much better prospect. Somehow – in her heavy woollen kirtle – she will have to get over the painted bulwark and onto the deck without looking like a turkey felled by a hunter's lucky shot. Crushing she can bear, but humiliation before Bruno's crew is another matter entirely. Summoning up her resolve, she manages it with no more indignity than having to reach out a hand to Luzzi, the sailing master, for assistance.

Inside the small cabin on the *Sirena*'s high, sloping stern, Bruno lies in his cot, propped up against a bolster. Bianca smiles as she sees he's waxed his mustachios into something approaching their former glory. He reaches out to clasp her hand, his voice still a dry husk compared to its former chirpiness.

'Graziano tells me I look like a wild savage with the flux.'

'You look a lot better than you did, Bruno, believe me,' she says, laying a hand on his cheek. 'And you may dispense with the deception, Cousin. I *know* who Graziano is.'

A flicker of alarm plays across Bruno's pale face.

'I had no choice,' the cardinal says, spreading his hands in admission. 'I've been keeping an eye on her while you were out of your wits. Your cousin is an enterprising young woman; though I have to say she seems possessed of a dangerous curiosity. It appears to run in the Merton family.'

The allusion to her father removes the last constraint on Bianca's temper.

'Not content with following me around like a common cut-purse, you've also tried to break into a chest of mine at the Jackdaw *and* stolen personal items from my physic garden!'

She stops, scarcely able to believe she's addressing a cardinal of holy mother church in such an insolent fashion. If Father Rossi could hear her now, he'd throw up his hands in horror and scuttle about on his ancient bowed legs like a crab poked with a stick.

Fiorzi, however, seems unperturbed; even amused. 'I think you'll find, Mistress Bianca, the items I took from your hiding place were not in fact yours.' He reaches inside his cloak and pulls out the sailcloth parcel. Untying the binding, he spills its contents out onto the little cabin table: Tyrrell's papers, the deciphered copies, and the two letters Nicholas wrote in his Poynes Alley tenement – the first of which she should, at this very moment, be delivering to Munt's warehouse on Petty Wales, but which now lie before her like damning evidence in a trial.

6

Nicholas lies on the cold stone floor of the lodge in the beech wood. He flinches as his tongue finds the rip Florin's fist has put in his upper lip. Through one eye he can make out a wash of pale light spilling through the windows. The other eye is too swollen to see out of. His medical opinion is that it could have been worse. His body will need some persuading.

Missing two teeth to the pommel of Nicholas's saddle, Florin's initial intent had been to batter Nicholas into insensibility and throw him in the stream with the carcass of the mare. Dunstan had allowed him his fun for a while, then – just as Nicholas had begun to think he was going to die – he'd casually suggested to Florin their master might not thank them for killing their prisoner before he'd been properly invited to explain his return to Cleevely.

But Florin said he hadn't enjoyed himself enough yet. So Dunstan had let him hit Nicholas twice more: two really vicious jabs that took the wind out of his lungs so violently he thought it had flown away, never to return. Then they'd thrown him over the saddle of Dunstan's horse and brought him back to the abandoned lodge, locked him in and ridden away – though, to be honest, that part is remembered only in fragments.

For a while now the only sounds have been the burbling of his own breath through the blood in his mouth, the ringing in his ears and the intermittent pattering of rain showers on the old slate roof. But now the ringing has faded, replaced by a dry, scratching noise he can't quite place.

Nicholas rolls onto his side and curls up. The posture gives him the opportunity to explore his arms and legs, to confirm that Florin's exuberant sallies with his boots haven't caused lasting damage. All seems to be intact. Mere bruises are easily dealt with, he thinks. Bianca would make up a balm of pimpernel, adder's tongue and mother-wort. Picturing her at work at her apothecary's bench in the little chamber beneath the Jackdaw's taproom, her amber eyes gleaming with satisfaction at her skill, the distance between them strikes home, filling Nicholas with a sense of almost unbearable loneliness.

✠

'Perhaps you could enlighten us as to how these came to be hidden away in your garden, Mistress Bianca,' says Santo Fiorzi, sweeping a hand above the papers strewn across the little table.

When she was young and her father had caught her red-handed at some mischief or other, her response had always been to maintain an innocent silence, betrayed only by the biting of her lower lip. By old habit, she does this now.

The cardinal's expression hardens. She wonders if he plans to strike her, beat a confession out of her. Being a member of the Holy Office of the Faith, he would be skilled in that line of work.

'I think you already know what they are, Your Eminence,' she replies at length, thinking how absurd it is to address a man in a sailor's jerkin and slops so formally, yet unable to prevent herself.

'I know one thing, Mistress Bianca: they were not intended for you to see.' A sudden flicker of admiration crosses his grizzled face. 'Let alone read.'

From his cot, Bruno stares at her open mouthed. 'She's *read* them? How?'

'She found the key to our cipher, Bruno – in your glove.'

'You should have had the stitching done better, if you didn't want anyone to notice,' she protests.

'Not content with that, she thought she would keep your appointment with Signor Munt,' says Fiorzi, as if he can't quite believe it himself.

'I was afraid Bruno was involved in something dangerous. I was right, wasn't I?'

'I followed her to Munt's warehouse, where – I presume – she presented herself as your emissary,' says Fiorzi. 'Because she came away with these.' He gathers up the papers and regards them like a hand of cards.

'Does His Eminence speak the truth, Cousin?'

'You could hardly have gone yourself. You were at death's door.'

'Oh, that's not all, Bruno,' Fiorzi says. 'Only the Almighty knows how, but by the look of it, she's even managed to decipher them and translate them into English! All save these two. They're still enciphered.'

'How in the name of all the saints did you break the code?' Bruno asks.

'Father Rossi taught us all the dates on which the Holy Fathers met their rewards in heaven. It was just a matter of trial and error to come up with the right page.'

'It's good to see our priests know how to school their flock,' says Fiorzi without the slightest trace of humour in his voice. He lays the papers back on the table. 'The question is: Do you understand what these are, Mistress Bianca? Do you comprehend their import?'

'One is a letter from Lord Tyrrell, addressed to "His Eminence". As there's unlikely to be another cardinal presently in England,

I assume that's you. All but two of the others contain the proof that you came all this way to receive at first hand.'

'And what manner of proof would that be, Mistress Bianca?' Fiorzi asks. 'Proof of what, exactly?'

He's still being cautious, she thinks. Even here, away from prying ears and eyes, he still won't put a name to his conspiracy. Doesn't he realize that if she was going to betray him to the Privy Council, she would have done so long ago?

'Proof the Brothers of Antioch have found Mary Tudor's living heir,' she says bluntly. 'That's what you've come all this way to see at first hand, isn't it?' Turning to Bruno, she adds, 'That was the "privy matter" you tried to embroil me in. What was it you told me – that day Munt came aboard the *Sirena*? Something about His Eminence needing someone he can trust in this den of disbelievers.'

Fiorzi's craggy face remains immobile. Bruno's, however, has drained of whatever colour it has managed to recover since he awoke. For a moment she fears he's about to suffer a relapse.

'And why would I – or your cousin – wish to see proof of such a thing?' Fiorzi asks calmly, still testing her.

'Because you intend to put Samuel Wylde on the throne of England, in place of Elizabeth. You want a holy war in this realm against those you consider heretics. And whether he's your grandson or Mary's, all you need is enough people to believe in him and then you can launch it!'

For a moment Fiorzi makes no response. His face remains so immobile it could be carved from brown Tivoli marble. If you speak personally to God every day, Bianca supposes, there's probably little that is likely to shock you.

From his cot, Bruno says softly, 'She won't betray us, Eminence. I'll stake my soul on it.'

Bianca wonders if he's just made a plea to spare her life. 'Well, you didn't come here disguised as a humble mariner simply to help my cousin sell his rice, did you?' she says defiantly.

'And how *should* I have come, Mistress Bianca? Do you imagine Robert Cecil would have welcomed me with open arms if I had arrived fully caparisoned in scarlet? Did your father not tell you the English have a tradition of beheading their cardinals?'

'To be honest, I don't care whether you wear a cardinal's cassock or a bishop's mitre. I don't care whether you pray in Latin or in English. I don't care if you think the wafer and the wine are the body and blood of Our Saviour or you don't. I just wish you'd all stop writing your arguments in other people's blood!'

'Is that truly what you think we came here for, Mistress Bianca?' asks the cardinal. 'To satisfy the fantasies of a cabal of embittered old men?'

Bianca stares at him. Even God, she thinks, couldn't read a man's thoughts through such impenetrable eyes.

'Well, *isn't* it?'

Bruno lies back in his cot with a faint smile of understanding playing on his bloodless lips. 'I suppose my cousin has a right to know, Eminence,' he says, turning his face towards Santo Fiorzi. 'Perhaps you had better tell her the truth.'

✠

Santo Fiorzi tells his story in a voice made for chapels and for altars. For Bianca, it is hard not to imagine she is once again sitting in the little church of St Margaret, listening to him explain why God has to punish, even when he loves. There's reverence in his voice, yet it also carries a warning. No longer the humble and insignificant ship's *portafortuna*, Fiorzi has become another man entirely. He has become the man she remembers.

He tells her how Arcampora appeared out of the blue at his chambers in the Holy Office of the Faith in Rome. 'He had somehow learned of my chaplaincy to Philip of Spain. He assumed that I had channels – privy channels – to his most Catholic majesty. He claimed he could provide Philip with proof that there had been a child – a daughter – born in secret to Mary Tudor. A child who had grown to womanhood and been delivered of a son.' Fiorzi spreads his hands to indicate how astonished he had been by the claim. 'You may imagine with what excitement I, a cardinal of holy mother church, received this news.'

Bianca says nothing. This is the man who'd once seemed able to look into her heart with ease. Now she'd rather he didn't.

'Arcampora said he had the backing of the Sworn Brothers of Antioch,' Fiorzi continues, 'I already knew who they were: three Englishmen – Thomas Tyrrell, John Lowell and Peter Kirkbie. I'd met all three in my time in England. I knew them as deeply pious men. I was therefore inclined to trust him.'

Fiorzi breaks his rhythm, sighs and allows her to see – just for an instant – a flicker of pain in his eyes.

'But Arcampora also tells me the boy is sickly; that he suffers from the sacred disease. And whether you are a cardinal or a tavern-mistress, you will know that a sickly king is no king at all.'

'And Arcampora told you he could cure him?' Bianca says boldly, remembering her conversations with Nicholas.

Fiorzi nods. 'What Arcampora didn't know was that my privy channels to Philip of Spain have long since been dammed up. That is because I have come to believe that war and violent suppression are not the way to change the hearts of the heretical. Nevertheless, he was offering me the opportunity to wrest England from the Antichrist. That, Mistress Bianca, is a desire that has burned in the hearts of followers of the one true faith for over thirty years. I hope it has not died in yours.' He allows himself a wry smile. 'I have to confess, *Passerotto*, I am almost proud of your achievement. I must have schooled you well.'

'I did need just a little help – with the Latin.'

'*Help?*'

Fiorzi grasps her arm as if he means to crush it. 'You have shared this knowledge with others?'

She wonders if this is the point where the man of God – the man who says he's turned away from espousing the violent overthrow of Protestantism – reverts to his old ways. What will he do now, if he decides she's more of a threat than an ally? Will he wait until dark and drop her over the side with a heavy chain around her ankles?

'It was Master Nicholas, wasn't it?' says Bruno. 'He was the one who helped you.'

Bianca tries to keep the truth from showing in her eyes. But it's too late.

'You need not fear him,' she protests. 'In fact he's trying to help the boy.'

'And why should Signor Shelby seek to help Samuel Wylde?' Fiorzi asks. 'What is the boy to him?'

It is the first time the cardinal has spoken the boy's name. Now, in this little stuffy cabin, Samuel finally exists. He cannot be denied. The conspiracy has a name. She wonders how much she should reveal about Nicholas's visits to Cleevely. If Fiorzi discovers they're at the behest of Robert Cecil, he's bound to think Nicholas a danger to his plan. 'Lady Mercy Havington asked him to observe Dr Arcampora's methods,' she says. 'She was concerned about Samuel's treatment.'

'Mercy Havington?' says Fiorzi softly. His face is no longer immobile, for conflicted emotions scud across it like cloud shadows. 'How does Signor Shelby know of that lady?'

'He served with her son-in-law, Sir Joshua Wylde, in the Netherlands.'

'Alice's husband?' Fiorzi's voice is now almost a whisper. 'Has he seen the boy?'

'Yes. He believes Samuel to be in great danger.'

'Given Arcampora's claims, Mistress Bianca, *that* is without question.'

'I mean danger from Arcampora himself.'

A flicker of uncertainty in Fiorzi's gaze.

'The Brothers of Antioch have entrusted Samuel to the care of a man who has killed – *deliberately* – to advance his own knowledge,' Bianca continues bluntly. 'Your Eminence, Samuel Wylde is in the care of a monster.'

Having set the match to the powder, Bianca braces herself for the blast.

But it doesn't come. For a moment she thinks Santo Fiorzi is going to tell her that consorting with monsters is a price worth paying to advance his cause. Then he says, 'You're quite correct, Mistress Bianca. Arcampora is indeed all that you say he is. And the Brothers of Antioch are scarcely much better.' He permits himself a grudging smile. 'You are quite right, *Passerotto*. Yes, I confess it – I would rather the English returned to the one true faith. But not at any price. Be you English, Roman, Spanish, French, Lombardy or Swiss, there is barely anyone alive on this continent who has lived a single year free from the war of the faiths; from the ambitions of kings, princes and bishops – cardinals, too, for that matter. But you are wrong in your assumption. I have not come all this way to put Samuel Wylde on the English throne. Quite the contrary.'

'Then what *have* you come here for?' Bianca's words sound to her like a tiny bell ringing in a vast cathedral.

'I'd have thought that would have been obvious to such a clever and tenacious woman,' Santo Fiorzi says. 'I've come to take my grandson home.'

7

Besides the pain, the beating has left a deep, aching lethargy in his bones. *Sleep*, it whispers. *Lie here on the cold flagstones and just sleep.*

But sleep means surrender. Sleep very probably means death. Because the hurt has a purpose now: it reminds him that Florin and Dunstan will return.

Like an old man climbing out of an uncomfortable chair, Nicholas eases himself up. He draws as many deep breaths as he can, until the pain becomes too great to bear. Then a wave of nausea makes the floor liquid beneath his feet, and he wastes precious moments regaining confidence in his legs.

He checks the door. It's made of stout timber, studded, with a covering of tar to stop it rotting. And it's bolted from the outside.

Inspecting the windows, Nicholas concludes they haven't been repaired since before the Dissolution. Those not blocked by moss and lichen let in a weak, watery light. Where the glass has gone from the iron latticework, the diamond-shaped spaces are too small to allow even his fist to pass through. He wonders if a heave of a shoulder might knock out the entire frame.

Stepping back, he hurls his bruised flesh against the ironwork. His efforts dislodge nothing but a few clumps of damp lichen and a shower of tiny rust flakes. The frame is set firmly into the masonry. He tries the others, grimacing at the agony of each impact. His only achievement is to open up his split lip again.

Nicholas turns his attention to the interior. The hall is utterly bare. The only furnishings are the festoons of spiders' webs and a few tendrils of ivy that have prised their way in from outside. It smells like an abandoned sepulchre after the dead have moved out in search of better lodgings.

He looks up at the roof. Perhaps if he could climb onto a crossbeam he could smash his way out. But the stone walls are slippery with damp. There's nowhere he can see that might provide even the most tenuous foothold.

At the centre of the inside wall is a cavernous fireplace, tall enough to stand in. The bricks are scorched black, the mortar wreathed in plump ermine collars of fungus. Perhaps there's a chance his limbs might support a squirming, rasping, lung-choking climb up the chimney. Nicholas plans it in his mind: brace the back against the brickwork... push out with the legs until they're rammed against the opposite side... propel yourself upwards inch by inch...

He walks in and looks up, expecting to see daylight at the top. Three feet above his head is a solid plug of dirt, crumbled masonry and broken birds' nests.

His despair is absolute. This is what it must be like, he thinks, to take your last look at the shore when you realize you can't tread water any longer.

Resigned to the knowledge there is no escape, he walks stiffly back to the far wall and slumps down to the floor, resting his jaw on his knees.

Why didn't I listen to Bianca when she warned me about going anywhere near Cleevely? he wonders. What will she do when I fail to return to Bankside? Will she dispatch Ned Monkton to come looking for me? Will Ned find my carcass, the way we found the remains of Tanner Bell?

It occurs to him there is one tiny glimmer of hope. Today, the first of his two letters will reach Thomas Tyrrell. In fact Bianca will have delivered it to Munt's warehouse by now. The instructions it contains should reach Cleevely inside four days. Perhaps there's a chance he can convince Arcampora to keep him alive that long.

As Nicholas considers how he might do this, he hears the same dry, scratching sound he'd heard on regaining consciousness. It seems to be coming from a curtain of deep shadow to the left of the chimneybreast.

Nicholas clambers to his feet. Crossing to the shadow, he sees a narrow door set into a solid-looking stone recess. Until now it has been hidden from him by the projecting wall of the fireplace and the pervading gloom inside the lodge.

The first thing he notices about the door is that there are no hinges visible. He'd expect to see stout iron bands reaching out across the planks from the frame. But the door must *have* hinges. Which means they're on the other side. The door must open into the space beyond. Away from him.

Up close, the scratching is much louder now. It sounds to Nicholas like a trapped bird. And a trapped bird must mean a hole in the roof. Or even a window. An *open* window.

He wonders what manner of chamber is on the other side of the door. If it's the lodge's former sleeping quarters, the lock should be on the door's other face. So why is the lock-plate and the sliding flat-bolt on *this* side? Unless it's been placed there not to allow admittance, but to prevent someone getting out.

Nicholas runs a finger along the flat-bolt. The metal is cold against his flesh. But it's not pitted with age. It's not rusted the way he'd expect, if it has been here since the time the clergy were expelled.

Out of nowhere, he recalls something Timothy had told him once, at the Jackdaw. The subject of the conversation had been

Bankside house-divers, and their ability to defy almost any lock constructed by mortal man. 'A lock is only as good as the door frame it's connected to,' Timothy had told him. And Timothy knew all about locks. Because his father was a locksmith, and it's only because Timothy is a second son that he's now a taproom boy and not his father's apprentice.

Nicholas squats again, ignoring the pain in his thigh where the tip of Florin's boot landed. He studies the bolt-keep on the door jamb with the one fully functioning eye Florin has left him.

The bolt-keep is kept in place by two iron brads, hammered into the frame. Nicholas reckons he might just be able to summon enough strength to drive in the door, ripping the bolt-keep out of the frame in the process.

Except that he's not built like Ned Monkton, and Florin and Dunstan have stolen away with most of his strength.

His first charge against the door brings a howl of pain from somewhere very deep inside his body. For a moment he thinks he's fractured his humerus, or at least dislocated his clavicle. And the door has yielded nothing, other than a little dust.

Nicholas steps back a couple of paces. He bends his knees, braces his palms on his thighs and tries to summon up the courage to do it again. Then he stands up, drops his right shoulder a little and makes a second rush.

A second howl of pain. Louder and more visceral than before. But still the door does not budge.

On the other side the trapped bird seems to have renewed its desperate attempts at escape. Nicholas can hear the thrashing of its panicked wings.

On the third charge he loses his nerve entirely, stopping the very moment before collision.

On the fourth he almost faints with the pain.

For the fifth attempt, he decides he needs help. He asks

Eleanor to give him the courage to continue. Or is it Bianca he asks? Somehow the fire in his shoulder seems to have fused the two images together.

Nicholas hits the door with the last of his strength, biting again at the gash Florin has put in his lip, spilling fresh warm blood over his chin.

As the bolt-keep tears out of the frame, Nicholas's own momentum carries him into the chamber beyond. It's all he can do to stop himself plunging on. He barely notices the door swinging loosely on one unbroken hinge behind him, as if all he'd really had to do was knock. He comes to a halt, half-crouched, hands on knees, gasping. But grinning, too. Grinning like a Jack o' Bedlam.

And as his functioning eye peers into the semi-darkness, he sees there is no window to escape through. No bird fluttering against the glass. Just a boy shackled by the ankle to a length of chain. A boy with a bloody rag tied around his head, every pore of his death-white skin weeping silent terror, while his right foot tries desperately to scuff out the necromantic symbols chalked into the flagstones.

8

'And what of *these*?' Santo Fiorzi asks, lifting Nicholas's two letters from the other papers on the table. He holds them between thumb and finger, as though the weight of the words might give him a clue to their value. 'They are still enciphered. Were you interrupted?'

'They're separate,' Bianca says, as though that explains everything.

'In what manner, separate?'

'They didn't come from the Brothers of Antioch.'

'Then where *did* they come from?'

The snowy wastes of Muscovy, she says in her mind. The ninth celestial sphere of the cosmos. The bowl in which her mother mixed her poisons. It doesn't matter where. They're not yours. Let me have them. Otherwise I can't keep the promise I made to Nicholas.

'They bear the same hand as the translations. So I assume they were written by Dr Shelby,' says Fiorzi in answer to her silence. 'What do they contain?'

'I don't know.'

'Did he not tell you?'

'No. He wrote them just before he left for Gloucestershire.'

The cabin has become unbearably stuffy. The swell has picked up and the *Sirena* is bumping against her rope fenders in a way that's making Bianca feel nauseous. She asks to be allowed out on deck for fresh air. Fiorzi refuses curtly. It's decided, then. She's not a guest, she's a prisoner.

'What did you do with the silk key, Mistress Bianca?' Fiorzi asks, in a voice that tells her that prevarication or evasion will be a greater sin than any he has yet heard admitted in the confessional – and likely to require more than a few Hail Marys to absolve.

'I put it back where I found it – in Bruno's glove.'

'And my gloves are where, Cousin?' Bruno asks.

'In the canvas sack I saw Luzzi carrying when you left the Jackdaw.'

The cardinal tidies the documents into a small pile and wraps them in the sailcloth. Then he leaves the cabin. She hears him speaking on the other side of the door, a low, insistent string of commands.

'This would all have been so much easier, Cousin, had you agreed to help us from the beginning,' says Bruno from his cot.

'Had you been more honest, I might have done so.' She rolls her eyes skywards. 'Rice, indeed. I should have known. You always hated rice.'

'His Eminence has risked everything by coming here. How can you not admire him for it? He has loved that woman for thirty-three years. Loved her as much as he loves God – perhaps even more.'

'How did he discover Arcampora's claim was false: that the child was never Mary Tudor's?'

'His Eminence had no notion Mercy Brooke had ever given birth to a child, let alone that Samuel was his grandson. But when he investigated Arcampora's fantastical claim a little more deeply, he came to realize Alice Havington must have been his daughter.'

'But why? She could just as easily have been Sir William's.'

'Because Cardinal Fiorzi's own mother suffered from the falling sickness. It runs in *his* family.'

'But how did he learn all this, when Mercy Havington was an ocean distant from him?'

Bruno gives a knowing smile. 'A cardinal of the Holy Office can call upon any number of eyes and ears, even in far-off countries full of heretics like this one. There are still those living here who are loyal to the true faith.'

If it's meant as a slight, Bianca doesn't rise to it. 'Then why did he think he needed *me*?'

'Because you were once his little sparrow. He trusted you. And you were *here*.'

Bianca looks up at the beams barely inches above her head. She smiles wistfully, as though she's seen a great and important truth written there. 'Tell him he can trust Nicholas not to betray him.'

'Are you sure about that? Master Nicholas may be a good man, but he is still of the corrupt faith.'

Bianca's reply is harsher that she intends.

'I'm not sure he has *any* faith. He too has lost the woman he loves. And a child. But if it were not for him, Cousin – if he hadn't worked his physic on you – you'd be lying unshriven in a foreign grave. You should count yourself lucky. When they kill a heretic here, they scatter his ashes into the nearest river, so that no trace of him remains.'

It seems an age before Fiorzi returns. When he does, he has a troubled, indecisive look about him. In one hand he's carrying a writing box. In the other, a sailor's knife, the blade sharp enough for splicing cables, carving lucky charms, opening up roughly stitched black doeskin gloves – or disposing of meddlers whose loyalty you cannot quite bring yourself to trust.

'I fear I may have badly misjudged the hazard,' he says.

The boy is an apparition, a creature conjured from a nightmare. When his mouth gapes to emit a howl of terror at Nicholas's explosive entry, no sound emerges. He screams silently, as though some dense but invisible barrier exists between them that sound cannot penetrate.

In the spill of light from the broken door, Nicholas notices the wounds on either side of the boy's neck. The *pig trick*, he thinks with a shudder; the great Galen's favourite public demonstration: cut the laryngeal nerves and turn shrieks of pain to a silent mime-show, to the astonishment and applause of the audience. Only instead of entertainment, here it's been done to keep the subject quiet. And the subject is not a pig, but a terrified young lad.

The air inside the room is rank with the smell of captivity, overlain with the cloying residue of burnt herbs and oils. Nicholas's senses begin to spin again. He has to steady himself.

He moves towards the apparition, raising his hands to show he means no harm. But the boy darts out of his reach. The chain rasps on the flagstones.

'Don't be afraid. I mean you no harm,' says Nicholas soothingly, though his face is contorted with disgust at what Arcampora has done to the boy.

The chain snaps taut, pulling the lad off his feet. He lies huddled on the flagstones, his mouth gaping silently like a hind brought down by a wolf. Nicholas catches a sour odour and realizes the boy has lost control of his bladder.

'I won't hurt you,' Nicholas repeats, squatting down on his aching haunches.

He studies the boy from a distance of two or three feet. He observes the streaks of black blood encrusting his face. He looks into a pair of eyes that stare wildly back at him, yet appear not to recognize any path that might lead to sanity. The knowledge of what might lie beneath the soiled linen rag tied tightly about the boy's head turns Nicholas's stomach to ice.

It takes a few moments for the realization to dawn that there's an odd familiarity to the boy's features. It's as if Nicholas has seen him before. He's looked into the same eyes; seen the same shape of the chin, the set of the mouth. The streaks of blood, the contorted features cannot hide the growing feeling that he knows this boy.

And then he has it.

You cannot watch a lad's face as he dies in your arms in a muddy Dutch field and not have his features seared into your memory. Nor can you sit across a tavern table from his father, while he recounts unimaginable horrors, and not recall the man's face. Dorney... Porter... Yes, the features are fuller, the body thicker, but the resemblance is unmistakeable, the kinship clear. This is Tanner Bell.

At first Nicholas can't believe it. Tanner Bell is dead. Tanner Bell's pitiful remains are lost in the beech wood. Then he remembers what Isabel Wylde said to him that day at Cleevely House, when Mercy Havington asked to see the boy: *I am compelled to disappoint... Tanner went with the other boy, Finney. They left for London some while ago...*

It must have been Finney's body that Buffle unearthed, Nicholas reasons. Tanner must have lent him Dorney's jacket. Or – more likely – Finney stole it.

Climbing stiffly to his feet, Nicholas makes a hurried inspection of the room. It's smaller than the main hall, with other doors leading off, presumably to other corridors, other rooms, perhaps even other horrors. The only furniture is a simple wooden bench and a chair. There's no mattress, so presumably Tanner sleeps on the floor – if sleep ever comes to him now. Nicholas thinks of Porter Bell's recounting of his time in the prison cell at Haarlem, waiting for Arcampora to make his selections. A terrible sense of desolation overwhelms him. It's followed by a desire for revenge that startles him with its murderous intensity.

Almost as disturbing as the damage done to Tanner himself are the chalk marks on the floor. Some have been scuffed into nothing more than grey smudges. But others Nicholas recognizes. He sees astrological symbols, such as a physician might use to draw up a diagnosis. He sees lines from the Bible, including one that he remembers from a sermon of Parson Olicott's. It's the answer Christ received from a demon who'd possessed a man's soul. Christ had asked the demon his name. The demon had replied: *My name is Legion, for we are many.*

Then there are symbols Nicholas doesn't recognize. There's the Hebrew סמאל and the Greek Ἀπόλλυον. Beside each, the writer has thoughtfully provided the English translation: *Samael* and *Apollyon*, presumably for the benefit of his assistants, Dunstan and Florin. Nicholas is familiar with the names, again thanks to the sermons he's endured on damp and misty Sundays in the presence of Parson Olicott. The Archangel Samael: the Lord's venom, the serpent who lured Eve to the apple. And Apollyon: the Destroyer. Old Testament terror, scratched in chalk on a stone floor in Gloucestershire. And woven like a thread throughout, a serpent...

St Margaret... a Christian martyr, he hears Bianca say. *She was swallowed by the Devil in the guise of a serpent. But she was so pious he couldn't digest her...*

Can it be, Nicholas wonders, that the monster responsible for this scene truly believes that – just like St Margaret – he can pass through the belly of the serpent and emerge unharmed? Does he imagine that when the history of physic comes to be written, by these acts he'll be ranked above Galen and Hippocrates? Is it twisted piety or monstrous ambition that drives Angelo Arcampora?

Because at that moment Nicholas finally comprehends the true madness of what Arcampora is doing. Now he understands why Finney and the poor creature writhing slowly in terrified exhaustion on the end of his chain have suffered the agony of trepanation. It's not solely to let sickness *out* – it's to let something else in. The great physician from Basle truly believes that not only can he cure Samuel Wylde of the falling sickness, but he can find a way to summon Mary Tudor's spirit and decant it into the brain of the sixteen-year-old boy he believes to be her grandson.

9

'The first of these purports to be from me,' says Cardinal Fiorzi, laying Nicholas's letters on the table in Bruno's tiny cabin. 'It directs Arcampora to bring Samuel to London for a proper examination by our physician.' He looks questioningly at Bruno. 'I wasn't aware we'd brought one with us. Were you?'

'I think he means himself,' Bianca says.

'Arcampora is to bring the lad to Tyrrell's house – at a place called Holborn.'

'It's in the country, to the west of the Fleet stream.'

'There they will receive further instructions on where Samuel is to be conveyed for the examination. Do you have any notion where that might be, Mistress Bianca?'

'Poynes Alley. It's across the river. You can see it from here. Or you could, if we were out on deck.'

'And what does Dr Shelby intend then?'

'He didn't tell me. But I assume he intends to prise Samuel away from them somehow, take him there and keep him safe until Arcampora is dealt with and Samuel can be returned to Lady Havington.'

Santo Fiorzi shakes his grizzled head, though whether in admiration or disbelief, Bianca cannot tell.

'How does he intend to keep a sixteen-year-old boy compliant and biddable during all this?' asks Bruno.

'He asked me to mix something. I suggested white poppy, henbane and mandragora.'

'You were prepared to *poison* my grandson?' asks Fiorzi, horrified.

Bianca rolls her eyes. 'He'd merely want to sleep a lot, that's all. Besides, I've already committed treason by carrying messages from Lord Tyrrell to a cardinal of the Catholic Church. Do you think adding kidnap and poisoning will make the axe feel any sharper when it falls?'

'Where is Dr Shelby now?' Fiorzi asks.

'Riding back from Havington Manor, I should imagine. That letter you've just read – I am supposed to deliver it to Munt this very day.'

'To be blunt, Eminence, it seems as good a stratagem as ours,' says Bruno grudgingly. 'Similar in some ways.'

'How far is this Cleevely from Holborn?' Fiorzi asks.

'About the same distance as Venice is from Bologna. Three or four days on horseback. Perhaps even longer if the roads are bad.'

Santo Fiorzi gives her a resigned smile. 'What are a few days compared to more than thirty years?'

'You must have loved her very much to risk coming here in person,' Bianca says, humbled.

'I loved her more than I have ever loved anyone, before or since. More even than the Church I swore to serve.'

I'm utterly unprepared for this, she thinks – receiving a cardinal's confession. I'm the one who should be unburdening herself.

Bianca considers the sins she has committed recently: asking God to make Rose lose her voice for a month... vanity... carnal thoughts... jealousy... and the really big sin: wanting to steal away Nicholas Shelby's love for his dead wife.

'Can you imagine,' Fiorzi asks, 'what it is like to know that when your daughter died, no one prayed for the easement of her soul? The heretics will not allow it. Isn't that so? They believe it has no purpose.'

'That's because they don't believe Purgatory exists.'

'Then you may tell your heretical friends, from one who's been somewhere very similar, that it surely must.'

That's the answer, she thinks. *Pray for Eleanor's soul. If she can escape Purgatory, perhaps Nicholas can, too.* 'When you have Samuel here, how can you be sure he will want to go with you?' she asks. 'Italy is as foreign a land to him as the moon.'

'He's Mercy's grandson. He'll know what to do.'

For a moment she's appalled by his selfish determination. And then it dawns on her: Mercy is going with him! They're abandoning faith, country – everything – to be together, to snatch whatever fragments are left to them of the life they were denied; the life they denied to themselves.

'Am I allowed to return to the Jackdaw, or am I now to be your prisoner?' she asks.

'Why should I wish to keep you a prisoner aboard the *Sirena*, Mistress Bianca?'

'Because I could go straight to the Privy Council and betray you.'

'Why would you do such a thing?'

'My father, for a start.'

He looks at her quizzically. 'Your father?'

'Simon Merton. I suppose the Holy Office of the Faith imprisons so many *heretics* you can't be expected to remember them all. He died in a miserable cell in Padua. It was the Holy Office that put him there. That is why I came to this country.'

'I'm sorry, Mistress Bianca, truly sorry,' Fiorzi says, his grizzled face suddenly softening. 'Of course I remember your father. He had written discourses on matters of physic that were considered blasphemous, is that not so?'

'They were just harmless books. He was eccentric, that's all.'

'I thought so, too.'

'Then why did you imprison him?'

'I didn't. It may have escaped your attention, Mistress Bianca, but I am not the sole member of the Sacred College of Cardinals. In the matter of your father's inquisition, I was a lone voice. I was unable to prevail. For that, I am truly sorry.'

From his cot, Bruno says softly, 'Eminence, we really must decide upon a course of action. Time will not abide prevarication.'

Fiorzi puts his head in his hands. He seems to be struggling with his thoughts, though Bianca suspects the conflict is far from theological. Then he gives her a resigned smile, as if admitting he's been outmanoeuvred.

'Very well, Mistress Bianca. You may have that letter. You had better hurry. I understand the English consider it the height of bad manners to keep someone waiting.'

'And the second letter?' Bianca enquires, the relief flooding through her body.

But Santo Fiorzi has already turned his back to leave the cabin.

✠

Nicholas sits beside Tanner Bell and tries to coax him down from his terror. He talks a lot about Dorney. About how he held him while he died. But even Dorney's eyes never showed such raw fear as he can see in Tanner's.

When Florin and Dunstan return to the lodge, the boy tries to slither out of their reach. But the chain stops him short. He curls up into a ball, howling silently into the darkest corner of the room.

'Hope you're going to pay the Professor for the damage to that door,' says Dunstan to Nicholas in a hideously cheery voice. 'Have you any idea how much locksmiths charge out here?'

'That's if you can find one,' says Florin, hawking a gobbet of phlegm onto the floor. Nicholas notices it has a skein of fresh blood in it. Otherwise, he seems unnaturally untroubled by the loss of two of his teeth.

'For mercy's sake, have pity on him,' Nicholas says. 'He needs help. He needs a physician.'

'He's already had one of those,' Dunstan says with a vile laugh. 'He's had the very best there is. Didn't get charged even a penny.'

'Tanner is playing his humble part in a great and wondrous enterprise,' Florin explains. 'You'd think he'd be more grateful, 'stead of pissing himself like a Bedlam madcap.'

Dunstan walks over to where Tanner lies at the end of his chain. He squats down behind him and gathers the boy's torso between his legs, almost as though he intends to calm him. But his voice sends an icy chill through Nicholas's heart. 'The Professor says you've played your part, young gentleman. He need trouble you no longer. You may be about your business.'

And before Nicholas can even begin to shout in protest, Dunstan wraps his arms around Tanner's head and with one smooth, practised and brutal movement snaps his neck.

For a moment Nicholas is speechless. He stares at Tanner's lolling head. The bandage has come adrift, and now he can see the suppurating hole drilled into Tanner's shaved skull. With a gentleness that turns Nicholas's stomach, Dunstan lays the body out on the flagstones and says to it, 'We'll come back later. Plant you somewhere nice, like we did with Finney. You'll like that.'

Then he and Florin advance on Nicholas.

For a moment he thinks they're going to beat him to death right here in the lodge. But they don't. Instead they bind him hand and foot and drag him outside, where three horses are tethered, grazing patiently. Dunstan throws him bodily over the back of the nearest, like the spoils of a day's hunting. Then they set off on a swaying, lurching journey that Nicholas assumes is going to end somewhere his body will be left to the foxes and the worms, just like Finney's. Just like Tanner's will be, soon.

In fact it ends at Cleevely House. In a deep cellar. In darkness. Where they throw him down and leave him to fitful dreams of a mad-eyed boy with a lolling head, who dances like a Bankside bear on the end of its chain.

10

Nicholas wakes to the sound of the cellar door opening and a woman's voice calling his name. The darkness is absolute. For a moment he thinks: they've killed me while I slept; the voice I hear is Eleanor's. Then he feels the ache deep in his bones and the cold, hard bite of the cobbles against his back and knows he's very much alive. But how long he's been asleep, or whether it's day or night, he cannot tell.

A brilliant light flares above and to the right of him, then descends, sloping through the blackness. Before he can make his eyes function properly, Isabel Lowell is standing over him. She's not so finely dressed as the last time he saw her: just a plain brown kirtle. And her auburn hair is worn loose. Lit by the glare of the burning torch, her round face takes on a pallid, pinkish hue. She reminds him of a creature born to live her life underground, without need of light. With her right hand she clutches the crucifix at her bloodless throat. Nicholas gets a shadowy impression of someone standing just behind her – a Cleevely servant, his fist gripping the shaft of the burning flambeau, his shadowy arm connecting the light with the darkness.

'Master Shelby, I urge you to deal openly with me,' she says, leaning down to untie Nicholas's bonds. The crucifix swings gently before his eyes, mesmerizing against her pale flesh. He can smell a cold, acidic perfume on her that makes him think of flowers slowly dying on an altar. Bianca could no doubt tell him what type, but he can't see how he might survive to describe it to her.

'Why have you come back to us?' she asks. 'Why have you not returned to my husband, as you told us? Have you lied to us, Master Shelby?'

Arcampora has sent you to soften me up, before the real business begins, Nicholas thinks, shaking his wrists to get the blood moving. He doesn't answer.

'Silence will not aid you,' she says, studying his bloodied features dispassionately in the torchlight. 'Dr Arcampora is possessed of a volatile impatience.'

Her eyes, he notices, are just as mirthless as he remembers, her piety still as polished as a communion chalice. But now he knows her for what she really is: a woman prepared to marry a man she does not care for, to turn her eyes from murder and mutilation, all in the service of her faith. Heartless expediency in the name of doctrine. He wonders how much she knows about what goes on in the lodge in the beech wood. Probably a lot, by the way her servants remain so untroubled by the presence of a bloodied prisoner inside their mistress's house.

She sighs, to let him know how much he disappoints her. 'Let me tell you what I believe, Master Shelby. I believe you do not serve my husband at all. You're not interested in Samuel's welfare. You're an enemy, come to steal him away from us.'

'So that he may be "delivered unto a place of protection against the malevolent designs of the ungodly",' Nicholas says, quoting the line from one of Tyrrell's papers.

In her eyes, he sees the martyr's conviction waver for an instant.

'What's your maiden name, Lady Wylde?' he asks, wondering what the point is of defiance, but choosing it anyway. 'It's Lowell, isn't it? You're John Lowell's daughter. Is that his crucifix you wear – to remind you of him while you're apart? To remind you of the Brothers of Antioch?'

Her intake of breath sounds like a draught in a crypt.

'What else do I know about you, Isabel Lowell? How about the fact that you sought out Sir Joshua Wylde in Holland and seduced him, solely to get close to his son? How much of a zealot does one have to be to consider such a course of action? Did *you* decide upon it? Was it your father? Or was it Arcampora?'

'The Bible tells us a prophet is often mocked in his own land, Master Shelby,' she replies, her eyes blazing with a troubling fervour. 'But I can tell you this. Professor Arcampora is gifted beyond ordinary measure. He is God's instrument. You would do well to remember that.'

You've bought the whole rotten edifice, Nicholas thinks. Like a country green-beard on your first visit to Bankside, you've swallowed every gull, dive and trick of it. Arcampora could have told you Samuel was Christ returned and you would have believed him. You would still have wed a man you had not the slightest feeling for, still stolen Charles Pelham's memories from him, still surrendered your stepson to Arcampora's insane experiments.

'I've heard enough from you,' she says tightly, as though she's had to listen to a blasphemous litany. 'Rest. Rest well. Very soon you will need all your strength and fortitude. God's wrath is going to scourge you, Master Shelby. Prepare for it.'

And then she leaves him to the darkness. And to the terrors that hide within it.

✤

'I shall be staying aboard the *Sirena* for a while, to look after Cousin Bruno,' Bianca tells Rose and Ned at breakfast as she entrusts the Jackdaw to their care. 'It won't be for long. Don't let

343

Buffle eat all the scraps, or she'll be the size of a horse when I get back. And no credit allowed while I'm gone.'

Rose, who has an unerring ability to know when her mistress is keeping something from her, says, 'Where's Master Nicholas? Why aren't I taking clean linen to Poynes Alley?' Her cheery eyes widen. 'I know what's going on. You're planning to elope! It was all a play!'

The few lodgers look up from their trenchers as the resulting thunderclap echoes around the tavern. No one can remember when they last saw Mistress Merton lose her temper so spectacularly. And on Easter Sunday to boot. Rose is left almost in tears. Timothy and Farzad hurriedly make themselves scarce, and Buffle can only be coaxed from beneath a table with a particularly succulent piece of brawn.

Not wanting to risk another storm, Ned Monkton stays silent as he carries a basket of bedding and clean clothes across the bridge towards Galley Quay, Bianca at his side. Halfway over, his fears get the better of him.

'You'd tell us, wouldn't you, Mistress Bianca – if you was planning to sail back to Italy, I mean.'

She's never before seen those great fiery brows, that vast neck, the huge arms, the beard like a great handful of tangled saffron seem so diminished – vulnerable even. She smiles appreciatively. 'Of course I'm not leaving, Ned. Why would I even think of such a thing?'

'But where is Master Nicholas?' he asks, summoning all his courage. 'His lodging on Poynes Alley is all locked up. No one's seen hide nor hair of him for days.'

She can't tell him the truth, though it would be good to confide in him. So a white lie seems the only alternative. 'He's returned to Suffolk – to see his family again,' she tells him. 'He'll be back soon.'

He seems relieved, though whether from the news or the fact she hasn't bitten his head off, she can't be sure.

At the quayside, one of Bruno's men takes the basket from Ned. As he turns to go, Bianca calls out to his broad, departing back, 'And tell Rose I'm sorry. I shouldn't have shouted at her like that. She may give Buffle a bowl of taproom scraps, if she likes. Just the one, mind – and small.'

✠

It is the old nightmare of his childhood: the monster waiting behind the closed door. He imagines the slow lifting of the latch, the pounding of the heart as the door opens. Only now the nightmare is real. And it lives somewhere in the darkness of the cellar, waiting for Nicholas's eyes to fall upon it.

He has lost all sense of time passing. Place, too, has come adrift. Sometimes he's chained up beside Tanner Bell, awaiting the sound of a key turning in the lock that will herald the beginning of some necromantic ritual Nicholas can only pretend to imagine. Sometimes he's with Porter Bell in his Haarlem prison, while Arcampora decides which of them will be the subject of his saw and scalpel today. Sometimes he's attending one of his physic lectures at Cambridge, only instead of old Professor Lorkin warbling on about the balance of the humours, it's Arcampora explaining in the most reasonable manner that if Kit Marlowe can make us see demons in a Bankside tavern, why should we think the world's greatest physician can't decant Mary Tudor's zeal for burning Protestants into the mind of a sickly sixteen-year-old boy?

In one of his more lucid moments, Nicholas wonders how long Porter Bell managed to survive before the terror broke him.

Thump-thump... thump-thump... like a heart beating: the slow, deliberate tread of two men descending the steps. When the door

345

to the cellar finally opens again, Nicholas has to bite his tongue to stop himself screaming. He curls himself into a ball, in preparation for the blows to begin again.

'Not yet, old fellow,' says Dunstan, giggling with amusement as he hauls Nicholas to his feet. 'Plenty enough time for sport of that nature when the master has done with you.' As they drag him up the stairs, Florin sings a childish air to the rhythm of Nicholas's ankles cracking against each step.

He wonders if he should pray. But although he's made his peace with Eleanor's memory, he has something else to hold against his Maker: His creation of a monster like Angelo Arcampora. So instead he thinks of Bianca. Of her amber eyes. Of that dark, unruly mane and the way she runs her hands through it around the hairline, as if preparing herself for action. Of her sudden explosive distempers, which have not a shred of malice in them. And, more practically, of her hurrying to Petty Wales to deliver his first letter.

And whatever Arcampora may have in store for him, all these images of her comfort Nicholas more than he ever expected.

✠

Arcampora is waiting for him beneath the tapestry of St Margaret of Antioch in the main hall. He'd seen it on his visit here with Mercy Havington. Then it had meant nothing to him. Now it is like an open shutter giving him a view of perdition. By the grey light spilling in from the windows, Nicholas realizes it's morning, though which morning he cannot be sure. He settles on Easter Sunday, on the assumption that Arcampora is not the sort of man to allow his enemies unnecessary sleep.

The physician is dressed in his doctor's gown, his raptor's face harsh and angular. There's no sign of Isabel Lowell or the servants. Perhaps they've been told to stay away, in case Dunstan and Florin find it necessary to encourage Nicholas to be more talkative.

'Have you rested comfortably, Master Shelby?' Arcampora asks.

'On a cellar floor? What do you think? I'd like the opportunity to wash, please.'

A tight smile from Arcampora tells him that personal niceties are, for the moment, not on the agenda. The Professor falls again into that strange way of speaking of himself in the third person.

'Do you know what Arcampora says to himself when Florin and Dunstan tell him they find you – what is the word? *Spiare* – spying in the woods?'

'I can't imagine.'

'Arcampora tells himself: let Dunstan kill you. Save everyone a lot of trouble.'

'Then why didn't he? The bastard killed Tanner Bell.'

At the edge of his vision, Nicholas sees Dunstan shrug and pout, as though he's been accused of wearing too bright a shirt to a sermon.

Arcampora studies Nicholas's bloodied face with professional detachment. 'Because yesterday was not an auspicious day to kill a man. Arcampora has decided this.'

'And I suppose today is?'

'Is too early to decide. Maybe Dunstan don't kill you. Maybe Arcampora kill you instead.'

Nicholas tries a wan smile with his swollen lips. It hurts. 'I assume at Basle you learned the oath of Hippocrates. The one about not killing your patients?'

'But you are not a patient, Master Shelby. You are a spy. Therefore, in your particular case, the oath does not apply. The question is: who are you spying *for*?'

'I don't know what you're talking about.'

347

'When you were last here, with Mercy Havington, I think you understood far more of what I said to you than you pretended to. So I ask again: *who* sent you?'

'No one sent me. I was visiting Lady Havington again, that's all.'

'What was in the sack you were seen carrying?'

'I told your friends here, I'd caught some coney from the journey. I object to paying tavern prices for my meals.'

'Do you know the greatest insult you can pay an intelligent man?' Arcampora asks. When he receives no reply from Nicholas, he supplies his own answer. 'It is to treat him as a fool.'

Florin and Dunstan move closer. Nicholas braces himself for the first blow, wondering how the fastidious Isabel Lowell will react to having her tapestry of St Margaret spattered with blood.

And then Arcampora raises his left hand to call them off. He leans over Nicholas like a hawk mantling over its prey. His voice is harsh and utterly without compassion.

'Answer me this, you know something of physic, yes? I realize this when you come here before – when you ask me about Samael.'

Had Nicholas not seen the chalk marks on the floor of the lodge, he might even now blame Arcampora's accent for the mispronunciation of the boy's name: *Samael* instead of Samuel. But now he knows the truth. He knows what this man genuinely believes he can do.

Samael, the Lord's venom, the Serpent who lured Eve to the apple...

'Yes, I know something of physic,' he admits in a weak voice, the dread beginning to rise in him like floodwater.

'You a physician, Shelby?'

'In a manner of speaking.'

'What manner? You tell Arcampora.'

'I studied medicine at Cambridge.'

'I knew it! I tell Isabel you were not a hired blade for the heretic cause!' Arcampora steps back and considers this for a moment. Then he asks, 'Tell me, Dr Shelby, are you a heart man or a brain man?'

What new madness has taken hold of Arcampora now? Nicholas wonders. Surely he hasn't called off the beating just so he can indulge in a medical debate.

'Come now – if you studied physic at Cambridge, you must know of the dispute,' he continues. 'Do our imaginings, our joys, our angers, our lamentations, flow from the heart or from the brain?'

'The brain, of course,' Nicholas replies, puzzled by where Arcampora's sudden and unnerving swerve is taking them both.

'Are you sure?'

'I'm not sure of anything, when it comes to medicine. Not any more. But, yes, Hippocrates says that what we sense and feel comes originally from the brain; not from the heart or the vitals. The thoughts are passed to the heart for action.'

'Because?'

'Because if it was the other way round, they would arrive at the brain too hot, too disturbed. We would constantly be in turmoil, like the beasts of the wild.'

'Very good, Dr Shelby. Clearly you are no charlatan.'

Jesu, you sound like the College Censors, Nicholas thinks.

'But there are those who say it is the other way around, that our lusts and our passions *prove* that the heart is the supreme organ. Shall we determine the argument once and for all?'

'Determine? What are you talking about?'

'A simple experiment, Dr Shelby. I cut out your heart and your brain to see who's right – unless you tell me the truth about why you came back.'

There's no doubting he'll do it, Nicholas thinks. Arcampora's eyes are those of a starving man contemplating a feast.

'Dr Shelby, I ask you again: *Who* sent you here?'

Nicholas decides it's time to try the explanation he's spent his wakeful moments in the cellar perfecting – the one he hopes will keep him alive long enough for his letter to find its way from Munt's warehouse to Cleevely.

'Dr Arcampora,' he begins in as strong a voice as his bruises will allow, 'in a very few days you will receive a summons from Thomas Tyrrell and the Brothers of Antioch. It will call you and the boy you claim is heir to Mary Tudor's crown to London, where certain people have an interest in examining him. By "certain people", I mean of course His Eminence. I've been sent by his emissary, Signor Barrani, to make sure Samuel Wylde arrives safely.'

11

Lord Tyrrell's courier arrives at Cleevely the following day, Easter Monday. He's made the journey from London at such a pace that his horse is all but spent. Nicholas watches his arrival from a window. By the urgent way the man takes a letter from his leather satchel and presses it into Arcampora's hands, Nicholas knows it's the first of the messages he instructed Bianca to give Munt. The timing, he thinks, could not have been better.

In the hours that have passed since his conversation with Arcampora, he's been treated better than he'd imagined. He's been taken to a pleasant chamber overlooking the privy garden. A tub was brought from the kitchens, followed by pails of hot water. Even a set of clean clothes, which – after he'd soaked away a little of the pain – just about fitted him. He'd wondered if they were Joshua Wylde's.

But he had noticed that the door had been locked behind him. His claim to be working for Bruno Barrani was clearly not yet believed without question. Not that that had stopped him sleeping. Not even the crack of doom would have achieved that.

On the courier's arrival, the atmosphere at Cleevely turns in an instant to purposeful action. Dunstan is dispatched to ensure there are enough fit horses for the journey, leaving Nicholas to dwell bitterly on the mare lying dead beside the stream at the edge of the beech wood. Arcampora sweeps in and out imperiously, but does nothing of any practical worth. Florin, when he encounters Nicholas, looks as though he's been cheated out of a fortune.

It is during this frantic preparation for the journey that Nicholas once again comes face-to-face with Samuel Wylde.

They meet when Isabel Lowell leads the boy out to the waiting horses. His face is shockingly pale. His thin fingers twist nervously, and his eyes look as though they're still getting accustomed to sunlight after a long imprisonment in a very dark cell. He seems eager to please. He stoops slightly whenever someone asks him to move aside. His Adam's apple rises and falls in his thin neck. His mop of corn-coloured hair droops in an unruly fringe, which he has to brush continually from his eyes. Nicholas is horrified. If the Brothers of Antioch are allowed to use this boy as they desire, if they proclaim him as Mary's grandson either in this realm or abroad, then Robert Cecil and the Privy Council – should they get their hands on him – will eat him alive and gnaw on his bones for the marrow.

Samuel is equally shocked by Nicholas's battered appearance.

'Is this not the gentleman my father engaged to bring news of me? He came here with Grandma Mercy. Who has used him so roughly?'

'A misunderstanding,' says Arcampora. 'It is resolved now. And he was not sent by your father. He was sent by certain friends of yours. Good friends.'

'My friends have gone away, back to London. I don't have any others.'

'You have more friends than you know, sir,' says Isabel Lowell. 'Powerful friends. You will meet them soon – in London.'

'As you can see, Dr Shelby, the boy is well,' announces Arcampora in an extraordinary display of bluster. 'I am encouraged by his progress. But we still have a distance to go. Once

Signor Barrani has had an opportunity to see him, I must be allowed to continue the treatment without interruption.'

That afternoon, beneath a pale sky that seems to Nicholas like a canvas stretched too tightly on its frame, ready to rip at the first touch, the small party rides out of Cleevely. Arcampora and Samuel take the lead. Nicholas follows. Dunstan and Florin ride close on either side of Nicholas, casting him the occasional hungry glance, as if to tell him they don't buy his alibi for a moment.

There's no escaping it, thinks Nicholas – it's going to be a miserable journey. It's not the stamina of the horses that will dictate how long it lasts, it is Samuel's ability to endure it. He rides well, but tires easily. Arcampora gives him frequent doses of a syrup of heart's-ease to help stave off his fits.

As for Nicholas, the pain in his body has barely eased. They've wrapped him in his gaberdine, the collar pulled up to hide most of his face. He hasn't looked in a mirror glass, but he doesn't need to – he knows instinctively that he looks like the loser in a fist-fight at a country fair.

The inns they stop at are low places. Nicholas is made to take his rest in barns and outbuildings, always in the company of Florin and Dunstan. And all the time he wonders: how long can this deception survive? Because reaching Lord Tyrrell's house is only the beginning.

✠

Bianca has been aboard the Sirena for four uncomfortable nights. Bruno has ordered a makeshift berth furnished for her in a rope-store on the deck immediately below his small cabin. It smells overpoweringly of hemp cordage. But the crew treat it almost as they would a shrine, lowering their voices whenever they are close, never daring to get within three feet of the curtain they've rigged up to provide privacy. Santo Fiorzi had told her more than once that she isn't a prisoner – so why, she wonders, does she feel so much like one? And not just a prisoner of the cardinal, but of her mounting fears for Nicholas. He left early on the tenth day of April. Today is Thursday, the eighteenth. He should have returned by now. *Where* is he?

Perhaps the roads are bad. Perhaps his horse has cast a shoe, somewhere far from a smithy.

But apart from the rain on Easter Eve, the weather has been good. So good, in fact, that if she were not cooped up on the *Sirena* she'd be taking a stroll along Bankside, or in the fields behind the ruins of Bermondsey Abbey.

Fine weather means more people on the road. That must be the reason for his delayed return – he's held up by farm waggons and other travellers. Rose will soon be here, bearing news of his arrival, just as instructed.

But by the next afternoon Bianca has become so concerned she mentions it to Bruno, while she's changing the dressing on his wound.

'He's probably entertaining himself in some tavern some-where,' her cousin says, trying to put her mind at ease. But his explanation serves only to make things worse.

As the bells call the faithful to Evensong in the churches beyond the waterfront, a stir goes around the *Sirena di Venezia*. Fiorzi appears in Bruno's cabin. He's no longer dressed in his mariner's jerkin and slops, but smartly attired in a plum-coloured doublet and black trunk-hose. With his runnelled face, the white stubble on his head and his dagger-blade of a beard, he makes a striking figure, though still as unlike a cardinal as she can imagine. His eyes gleam with anticipation.

'She's arrived,' he says to Bruno, a trace of awe in his voice. 'She's lodging at the sign of the Blind Archer on Botolph Lane.'

Bianca knows at once he's speaking of Mercy Havington.

Fiorzi turns his head towards her. The years seem to have released their grip on him. He looks younger, more vigorous. 'Is that far?' he asks.

'It's just the other side of the Customs House,' she says, trying to smother an involuntary smile. 'A quarter of an hour at the most.'

'Will you accompany me, Mistress Bianca? I find this city of yours a veritable labyrinth.'

'I'd be honoured, Your Eminence,' she says, grinning.

'I think you'd better get used to calling me plain "Signore", Mistress Bianca. When the Sacred College of Cardinals finds out what I'm up to, the nearest I'm likely to get to a position in the church is a job as Father Rossi's gardener.'

At Botolph's Wharf, Bianca and Fiorzi put the river at their backs and head north towards St George's church. The lane is quiet, the people mostly at church.

'Do you not fear the Brothers will seek revenge, when Samuel is stolen from them?' Bianca asks.

'Once again, Mistress Bianca, your idea of theft is somewhat at odds with mine. Just as Tyrrell's letters were not yours to lose, so my grandson is not theirs to keep. Besides, Tyrrell, Lowell and Kirkbie are men of the past. They have no real power – that is why they were so eager to embrace Arcampora's insane story.' He sees the confusion on her face and laughs. 'Oh, they may sit behind the walls of their seminary at Douai, plotting until they wither, but it is too late. They cannot see how the world has changed.'

'What do you mean, *changed*?'

'After Spain's great Armada was scattered three years ago, her coffers are exhausted. Philip does not have the money, let alone the power, to wage a war of faith with England.'

'So Nicholas was wrong – about Samuel's value to them?'

'Oh no, child. Zealots like that will clutch at any straw, even if by doing so they crush it between their fingers. They will care only that they fan the flames of hatred between the faiths.'

On Botolph Lane they find the sign of the Blind Archer fifty yards south of Thames Street. A more salubrious establishment than the taverns along the wharves, it boasts a decorated timber frieze running along the overhang of the first floor, freshly painted in vivid red, yellow and green. Bianca decides it's just what the Jackdaw needs.

She will not enter with him. The last part of Santo Fiorzi's extraordinary journey must be made by him alone. But she does have a parting question – not for him, but for Mercy Havington.

'Please, Your Eminence, will you ask her if she has any news of Nicholas?'

The fact that he doesn't answer is lost on her, because she's too busy watching Santo Fiorzi step through the doorway into the shadows beyond, too busy taking innocent pleasure in the pride in his gait, the anticipation in his step – though what tumult of emotions he must be suffering, she can only imagine. As he disappears, her last mental image of him is not as a scarlet-robed cardinal with a voice like God's holy thunder, but as a young man who simply forgot to fall out of love.

12

Nicholas can hear the church bells proclaiming Evensong when Arcampora leads the riders into the courtyard of a fine half-timbered mansion, one of a number of newly built houses in the fields and orchards between Holborn and Gray's Inn.

Thomas Tyrrell receives them in a spacious panelled upstairs room at the back of the house. The windows look out over Gray's Inn. Nicholas can just make out a scattering of black-gowned lawyers strolling leisurely towards the chapel. They'll have plenty of work drawing up the arraignment, he thinks, when Robert Cecil gets to work on their treasonous neighbour. But not yet. Not until Samuel is safe, and Bruno is well on his way to Venice. Though quite how he will achieve this, Nicholas still hasn't determined.

With his scowling face and his martial beard, Tyrrell would make a perfect portrait to hang at Cleevely House alongside all those Wylde ancestors. He looks ready to bow to no man. Yet as soon as he sees Samuel, he drops to one knee in obeisance.

Another one well and truly gulled, thinks Nicholas. Just like Isabel Lowell, Tyrrell has bought every last piece of Arcampora's great lie.

'Why did you not make yourself known immediately?' Tyrrell asks Nicholas, when Arcampora introduces him as another of Bruno's emissaries. 'You could so easily have avoided such rude handling.'

'I was on my way to Cleevely to do just that, when this pair of bravos' – a nod towards Florin and Dunstan – 'decided to have their sport with me.'

'Do you have proof of who you say you are?'

'I knew when your letter would arrive at Cleevely. I knew what it would say. If I wasn't in the intimate service of Cardinal Fiorzi, how else could I possibly possess such knowledge?'

'But do you have material proof?' Tyrrell says, offering his right hand, palm upwards, fingers spread, in the expectation that Nicholas has something to offer him.

Nicholas feels the heat drain out of his body. In its place comes the clammy dread of exposure. What is it Tyrrell expects him to offer?

It was something Munt let slip... he hears Bianca say in his head, as she comes to his aid. *He and Bruno each have a medallion... proof of identity...*

Even so, Nicholas can't answer for a moment because the breath won't come back into his lungs. Tyrrell's face clouds with suspicion.

'If you're speaking of the medallion of St Margaret of Antioch,' Nicholas manages at length, 'only Signor Barrani and Mistress Merton are permitted to carry one. His Eminence doesn't hand them out like trinkets. What if I were to be taken by Privy Council watchers? They could use it to trap every single one of His Eminence's agents.'

Is Tyrrell satisfied by this explanation? It's impossible for Nicholas to tell. But he drops the expectant hand. 'You have had a long journey,' he says, addressing the others as though Nicholas is no longer of importance. 'Take your ease. Word should come soon about the time and place of the examination. In the meantime, the prince should rest.'

Tyrrell guides Arcampora to the window, away from where

Samuel – flanked by Dunstan and Florin – is standing. He lowers his voice, but Nicholas is just close enough to hear the exchange.

'How goes the prince's cure, Dr Arcampora?'

'Steadily, milord. Do not forget, I counselled patience from the very start.'

'But you are content?'

'Cautiously so. When this business with Barrani is over, and I am permitted to return to Cleevely, I expect to make swifter progress. I will need further subjects, of course.'

Subjects.

Nicholas thinks of Tanner Bell's silent howls of torment and of Finney's fox-chewed remains. He gives serious consideration to lunging at Arcampora and attempting to strangle him with his bare hands. He wonders if he could inflict fatal damage before Dunstan and Florin stopped him. But Tyrrell's next question roots him to the spot.

'And what of the Havington woman? Has Mistress Isabel succeeded in determining if it was she alone who stole away the prince's mother from the queen's lying-in chamber, or was the crime committed by others of her heretical faction?'

'That, milord, remains unknown as yet. Arcampora is sure only that the child was taken because the heretics feared for the survival of their abominable superstitions, if her true identity became known. As to exactly *whose* hands took her from the cradle...' He shrugs, like a hawk disgorging a pellet. 'We should be thankful they did not kill her.'

'Whatever the truth, there will have to be a reckoning when this matter is concluded, Dr Arcampora.'

'Arcampora would not have it otherwise, milord. You may rest assured, there will be no womanish tears spilt by me, or by the Lady Isabel.'

'But the prince may still harbour a fondness for the woman, given how long he has believed her to be his grandmother.'

'Fear not, milord. The prince will look to me, when the time comes for a reckoning. In the meantime, I urge that we get this inconvenience over as swiftly as possible.'

Nicholas tries desperately to look disinterested as he seizes his chance. 'I could go to Signor Barrani now, if you wish, my lord. I could press him to agree the place and time of the examination,' he says. 'Dr Arcampora is correct: the sooner Cardinal Fiorzi's emissary is satisfied, the sooner the prince will ascend his rightful throne.'

'That is an eminently practical suggestion, Dr Shelby,' says Tyrrell. 'We have all waited long enough. Perhaps you will make that point to Signor Barrani on my behalf.'

Nicholas can't believe his luck. He struggles to remain impassive, allowing Tyrrell to show him down the wide stairs and to the door, where he stands looking out over Red Lion Fields in the dusk, while his horse is retrieved from the stables. He's not yet sure where he'll go: the *Sirena*... the Jackdaw... Poynes Alley... All he knows is that it will be anywhere but here. And when he's decided, then he'll try to resurrect his plan from the thicket of thorns in which it's become entangled.

'This gentleman will accompany you, Dr Shelby,' he hears Tyrrell say behind him, just as a groom emerges from the stables with his horse.

Startled, Nicholas turns to look back into the house – and finds himself staring into the malmsey-veined face of Walter Burridge.

13

Aboard the *Sirena di Venezia* the lanterns are being lit. Standing at the stern rail, Bianca watches them glint in the twilight, casting little pools of gold on the holystoned deck planks. She imagines Rose setting the tapers to the rushlights in the Jackdaw, the raucous chattering of the watermen as they drink to the day's labours, the cries of the card players at their games of *primero* and *one-and-thirty*, the rattling and the roaring as the pieces roll across the *hazard* board. She hopes Ned Monkton is keeping his eyes open. The Jackdaw has a reputation for honest gaming – as rare in Southwark, she thinks with a wry smile, as Catholic cardinals. She doesn't want to lose it.

'It will be tonight, *Passerotto*,' Santo Fiorzi says softly, appearing beside her. 'We sail on the next tide.'

'Is she coming with you?'

Fiorzi nods, doing his best to stifle a grin.

'I'm glad. I could use some good news.'

'You are still concerned for your friend, Signor Shelby?'

She turns to face him, unable to match his self-control. 'Some ill has befallen him; I'm sure of it.'

'He left Havington Manor on Monday last. That's all I know.'

'Then he should be here by now.'

'Put your trust in God, my child,' he says, handing her a small square of folded paper, sealed. She doesn't need lantern light to tell her the wax bears the impression of St Margaret and the serpent – she can feel the design beneath her fingertips. 'This is the note you are to deliver to Munt. It is signed by Bruno. It summons Samuel here, for his examination.'

'When will they come?'

'In a matter of hours.'

She wonders how he can be so sure. Perhaps at this very moment one of Bruno's crew is trying to explain to the watch in broken English that he got lost coming out of a tavern in a strange city, which is why he's unaccountably found himself on Petty Wales, or even on Holborn Bridge. Then she remembers what Bruno had told her: *A cardinal of the Holy Office can call upon any number of eyes and ears, even in far-off countries full of heretics like this one...*

'Will you reveal to them who you are?' she asks.

'I think not. Let them assume I am still sitting in my quarters at the Holy Office of the Faith, resplendent in scarlet, drinking the finest wine and eating the best food, as befits a prince of the Church.' He casts a glance around the spartan deck. 'Ah, the sacrifices one is forced to make for love!'

'Are you not troubled by the risks you're taking?'

'What risks, *Passerotto*?'

'Taking Mercy Havington back to Italy.'

'Mercy Havington no longer exists. But I shall offer up a prayer for Sir William's immortal soul, for caring for her these long years past. No, the woman who has chosen to accompany me is named Mercy Brooke.'

'Even so, having a woman live openly in your household – do you not risk the opprobrium of mother church? Even excommunication?'

He laughs like a Paduan gravedigger. 'Pope Alexander VI had at least four acknowledged illegitimate sons. One of them, Cesare Borgia, became a cardinal. Sixtus IV swelled St Peter's treasury by charging his priests for the privilege of keeping their mistresses. I know several members of the Sacred College who are at this moment likewise occupied. They know it's best to let sleeping dogs lie. Besides, my lack of zeal for overthrowing heretic nations by force means that nowadays they mostly leave me to my gardens and my art collection.'

'And Samuel? How will he fare in this new world you're taking him to?'

'He will have love – unpaid-for, unjudging love – and the finest physicians in Italy.'

She allows him his moment of victory. Then she says, 'I must have the other letter – the second one Nicholas wrote. He insisted that I deliver it to Munt, so that it could reach Arcampora without delay.' A flash of raw fear disfigures her amber eyes for an instant. 'I must have it – for when he comes back.'

Santo Fiorzi looks troubled. He seems reluctant to answer her. For a moment he just stares towards the far bank. Out in the river, the sail of a tilt-boat returning from depositing its passengers at the Marigold stairs flaps noisily. Then, his voice sounding uncertain, Fiorzi says, 'I think before you deliver it, you should read it. You may find it will change your opinion of him.'

'What do you mean, Eminence?'

Santo Fiorzi reaches into his doublet and extracts a folded sheet of paper. He hands it to her. The sadness in his eyes sends a shiver of fear coursing through Bianca's heart.

'I fear, *Passerotto*, that your Dr Nicholas has betrayed us all.'

Opening the letter, Bianca begins to read the words the cardinal has deciphered:

To my well-regarded and worthy friend in physic, Angelo Arcampora, greetings. If you value your life, read this and heed its warning. By means of a traitor to your cause, the

queen's ministers have learned of your past deeds in the
service of the Duke of Alba...

Her eyes fly over the words. She shakes her head in disbelief.

Plans are already afoot to take under arrest you and the
emissary to His Eminence, Cardinal Santo Fiorzi, along
with all others involved in the matter of her late majesty's
grandson. Unless you desire to meet a cruel fate upon the
scaffold, you must with all haste flee out of this realm...

'It would appear, Mistress Bianca, that your Dr Shelby is a
deceiver,' says Fiorzi from somewhere very far away. 'The English
plan to arrest us all. He's giving his fellow physician time to escape.'

'I don't believe it,' Bianca says, breaking off from the letter.
'Nicholas despises men like Arcampora. He'd *never* help him. I
know he wouldn't.'

'Perhaps there is a bond between men of medicine, just as
there is between men of faith.'

'It can't be true! Perhaps you've deciphered it wrongly.'

'Come, *Passerotto*, you know that is implausible.' Fiorzi glances
at the letter that Bianca is in danger of crushing in her palm. 'He
says the arrests will commence upon St George's Day. When is
that? I am not so familiar with English feast days.'

'On the twenty-third day of this month.'

'A mere four days' hence! They're preparing a trap for us.'

Bianca feels a hot bloom of sweat on her cheeks, even though
a cool wind is rising from the river. 'I cannot believe Nicholas
would sell us all to Robert Cecil!' she says, the tears starting to
well in her eyes. 'The money was for his services as a physician.'

'Money?' echoes Fiorzi in his end-of-days voice, the one she
remembers from her childhood; the one she's always thought
he'd borrowed from God. 'Are you telling me Nicholas Shelby is
in the pay of a minister of the English queen?'

'It was only to recompense him for his visit to Samuel,' she protests weakly, battling the worm of doubt that has suddenly entered her stomach. 'He talked of using the money to fund a practice on Bankside.'

Again, as when she watched him disappear into the Blind Archer, she gets a glimpse of Fiorzi the man, rather than Fiorzi the cardinal.

'I am so sorry, child. At your tavern I could see clearly how you were beginning to care for him.'

Bianca turns away from Fiorzi, shaking her head vigorously. 'He wouldn't *do* this! I know him too well. Eleanor would never forgive him!'

'Eleanor?'

'His dead wife. She's his lodestone. His guiding star. He'd never ally himself to a man like Arcampora – she wouldn't approve.'

And then the prince of the Church reasserts itself.

'I don't have time to debate Dr Shelby's code of morality with you. The tide will not wait. I will not wait. If what he has written is true, we are all in great peril.'

On the main deck the crew are moving purposely in the misty twilight. The *Sirena di Venezia* is preparing to sail.

'Hurry, child,' Fiorzi says insistently. 'You must deliver Bruno's summons to Tyrrell at once. It will take some time for him to bring Samuel here.'

Even now Bianca hesitates.

'Go! Everything now depends upon you. We are in your hands.'

Folding Nicholas's letter, she slips it away in her gown. From habit, she makes a deferential bob before the cardinal. Then she descends the stern-castle ladder with the last of the composure Fiorzi has left her, crosses the main deck and goes down the gangplank onto Galley Quay.

Dark hills of unloaded cargo line the wharf. She imagines

them as living sentinels waiting to pounce upon her – to steal away everything good she has come to believe in, since Nicholas Shelby entered her life. With a growing sense of desolation, Bianca hurries past them, skirts the silent mausoleum of the Customs House and sets off towards Petty Wales.

14

'Sit down, Shelby,' says Tyrrell, gesturing to the brick floor. 'And if you don't want Dunstan here to cut out your tongue, I suggest you deal plainly with me.' For emphasis, Dunstan sticks out his own tongue and waves his dagger in front of it. Nicholas does as he's told.

No nice, airy room with a view over Gray's Inn this time. Instead an unoccupied part of the stables, the air heavy with the acidic smell of soiled hay.

It suggests Tyrrell is having second thoughts about him.

Arcampora watches Nicholas intently. He seems unwilling to accept that his judgement has played him false.

'How do you know this man Shelby, Master Burridge?' Tyrrell asks.

'He is Mistress Merton's fellow, at the Jackdaw. I understand he was once some sort of physician.'

'But is he trustworthy? And is he, as he claims, Cardinal Fiorzi's man?'

'He tended Signor Barrani, after he was assaulted,' says Burridge, clearly uncertain what to make of Nicholas's presence. 'I know that much. But I didn't know he was in Barrani's service. He gave no sign of it.'

So that's why Burridge chose the Jackdaw for Marlowe's play-practice, Nicholas thinks – so that he could keep watch on Bruno for Thomas Tyrrell. And when Bruno was confined to his chamber, insensible after the brawl, he enlisted Marlowe, hoping he could entice Bianca into indiscretion.

Keep your nerve, he tells himself. All is not yet lost.

'Mistress Merton and I are both servants of His Eminence,' he tells Tyrrell, trying to sound affronted. 'Why should I have confided in Master Burridge here? I had no idea he was in your service. But I do know he has the loudest voice in London. Who knows what he might have let slip after a jug or two?' He looks at Burridge with disdain. 'Besides, if he's had his ears open recently, he'll know Mistress Merton and I are lovers. It's common knowledge all over Bankside.'

Lovers.

Despite the tension, despite the imminent threat to his life, Nicholas actually smiles. We've made such a pretence at denying it, he thinks, yet when I proclaim it now to Tyrrell, it doesn't seem like a pretence at all. In fact it seems utterly reasonable.

'It is true,' says Burridge cautiously. 'I have heard the very same.'

And then Dunstan speaks. Dunstan, who likes breaking necks.

'There is an easy enough way to discover if his heart is false or not.' He squats down beside Nicholas. He slowly circles the tip of his dagger's blade in the air just in front of Nicholas's face. Nicholas can almost smell the heat of his desire to hurt.

'And pray, what is that, Master Dunstan?' Tyrrell asks.

'If you want to know where his loyalties lie – if you truly want to know whether he's lying – ask him to recite a line or two from the Holy Mass.'

15

The Sirena's deck is bathed in moonlight when Bianca returns. The masts and cordage strike angular shadows across the pale planks. Lanterns burn at prow and stern-castle. As she watches the crew going quietly about their preparations, she notices most of them are armed, with wicked-looking blades at their belts. She wonders if Santo Fiorzi is expecting resistance.

Bianca knows little about ships, other than that they are cramped, uncomfortable and insanitary, though thanks to Bruno, she understands something of the Sirena's imminent departure. The correct papers have been lodged at the Customs House listing Bruno as master, an AL for Alienigena – alien – neatly annotated beside his name. The Comptroller of Customs has received the warrant from the searchers to show the Sirena carries no contraband or, more importantly, no traitors fleeing from justice. The letter of safe-passage has been received to protect the vessel from the attention of English privateers, who are in the provocative but highly lucrative trade of preying on foreign merchantmen. More immediately, watermen have been hired for the morrow. At dawn they will row the Sirena's kedge-anchor out into the river and drop it overboard, allowing the ship's crew to haul on the cable and swing her away from the wharf and out into the current.

Now there is only the waiting left.

Bianca stands at the furthest end of the high stern-castle, looking out over the river. Ships' lanterns glitter like sprites dancing in a dark forest. To her left is the menacing silhouette of the Tower. To her right, across the river, she can just make out the dark bulk of the grain mills beyond Bermondsey House.

Where are you, Nicholas? Why have you not returned? Is it because you've betrayed us all? Have you sold us all to Robert Cecil?

She takes his second letter from her kirtle. She had barely managed to get halfway through it before Santo Fiorzi hurried her to deliver the summons to Munt. Now, by the lantern light, she starts to read again:

> To my well-regarded and worthy friend in physic, Angelo Arcampora, greetings. If you value your life, read this and heed its warning. By means of a traitor to your cause, the queen's ministers have learned of your past deeds in the service of the Duke of Alba. They are now privy to your actions at Naarden, and most crucially to your present dealings with the Brothers of Antioch. Plans are already afoot to take under arrest you and the emissary to His Eminence, Cardinal Santo Fiorzi, along with all others involved in the matter of her late majesty's grandson. Unless you desire to meet a cruel fate upon the scaffold, you must with all haste flee out of this realm. These arrests will begin upon St George's Day...

It's the starkest betrayal she can imagine. Nicholas has delivered them all to Robert Cecil. The only person he intends to spare is a fellow physician – the man to whom the letter is addressed.

How could he do this? she wonders. When did the man she was beginning to love decide to become Arcampora's creature? She remembers how insistent Nicholas had been, the day Bruno had returned to the *Sirena*; how he'd given her precise instructions on delivering this very letter to Munt: *Make all alarm... Hammer on the door, appear breathless – frightened even...*

Did he mean to give the warning added impetus, she wonders. Or is there another reason? She holds the letter closer to the lantern and reads on:

> The *Sirena di Venezia* will make sail with all haste. But you must eschew this means of escape, for her interception off the North Foreland has already been planned. All aboard her will be taken. There are, however, still those loyal to our great cause...

In the next sentence she sees an unexpected name written. It jumps out at her, throwing her off-balance. She reads the line again. Then a third time, just to be sure the flickering lantern light and the state of her fevered imagination haven't made her see something that isn't there.

And then she begins to smile.

16

Like many weak men, Walter Burridge finds the brutality of others a spur to violence that he would never dare commit alone. As Dunstan and Florin bind Nicholas's hands and feet, he takes the opportunity to slap him across the face. Matched against the new blows Arcampora's two companions have landed on Nicholas's already bruised body, the strike is ineffectual. But it still hurts.

'Heretic!' he hisses, almost jumping up and down with a mixture of rage and excitement. The malmsey veins stand out on his jowly face like skeins of blood. 'You are nothing but piss, to be washed off the marble floors of God's hallowed heaven. We should let Dr Arcampora do his work upon you. Even a heretic may be useful!'

A sickening comprehension forms in Nicholas's mind: it's the seemingly avuncular Walter Burridge who's been recruiting young lads to Tyrrell's company of players, picking those who won't be missed for Arcampora's murderous physic. And an unsuspecting Joshua Wylde has been paying for it, thinking he's soothing his conscience by sending companions to his son. It's Porter Bell's Dutch cell transported to Bankside: *Today I choose to pass you by... tomorrow I shall return, and maybe then it will be you...*

'I'm not to be held in such disregard now, am I, Shelby?' Burridge sneers an inch from Nicholas's face. 'I have served Lord Tyrrell and the true faith all my life. I have seen my religion trampled in the dust. But I have been as much a soldier as any man.'

Tyrrell inspects the cords that bind Nicholas. He declares himself satisfied. Arcampora looks on, a malevolent anticipation in his eyes that turns Nicholas's stomach.

'I think we're done with you, Dr Shelby,' Tyrrell announces. Then he turns to Dunstan and Florin and says, as if he were ordering them to take out the night-soil, 'Get him out of my sight. Dr Arcampora and I have pressing business to attend to. When we're done, we'll find out whose man he really is – then you may gladly kill the heretic.'

✠

Bianca hears a noise on the deck behind her. She folds Nicholas's letter and returns it to the hiding place in her kirtle. Turning, she sees Santo Fiorzi approaching. Bruno is with him, one arm thrown over the cardinal's shoulder for support. Her cousin has attired himself in his fine black satin doublet, the one he'd been wearing that day she'd first seen him on the quayside.

'I have just received word from the man I sent to keep watch on Tyrrell's house,' Fiorzi tells her. 'Tyrrell and the physician are on their way. Samuel is with them.'

'You were wrong, Eminence – about Nicholas,' Bianca says confidently. 'He hasn't betrayed us.'

A momentary flicker of irritation in the cardinal's eyes. 'You harbour an attachment to him. It is clouding your judgement.'

'It's not clouding anything. I *know* Nicholas. He wouldn't sell us all to Robert Cecil. He just wants Arcampora to believe that he has.'

'His Eminence is right, Cousin,' says Bruno regretfully. 'His letter was unequivocal. Besides, if he hasn't betrayed us, then where is he?'

'I don't *know*,' Bianca snaps. 'Perhaps Tyrrell has him.'

'If you're right, he's dead anyway,' Fiorzi says. 'But my man saw no one else leave the house but Tyrrell, Arcampora and Samuel – save for two servants and a carter with his waggon.'

'I'm truly sorry that he deceived you, Cousin,' Bruno says. 'But we must sail on this tide. If Tyrrell does have him and the English discover it, they will not wait for St George's Day to move against us.'

'The English plan was set down plainly in his letter, child,' says Fiorzi. 'They intend to intercept the *Sirena* off the North Foreland, on our way out to the Narrow Sea. Needless to say, that is not the course we shall steer.'

'But that's exactly what Nicholas *wants* Arcampora to believe!'

'For what possible reason?' asks Bruno.

Bianca is only too aware of what her cousin might think of her if she tells him what she believes Nicolas intends. She gives Fiorzi a pleading look. 'Eminence, you *have* to let me give Arcampora Nicholas's letter. If you don't, you will have allowed a monster to escape all retribution for his crimes. By all means, tell Tyrrell that the Brothers of Antioch have been discovered. Give him warning if you must. But *please*, let me give Arcampora Nicholas's letter.'

As she waits for his response, Bianca prays that if God is inclined to forgive any of her many sins, He forgives her this one.

17

The cart rolls through the empty lanes beneath a cloudless sky frosted with stars. Nicholas lies in the darkness beneath a pile of hemp sacks, gagged so tightly he is close to suffocating. He can feel every rut and cobble of the journey. He can hear the faint murmur of voices: Dunstan and Florin chatting happily as they ride close by, like two old friends anticipating a pleasant day hunting wildfowl in the marshes around Barnthorpe.

He has no idea where they are taking him. Perhaps to the silent emptiness of Moorfields, or Finsbury Park, or Spittlefields. All he knows is that wherever it is, he will meet his death there. He imagines the dawn rising, an unknown washerwoman approaching a hedge intending to lay out her laundry to dry, finding his body beneath it – just another victim of a violent London quarrel.

Or perhaps he will not be found. Perhaps they mean to dispose of him in the river. That would be ironic, he thinks. The river let him go once before. It has never occurred to him that it was only a temporary reprieve.

They are heading deeper into the city now, he's sure of it. By the number of turns the cart is making, Nicholas reckons they must be avoiding the main streets. He wonders how long he will be able to resist Florin and Dunstan when they go to work on him. The thought of what they might do, before they kill him, turns his stomach to ice. But what is even worse is the prospect of his utter humiliation in the face of unendurable pain, and the enjoyment Dunstan and Florin will take from inflicting it. When they have killed him, they will go on their way without the smallest sliver of remorse. They will laugh about it, as he can hear them doing now. In their hard, uncaring eyes, the love he had for Eleanor, his growing feelings for Bianca, his desire to heal – all the things that make him better than a beast – will be worthy of nothing but their derision.

The cart stops. Nicholas hears footsteps. The weight of the hemp sacks is lifted from him. What he sees is beyond all expectation. If he were able, he would open his mouth in wonder.

He's staring at the beauty of a full moon. It's the most magnificent moon he's ever seen. A terrible longing comes over him: the overwhelming desire to gaze on this brilliant white beautiful disc until his sight freezes over, until it becomes the only thing he will ever see again.

Then the smoky glare from a burning torch blots out the pristine image. Hands seize him by the shoulders. He feels himself lifted up, dragged roughly from the back of the cart and onto his feet. He turns his head, longing for one last sight of that glorious moon, and by its light sees the high, grey stone wall of the Bulwark Gate of the Tower a short distance away. He realizes he's in Petty Wales. They're going to kill him in Tobias Munt's warehouse.

He hears the rasping of a heavy door opening. Florin and Dunstan drag him inside like a laden sack. Someone slams the door behind him, shutting out the clean, pure moonlight and leaving only the oily flames of the carter's torch to show the way.

Nicholas catches glimpses of columns of casks and wicker tubs, hemp sacks and wooden boxes, towering upwards into the darkness. He smells the heavy odour of grain and timber, oils and spices, animal hide and unwashed wool, all mixed together in close confinement.

He is brought to a halt before a stocky figure in a leather jerkin. The man has a lazy, shiftless face, with a thin mouth that cuts across his face like a slash.

'What is this you've brought me, Master Florin?' the man asks.

'No sale required for this one, Master Munt,' says Florin with a coarse laugh. 'You can write him off as spoiled goods.'

'He's a spy,' says Dunstan. 'To be put to the hard press before we kill him. Lord Tyrrell wants to know who employs him. Watch if you want, or go about your business. It's all the same to us.'

'I really would like to stay for the spectacle, Master Dunstan,' Munt says. 'But a note has been delivered to me, which I must convey to his lordship without delay. I'd be obliged if you didn't spill more blood than I can scrub off the floor, if it's all the same to you. Sometimes the customs searchers come calling, and I don't have a licence to run a butcher's shambles.'

'You won't even know he's been here,' says Florin.

'Unless the bowels go,' Dunstan adds. 'That's always a risk.'

Florin looks up appreciatively at a hook set into a beam above his head. 'Any means of suspension, perchance, Master Munt? Chain or hemp – makes no difference.'

Munt disappears into the darkness, returning a few moments later with a coil of rope.

'This will do nicely,' says Florin. He takes the rope from Munt and, with practised ease, tosses it over the hook at only the second attempt.

For a moment Nicholas thinks they intend to hang him right here. But Dunstan has spoken of employing the hard press to make him talk. And as he feels one end of the rope being tied around the bindings that pin his wrists behind his back, he realizes how they're going to do it: *strappado*. They will haul on the other end of the rope, pulling his arms out and upwards until he's suspended by them. Then his own weight will rip his shoulders out of their sockets. He has treated freed prisoners of the Spanish who'd been tortured in such a manner. They had described pain beyond endurance. In a bizarre moment of detached observation, he wonders if his screams will be heard on the far side of the Bulwark Gate.

But Florin has one final terror in store for him. One last act for when he's told them everything they want to know. Florin takes the carter's torch and stands in front of Nicholas, the grin on his face revealing the missing teeth he'd lost to Nicholas's saddle in the beech wood. He raises his other hand so that Nicholas can see what he's holding. Clenched in his fist is a twisted length of iron, a wooden handle at one end and a broad, circular cutting blade at the other – a carpenter's auger – just made for drilling through living bone.

18

Luzzi, the sailing master, appears on the stern-castle. Seemingly oblivious to the tension, he takes off his cap before addressing Santo Fiorzi. 'They are on Lyon Quay, master,' he says. 'It is time to go below, I think.'

Bianca helps Fiorzi lead Bruno down the steps of the stern-castle and onto the main deck. Her cousin moves carefully, like an old man unsure of his legs.

The grating over the wide hatchway to the cargo hold has been pulled aside, exposing what looks like a black hole leading into the depths of the river. Peering in, Bianca sees an almost vertical ladder. At the bottom, a flicker of lantern light appears as one of the *Sirena*'s crew positions himself to help Bruno descend. Then the river lifts the *Sirena*'s hull and the floor of the hold seems to rise towards her, bringing with it a wave of nausea. Bianca steadies herself, checks Bruno is safely down and then – summoning all her courage – slips her legs over the edge of opening.

Reaching the deck below, Bianca imagines she has entered the gut of St Margaret's serpent. Huge wooden ribs twice the width of a man's thigh rise out of the darkness on either side. She makes a hurried sign of the cross over her breast as she steps away from the ladder.

The crewman sets his lantern on a hook in a nearby deck-beam. It begins to turn gently to the movement of the river, striking fragments of detail out of the darkness: casks of fresh water; sacks of victuals for the voyage back to Venice; coils of hemp cordage and spare yards for sails; even a small demi-culverin, for defence against the Barbary pirates who roam into English waters, and which will be brought up and mounted when the Sirena is at sea. And set into a small clearing is a makeshift throne for Bruno the cardinal's emissary to sit upon, made out of bags of flour. Still weak, he sinks onto it gratefully, a diminutive doge of his own little republic. Bianca and Fiorzi – who is now clad in his usual disguise of plain jerkin and slops – take up their positions as his loyal ministers on either side.

They don't have long to wait.

Bianca hears hushed voices on the deck above. She looks up as three dark figures appear at the edge of the hatchway. There's no mistaking Tyrrell, his great beard frosted by moonlight. Arcampora is just a silhouette to her, angular and infinitely menacing. Between them stands a willowy figure, slightly hunched, like a prisoner being led to the scaffold. They begin to descend the ladder, Tyrrell first, then Samuel Wylde, then Arcampora. Bianca notices Tyrrell has a sword at his belt.

When they reach the deck, Tyrrell pulls back the cowl of his cloak and nods to her in recognition. He's lost none of his scowling menace. His eyes blaze as he pushes Samuel forward, as though he expects everyone to kneel. What Arcampora is thinking is impossible to say. His hawk-like features seem frozen. Only Samuel Wylde shows emotion. He stares around in alarm, as if he thinks he's about to be incarcerated, left to a lingering demise in a dark cell. He looks, to Bianca, like the most unlikely pretender to a throne she can imagine. It occurs to her that neither Tyrrell nor Arcampora has thought it necessary yet to tell him what the Brothers of Antioch have planned for him.

'Signor Barrani, I am pleased to see you restored to health,'

Tyrrell says, his voice flattened by the timber walls of the hold. 'We had heard your injury was severe.'

'God favours our work, my lord,' says Bruno from his makeshift throne. 'He has spared my life for a purpose.'

He; me; but mostly Nicholas Shelby, thinks Bianca.

'Then let us hope he spares it a little longer,' says Tyrrell coldly. 'Because we have a spy in our midst, Signor Barrani. Dr Arcampora's men found him sniffing around at Cleevely, like a dog on heat.'

The timbers of the *Sirena* seem to part beneath Bianca's feet, plunging her into the deepest of whirlpools. She has to bite her tongue to stifle a cry.

'He claimed to be in the service of His Eminence, Cardinal Fiorzi,' she hears Tyrrell say, as if from behind a mask. 'So we put him to the test. It swiftly transpired that he's a heretic. Who he's working for, or how much he knows, we'll find out when we've completed our business here. Then we'll dispose of him.'

Bianca's whole world seems to have toppled off its axis. The darkness of the hold pours over her in a crashing wave of hopelessness.

'Does this spy have a name, my lord?' Bruno asks.

'*Nicholas Shelby*. Apparently he's a physician.' Tyrrell fixes Bianca with a hard stare. 'I'm told he was in your service, Mistress Merton. Were you not instantly suspicious of a man who is so obviously an apostate?'

Bianca opens her mouth, but cannot speak. She knows that one wrong word from her, and the masque Bruno and Fiorzi have created will be revealed for the fiction it is.

It is Bruno who comes to her aid.

'We know all about Dr Shelby, my lord,' he says casually. 'In truth, it was Mistress Bianca who alerted us to him. That is precisely why I summoned Dr Arcampora and the boy to London.

We do not intend to examine him here – but he cannot possibly remain in England. It is too dangerous now.'

'Where then?' asks Tyrrell.

'Samuel is to be delivered to the care of Masters Lowell and Kirkbie at the English seminary at Douai in the Spanish Netherlands,' Bruno says. 'He will be safe there.'

Bianca stifles the urge to smother her cousin with gratitude, but she wonders how long they can play this impromptu game with Tyrrell and Arcampora before one of them makes an obvious error.

Samuel Wylde turns to Arcampora. Bianca can clearly see the alarm etched into his young features. 'I don't understand what is happening,' he says. 'I do not wish to go to Douai. I wish to go back to Cleevely.'

'I fear that will not be possible, Samuel,' Bruno says in a gentle voice. Then, to Tyrrell, 'It is essential we sail on the next tide. If the boy falls into the hands of the heretic queen and her council, all will be lost. I need hardly remind you of the fate that awaits *you*, were you to be arrested.'

Bianca watches helplessly as the fear begins to flood into Samuel's eyes.

'Spies... heretics... arrests... I don't understand what you are talking about. Why would anyone wish to arrest *me*?'

'You are in grave danger, Samuel,' says Bruno. 'We must get you away from England with all possible speed.'

'But *why* am I in danger? I haven't done anything.'

Bianca glances at Santo Fiorzi. She can see in his face that he's struggling to remain silent.

'You have enemies, Samuel,' she says. 'Men with hard hearts. Men who do not know the meaning of mercy.' Even as she speaks, she's thinking: *And they're not who Tyrrell or Arcampora might tell you they are.*

'This is too precipitous!' says Tyrrell angrily. 'Putting Shelby to hard questioning will tell us who employs him and what he has revealed. We may have caught him early enough.'

'I know exactly who employs him, my lord,' says Bruno, half-rising from his seat of flour sacks. 'It is the heretic queen's Privy Council.'

For the first time there is uncertainty in Tyrrell's voice, Bianca notices. 'Jesu! Are we then already discovered?'

'I fear we are. But we must hold our nerve.'

'Then what is it His Eminence would have us do?'

'You must leave the prince with us,' Bruno continues. 'If he is not out of England on this next tide, all could be lost. *Everything.* Your friends in Douai will hold you responsible for that, my lord. Cardinal Fiorzi will hold you responsible – and you know to whom he reports.'

Still Tyrrell hesitates. 'I cannot permit you to take His Grace without the authority of Master Lowell and Master Kirkbie!'

'It is holy mother church who is the authority in this matter, not the Brothers of Antioch,' says Bruno decisively. 'And as Cardinal Fiorzi's emissary, it is I who speak for her here.' Bruno jabs one arm in the vague direction of London Bridge. In as strong a voice as he can muster, he almost shouts, 'And unless you want your head rotting on a spike, my lord Tyrrell – act now!'

Bianca fears that if she so much as breathes, the spell Bruno has cast will be broken. Moonlight spills over the hatchway like a ghostly waterfall. Looking up, she sees the full moon hanging directly over the *Sirena di Venezia*, the masts and rigging frozen against the sky. She wills a weight into Bruno's words that will make Tyrrell unable to deny them. *Believe them. Act on them. Give us the boy and be gone!*

And then she hears Arcampora say, 'You must go with Signor Barrani, Samael. He will take care of you. We will meet again very soon, in Douai. You have Arcampora's word on it. This enterprise is too great to risk it with indecision.'

Noticed only by Bianca, Fiorzi shuts his eyes in what she knows must be a prayer of thanksgiving.

Then Tyrrell is pushing Samuel forwards, towards Bruno, as though he's a neophyte at some mysterious pagan ceremony.

Running to the boy, Bianca folds an arm around his thin shoulders. 'You're safe with us, Samuel,' she whispers, thinking her sudden release of breath must sound like a roaring gale in his ear. 'Safer than you can imagine.' To her relief, she feels him lean into her, as if all he really wants is to sleep against a mother's breast.

'Masters, we will be in Douai within six days, God willing,' Bruno says. 'I suggest you make all speed to join us there.'

And then Arcampora turns everything on its head.

'Arcampora is his doctor!' he announces. 'Arcampora shall accompany him. The prince must have his physician.'

For a dreadful instant Bianca fears Bruno is going to agree. She knows he'll probably have the crew hurl Arcampora over the side the moment the *Sirena* is out of sight of land, but that is not the justice Nicholas intends for him. And whether Nicholas lives or dies, she knows it's up to her now to see his plan through.

Remembering how Bruno had described the process of the vessel's departure to her, she says confidently, 'I fear that is impossible, Dr Arcampora. Signor Barrani has declared the number of crew to the English, accounting for Samuel's presence. If we were to be boarded, the searchers would find one man more than admitted to, in the letters of dispatch. They would at once think we had put into some creek or estuary to take aboard a Jesuit fugitive. I'm sorry, Dr Arcampora. You and Lord Tyrrell must make your own arrangements.'

Bruno is watching her, puzzlement in his eyes. But before he can speak, Tyrrell regains his resolve. 'We are wasting time. We can resume our enterprise when we are all safely across the Narrow Sea. In the meantime, I intend to make this heretic spy tell me how much he knows and how much he has revealed to his masters.'

Bianca sinks her nails into her palms to stop herself crying out in protest. Samuel in return for Nicholas's life – it's not the exchange they'd planned.

Time, she thinks. I need to purchase time.

'I want to be there, Lord Tyrrell,' she says, without a single thought as to what her presence might accomplish, other than to be a comfort to him as he dies in agony. 'Nicholas Shelby has betrayed my trust just as much as he has betrayed our cause. I want to hear what he has to say. Besides, His Eminence must know the interrogation was forceful enough.'

'Putting a man to the hard press is not for a woman's eyes. It would be better if Signor Barrani were a witness.'

'Signor Barrani *cannot* be a witness. Look, he can barely stand, let alone walk to Petty Wales. Let *me* hear the heretic's confession!'

'I fear you will find it an affront to your sensibilities, Mistress Merton,' says Tyrrell. 'Women should not see what men are sometimes forced to do.'

Bianca does her best to sound contemptuous. 'I was born in the Veneto, Lord Tyrrell. I have witnessed heretics burning. Now I live on Bankside, a stone's throw from the bear garden, where Englishmen come to watch chained beasts being tormented by dogs,' she says with a defiant lift of her chin. 'Do you really think I'm going to wilt at the sight of flesh being torn asunder? And if you seriously believe you can put a man to the press more efficiently than the Holy Office of the Faith, then I, for one, will be fascinated to observe it. I will pass on your techniques to His Eminence, for his better instruction.'

Out of the corner of her eye she sees Fiorzi shift uncomfortably. But Tyrrell smiles at her in admiration.

'Our enterprise could make use of your mettle, Mistress Merton. But we must hurry. We do not know how much Shelby has revealed.'

'I will be with you anon. But first allow me to ensure Samuel is content and comfortable,' Bianca says, as though Tyrrell is her favourite customer at the Jackdaw. 'And do nothing to Nicholas Shelby until I am there to witness it.'

Tyrrell nods curtly and starts to climb the ladder to the upper deck. Arcampora turns to follow.

Samuel watches him anxiously. Bianca whispers into the boy's ear, 'Fear not, Samuel. Someone you know and trust will be here very soon.' She hugs him, wondering how he will react when Lady Mercy Havington arrives and he discovers who the grizzled man in the sailor's slops standing silently beside Bruno really is.

Then, her heart racing, she takes a few brisk strides to the foot of the ladder, where Arcampora is about to follow Tyrrell out into the moonlight. Grasping the physician by the arm, she says softly into his ear, 'It is worse than my cousin admitted, Dr Arcampora. Much worse. Take this.'

And with that, she presses Nicholas's second letter into Arcampora's hand.

19

They have left him alone in the darkness of the warehouse. Florin and Dunstan have tied the free end of the rope to a nearby pillar, putting just enough tension in it to pull his arms away from his back a little, so that whether he stands still or moves, there is always a fiery ache in his shoulders. There is no escaping it. If his legs sag, the pain becomes excruciating. And they haven't even begun the *strappado*.

He presumes they're waiting for Tyrrell to arrive before they begin, because sometimes he can hear movement in the chamber above. The fear in him is starting to suppurate like a diseased wound. As if designed expressly to stretch his nerves even tighter, Nicholas can hear the occasional dry rasping of rats' claws amongst the barrels and sacks.

His fear, too, has a sound of its own – part laboured breathing, part pounding heart, part coursing blood. It's roaring in his ears. He imagines he's caught in a hurricane, clinging desperately to the weakest of branches, while all around him the world is being ripped apart by the howling wind.

To steady himself, he thinks of the beautiful moon he'd seen when they dragged him from the cart on Petty Wales – the sight he'd wished he could gaze on until the darkness comes to take him. He tries to conjure up the vision now. But it does not come.

In his despair, Nicholas calls out a woman's name. A plea for help. Or absolution. He's not sure which.

And to his surprise – though it *does* calm the tempest in his mind – the name he calls is Bianca's.

✠

'He saved your life, Cousin. And now they're going to kill him! You *have* to help me,' says Bianca, close to tears. She knows any hope of saving Nicholas is seeping away with every moment she remains aboard the *Sirena*.

'Bianca, that is impossible. We must be ready to sail at dawn, when the tide is in our favour.'

'I'm afraid your cousin is correct, my child,' says Santo Fiorzi. 'We have a long journey ahead of us if we are to avoid the English ambush. We cannot linger here.'

'But there isn't going to *be* an ambush!' cries Bianca in exasperation. She wonders if laying violent hands on a cardinal counts as a sin, in the eyes of God. 'Can you not see? That second letter: Nicholas made it all up. It's a fiction. He's trying to flush Arcampora from cover – to make him think he needs to flee!'

'If that is true, then we've already accomplished what he desires,' says Fiorzi. 'But on the evidence of his letter, I cannot take the risk.'

Suddenly Samuel Wylde makes a break for the ladder. As he reaches out to climb, one of the sailors appears over the edge of the hatch to block his way. Santo Fiorzi takes Samuel gently by the arm and draws him back. 'Peace, *ragazzo prezioso*. Do not be afraid. We are your friends here.'

The boy's eyes are wide with fear. 'I don't want to go across the Narrow Sea,' he pleads. 'I don't want people to call me "prince" any more. I'm *not* a prince. I'm Samuel, and I want to go home – to Grandam Mercy.'

Bianca takes the boy's hands in hers. She can feel them trembling. She cannot begin to imagine how confused and frightened he must be. 'Your grandmother will be here very soon.' She glances at Fiorzi. 'Isn't that so?'

'She is already on her way, Samuel,' the cardinal says, with a smile that lights up his grizzled face. 'When she arrives, she will explain everything to you.'

Bianca gently touches Samuel's cheek. 'I would stay with you if I could, Samuel. But Dr Arcampora is not the man you believe him to be, and if I don't hurry, he will hurt someone I care for.' She crosses to where her cousin is sitting on his throne of sacks. 'Two men, Bruno. That's all I ask. Ned Monkton will count for three more. It's the very least you owe Nicholas. If it were not for him, the *Sirena* would not be carrying Samuel to safety – it would be carrying your body home to Padua!'

Bruno closes his eyes and raises one hand in defeat. 'Perhaps I could spare one man.'

'Two! And handy with it.'

'Enough, Cousin! God help your poor husband, when you find one,' Bruno says, waving a cautionary finger in her direction. 'Two it is. But if the work is not done by sunrise, they will have orders to leave you to whatever madness it is you're planning now.'

20

From somewhere in the lanes nearby, the watch cries the midnight hour: *Twelve of the clock, look well to your locks...*

'Where are we going, Mistress?' asks Ned Monkton as they duck beneath the curfew chain strung across the gatehouse on the Southwark side of London Bridge.

'Petty Wales, by the Tower. And hurry, we don't have much time.'

She has wasted precious moments sprinting between Ned's father's house on Scrope Alley and the Jackdaw, where she'd caught Ned and Rose about to retire for the night to one of the lodging rooms. (She'd be having words with them both in the morning about *that*.) Since then he has remained unusually reticent. And she knows it's not through embarrassment.

She has tried to explain why she and Nicholas have stayed silent about Samuel Wylde – how they had not wanted to risk embroiling people they cared for in such a lethal conspiracy. But she fears he's taken it as a sign of mistrust. Somehow she will have to make it up to him.

Ahead of them, the street disappears into the very heart of the bridge, a tunnel drilled through a procession of grand buildings, a whole city thoroughfare – three hundred yards long – laid out across the Thames. Most of the inside frontages she passes are shops: a milliner's... a silk-maker's... a grocer's... There's even an old chapel turned over to private lodgings, six storeys high, at the centre point. At only three places does the bridge open itself to the night. Then Bianca hears the roar of the river surging between the huge stone starlings set into the river, glances up and sees that perfect moon. Then it's back into the belly of the worm.

Here and there lanterns burn, spilling a smoky mist around the doorways and boarded-up counters. In a doorway lies a reveller snoring drunkenly in a pool of vomit. As Bianca passes, she sees a neat rip in his grubby jerkin – Bankside's parting gift has been to cut away his purse while he sleeps.

She is certain the echo of their hurrying footsteps on the cobbles will wake the entire bridge. All the way across she waits for the first opening of a window, the first challenging cry, the first shout for the watch. For who else can be dashing through the night at this hour but brawlers, felons and vagabonds?

The help Bruno promised is waiting for her on the quayside in the shadow of a tall wooden crane: two wiry little knife-fighters from the slums of the Venetian *Giudecca*, named Cesare and Marcello. Cesare has a vertical scar running from just beneath his right eye to his jaw, which makes him look as though his face has been assembled from two different people. Marcello has a broad, boyish face and the flinty eyes of a practised killer. She recalls both had been at the Jackdaw the day Bruno was hurt – how they'd watched anxiously as Nicholas had saved his life. Now they're eager for a quarrel with anyone who would do him harm. Silently she thanks her cousin for keeping his word.

Halfway up Petty Wales, Munt's warehouse stands gaunt and grey in the moonlight. The sign of the three tuns hangs over the street like the banner of an enemy army. Suddenly a fire begins to burn in her with a heat she has never felt before. The night is hers alone to win or lose. And even though the stakes could not be higher, Bianca discovers she is smiling.

'If anyone addresses you, Ned, say nothing. Just look at them as if you don't understand. They'll assume you're Venetian.'

'Aye, Mistress.'

'And don't *do* anything unless I give you a clear sign. They could kill Nicholas before we can intervene.'

'No, Mistress.'

'Promise me – no sudden foolish attempts to save him. Move only at my instruction. Understood?'

'Clearly, Mistress.'

Bianca turns to Cesare and Marcello and gives similar orders in Italian. Then she nods towards the broad double doors of the warehouse. Ned raises a giant fist and raps three times on the planks.

The answering silence seems to last an age – an age in which she imagines she's too late. She sees Nicholas in her mind, lying on the other side of the door, bloodied and broken, his death a slow, drawn-out masque of agony staged for the entertainment of Thomas Tyrrell and Angelo Arcampora.

And then she hears Munt's muffled voice coming from the narrow gap between the doors. 'Who calls? Name yourself!'

Bianca fills her lungs with night air to steady her racing heart. Then she says softly, but in a commanding tone, 'It is Mistress Merton! In the name of His Eminence Cardinal Santo Fiorzi of the Holy Office of the Faith, open these doors!'

She hears the rumble of a wooden beam sliding through iron hoops. Then one of the doors opens outwards just enough to let one person through.

Bianca goes first, Cesare and Marcello next. Ned casts a glance over his shoulder to check the street is empty, pulls the door a little wider to allow his great bulk to pass through and steps in after them.

✠

Clouds of hemp dust hang slackly in the flickering light of Munt's burning torch. Ahead of her, Bianca can make out a dark maze piled high with sacks of spices, lengths of Baltic timber, barrels of Dutch salted herring... When she breathes the air it has the sour tang of unwashed trencher boards about it.

She follows Munt down an avenue of wooden pillars supporting the ceiling beams, Cesare, Marcello and Ned close on her heels. Munt seems more respectful than when she saw him last. Has Tyrrell told him of her supposed desire to witness what is to come? she wonders. Does he think she has a stone for a heart? If they only knew the truth.

And then she sees him.

His body is at the centre of a cleared space, limp, pitched forward a little, like a martyred saint. A rope disappears into the darkness above him.

Oh, my poor Nicholas: I'm too late. They've hanged you!

But then he moves – like an old man trying to find a stance that eases the aches of a hard life lived too long.

A wave of relief sweeps over her, then breaks on the realization of what they've done to him. Or are about to do. *Strappado*. It's what the Holy Office of the Faith did to her father to make him confess that the Devil had guided his pen. It had broken him. She fights the overwhelming desire to rush to Nicholas's side, to take him in her arms, to hold him and protect him. To make him whole again.

In the semi-darkness she can sense Ned Monkton battling the almost overwhelming urge to act. She wants so much to let him loose, but it would destroy everything Nicholas has risked his life for. Unseen, she lays a restraining hand against his arm. Cesare and Marcello she keeps leashed in with a single shake of her head.

Tyrrell is standing by Nicholas's body. Two paces behind him is Arcampora. The physician looks up at her approach. She sees that cold mouth twitch. It's almost a smile of gratitude. She guesses he's already read Nicholas's second letter and believes every word of it. If that is the case, whatever happens now, his fate is settled.

Behind Arcampora stand two heavyset men. One of them is holding a wicked-looking iron rod with a wooden handle at one end and a flattened, circular cutting blade at the other. She doesn't need to know much about instruments of torture to guess its purpose.

Nicholas turns his head towards her. He looks almost unrecognizable. One eye is closed and swollen. His face is streaked with dried blood. It has spilled onto his ruined shirt in a dark tracery of pain.

Does he know it's her standing in the shadows, almost within reach? He makes no sign of it.

'I have to confess I thought you would lose your nerve, Mistress Merton,' says Tyrrell in a disdainful voice.

'Well, you thought wrong.'

'And, pray, who are these fellows with you? This is not some Bankside entertainment for the lower sort. We are not at the play-house now.'

'I am a cardinal's emissary,' Bianca says as haughtily as she can manage. 'Would you have me wandering the streets alone at midnight, like a common doxy? They're from the *Sirena*. Signor Barrani has sent them for my protection.'

Tyrrell gives a grunt of indifference. He yanks on the rope, wrenching Nicholas's arms away from his back and tearing a rasping moan from his upturned throat. Bianca feels Ned begin to move. She steps directly in front of him, blocking him, although if he was of a mind to, he could flatten her just by pushing forward.

'Master Florin, Master Dunstan, the heretic is all yours,' Tyrrell says. 'Serve him well. Give him all the misery he can swallow!'

'Strappado or the auger, my lord?' asks Florin, as if he's offering Tyrrell wine at supper.

They haven't begun the torture! Bianca stifles a gasp of relief. There's still a chance.

'The auger, I think. More fitting to Dr Arcampora's presence. Besides, the spy will talk sooner and die quicker. We don't have much time.'

Florin unties the other end of the rope from its anchorage around a pillar. Nicholas immediately falls to his knees. Dunstan steps forwards, kneels and folds an arm around his lolling head to hold it steady. To Bianca's horror, Florin stands over him and places the blade of the tool against Nicholas's skull.

'Tell me, heretic: who is your master?' asks Tyrrell, squatting down beside him.

It's all Bianca can do to remain motionless. She senses Ned, Cesare and Marcello losing the same struggle. If just one of them springs to Nicholas's defence, the pretence is over. Her cry is directed to them as much as to Tyrrell.

'Wait!'

Tyrrell rises to his feet. 'I did attempt to warn you, Mistress Merton,' he says, a smirk of vindication on his face. 'If you would rather leave—'

But Bianca matches his sneer with a venomous smile. 'Lord Tyrrell, if you're going to spend all night asking questions to which we already know the answer, we'll still be here when the Privy Council's men arrive to arrest us all.'

Where the audacity comes from, she has no idea. But she airily waves Tyrrell aside and squats down in front of Nicholas.

At once she can see the confusion in him, the incomprehension at her sudden presence. Her heart is close to breaking for what they've already done to him. It takes all her will to stop herself reaching out to caress his bloodied face.

'Can you hear me plainly, Master Shelby,' she asks.

To her joy and relief, he nods.

'Do you know who I am? Do you recognize me?'

He nods again. Mouths the word 'yes'.

She prays his senses are not so battered that he cannot think straight – because if she can get him to say the words she needs Tyrrell to hear, if she can somehow coax him into following her lead, then there may just be a way out of this nightmare.

'Look at you,' she says haughtily. 'You are no better than a dog. A heretical dog. Do you understand me?' She places her face close to his. 'A *dog!*'

Another swift prayer – that the single word has penetrated the fog of his pain.

'You would do well to follow what I say closely, Master Shelby,' she urges, still with her face close to his. 'Because if you play the buffle-head with me, your end will be a torment beyond enduring.' She stares deep into his eyes, hoping his senses aren't so bruised that he can't remember the present Ned brought back from Gloucestershire for Rose. 'Do you understand me, *buffle*-head?'

Nicholas searches her face. For a moment she thinks he hasn't understood her. That he doesn't realize she's trying to lead him. And then the faintest hint of a smile creases his mouth, followed by a wince of pain and a dribble of blood from one corner. But it's the final slow nod he gives her that fills her heart with joy.

Bianca waits a moment, holding his gaze with hers, while her racing thoughts search out the path she must take to lead him out of this horror.

'We already know who you work for, Master Shelby,' she says. 'Your master is Robert Cecil – am I correct? That's true, isn't it?'

A moment's silence, during which Nicholas holds her gaze like a man clinging to the edge of a precipice. Then, very softly: 'Yes. My master is Robert Cecil.'

'And Robert Cecil sent you to the Jackdaw, didn't he?'

'Yes.'

'For the purpose of worming your way into my confidence. That is so, isn't it?'

He nods. Another bloody trickle from the corner of his mouth.

'He sent you to spy on my cousin, Signor Barrani, didn't he?' Bianca continues, skipping ahead of herself in her mind, trying to steer the questions where she needs them to go.

'Yes. It's true.'

'How much have you learned, heretic? Everything?'

Nicholas dips his head in acquiescence. 'Everything.'

'Do you know the true identity of Samuel Wylde? Do you know that he is the rightful King of England?'

'Yes. I know it.'

She looks at Tyrrell as if to say, *Do you see how easy it is, if you use brains in place of pain?* Then, to Nicholas again: 'A trap been laid for the *Sirena di Venezia*, has it not?'

'It has.'

'Where? Tell me – to the letter. To the very *letter*, mind.'

'Off the North Foreland.'

'Christ's holy wounds!' Tyrrell cries. 'Did you *know* that?'

'Of course we did,' says Bianca calmly, casting the merest hint of a glance at Arcampora.

'Then the prince must not sail tonight. Return him to us. I have friends – I can arrange for another vessel...'

'You need have no fear for Samuel,' Bianca says calmly. 'Signor Luzzi, the sailing master, has plotted a course well to the north. When the English arrive, they will find nothing but empty sea.'

She returns to her play-acting with Nicholas. 'And the arrests of those who remain: Lord Tyrrell, Dr Arcampora, Isabel Wylde? When will they occur?'

Nicholas looks at her blankly. Then he remembers what he'd written. 'On St George's Day.'

Munt is the first to break. From the darkness, Bianca hears him mutter, 'God's wounds, that's only three days away!'

Tyrrell curses him to silence. 'We can be across the Narrow Sea in two! Where's your courage, man?'

'Why do they delay?' asks Arcampora.

'Yes, why?' says Tyrrell. 'Why wait until the twenty-third?'

Now it's Bianca's turn to struggle for an answer. She doesn't know. A surge of panic rises in her throat.

Nicholas's voice is barely audible. But it rescues her. 'They need time to get men in place. So that the arrests can be made simultaneously. No warnings passed. Everyone taken together.'

Bianca rises to her feet. She hopes Tyrrell won't notice her legs are shaking.

'Do you see, Lord Tyrrell, what a woman's gentling can achieve? If I'd left it to your bold fellows here' – a contemptuous glance at Dunstan and Florin – 'you'd still be waiting for the heretic to regain his wits enough to confess his own name.'

Tyrrell stands with legs apart and hands on hips, appraising her. 'I confess my admiration, Mistress Merton. Most neatly done.' He turns to Florin and Dunstan. 'We need tarry here no longer. Dr Arcampora and I will return to Holborn immediately to prepare for the journey. Join us there when you've done. You, too, Master Munt.' He seizes a fistful of Nicholas's hair, yanking his head back. 'In the meantime you may send this meddling heretic to his rightly deserved hell!'

Dunstan steps forward and once again enfolds Nicholas's head in one arm. He forces it downwards, so that the crown is offered to Florin's auger. Florin's face twists cruelly with the anticipation of driving the cutting blade deep into Nicholas's skull.

This time it's too much for Ned, Cesare and Marcello to bear. They almost sweep Bianca aside, stopping only when she raises her arms from her sides to restrain them. To her relief, everyone else is too busy watching Florin position the auger to notice.

'No! Wait!' she shouts, again directed as much to her companions as to Tyrrell.

'Mistress Merton?' he says, a look of surprise on his face as he turns to her.

Bianca wonders how long she can maintain this act before she collapses on the floor in a sobbing heap. It's all she can do to keep her voice steady.

'Master Munt,' she says, 'the Customs House searchers make unannounced inspections of the warehouses along the wharves, do they not?'

Munt nods.

'Looking for contraband, I suppose?'

'Aye.'

'Of course you don't *have* any contraband here, do you, Master Munt? You're an honest man. You pay your taxes.'

Munt declines to answer the question. His silence tells her all she needs to know.

'I saw some rogues coming out of the Customs House this evening. They looked very much like searchers to me,' she says. 'What if they were to find bloodstains here? Half of them work for Robert Cecil anyway. They'd soon put two and two together. Cecil will realize we've made his spy talk and start the arrests immediately.' She looks at Tyrrell with an expression that says: how is it a clever man like you needs a mere woman to point this out?

'What are you proposing, Mistress Merton?' he asks.

'Let the river have him.'

'The river?'

She glances over her shoulder. 'My gentlemen here can take him for a walk along the shore. It's a pleasant night, as long as we watch where we step.'

Tyrrell commands Florin to lay aside the auger. Then he takes Bianca's hand and bestows a kiss upon it. His lips are like ice against her skin. 'What a remarkable young woman you are, Mistress Merton. I hope His Eminence knows how blessed he is to have your services. If only we had more of your mettle in the Brotherhood, England would never have fallen to the heretics in the first place.'

Bianca smiles graciously, though her heart is hammering against her ribs.

'But let us not take foolish chances. They're slippery creatures, heretics,' says Tyrrell, releasing her hand. 'Dunstan and Florin will go with you – to ensure it's done properly.'

21

The night air is cool. The moon dusts the city with a frosty coating of grey light. Keeping close to the menacing wall of the Bulwark Gate, Bianca leads the little group south towards the river.

Nicholas has said nothing since they left Munt's warehouse. He has surrendered his fate entirely to Bianca. He might not understand what's happening. He might be too bruised and battered to care. He might be so damaged that he's already dying.

Supported by Ned Monkton, he seems content to be borne down Petty Wales like a reveller who's been a little injudicious with his ale. The only sound he makes is an occasional groan when he stumbles on the cobbles.

Ned glances at her as if to say: how long are you going to let this play-acting go on? But she dares not say or do anything that might make Dunstan and Florin suspicious. Because one thing is certain, and it troubles her deeply: Florin and Dunstan must die. There can be no other way. It became inevitable the moment she uttered the words *Let the river have him*. They cannot be allowed to tell Tyrrell that Nicholas has escaped, and that it was Bianca who made it happen. What troubles her most is the knowledge that she wants them to die – for what they have done.

Reaching the wharves, she calls to Cesare and Marcello in Italian, 'What ugly dogs these two English are! God must have had his eyes closed when He made them.'

'As ugly as sin,' Cesare replies, laughing.

'And they stink like dead fish,' agrees Marcello. He nods at Nicholas and Ned. 'But these two – they're alright. It's just a shame God didn't make them Venetian.'

Bianca studies Florin and Dunstan. They give no indication they appreciate they've been so roundly insulted. Now she knows she can safely explain her plan to Cesare and Marcello without fear of them realizing what is to come.

She wonders whether it's right to pre-empt God's justice, and whether He will forgive her. Then she considers what Nicholas has told her about Tanner Bell, and about Angelo Arcampora. She thinks about the apocalypse Tyrrell and the Brothers of Antioch intend to unleash in the name of an innocent, sickly sixteen-year-old boy. A sin committed to prevent a much greater one – surely God can forgive her for that.

In a fast stream of Italian, punctuated with laughter to make it sound utterly innocent, she gives her instructions. Ned will know his cue when it comes.

They pass the *Sirena* and the Customs House. They pass the water-stairs at Billingsgate. They cross Botolph Lane and Fish Wharf, where the Dutch hoys are moored, and all the while the rumble of the waterwheel in the northern arch of London Bridge gets louder, a drumbeat ordering her on.

The bell at St Magnus tolls two o'clock, a slow, sonorous prelude for what is to come. And then the moon and its canopy of stars vanish, as Bianca steps into the arch of the gatehouse on the northern end of the bridge.

The tunnel echoes to their footsteps. The smoky haze from the scattered lanterns robs the shop fronts of their solid form, turning the way ahead into a shifting, mystical passage through a childhood dream. Bianca almost believes it is not a bridge she is on, but a ramp descending into the Underworld.

As she approaches the end of the first block of buildings, where the bridge is open to the night for a few short yards, she slows. Her heart races. She can hear the roar of the river as it tumbles between the stone starlings beneath her feet.

'Sancta Maria, Mater Dei...' she begins, 'ora pro nobis peccatoribus... nunc et in hóra mórtis nóstrae...' Though she does not read Latin, the words are as familiar to her as the rhymes her mother taught her as a child in Padua: Holy Mary, Mother of God, pray for us sinners, now and at the hour of our death.

Cesare and Marcello make their reply. Amen.

Dunstan and Florin make their reply. Amen.

Two of them, however, are entirely mistaken about which sinners they're praying for.

Bianca has brought them all to the centre of the open space. Looking east towards Wapping marsh, she can make out the masts of the ships in the Pool standing out against a wash of stars. She casts a brief glance over the balustrade and sees the foaming white water surging around the sides of the arch, some thirty feet below. She wants so much to turn away, to distance herself from what is about to happen. But then she thinks: if I cannot face the consequences of what I have done, I will reproach myself as a coward for the rest of my days.

She turns to Ned, taking Nicholas gently from him, feeling the weight of him against her, the way she did when the watch found them at the top of Black Bull Alley.

'Let it be now,' she says clearly, looking up into Ned Monkton's eyes. And for Cesare and Marcello, 'Adesso!'

Even though she's prepared herself, the speed and the violence of it appal her.

Tyrrell's men step forward eagerly to seize Nicholas. As they do so, Ned moves faster than she could ever believe possible for such a big man. Dunstan is on the cobbles in a spreading pool of blood before her ears register the sound of Ned's giant fist striking home. Cesare and Marcello fall upon the startled Florin like a pair of starving wolves. Bianca hears, briefly, what sounds horribly like a man trying to breathe while someone stands on his throat. She stares into the night and tries to stop her legs buckling.

And then it's over. Almost as if she's imagined it. Only in her mind does she hear the impact as the two bodies hit the water in quick succession, plunging into the churning foam between the starlings.

On the bridge not a single window opens. Not a torchlight flares. Not a single cry of alarm disturbs the night. Just a dog howling mournfully somewhere in the darkened alleys of the northern bank.

Bianca looks round to be sure it's actually happened, tears welling in her eyes, an uncontrollable trembling in her limbs.

Further down the bridge, the same drunken reveller still lies in his doorway, contentedly snoring his way towards the dawn.

22

The river is coming alive, the crisp morning calm broken by the shouts of the labourers and the watermen, the metallic yelps of block and tackle, the taut creaking of cable and hawser. In the Customs House the clerks are opening their ledgers. Out on the water the tilt-boats and wherries ply for early trade. Weaving imperiously between them are the silk-canopied private barges bearing the lawyers and the churchmen, the courtiers and the privy secretaries to the grand houses and the palaces along the Thames: Greenwich and Richmond, Whitehall and Lambeth, Baynard's Castle and Hampton Court.

Bianca stands sore-eyed with Bruno and Nicholas on the forecastle of the *Sirena di Venezia*. Below them, on the wharf, men stand ready to untie the lines that hold the vessel fast. In little more than a few minutes, the *Sirena* and her precious cargo will be on their way. To the east, the sun has already cleared the rooftops and spires of Gravesend and Tilbury and the desolate flatness of the estuary beyond.

Bianca turns to look back at the busy main deck. By the larboard chains, she sees Samuel deep in conversation with his grandmother. Santo Fiorzi is standing close by, beaming with pride and contentment. She wonders what the boy must be thinking, facing a future that only hours ago he could not possibly have imagined: no longer discarded and shut away, no longer subject to the dangerous ambitions of others, but loved, safe amongst his kin.

'Come with us, Cousin,' Bruno says, scanning her face for the slightest sign that Bianca might consent. 'It's not too late.'

'I told Arcampora another person aboard would be too risky,' she says with a grin.

'That was a lie, Cousin – though it was told for a just reason.'

'And it would be a lie if I were to tell you this is not my home now, Bruno. No, I will not come with you. But remember me to everyone who might have cause to wonder what became of Bianca Merton. Tell them she is happy – mostly.'

Bruno sighs in resignation. He turns to Nicholas, who looks a little less alarming now that Bianca has had time to wash the dried blood from his face and tend his bruises. 'Signor Nicholas, you saved my life. I owe you my enduring gratitude. Though I confess you had us all somewhat mistrustful last night – until Bianca explained everything.'

Nicholas tries to return Bruno's thanks with a self-deprecating smile, but the crack in his lip turns it into a twisted grimace. 'I'm truly sorry for that. But a certain kind of crime requires a certain kind of justice. There was no other way.'

Bruno nods gravely. Then he puts aside whatever dark thoughts he might be harbouring. 'I would ask one last service of you, Nicholas.'

'You have only to name it.'

'Take care of my cousin Bianca for me.'

Not even the damage to his lip can stop Nicholas laughing at *that* request. 'If you care for my opinion, Signor Bruno, I can't think of a maid in all London who needs *less* taking care of.'

'Then *please*,' says Bruno, rolling his eyes skywards, 'at least try to keep that curiosity of hers from biting anyone. It's as dangerous as a rabid dog!'

They make their way down the larboard ladder and onto the main deck, where Mercy Havington takes Nicholas by the hand.

Her eyes are sparkling with a girlish delight and the years seem to have fallen from her face.

'Dr Shelby, when we last said farewell, I did not think to see you again. I'm glad I've had the chance to take a proper leave of you.'

'And I hope you've managed to convince the cardinal that I am no traitor to his enterprise, madam.'

'He knows, Dr Shelby. He knows.'

'There is, however, the small matter of Robert Cecil,' says Nicholas, wondering how he's going to explain the disappearance of Mercy Havington and her grandson to the Lord Treasurer's son. And whether he'll want his money back.

Lady Havington squeezes his hand. 'After our last conversation, I have no doubt your imagination will come up with a convincing enough tale. You'll find a way. If it's of any assistance, I'd rather everyone thought Samuel and I had simply disappeared. Make them believe we're dead, if you must. It will be better for everyone. Even my son-in-law Joshua.'

From out in the river comes the splash of the kedge-anchor being dropped. The saturnine figure of sailing master Luzzi steps up to tell Nicholas and Bianca it is time to go ashore.

'Pray, give me a just few moments more, Signor Luzzi,' Bianca says.

Seeing something in her eyes, he concedes. 'The tide is fair for a while yet, Mistress. The fellows on the lines will be grateful for a little extra ease.'

Bianca kisses Samuel on the cheek and bids him farewell. Then she crosses to where Santo Fiorzi is taking his last look at the great span of the bridge, the multitude of windows reflecting the light of the morning sun.

'Your Eminence, I would beg a kindness of you before you go.'

'Name it, *Passerotto*.'

She drops to her knees, looks up into the cardinal's stern grey eyes and makes the sign of the cross over her breast, as she remembers the sound of two bodies hitting deep water.

'Bless me, Holy Father, for I have sinned. It is over three years since my last confession...'

✚

From the wharf they watch the anchor cable lift from the river and spring tight with tension, scattering cascades of watery jewels into the morning air. Slowly the *Sirena di Venezia* begins to swing away from Galley Quay.

'She's a fortunate woman, Mercy Havington,' Nicholas muses.

Without consciously thinking, Bianca slips her arm through his. 'She has a long and uncomfortable journey ahead of her. She's given up her home and her faith, and she has a grandson with the falling sickness to look after in a foreign land.'

'Yes, that's all true,' says Nicholas, his eyes holding Bianca's gaze. The crack of unfurling sails reaches them from out on the river. 'But she's also been given a second chance at happiness. More to the point, she's had the courage to seize it.'

'Has the clever physician learned something he didn't know, Dr Shelby?' Bianca says with an impertinent smile.

'That's the wonderful thing about healing physic,' he replies. 'If you're brave enough to look, you can discover new cures in the most unlikely places.'

✚

Nicholas does not return to Poynes Alley. Bianca will not hear of it. He spends the next two days recovering under her care – and considering carefully the letter that had arrived barely an hour after they'd left Galley Quay together. It is from the College of Physicians. The Censors have reached a verdict.

He almost doesn't go. Only Bianca's gentle urging, and a sense of duty to a father who has invested so heavily in him, persuades Nicholas.

The fish stalls are closing when he arrives at the guildhall on Knightrider Street a little before midday. The fish has all been sold, the bloody boards washed down, the customers gone home. Men in leather aprons and women in smocks are clearing up, but the smell of eel, herring, pike and oyster lingers, trapped by the closeness of the buildings. The windows of the guildhall are closed, he notes. The mood inside the College will not be forgiving.

'God give you good day, Mr Shelby,' says Arnold Beston from behind his freshly starched ruff when Nicholas is ushered into the same upstairs chamber. Censor Frowicke sits on one side of him, Censor Prouty on the other. Faces like slate. And *Mister*, Nicholas notes. Not *Doctor*.

I've been tried, condemned and executed, he thinks. They just haven't got round to telling me yet. But I don't really care. Because two days ago someone tried it for real – and I'm still here. So do your worst. Throw me out of the College. I'll go and get a licence from the Worshipful Company of Barber-Surgeons. I'll suture wounds, mend broken bones, pull teeth, if necessary. I'll do what I know works: practical physic. Meat-work. I'll leave you fine physicians to study your beakers of piss, consult the lie of the heavens, feast yourselves into a torpor, quote at length in Latin from your musty old books and draw up your bills.

'Mercy, whatever has befallen you, Mr Shelby?' Beston asks, staring at Nicholas's bruises. 'Please do not tell us you've been quarrelling again.'

'No, sir. I was attacked – by cut-purses.'

It's the easiest explanation, Nicholas thinks. And Beston probably wouldn't believe the truth even if I dared tell it.

'Still not wearing your gown, I see?' observes Frowicke.

'As I informed you last time I was here, sir, I got rid of it.'

'How long have you been practising?' Beston asks. 'Three years?'

'A little longer.'

'And in that short time you have lost a practice, run riot, fallen into vagrancy and apparently decided you know more than any of us. That's quite a start to a medical career, Mr Shelby.'

Nicholas has no answer. And his bruises are throbbing.

Beston shakes his head despairingly. 'We have tried very hard to look sympathetically upon your case. It was clear from the answers you gave us that your knowledge was more than sound – even if you *do* hold that knowledge to be all but worthless. And from what we have learned, your work at St Thomas's amongst the poor last year was exemplary.'

Here it comes, thinks Nicholas.

'So it is not your level of ability for which we punish you,' Beston intones gravely, as though he's coming to a judgement in a treason trial in the Star Chamber, 'but rather for your youthful contempt for this great and noble calling. The verdict is unanimous. It is the decision of this College that you be banned from practising physic within the bounds of the City of London.' He pauses, drawing himself to his full height for greater gravitas. 'Banned for a period to last the length of one single day – starting upon this hour. Do you wish to appeal?'

In the circumstances, Nicholas finds dropping his jaw somewhat painful.

Beston engages him with a smile of deep compassion. 'You are a fine physician, young man. But this board of Censors suggests you use the time during which you are disbarred to consider the restorative properties of humility – Dr Shelby.'

✠

That evening, in a quiet moment at the Jackdaw, Nicholas sits down to write a letter to Sir Joshua Wylde. He stares at the pristine sheet of paper, wondering what to tell him. Then he remembers what Mercy Havington had said aboard the *Sirena*: *I'd rather everyone thought Samuel and I had simply disappeared. Make them believe we're dead, if you must. It will be better for everyone...*

Nicholas suspects that for all Wylde's rejection of his sickly son, Sir Joshua is not a complete stranger to grief. So he invents a story in which Isabel Lowell, Arcampora and Tyrrell have contrived Samuel's murder, in revenge for Wylde taking up arms against their faith. It's better, Nicholas thinks, than Wylde knowing that his son has chosen to live amongst his enemies. He closes the letter with a sentiment that he hopes will allow Joshua Wylde to think better of his Samuel: *Samuel gave his life most bravely, resisting the papist plot...*

Who knows? One day there might even be a portrait to hang beside the others at Cleevely.

✶

The next morning, Nicholas goes to the Mutton Lane stairs and boards a wherry to Cecil House. The waterman takes one look at his bruised face and laughs loudly, 'Another green-head takes a tumble on his first visit to Southwark, eh? When will you fellows ever learn?'

As the slow rise and fall of the river lulls him almost into sleep, Nicholas rehearses the tale he's going to tell Robert Cecil.

The moment he arrives, he senses something has changed. A mood of quiet satisfaction pervades Cecil House. The lawyers, the clerks, the scurrying blank-faced factotums – all seem to have a more assured stride. The secretary who escorts him to the presence chamber explains.

'He is Sir Robert now. A seat on the Privy Council is sure to follow. We serve a gentleman who is bound for greatness in this state.'

To Nicholas's surprise, Burghley's son makes no objection to the suggestion that they speak alone. When the clerks and secretaries have gone, he listens to Nicholas's story without interrupting, staring out of the high window at the fields of Covent Garden. He looks like a child actor fixated on something at the back of the stage, framed as he is by the window and flanked by the panelled walls. It's a struggle to stop his eyes settling on that malformed body beneath the expensive damask doublet; yet to do so, Nicholas thinks, would be an unkind intrusion.

Why do I suddenly feel compassion for this driven man? he wonders. Is it that we share a certain solitude of the heart? Is that the price those of us prepared to inflict pain in defence of what we love most dearly – in my case, Eleanor and Bianca; in his, the very realm itself – must pay?

'They should have a proper Christian burial – Mercy and Samuel,' Cecil says when Nicholas has finished. 'They are not carrion. They are my wife's kin.'

Not expecting such open humanity, Nicholas almost stumbles over his next lie. 'Finding the... the bodies... in that beech wood at Cleevely will not be easy, Sir Robert. It may take weeks. Even if the search is successful, it will probably be impossible to determine which set of remains is Mercy Havington's and which is Samuel Wylde's. I fear you must accept they are lost.' He offers up a short prayer of atonement to the souls of Tanner Bell and Finney.

'Sir Joshua must be informed, before he hears by rumour.'

'I have already written a letter,' Nicholas says, drawing the paper from inside the laces of his white canvas doublet. 'I wondered if one of your couriers to Holland...'

'Of course.' Robert Cecil turns back to face Nicholas. There is anger in that pale, sensitive face. The inner man has broken through. 'What kind of Christians are these Brothers of Antioch? Murdering a woman and a sickly young boy. They think themselves pious, yet in truth they are the very minions of the Antichrist!'

Nicholas has only a few more lies to tell. 'I can only imagine that somehow Lady Havington learned of their intent,' he says. 'She must have gone to Cleevely to warn Samuel; paid the price for it. She is a brave woman.' He quickly corrects himself. 'She *was* a brave woman.'

'I'm sorry you were so ill used by those monsters.'

'I mend well enough, Sir Robert.'

'Had you been able to bring me word earlier, it might have been possible to apprehend them. Still, it may not be too late. I'll send word to the ports to be on the lookout for them. We shall have them yet.' He offers Nicholas a glass of sack, pouring it from a silver ewer on his desk. 'Tell me, how did you manage to escape?'

'They were taking me to Lord Tyrrell's house at Holborn, for further examination. I was able to overpower the man they set to guard me,' Nicholas says. He tries his best to look contrite. 'I suppose you'll want your money back. After all, you told me this was a match you expected to win.'

But Robert Cecil barely remembers giving him the purse. 'You've been put to severe discomfort on my family's behalf, Dr Shelby. Keep it. Call it a bounty, to celebrate my own good fortune.'

'That is generous of you, Sir Robert.'

Cecil gives him an admiring look; the sort he might give to some expensive trinket he was thinking of buying. 'You know, you really ought to consider joining my household in a more formal capacity. What say you? We could soon burnish those rough yeoman's edges.'

'I'm not sure I'm cut out for the work of an intelligencer, Sir Robert.'

'As a *physician*, Dr Shelby.' Cecil studies the rim of his sack glass. 'Though I confess, it would be a foolish man who disregards your other skills.'

'Oh. I hadn't expected—'

'You might know that I have a son now: William. He's three months old.' Sir Robert places a hand on his own left shoulder in the merest acknowledgment of his deformity. 'I would like him to have at least *one* competent doctor.'

It's a tempting proposition. But Nicholas knows what's likely to accompany it. 'I *am* humbled by the offer, Sir Robert,' he says. 'And I will consider it most carefully. In the meantime, although this enterprise has not concluded the way either of us hoped, there is one small favour I would ask of you – if you think it not too impertinent.'

'I'm listening, Dr Shelby,' says Sir Robert Cecil, draining his glass of sack.

✠

Cecil House has one final surprise in store for Nicholas. As he crosses the busy courtyard towards the street gate, he sees Kit Marlowe striding towards him.

'Jesu, Dr Shelby, I had no notion we both served the same master,' the playwright drawls. 'I hope he's rewarded you well. You look as though you've been wrestling the bear, old Sackerson.'

Nicholas smiles as the realization dawns. '*Now* I understand. You were hanging around the Jackdaw like the smell from the flux just so you could keep an eye on Signor Barrani for Robert Cecil, weren't you?'

'And profitless it was, too! Mistress Bianca wouldn't let me get within sight of him. Pity. I rather like the fellow. Short, but devilish easy on the eye. How does he fare?'

'Don't you know? The *Sirena* sailed days ago.'

A sudden flash of panic on Marlowe's face tells Nicholas all he needs to know.

'Oh, I see – not paying attention. Still, I suppose one barque looks much like another when they're all tied up at the same wharf. What got in the way of the work, Marlowe: selling your soul to feed your appetites?'

'I only 'ave two legs, Shelby,' Marlowe protests harshly, the Kentish shoemaker's son and the fashionable London playwright suddenly, and without warning, staging a fight for his voice. The cobbler's boy wins hands down. 'Can't be fuckin' everywhere, can I? The Jackdaw... Galley Quay... back to the Jackdaw – Christ's wounds, a fellow 'as to take *some* ease.'

Nicholas doesn't laugh at the joy of besting a rival; he's too busy stifling the appalling thought that Marlowe could have stumbled across what had occurred aboard the *Sirena* – if he hadn't been soiling some unknown bed at the time. 'Your secret is safe with me, Kit,' he says nonchalantly. 'As is the other one.'

'Other one? What other one?'

'The fact that you've been serving *two* masters these past weeks.'

'*Two*? What do you mean?'

'Walter Burridge.'

'Burridge!' spits Marlowe, as though he's trying to eject a morsel of bad meat from his throat. 'I don't serve that rogue. He serves *me*.'

'Walter Burridge is a papist agent – currently on the run. He duped you into spying on Bruno Barrani for his own ends. That's another secret of yours I'll keep, just as long as you stay away from the Jackdaw. Good luck with the play, by the way. Let's hope the audience can stomach it for more than one performance – though judging by the riot at the Jackdaw, I somehow doubt it.'

Kit Marlowe's mouth gapes like a distressed salmon's.

'It's good sport, this intelligencing,' says Nicholas casually over his shoulder as he departs. 'I think I'm beginning to like it.'

✠

Nicholas Shelby steps out of a late wherry and onto the Mutton Lane water-stairs on Bankside. The sun has almost sunk below the horizon, just a smudged orange arc lingering above the Lambeth marshes to the west. The evening air is cool. The cloying smell of the river hugs the shore, earthy, sulphurous, the smell of rotting fruit or long-forgotten graves. He looks back at the dark water, then across to the white foam in the arches beneath London Bridge. The tide is ebbing, the dark, indifferent water flowing out towards the Hope Reach and the sea. A good place, he thinks, in which to let secrets lie.

At the Jackdaw, the lights are burning. As he steps across the threshold, the sound of Timothy's lute reaches him, a Venetian jig full of lively twists and turns. Full of joy. Full of life.

In the taproom doorway Ned Monkton is petting Buffle. The dog nestles in his huge arms, licking his great auburn beard deliriously. Rose is carrying trenchers to the tables, her dark curls gleaming like ebony in the candlelight. The smells emanating from the kitchen suggest Farzad has produced another of his strangely flavoured dishes – the fiery flesh of the Devil himself, according to Rose.

And there's Bianca, in her emerald-green kirtle and her carnelian bodice, her face flushed from the measure she's just been cajoled into dancing with old Walter Hyssop, who was born in the year the queen's father married his Aragon queen, Catherine. She sees him. Waves him in.

'How did you fare with the crab?' she asks, brushing her hair from her temples with her slender fingers.

'Well enough. I think he believed me. And he's not a crab. Not really.'

'Perhaps not. But he is a man prepared to use great violence to achieve his ambitions.'

'To protect the things he holds dear. That's how he would see it.'

Bianca blushes. Her lips tighten as she stares at the floor. 'Yes... well... according to Santo Fiorzi, that's a forgivable sin.'

She glances at the parcel he's carrying, a parcel wrapped against the spray of the wherry journey.

'You've brought me a present?'

Nicholas tries to stop the smile from spreading across his face. 'Ever since Ned brought Buffle back from Cleevely for Rose, I've reproached myself for not bringing you a gift at the same time. This is to make amends.'

He hands her the parcel and watches as her expression slowly changes from curiosity to tearful astonishment.

Lying inside are her father's books on physic, the ones she'd brought all the way from Padua, the ones Robert Cecil had once considered heretical: *Work for me*, he'd said to Nicholas on that occasion, *or Bianca Merton hangs for a witch*.

For a long while Bianca just stares at the thin, leather-bound volumes. Then, without thinking, Nicholas reaches out to brush away a single pearl of liquid that threatens to spill from the lip of her right eye. She makes no move to avoid him.

'Do you remember what I said at Galley Quay?' he says. 'About Mercy Havington and Santo Fiorzi having the courage to seize a second chance at happiness?'

'Yes, of course I do. I thought it prettily said – for a yeoman's son.'

'And do you recall, at Gravesend, when I said we ought to talk?'

'Yes. And it turned out to be about those letters of Tyrrell's. And look where that led us.'

'You fetched me a mighty blow, I remember.'

'Which you richly deserved, Nicholas Shelby.'

'You were expecting me to speak of something else, weren't you?'

'I may have been. I can't recall.'

Nicholas smiles broadly, ignoring the pain of the half-healed tear in his lip. Ignoring the noise of the taproom. Ignoring everything but those startling amber eyes.

'If I were to suggest we began the conversation anew,' he says, reaching out once more, now to brush an unruly twist of hair from her temple, 'would you promise to treat a poor invalid more gently this time?'

✠

At Gravesend the Thames stretches away in the twilight to the low ramparts and the marsh fever of the Tilbury shore. The ships anchored in the Reach seem to be melting into the leaden darkness like upended tombstones in a darkening graveyard. The air is cold here, chilled by a wind blowing in from the sea.

As he walks down the Hythe towards the water, Angelo Arcampora pulls his cloak close about his shoulders and wonders which vessel is his. He hopes she will be fast. Born in a Swiss mountain canton, he is not by nature a sailor and, even with this running tide, he does not expect to step foot on the French coast until late tomorrow afternoon.

Drawn up on the shingle is a small Kentish skiff, barely large enough for half a dozen people. A lantern burns in the stern, striking tight little beads of reflected flame from the lapping water.

The oarsman stands by the prow. He's a thin, hollow-eyed man who looks to Arcampora as though a trip out to an anchored ship might well be beyond him. But Arcampora doesn't have a choice; the Hythe is otherwise deserted.

'God give you good evening, Master,' says the oarsman as Arcampora reaches the skiff. 'I feared you might not come.'

Arcampora says nothing. The man is of no consequence to him, other than to bear him to safety. He makes himself as comfortable as he can on one of the hard wooden transverse boards, his back to the oarsman, who pushes the skiff off the shingle and jumps in effortlessly. In a moment they are rowing away from the Hythe and out into the dark river.

Watching the shore recede, Arcampora takes from his cloak the letter that has brought him here, the letter Bianca Merton pressed into his hand as he left the *Sirena di Venezia*. In the dancing lantern light the words are not easy to read, but he knows them almost by heart now:

> If you value your life, read this and heed its warning.
> You are betrayed... Unless you desire to meet a cruel fate
> upon the scaffold, you must with all haste flee out of this
> realm... At Gravesend you should seek out one Porter
> Bell, a waterman. He is forewarned, and will convey you
> secretly to a barque bound for Calais... Trust no other man
> but him...

The day has almost ended. Only the lantern light and the smudge of the Tilbury fort ramparts on the horizon hold out against the gathering darkness. Arcampora's hands are numb with the evening chill. He massages his right hand with the left, marvelling at the miraculous skills they possess. Skills that no other physician can claim. And he thinks of meeting Samuel Wylde and the others at Douai. These hands, he tells himself, will soon have new employment.

The skiff moves through the water with the slow, weary plod of an exhausted beast of burden.

And then it stops.

Now they are far out in the open Reach. Raised in a cosseting, pine-clad alpine valley Arcampora finds the emptiness overpowering. Malevolent. Out here, even the greatest physician is nothing. Less than nothing.

He turns wildly about, searching for the silver flash of a wave breaking on shingle, a glimpse of the Tilbury ramparts to tell him that safety is his for the price of a waterlogged boot. But there is nothing. Nothing but the river and the darkness stretching away without limit.

The little skiff rocks violently as a wave strikes it. Angelo Arcampora grabs the sides of the boat, terrified he's about to tumble out into this all-enveloping void, into ink-black water twice as deep as hell itself. His heart pounds wildly in his chest, filling his entire body with a drumbeat of mounting terror. A drumbeat so loud that he quite fails to hear the rasp of steel against leather, as behind him Porter Bell savours the slow drawing of the wickedly sharp blade from its sheath.

Author's note

The practice of trepanning continues still. In the early 1970s an English woman, Amanda Feilding, underwent the procedure. She couldn't find a doctor to do it, so she performed the operation herself, with the aid of an electric drill. She wanted to expand her consciousness. She's still alive, the Countess of Wemyss and March.

The drilling of a hole in a patient's head, while the subject is still alive, has been more common than one might think. Carried out since ancient times, trepanning was recommended in Hippocratic medicine as a way of treating skull injuries. In the early nineteenth century Cornish tin miners were said to insist upon the treatment if they sustained wounds to the head. The process was a forerunner of lobotomy.

Nicholas was right to worry about Kit Marlowe's rehearsal of *Faust*. There are reports that at one performance a real demon appeared – though perhaps this was due more to clever pre-show marketing than to the effective reciting of incantations. Nevertheless, in Nicholas and Bianca's day, such things were believed to be eminently possible. And if trepanning was an acknowledged way of letting out noxious airs, then it would be entirely reasonable to Dr Arcampora that it might allow something to travel in the opposite direction.

I must thank Philip Ball for *The Devil's Doctor*, on the life of the Swiss physician Paracelsus, and Charles G. Gross for his *A Hole in the Head*, both of which were invaluable in the making of this story. Colin Grant's moving tale of epilepsy, *A Smell of Burning*, and Andrew Wickens's *A History of the Brain* also provided rich inspiration.

Once again, I must thank the following people: Jane Judd for her wise counsel and support; Susannah Hamilton, Sara O'Keeffe, James Pulford and the team at Corvus Books – whose patience and forbearance seem unquenchable; Mandy Greenfield, whose eagle eye has prevented any number of howlers; and, finally, my wife Jane, without whose unshakeable belief in the author none of this would have happened.

Read on for an extract from . . .

1

Marrakech, Morocco, March 1593

In the moment before they caught him Adolfo Sykes was dreaming of oranges.

It was an hour after sunset, the last night of the time the Moors called `Ushar. The moon was almost full, her brilliant ivory face softened by a thin desert mist. In the gardens of the Koutoubia mosque the sellers of holy texts had packed away their books. The professional storytellers had departed and their audiences dispersed. From their high minarets the muezzlns had called the city to the al-'isha prayers, leaving the medina to the shadows and the scavenging dogs.

He loved the city at this time of night. He felt enfolded within its protective red walls, the cooling breeze from the Atlas Mountains filling the streets not with the scents of spices and human sweat but with cleansing citrus.

Until he'd come to the land of the Moor, Adolfo Sykes had barely seen an orange let alone tasted the succulent golden flesh. But now, after three prosperous years in Morocco, this agent of the Barbary Company of London – founding stockholders the noble earls Warwick and Leicester – was ready to believe that paradise itself might smell like one vast orchard of orange trees.

This agreeable reverie was shattered in a single heartbeat.

He had almost reached his destination, the city hospital – the Bimaristan al-Mansur. Its high mudbrick walls were barely twenty paces ahead him, a dark cliff face looming in the darkness. And then, out of the night, stepped two figures, their heads bound in voluminous *kufiyas*, a pair of monstrously fat-headed demons conjured up by some devilish *jinn*. In that instant Adolfo Sykes realised he had been a dead man from the moment he'd left his lodgings on the Street of the Weavers.

Until now, he had thought himself unobserved, no easy accomplishment for a small, somewhat bow-legged half English, half Portuguese merchant with a threadbare curtain of prematurely white hair that clung to the sides of his otherwise unsown pate. An involuntary grunt of surprise escaped his lips. He stopped. Then he did what many men are inclined to do when they've stumbled into what they suspect to be mortal danger: he came up with hasty reasons to believe he hadn't.

They are fellow Christian traders, he told himself confidently. Indeed, how could they be otherwise? The Mahometans were all at their devotions. Only we foreign apostates, tolerated out of commercial necessity, are out of doors at this hour.

But these two didn't look much like Christian traders. Besides, Adolfo Sykes was an upstanding member of that very same community. He knew them all. They knew him. Surely by now they would have extended a courteous 'How now, Master Sykes. A fine night, is it not? If perhaps a little on the chilly side.' So far they hadn't spoken a word.

If not Christian traders, then perhaps they were Jewish moneymen from the El-Mellah quarter; two of those clever fellows without whom trade between Moor and European would seize up like an axel without grease.

But he knew most of them, too. The night suddenly seemed colder, despite the *djellaba* he was wearing, woven from the best English wool and evidence – if any were needed – of the superiority of his merchandise.

Christian traders. Jewish money-lenders. Perhaps even messengers sent from London to tell him it was time to come home and receive the accolades due to a very model of the English merchant venturer class. Whoever they were, they were not, under any circumstances, real or imagined, *assassins*.

'Boa noite, senhores—'

Adolfo Sykes began the bid for his life – for that is what a small voice deep in his head was now proclaiming it was – in Portuguese, the lingua franca of those foreign merchants who found Arabic too strange for their European tongues.

But his greeting received no answer. Fighting against a rising tide of panic, Sykes glanced quickly over his shoulder. A second pair of shrouded figures were standing barely two paces behind him, cutting off his retreat.

What happened next began with a moment of awkward comedy. First there was an odd little dance, as though five late-comers to a feast had all converged at the one remaining empty chair. Sykes, being a diminutive fellow and as wiry as a Barbary macaque, dodged sideways. He had a brief glimpse of himself as a free man, speeding through the darkened streets to safety – then to a ship that would carry him back to England where, as far as he knew, no one intended him violent bodily harm. Then a grasping hand caught a fold of his *djellaba* and a sideways kick swept his little bowed legs from under him. He went face down onto the dirt. A plaintive grunt – half expelled breath, half a cry of protest – burst from his lungs. He felt warm blood pool in his jaw, and the weight of a man's knee in the small of back, almost breaking him. The darkness took on an even thicker patina as the man leaned over him, enveloping him in the folds of his robe like a falcon mantling over a stunned hare.

Even then, Adolfo Sykes was not yet ready to fully acknowledge the truth: that they'd known he was coming, known where to lie in wait. That he'd been driven like game, the way the Berber tribesmen drove the desert gazelle towards their bows. In his tolerable Arabic he gasped 'Purse...left side...my belt...take it. If God wills it, it's yours.'

The answer ripped away the last shreds of self-delusion.

'Do not insult us, Master Sykes; we are not common thieves,' said a voice very close to his left ear. 'It is not your purse we desire; it is the secret that you keep hidden from us in your infidel heart.'

English. Spoken with an Irish accent. The very last thing he'd been expecting to hear. The tone, young. Not the voice of a lad of quality, but a carpenter's son perhaps, or a glover's, a cooper's. An apprentice to a respectable trade.

In confirmation, as he turned his head to the speaker, Sykes saw a cheek as pale as porcelain in the moonlight, a cheek flecked with a boyish attempt at a beard. And though the eyes were all but lost in the shadow of the kufiya, he got the distinct impression they were the eyes of a someone barely out of childhood.

The voice then spoke some words in Arabic, presumably for his companions' benefit. Not the unrefined language of the streets, Sykes noticed abstractly, but formal, classical Arabic – as if it had been recently learned by rote at the feet of a teacher. Sykes picked out the phrases 'It is him... It's the infidel who steals from the faithful.'

This offended Adolfo Sykes almost as much as the assault upon his body. He had never stolen from anyone. Ask his customers. Ask the Christian merchants. Ask the Jews from the El-Mellah. Ask the forty God-fearing English merchants who comprised the body of the Barbary Company – licenced by the queen's seal to hold the monopoly of trade between the princely states of Morocco and England, fine upstanding men who would expel him at the merest suggestion of it.

But what troubled him more than the slander was the voice: the voice of his homeland, laden with all the old safe familiarities of place and class, the English voice that had just called him an infidel.

Rough hands hauled Sykes to his feet. Making a poor attempt at bluff, he protested, 'I am the factor for the Barbary Company of London. As such, I am protected by the mercy of his majesty Sultan Al-Mansur. I have his written word upon it. I can show you.'

And it was true, after a fashion. The passport was in his lodgings, penned by one of the sultan's army of clerks, though as it was written in Arabic – which he could speak but not read – it might, for all he knew, be a shopping list.

Their answer was brutally unapologetic. First there was a blow to the side of his head that made his knees buckle and the stars above him reel. Then they bound his hands and gagged him. He could tell at first bite the gag was of a wholly inferior quality cloth. Probably homespun by Berber tribesmen. It seemed to Sykes like the final, deliberate insult.

✠

They manhandled him roughly through the same narrow doorway cut into the mudbrick wall of the bimaristan from which they had emerged. He didn't struggle. They were young and much too strong for him. They had the law of the desert on their side: the weak always die first; resisting only prolongs the agony.

Once inside, Sykes saw by the meagre light of an oil lamp an old watchman sitting in an alcove. His skin was as dark and furrowed as argan bark and he wore a short white beard. He left his seat, turned away and dropped to his knees, taking up the posture of a Moor at prayer. Sykes understood at once: this was not religious devotion, this was done so that he could later claim never to have witnessed the furtive, nocturnal arrival of a bound and gagged European.

His only understanding of a hospital for the insane was London's Bedlam. Consequently, he had imagined the bimaristan al-Mansur to be a place of stinking straw and demonic shrieking, of drooling, tormented creatures who had lost the light of God's mercy. What he saw now was nothing like that.

A score of individuals sat or lay quietly on cushioned mattresses, their faces washed by the weaving light from oil lamps set on intricately tiled plinths. Some lay curled up like infants, others sat with their knees under their chins, gently rocking, as if they were soothing themselves into slumber. The air was heavy with the palliative scents of herb-ivy and camomile. A deep serenity seemed to fill the long chamber. Four women wrapped almost entirely in plain Berber cloth moved amongst the inmates, dispensing water from wide bowls of beaten brass. As Sykes passed, they too turned away. They have seen me, and they know my fate, he thought. But they too, like the watchman in his alcove, deny my existence, even to themselves. I wasn't here. I never passed this way.

For the place of execution, they had chosen a room seemingly at the very heart of the bimaristan, a chamber tiled from floor to ceiling with intricate mosaics, each tiny square of stone as polished as a mirror glass. He heard the one with the English accent engage in a brief but tense conversation in Arabic with his companions. He could understand only intermittent words, but he knew they were fortifying their own courage – boys on the verge of manhood, steeling themselves for a harsh rite of passage. He heard the prayer begin. 'All hu akbar—'

In a way, he was glad it was to be here, in this little bejewelled chamber. Because cut into the flat ceiling was an opening in the shape of a six-pointed star, a window onto the limitless night, and once more he could catch the scent of oranges on the air. Paradise. Waiting for him. And all he had to do now was steel himself for the journey.

2

One month later.

The south bank of the Thames river, London

In the small hours of a deathly still April morning two miles downriver from Westminster, three men capped and cloaked against the bitter cold climb silently from a private wherry. With an urgency that has more to do with the impatience of the man who sent them than simply keeping warm, they strike east from the Mutton Lane river stairs. They are heading for Long Southwark, guided through the empty lanes by the twisting flames of a single torch. Bankside is deserted. The unseasonable night is too raw even for thieves and house-divers. The timbers of the close-set houses rear out of the mist like the ribs of a fleet of galleys wrecked in the surf.

At the gatehouse on the southern end of London Bridge they come across the night watch, warming their tired bones around a brazier that burns like a beacon warning of invasion. The three men pause, but only to confirm the address they have been given. There is a practiced hardness in their faces that hints they might be bearing steel beneath their cloaks. The watch lets them pass without question. They know government men when they see them. And arrests are always best made at times like this, when the subject is too sleep-befuddled to put up a fight.

Entering a lane close to the sign of the Tabard inn, the three men count off the houses until they reach a modest two-storey property of lathe and plaster, close to a row of trees that marks the western boundary of St Thomas's hospital for the poor. With no show of pleasure at having reached their goal after such an uncomfortable journey their leader begins to hammer violently on the front door, as though its planks and hinges are personally responsible for the night's discomforts.

✠

Nicholas Shelby wakes with a start. He feels the rhythmic blows through the floorboards, through the frame of his bed, through the straw in the mattress, even in his bones. It is the sort of hammering that constables employ when arresting traitors – or calling physicians from their warm beds to tell them that the plague has finally crossed the river into Southwark.

He has been awaiting a call like this since the first cases of the new pestilence came to light last year. So far, the outbreak has stayed confined to the poorer lanes on the other side of London Bridge. But that hasn't stopped the Courts of Chancery, Wards, Liveries and Requests taking themselves off to Hertford to consider their business in healthier surroundings. So far, the liberty of Southwark has escaped. In the Bankside taverns, more than one wag has made the connection between the decrease in lawyers and the absence of plague south of the river where the bawdy houses lie.

But Southwark has not escaped entirely. The Lord Mayor has ordered the closing of the play houses and the bear-pits. A strange lethargy has descended on the southern shore of the Thames. The purse-divers and coney-catchers have lost half their trade at a stroke. In the stews, there are whores who've had only themselves for company since Candlemas, and the kindlier church wardens have stopped asking them their trade when assessing the need for charity. Cynics say there are only two types of public places the authorities dare not shut for fear of riot: churches and taverns. It all seems to Nicholas a grim prelude for what would otherwise be a time of joy and festivity – an impending wedding.

Fully awake now, he opens his eyes to the semi-darkness of his rented room. On the clothes chest a single candle stands close to guttering, as squat and fat as a lump of yellow clay thrown on a potter's wheel. It fills the room with the smoky smell of mutton grease. A film of moisture on the inside of the window and the absence of anything other than watery blackness beyond tells him dawn must still be some hours off. It is that hollowed out time of the night, he decides, when it is better not to wake; when thoughts unchain themselves; when spirits walk and old men die.

'The Devil take you and your godless knocking!' The voice of his landlady, Mistress Muzzle, penetrates the floorboards, caustic enough to strip limewash off a wall. Nicholas hears a wheezing snort of indignation, followed by, 'I hope this is not one of your patients, Dr Shelby! If it is, I'd be indebted if you would ask them to fall sick at a godlier hour.'

Nicholas knows it will take his landlady a while to reach the front door. She is a woman ill-designed for velocity. Struggling into his hose and shirt, he wonders if he can beat her to it. As he steps out onto the landing, he sees the flicker of an oil lamp moving ponderously through the darkness, and hears her voice again, full of injured propriety: 'Anon! Anon! Do you expect me to open the door in naught but my shift? What manner of place do you think I keep – a bawdy-house?'

Even on Bankside no one would confuse the upright Mistress Muzzle's dwelling with a bawd's premises, thinks Nicholas as he stumbles down the stairs. It is however the perfect place in which to start a medical practice: one room at street level for seeing patients, accommodation above; the landlady – the fearsome Mistress Muzzle – safely in her own domain at the rear of the house. The only part they are forced to share is the front door.

And that is where he joins her a moment later.

In the light from the lamp, her pouchy face has the discomforted look of someone suffering a mild bout of colic. With an indignant explosion of breath and a theatrical jangling of her keys, she opens the door. Over her expansive shoulders, Nicholas can just make out three heads silhouetted against the misty night, a night turned a wet muddy ochre by the light of a single flickering torch. A disembodied voice reaches him; no apology, just a bald statement:

'These are the lodgings of Dr Nicholas Shelby. Correct?'

'I am Dr Shelby,' Nicholas says, rubbing the sleep from his eyes.

'You are to come with us – at once.'

'By whose command?'

The answer serves only to make the night even colder. 'By Sir Robert Cecil's command.'

So then, not the pestilence – but a close enough second.

Mistress Muzzle turns back from the door. Nicholas sees her little eyes flicker over him, full of sudden mistrust. He knows what she's thinking: a member of the queen's Privy Council has sent for her tenant in the middle of the night. Therefore, at the very least he must have poisoned someone. Has he been distributing papist pamphlets instead of medicine? Is he no doctor at all, but a charlatan prescriber of fake elixirs? And more importantly, by taking his rent is she guilty by association?

For a moment Nicholas enjoys her confusion. But spacious, sanitary lodgings are not easy to find on Bankside. So he tells her reassuringly, 'I'm not a wanted felon, Mistress Muzzle. Or a

Jesuit – if that's what concerns you. And I *have* paid my rent until Trinity term.'

Unconvinced, she turns her head back towards the door and the men in the street. 'Is Dr Shelby under arrest?' she asks.

'Not at the moment,' says the one holding the burning torch. Wisps of smoke swirl upwards, disappearing into the cold damp night and making Nicholas think of souls rising from a graveyard. 'But if you want—'

The hammering has sounded so official that not a single occupant has dared open a window to see what is happening. No one wants to risk witnessing the apprehending of a traitor or the flushing out of a papist priest. Too many questions get asked, and there's always the chance of being mistaken for an accomplice. Much safer to wait for the public finale on Tower Hill or at Tyburn.

And even though he knows himself to be an *almost* innocent man, Nicholas can't help but acknowledge the little wormy knot of cold fear that writhes in his stomach.

'Do I have time to make myself a little more presentable?'

'Be quick. This is not an invitation to a revel, Dr Shelby. We have a wherry at the Mutton Lane stairs and the tide will soon begin to ebb. Bring what items a physician might normally have about him.'

'For what malady?'

'Sir Robert did not say.'

'Then how in the name of Jesu may I know what to bring?'

The irritation is clear in the man's terse reply. 'Whatever else is required, Sir Robert will provide it. Now *hurry*.'

'How long will you be away?' asks Mistress Muzzle.

'I don't know. Ask *them*,' Nicholas says, nodding at the men in the street, who seem disinclined to answer. 'If anyone comes here needing medicine, tell them to seek out Mistress Merton.

She'll be either at the Jackdaw tavern, or at her new apothecary shop on Dice Lane. Bianca will know what to do.'

For the first time that Nicholas has witnessed since he moved out of the Jackdaw and into Mistress Muzzle's lodgings, his landlady favours him with a smile. It is the warm, indulgent smile that some women are inclined to whenever they think of impending nuptials. 'And if Mistress Merton herself should call here while you are away?' What am I to say to her?'

'That's easy to answer, Mistress Muzzle. One way or another, I will be back in time for the wedding.'